POWER

THE SANTINI ASSASSINS, BOOK ONE

STONI ALEXANDER

This book is a work of fiction. All names, characters, locations, brands, media and incidents are either products of the author's imagination, or have been used fictitiously. Any resemblance to actual persons living or dead, locales, or events is entirely coincidental. The author acknowledges the trademarked status and trademark owners of various products referenced in this work of fiction, which have been used without permission. The publication/use of these trademarks is not authorized, associated with, or sponsored by the trademark owners.

Copyright © 2025 Stoni Alexander LLC
Cover Design by Better Together

All rights reserved.

In accordance with the U.S. Copyright Act of 1976, the scanning, uploading, and electronic sharing of any part of this book without the permission of the publisher is unlawful piracy and theft of the author's intellectual property. Without limiting the rights under copyright reserved above, no part of this publication may be reproduced, stored in or reproduced into a retrieval system, or transmitted, in any form, or by any means (electronic, mechanical, photocopying, recording or otherwise) without the prior written permission of the above copyright owner of this book.

Criminal copyright infringement, including infringement without monetary gain, is investigated by the FBI and is punishable by up to five years in federal prison and a fine of $250,000.

Published in the U.S. by SilverStone Publishing, 2023
ISBN 978-1-946534-32-3 (Print Paperback)
ISBN 978-1-946534-33-0 (Kindle eBook)

Respect the author's work. Don't steal it.

NOVELS BY STONI ALEXANDER

THE TOUCH SERIES

The Mitus Touch

The Wilde Touch

The Loving Touch

The Hott Touch

In Walked Sin

Dakota Luck

THE VIGILANTES SERIES

Damaged

Vengeance

Savage

Wrecked

Broken

Rebel

Fury

THE SANTINI ASSASSINS

Power

BEAUTIFUL MEN COLLECTION

Beautiful Stepbrother

Beautiful Disaster

Available on Amazon or Read FREE with Kindle Unlimited

ABOUT POWER

POWER. Power is *everything*. It's a magnet for wealth, success, and living the good life.

I grew up with nothing. My father built his business one dirty deal at a time. Then, he got himself killed. Here one minute, gone the next. But he taught me three powerful lessons.

One, be shrewd.
Two, trust no one. *Ever*.
Three, energy is finite. Need more? Take it from others.

When I lost what mattered most, my heart turned to stone. That's when I learned the true meaning of ruthless.

Now, I'm one of the most successful men in the world. I run a global empire worth billions, but my soul demands vengeance. Revenge drives me forward.

When I catch *her* spying on me, I let her have her fun until it's time to make my move. The hunter becomes the hunted.

I hope she enjoys the chase.

I know I will.

To the one who continues to zhuzh me...
all these years later

and

To the one who holds all the power

1

LUCIANO'S TARGET

LUCIANO

Luciano Santini stepped out of his chauffeured Rolls Royce and buttoned his hand-tailored suit jacket. He breathed in the brisk October air, welcoming the cool evening. After a nod to his driver, he tied on a simple black mask, collected the designer shopping bags from the back seat, and made his way up the stone stairs toward the etched-glass front doors.

Every last one of the estate's front-facing windows was illuminated in a freakish red glow.

It's like I'm walking into hell.

Saturday night, after eleven, and the party was well underway. It had been years since he'd been to one of Burke's soirees, but he was setting a trap, and it had to be there.

Time to make my move.

One quick glance over his shoulder confirmed that his younger brother, Teddy, was seconds behind him, also in a chauffeur-driven sedan, also wearing a Santini suit.

Just as he reached for the front door, it swung wide. Two

women, both wearing French maid outfits, stood in the foyer, their faces concealed behind elaborate feathered masquerade masks.

He liked birds, just not on a woman's face.

Less is more.

"Good evening, Mr. Santini," said the petite, light-skinned one.

"It's a pleasure," said the taller, dark-skinned woman.

He waited for Teddy before entering the home. Red lighting bathed the home in an eerie glow that added to the already edgy vibe.

"Ladies," he replied. "Same rules?"

"No, is no," said the tall one. "Consent is king."

"We're also available to play," said the small one.

Luciano wasn't there to play with the members, and he wasn't there to play with the lovelies posted around the mansion either, but they didn't need to know his *real* intention.

Barefaced, Teddy appeared in the doorway and Luciano threw him a disapproving glance.

"Right, my mask." Teddy pulled a black one from his suit pocket and fitted it over his eyes.

"Hello, sir," said the dark-skinned woman. "Name please."

"He's with me," Luciano said.

"Sorry," blurted the light-skinned woman. "No exceptions."

Luciano let his gaze linger on one before sliding his attention to the other. Then, he flashed them a smile. One sighed, the other bit back a moan.

Worked every damn time.

"Let Burke know Tank is with me," Luciano said.

"No need," said Burke as he joined them. The two men shook hands. "Luciano, you look perfect and I fucking hate you for it."

Teddy snort laughed as Burke extended his hand. Teddy shook it. "Tank, you look too damn good yourself."

Luciano's youngest brother, Theodore Santini was Teddy to the family, Tank to everyone else.

Burke had put on fifty pounds, his large paunch protruding over his polyester blend lounge pants. The leopard-print robe hung open, revealing tufts of graying chest hair.

Luciano wouldn't be caught dead designing leopard-print loungewear for men.

Luciano handed Burke a shopping bag. "For the host."

Burke held up the bag, admiring the gold, embossed lettering.

SANTINI

"Very generous." Burke pulled a black, pure-spun, organic silk smoking jacket from the bag. "It's magnificent." He dropped the unattractive robe off his shoulders and slipped into the luxury garment.

"My skin is having an orgasm," Burke blurted, as he ran his pudgy fingers over the finely woven material.

Luciano and Teddy laughed.

Burke slung his arms around both men. "Tank, you get more muscular every time I see you, but look at me... I got fat." His boisterous laugh filled every inch of the spacious foyer.

After Burke settled down, he escorted the brothers toward the kitchen.

The living and dining rooms were crowded with furniture, most of it outdated and hideous, but Luciano didn't give a damn about the decor. He was there to meet someone. Someone who'd been lurking the shadows for well over a month. After doing his due diligence, he was done being the hunted. Time to become the hunter.

A charge of adrenaline spiked through him.

Nothing better than the thrill of the chase.

In the spacious kitchen—also in desperate need of a

makeover—the bartender was chatting it up with several guests perched on the counter stools as he topped off their white wine. Burke opened the refrigerator, extracted a bottle of champagne, popped the cork, and poured three glasses.

After the men toasted, Luciano glanced around. Though the party was downstairs, several guests chatted in small groups nearby.

She's not here... yet.

Luciano sipped the bubbly while Burke chatted about his business. When the glasses had been drained, Burke escorted them to the lower level.

"Enjoy, and thanks for the gift," Burke said before walking toward his seat in the front row.

The lower level boasted a seventy-five-seat theatre where a cast of six titillated and enthralled their audience with their well-rehearsed sex show on a red-lit stage.

For over a decade, Burke and his wife Morticia, had been hosting these free-for-all spectacles. Years earlier, Luciano's close friend, Colton Mitus, had dragged him to one. He'd hooked up with a woman, then hooked up with another. There had been a third, then the night evolved into an orgy. The intense evening had lasted until daybreak. It had been fun, but he'd never returned. Random hookups weren't his thing.

Standing in the back, Luciano and Teddy watched the hedonistic performance. Sex used to mean something to Luciano. Nowadays, it was a necessary evil, devoid of any emotional connection.

Though his cock stirred, Luciano wasn't drawn to the scene, so he shifted his sights to the audience. Row after row of perfectly aligned seats packed the finished lower level. His target would be easy to spot. A leggy beauty with long, wavy chestnut hair, unremarkable clothing, and a pair of binoculars in hand. Tonight, however, she wouldn't have the binos to hide behind.

He'd been looking forward to turning the tables on her. Nothing like confronting the enemy.

"Is she here?" Teddy whispered.

"I don't see her."

"Are you sure she's coming?"

"You tell me," Luciano murmured. "You hacked into Burke's computer and saw the guest list."

"She was on it, but that doesn't mean she'll be here it. Check the tracker," Teddy said.

With his phone in hand, Luciano tapped on the app. After Teddy couldn't find out anything about her, he'd attached a tracker to her vehicle.

Did these silent enemies expect Luciano to do nothing?

A charge of energy bolted through him. "She's here," Luciano murmured, still eyeing the tracker.

"It's go-time, baybeeee!" Teddy exclaimed.

Several guests in the back row craned around. One woman shot him a dirty look. "Shhhh!"

A growl rolled from Teddy. He hated—fucking hated—to be challenged on anything. The woman flicked her gaze at Luciano and he shot her a smile. The corners of her mouth curled up and her tight shoulders dropped back down.

"She's cute," Teddy whispered.

"Go for it," Luciano said.

Teddy shook his head. "I'm working."

Luciano appreciated that his baby brother took his job seriously. Teddy was amongst a few Luciano could trust.

"Once I find her, you can go have fun," Luciano murmured.

Teddy shot him a grin. "There's my motivation."

Hugging the wall, Teddy walked toward the front while Luciano shifted his attention to the performers, their guttural grunts and groans filling the air with sensuous sounds. As they cried out through their collective orgasms, Luciano scanned the room again, but couldn't locate his target in the darkened space.

Teddy returned, shook his head, then turned his full attention on the show.

When the performers finished their real or fake climaxes, the curtain dropped and the lights brightened, casting a reddish glow on the audience. Most guests rose, but a few remained in their cushioned seats making out. Two rows up, one woman pulled up her skirt and mounted a very-ready guy in the chair next to her.

Monkey see, monkey do.

Maybe I've become too damn uptight. It's just fucking.

Burke's wife Morticia sidled over. Like her husband, she'd put on weight since the last time he'd seen her. After he kissed her cheeks, she clasped his hands and squeezed.

"Hot, hot Mr. Santini. Please tell me tonight's my very lucky night."

Despite Morticia's short silk nightgown that left little to the imagination, Luciano wasn't tempted. He wasn't screwing another man's wife. Even if she'd been unattached, he wasn't screwing her. She didn't rev his motor... or any other part of him.

He held out the Santini shopping bag.

She batted her ultra-long faux lashes as him, laid her hand over her breast. "For meeee?"

He chuffed out a laugh. When surprise flashed in her eyes, he realized she wasn't being playful. She was coming on to him.

"A little something for the lovely hostess," he said.

She accepted the gift, pulled out the red tissue paper, and extracted the black negligée laced in small rows of diamonds that flanked the side slit.

Her scream sent a bolt of energy charging through him.

"What the fuck," Teddy blurted, but Morticia was too busy

jumping up and down, her giant implants flopping out of her nightgown.

Then, Teddy started laughing and Luciano knew he was screwed. Teddy's laugh was infectious. Trying to control himself, Luciano snickered as Teddy escaped into the crowd.

"A Santini Original!" Morticia threw her arms around him. "This is super thoughtful of you. I have got to introduce you to my best girl! You two will hit it off, for sure. And her boobs are bigger than mine."

No thanks.

Someone slinked by, and he glanced over Morticia's shoulder. A hit of energy powered through him.

Gotcha.

Up close, Simone Redding was stunning. Layered brown hair with chestnut highlights, pulled into a high ponytail, leaving wavy strands framing her face. Electric-green eyes shone bright from behind her black mask while her heart-shaped lips had him biting back a groan.

Her sexy mouth around my cock would be so damn good.

And she was tall. Had to be six feet in heels. Nothing sexier than a beautiful, long-legged woman.

As he'd expected, her clothing was nondescript and unflattering. But he was a self-admitted garment snob. Running Santini International—one of the world's premier fashion houses—had done that to him. Clothing was meant to accentuate the good, hide the bad. It was designed to augment a person's personality, maybe even create one.

Her white shirt didn't cling, but it wasn't baggy either. It was simply boring. Though her tight, black skirt showed off her ass, it was her shapely legs that snagged his attention.

Stop.

To his surprise, she hadn't seen him... or if she had, she was playing things chill as she disappeared into the crowd. Either way, it was *his* turn to pursue *her*.

"Whew," Morticia said, regaining his attention. "That was a long-winded explanation as to why this stunning gift means so much to me."

Luciano offered a polite nod, having missed what Morticia had just said. Simone Redding had taken him off his game.

Get it together, Santini.

"I'm sure *you* think we should sell the house," Morticia continued.

Dammit.

He had no idea what she was talking about. "Would that relieve your anxiety?"

Morticia pushed onto her toes, leaned close. "We're in debt up to my tits. Credit cards are maxed out. The house has a second mortgage... as big as my boobs!" She laughed.

Luciano was not about to talk finances in the middle of a kink party. "What does your wealth manager say?"

"He agrees with me. Sell the house, pay off the debt."

He kissed one cheek, then the other. "You're a smart woman. You'll do the right thing." He flashed a smile before taking off into the crowd.

As Luciano weaved his way through the partygoers, he eyed the closed door in the corner. Behind it was a large room where guests could talk, play, screw, whatever. On the other hand, if they wanted privacy, they could retreat into a bedroom on the second floor.

Regardless of the fancy digs, it was one big fuck fest.

He spotted his brother chatting it up with three women. A smile ghosted Luciano's face. He hoped his brother was about to get laid... times three.

Not seeing his target, he made his way to the corner door and entered the room. The smell of sex tornadoed through him, and his senses came alive. A half-naked couple hurried by, eager to have some carnal fun. Strolling around the room, Luciano took in the sights. Beyond the obvious gyrations of naked bodies, the cacophony of moans and groans made him growl. Sex soothed the demons that haunted him, but the sex high never lasted long.

While he'd done a background check on Simone—learning very little—he knew nothing about why she was at the private party. Was she there to play? To watch? Was she there for work? He was at an unusual disadvantage.

"Oh, fuck me harder," a woman cried out while her partner thrust into her.

Luciano kept moving through the spacious room.

She's not here.

He exited, swept his gaze over the rows of cushioned chairs, but she wasn't there either. Up the stairs he went. A woman with long auburn hair caught his eye, but when she turned—not Simone.

He walked the first floor, then took the stairs to the second. He'd be damn pissed if she'd left. Like the rest of the home, the hallway was bathed in more red lights. Most of the bedroom doors were shut, but three remained opened.

He entered the first one. Empty. In the second room, two women were fooling around on the bed while a masked man watched from a corner chair.

"You're welcome to stay, man," said the guy.

"I'm good," Luciano replied.

"Hey, I know you," said one of the women. "I'd recognize you anywhere. You're somebody famous. Wait, don't tell me." She stared at him. "I know! You're Luciano Santini!"

She pushed off the bed, picked up a garment, and held it out. It was from his Demure collection.

"You have excellent taste," he said.

"Pleeeease stay," she begged. "I'd love to say I fucked you."

He walked up to her, tipped her chin with his index finger, leaned down and dropped a light kiss on her lips. "I'm meeting someone." With a wink, he walked to the doorway, tossed the man a nod, and left.

As he made his way toward the third and final open door, his phone buzzed with a text from Teddy.

> I'm going upstairs to play

> Enjoy

Luciano strolled into the room.

An unmasked woman sat in the corner chair, the red lights illuminating her face in a smoldering glow. His heart pumped faster.

It's her.

He shut the door behind him. His mark had set the trap and he'd walked right into it. She sat still, like a cat about to pounce on its prey.

"Ms. Redding," he said.

"Mr. Santini," she replied.

The timbre of her voice sent desire trailing down his spine. Sexy, soft, and filled with so much promise.

"Have I kept you waiting long?" he asked, before removing his mask.

For over a month, he'd seen her from a distance only. Now, mere feet away, the pull to go to her was strong. Very strong. But he had more control than that and he stood his ground. She'd been tailing him... he would force her to make that first move.

"How do you know I'm waiting for *you*?" she asked.

Nice.

She pushed effortlessly out of the winged chair. "I didn't expect to see you here."

His gaze dropped slowly. *She's got a killer body.*

Stopping a foot away, she hitched a hand on her hip and

drilled him with an unblinking stare. Simone Redding was drop-dead gorgeous.

"You've been watching me from a distance for over a month," he said. "Time for a closer look-see."

Her laugh filled him with a lightness he hadn't felt in a long time. She took one more step, then tilted her head. "You're taller in person."

He had come to the party to find out why she'd been tailing him. But the change in her breathing—though subtle—was throwing him off his game.

But not off balance.

He trusted scant few. Better to count her as an enemy until he had all the facts. And even then, he still wouldn't trust her.

She slinked right up to him, lifted her beautiful face toward his, and pinned him with a heated stare. "And much more muscular."

Her baseline scent wafted in his direction. She smelled of lust.

"Why have you been tailing me?" he growled, desire coursing through him.

He hated the control she exhibited. Hated that she'd barely uttered a word. She hadn't apologized for stalking him, hadn't even admitted to it. She was eye-fucking him in a way that stripped him bare... and he loved it.

Fucking loved it.

Her breathing thundered in his ears, but when a moan slithered from her sensual mouth, he snaked his arms around her waist. Their lips came together in a kiss that felt more like an attack than an embrace. She pressed herself close, slipped one hand into his hair while the other wrapped around his shoulder.

On a groan, she pressed her hungry tongue into his mouth and unleashed a torrent of energy into him. Normally one to take the lead, he liked her aggression, liked how she took him hostage in her arms.

Between kisses, she said, "Grab my ass."

If he did, he'd have her on the bed in a second. Naked in five, and buried deep inside her moments after that.

In one fluid move, he grabbed her ponytail, slowed the kiss, and pulled her off him.

Panting, she stared into his eyes. "Are you here to talk?" She heaved in a deep breath. "Or fuck?"

His hardened shaft pressed against his boxer briefs, eager to break free and root inside her. Forcing himself to gain control, he released her, but he didn't step away. Now, inches apart, he waited while her jagged breath returned to normal.

"Aren't I doing it for you?" she asked.

He placed her hand over his hardened cock.

"That's your dick talking," she said matter-of-factly. "What do *you* say?"

Leaning down, he nibbled her earlobe, then bit it. "Why don't you tell me why you're stalking me?"

She smiled. "I like pain, and I have a very high threshold."

"Mmm, good to know."

"I'm *not* following you, but I can see how someone with your massive—" she rubbed his hard shaft— "*ego* would think that."

Luciano was done playing word games. She wasn't going to answer him and he wasn't about to walk. There was no way he would get the same satisfaction from his damn hand. Not when someone this intense and this beautiful was *this* ready to screw.

"How 'bout I fuck the answer out of you?" he proposed.

"How about we just fuck?" she replied.

SIMONE

Simone Redding—Red to her friends—was a ball of fire. A volcano coiled to erupt. Inches away from Luciano Santini was a very different experience than watching him from afar with binos.

Holy hell.

Normally chill, she was quivering with pent-up desire. Logic had flown out the window. If she had a modicum of sanity, she would walk away, drive straight home, and pretend their chance encounter had never happened.

But this was *no* chance encounter and it *was* happening. He'd turned the tables on her, cornering her at her one hedonistic escape.

Hooking up with Luciano Santino sounded like a sinfully perfect way to spend an hour... or several. As she stared into the eyes of the devil himself, he flashed her a wicked smile.

Do it.

She grasped his shirt, tugged him close, and kissed him. Hard. He slithered his arm around her, pulled her tight against him, and slid his tongue inside her mouth with a sweeping motion. The gentle way he kissed her was in sharp contrast to the possessive way he held her.

And she loved it.

Then, he placed his other hand on the small of her back, just above her ass, and locked her into place. Trapped, she released a groan so gritty she didn't recognize her own voice. She pressed her tongue against his, tasting this sinful man for a second time.

Damn, he tastes good.

She pressed her hands against his pecs and was rewarded with bulging muscles straining against his white dress shirt. In one swift move, she slid her hands under the suit jacket and onto his shoulders, forcing him out of his garment.

"Nice," he murmured. "I like a woman who strips me naked."

As she unbuttoned his dress shirt, she stared into his eyes while his steely gaze never left hers. Her heart was pounding, her breathing fast and shallow, and her insides wet with desire.

She was loving every single second with a man she shouldn't be within fifty feet of.

After tugging his shirt out of his pants, she finished unfastening each button before raking her fingers down his hard pecs. The red-lit room bathed him in a seductive glow, but it was the heat from his perfectly-sculpted torso that had her pressing her mouth against his skin. Her eyes fluttered closed and she kissed his chest, then kissed him again. Soft skin over hard muscles. But she returned her gaze to his strikingly handsome face while she unbuckled his belt, unzipped his pants, and let them drop.

She massaged his shaft, trapped beneath his black boxer briefs, then before she could check herself, she slipped her hands inside the material, pulling it over his cock, and letting it pool at his ankles.

His breath hitched, once, and she bit back a smile. Maybe, just maybe, she was having an effect on him, but he was impossible to read... beyond his jutting cock.

She wrapped her fingers around his shaft. His thick, stiff rod sent a moan ripping from her chest. Her insides were pulsing hard, her pussy desperate for his touch, but it was the fire in his eyes that made her wild with need.

"If I suck you—" she murmured.

"I'll come."

"Been a while?"

"You're very sexy."

"Are you clean?" she asked.

He ran the back of his hand down her cheek, and she inhaled a jagged breath. "I'm clean."

She knelt at his feet, stared up at him. The need to take him in her mouth, to taste his juices had taken control of her senses.

She had to have him, something she would regret in the light of day.

But he'd stepped into her world. Here, the only thing that mattered was consent. She would deal with reality when the day dawned.

Taking the smooth head of his cock into her mouth sent streaks of white-hot energy soaring through her. She ran her tongue over his skin and was rewarded with a salty sampling and a throaty moan.

"You feel fantastic," he said.

A groan ripped from her throat as she pushed him in deeper while cradling his balls in her hand. Her insides were throbbing hard, the desire to take him inside her had her sucking him with a ferocity she'd never known. Hard and fast, over and over again.

In this moment, she held the power, and she was unleashing it all on him.

"Jesus," he bit out as his fingers sunk into her hair. "So fucking good."

Luciano Santini was a big boy, but she pressed him farther back, until he choked her with his thick, hard rod. Then, she dragged him over her lips while curling her tongue around the oozing head.

"I'm gonna come so hard. Pull off if you—"

She didn't want to take him out. She *needed* to taste every last drop of him and swallow him down. Drunk on his essence, she massaged his shaft while bobbing wildly on the head. And she hadn't stopped cradling his tightening balls with her other hand.

Her reward?

Him, roaring through his massive orgasm while he released himself into her.

When he finished, she slowed to a stop, and pulled off him.

With a firm touch, he pulled her into his arms, kissing her with a wildness that left her gasping for air.

Being with him was wrong, swallowing him down was a dirty little pleasure she hadn't done in years. And she loved every minute she was spending with someone she shouldn't even be speaking to.

So much for following protocol.

His ringing phone interrupted their lusty moment with the reality that the outside world still existed. He silenced it, toed off his shoe boots, and stepped out of his pants. With his fiery gaze drilling into hers, he unfastened her shirt's buttons, slowly revealing her breasts. She pulled it off her shoulders, letting it tumble to the floor.

Bare chested, she felt comfortable topless. While her breasts were smaller than most, she had great ones. And she loved her large nipples which, at the moment, stood very erect. Couldn't miss those high beams, even in a dense fog on a stormy night.

Luciano caressed her chest, running his fingers over the swell of one breast, then the other, before teasing her hard nips with his thumb.

"You're a naughty woman, Simone," he growled before latching onto her nipple and sucking.

Desire throbbed through her and her eyes fluttered closed. Forcing them open, she watched as he expertly licked and tongued one nipple, then the other. His gritty groans charged through her, each landing between her legs. Eager to touch him, she sunk her fingers into his thick, almost jet-black hair, and a whisper-soft sigh escaped her throat.

He's total male perfection.

While sucking her nipple, he reached around, unzipped her skirt, sending it plummeting to the floor. His fingers skimmed her exposed pussy, and she trembled with excitement. Wearing only stilettos, she heaved in a slow, deep breath, hoping to calm her palpitating heart.

"Please," she murmured.

He lifted her in his arms, laid her on the bed. One panty-searing kiss had her writhing beneath him. Pausing, he stared into her eyes, and this random hookup turned a little too intimate for her. As he kissed his way down her heated body, hit after hit of glorious pleasure had her moaning on every breath. When he settled with his face between her legs, she couldn't take her eyes off him. Nothing sexier than a gorgeous man feasting on her.

Nothing.

And Luciano Santini was as hot as it got. She ought to know. She'd been tailing him nonstop for weeks.

His penetrating gaze stole her breath. "Bellisima."

"Thank you," she whispered.

"First, I ravage you with my mouth," he murmured. "Then, we fuck."

"Yessss," she hissed.

Luciano pressed his mouth to her pussy and licked her soaking wet opening. Mini explosions powered through her, but when he slid a finger inside her, she cried out.

"So fucking good," she groaned.

His phone rang as the bedroom door burst open. In the red-lit hallway stood his brother, Theodore Santini. Known nicknames: Teddy and Tank.

Fuck. Fuck me.

"We gotta go," Teddy blurted before he regarded her. "Sorry to interrupt."

Luciano pushed off the bed. "What's going on?"

"Dulles," Teddy replied.

"Five minutes," Luciano said.

"I only need two," Simone blurted.

"It's urgent," Teddy insisted.

Luciano kissed her cheek, then the other. "I have to go."

In seconds, he'd pulled on his boxers and pants, collected his shirt and suit jacket before following Teddy out. At the door, he turned back. "I'm sorry."

After he shut the door, she murmured, "You owe me an orgasm."

Frustration had her pushing off the bed. As she dressed, she knew that karma wasn't just a bitch, it was the universe's way of reminding her that she should never, *ever* get close to a mark.

While she could have stayed to watch the second live performance or she could have found another willing partner, she was done. Down the stairs and out the front door. The October breeze cooled her still-heated skin. Pulling out the ponytail holder, she ran her fingers through her long, wavy hair.

"What the hell is wrong with me?" she asked herself as she slid behind the wheel of her SUV.

I got caught up in the cyclone that's Luciano Santini.

As she drove toward home, she vowed, "Never again." But she wondered if she'd be able to keep her distance. She'd had a taste of him and she wanted another.

Not to mention he owes me one.

A smile tugged at the corners of her mouth. Without a doubt, she would definitely be interested in collecting on that.

2

THE TERRORISTS

LUCIANO

As his driver sped toward the airport, Luciano scrolled through the unread texts. His brother, Gabriel, had sent several cryptic ones, then Teddy had sent a few of his own before he'd started calling.

Luciano had turned on Do Not Disturb.

"For a fucking reason," he ground out.

"Say what?" Teddy asked.

"Talking to myself."

"You do that a lot, you know."

"What am I walking into?" Luciano asked as he closed the privacy screen. Though he trusted his driver, Stuart, the less he knew, the better.

"Gabriel called," Teddy began. "Three terrorists on the No-Fly List from the Haqazzii terror cell were detained at Heathrow. They were five minutes from boarding a flight to Dulles. Scotland Yard detained them, but Gabriel is having them moved. They're traveling under legit US passports with aliases." Teddy checked the time on his phone. "You're cutting it close, which is why I had to, um, step in."

"I'll finish what I started when I get back."

"You shouldn't even be talking to her," Teddy said.

"We *weren't* talking."

Teddy chuffed out a laugh before running his hand through his long, blond hair. "No, you weren't."

The brothers grew silent as the sedan sped toward the airport, then over to general aviation. Luciano extended his hand. When Teddy clasped it, Luciano said, "Join me. You love roughing up the bad actors."

"No thanks," Teddy replied.

His brother hadn't stepped on an airplane in years, and not even taking out known terrorists would change his mind.

The back door opened. Luciano exited the vehicle, and Stuart handed him his laptop satchel and a black leather duffle bag. "Safe travels, sir."

Luciano entered the building, made his way to the check-in counter. "Suzie, working the late shift again."

"Mr. Santini, hello." Her round face flushed crimson.

Minutes later, Luciano walked onto his private jet and said hello to his pilots.

"Are we waiting for anyone else?" the co-pilot asked.

"No."

"How long will we be there?" asked the pilot.

"Two hours, three tops," Luciano replied.

"We've got good flying conditions, so we'll get you there as soon as we can."

"Flight time?"

"About seven hours," replied the pilot.

Luciano retreated into the twenty-seat cabin, set down the bags before sitting at a four-person table. He extracted his laptop, signed in, and opened the file called Background

Checks. After finding what he needed, he called his personal assistant.

"Good evening, Mr. Santini," answered Dominic.

"I need a large bouquet of flowers sent to Simone Redding," he said. "Include birds of paradise and roses."

"What do you want the card to say?"

"Next time, ladies first," Luciano replied.

"Where is it being sent?"

He rattled off her home address and phone number from the report.

"Anything else?"

"Have it delivered tomorrow midafternoon and *don't* add my name to the card. Just the note."

"Yes, sir," his assistant replied.

Luciano ended the call, logged into his personal email account.

"Mr. Santini, we're cleared for take-off," said the co-pilot through the intercom.

Luciano snapped the seatbelt into place, opened the window shade, and stared into the night. As the bird taxied toward the runway, his thoughts jumped to a very seductive, very naked Simone Redding, sprawled on the bed. His cock stirred.

Stand down. You had your fun.

He hadn't planned on hooking up with her, but Simone Redding was impossible to refuse. His stalker had it all. But it wasn't only her physical beauty that had interested him, it was the intense energy she brought with her. Currently, she held *all* the power.

And *that*, he found irresistible.

The aircraft gained speed as it raced down the runway, then lifted effortlessly off the ground. Luciano glanced down at the sights below, but the bing of an email diverted his attention.

When he opened it, the faces of three men appeared on the screen. All three were members of Haqazzii's organization. Despite the deaths of the senior Haqazzii and his eldest son, the others—led by the only living son and run by his cousins—were reemerging as one of the most dangerous threats on the planet.

They lived to terrorize, torture, and eliminate innocent souls.

A growl shot from Luciano. He would travel to the ends of the earth to hunt down men like this. As he studied their mug shots, he wondered how'd they'd gotten into the UK with US passports. He had two goals? Extract information, then terminate them.

Something he was more than willing to do.

He spent the majority of the flight working. As CEO and President of Santini International, he could work nonstop and never get it all done. He had big goals, bigger dreams, and a passion for creating. It was a blessing and a curse because he was like a damn cat chasing its tail.

A few hours into the flight, while reviewing sketches for next fall's lines, his thoughts drifted to Simone again.

Over the past month, he'd spotted her outside his gated mansion more than once, he'd seen her on the banks of the river during his cousin's wedding, and he'd eyed her waiting for him when he got into his limo at the end of a workday. Always hiding in the shadows or behind a pair of binos, she'd been impossible to ID.

That's where Teddy had come in. He'd snapped a pic of her and uploaded it to Stryker Truman's propriety IDWare. That gave him a name.

Simone Redding.

But the background check had been useless. Beyond her name and address, there was nothing. Since Luciano had enemies, he couldn't begin to know who had hired her to watch him. Rather than try to figure it out, he decided to confront her directly.

Some good that had done.

His lips quirked into a sliver of a smile.

It did me a lot of good... and gives me a legit reason to see her again. We have unfinished business.

With his duffle in hand, he retreated into the restroom. Unlike a commercial jet, he had a large lavatory equipped with two sinks, a small shower, and a water closet. He changed from his white dress shirt and black suit to a black turtleneck, black pants, and black boots, then shoved a black ski mask into the pocket of his black leather jacket.

He pulled on his shoulder harness, pulled one Glock from the bag and fitted it into the holster, then slid the second Glock into the other jacket pocket. He strapped a holster around his ankle, secured a small sidearm in that. After exiting the restroom, he locked his duffle in the closet.

At the expected hour, the jet touched down at Heathrow. Before deplaning, he locked his laptop in the closet, thanked the pilots, and told them he'd text them when he was ready to fly home.

Though he didn't change the time on his Omega watch, his iPhone automatically adjusted to the new time zone thrusting him five hours into the future. He walked through the terminal and exited out the front, sliding on his shades despite the light rain and cloudy day.

He pulled up the photo of the driver Gabriel had hired, then scanned the line of waiting limos at the curb. A woman exited one of the Bentleys, opened the back door. Luciano walked over, shook her hand. She offered a tight smile before he slid into the back seat.

Though the privacy screen was down, she made no small talk. He fixed his gaze out the window, the kilometers ticking by, the buildings becoming more rundown as they got closer to their destination. She pulled in front of an abandoned one-story building at the end of a quiet street.

"I'll wait down the street," she said, her British accent catching his ear.

Luciano exited the vehicle, tried the front door. It was locked. He sent Gabriel a text.

> I'm here

Seconds later, his brother opened the door, and Luciano slipped inside. They greeted each other with only a nod. No words needed.

The rundown space was cavernous, gray light from outside bathing the room in somber shadows. Rain started coming down harder, the pitter-patter on dirty windows sounding like the tapping of anxious fingers against the glass panes. Empty booze bottles were strewn about and several long-deserted conference-room tables and chairs stood nearby in various stages of disrepair.

Luciano eyed the three men seated at a table, their wrists bound behind their backs, their ankles secured with zip ties, and black cloth sacks covering their heads.

As he stood across the table from them, Gabriel removed their head coverings. One spit at Luciano. The second was sweating profusely. The third glared at him.

Gabriel stood next to Luciano and held up three passports. "How'd you get these?"

Silence.

Then, the first man said something in Arabic.

"English!" Gabriel demanded.

"I speak little," said the second man.

"Fuck you," said the third.

"We can do the question-and-answer thing all day," Gabriel said, "or you can tell us how you got these."

"What we get if we talk?" asked the second man.

Gabriel pulled a folded map from his pocket, handed it to Luciano. "Found this on the third guy."

Luciano opened the tourist map of DC. Six buildings were circled. The White House, the U.S. Capitol, the J. Edgar Hoover building, Justice, State Department, and the Supreme Court. An arrow pointed toward Arlington with the word Pentagon scribbled in ink and a second arrow pointed toward Northern Virginia. On that arrow, someone had written CIA.

"What do you get if you talk?" Luciano repeated. "You don't *get* anything. This isn't a negotiation. We aren't the good guys." He glared at them. "We're here for answers. Talk."

The first man shoved back in the chair, then pushed to his feet. He screamed, "Death to Americans!" in a thick accent, but his bound ankles restricted his ability to move. He lost his balance and fell on the hard, concrete floor.

"Fuck!" he hollered, then screamed more obscenities in his native language.

"Shut-up," yelled the second man.

Gabriel opened one of the passports. "These are authentic, and your aliases checked out." He eyed the first terrorist lying on the filthy floor. "You're a professor at American University." He shot the second man a cool stare. "You're a translator with the State Department." Gabriel shook his head. "Not buying that either." And you, my friend—" He glared at the third man — "You're a newspaper reporter."

Luciano's patience had run out. These men weren't going to divulge anything. They were bound by their loyalty to their terror cell.

"Haqazzii," Luciano said. "You going to blow up these buildings? Who do you work for?"

"The Bomb Maker," said the second one. "We work for him."

"Tell us his name," Luciano rasped.

Gabriel walked over to the man on the floor, pointed his Glock at the man's head. "Someone tells us or this one goes."

The third one shoved out of his chair and lunged for Gabriel.

BANG! BANG! BANG!

Luciano opened fire and the man dropped, blood pouring from his wounds.

The one on the floor started crawling toward Luciano. "You die! You die!"

BANG!

Gabriel shot him in the head and he stilled.

"Last chance," Luciano said to the second one. "Who is The Bomb Maker?"

"He is in America and he will kill you all," said the thug. "I die to honor him."

Movement caught Luciano's eye. From the back of the building, a man dressed in black ran toward them, a rifle cradled in his arms. He eyed the man on the floor, shouted in Arabic, and pulled to an abrupt stop, hatred spewing from his every pore.

The second man jumped up. "Kill them!"

"Death to Americans!" screamed the armed terrorist.

Luciano and Gabriel opened fire on both men.

BANG! BANG! BANG! BANG! BANG! BANG!

The terrorist dropped, his body riddled with bullets, and the second slumped forward on the table, blood oozing from his head.

"Who the hell is The Bomb Maker?" Gabriel asked, as he holstered his weapon.

"I don't know," Luciano replied, doing the same with his Glock. "But I know someone who will."

Moving swiftly, they exited the warehouse. The waiting limo had moved down the street. It flashed its lights, drove toward them. Luciano texted the pilots that he was returning to

Heathrow and received confirmation they were ready to depart.

"Where are you headed?" Luciano asked.

"Back to Italy," Gabriel replied. "I need a ride to the airport."

"How did you get here?"

"My contact. The one who drove the van of prisoners."

"Someone you can trust?" Luciano asked as the driver exited the vehicle, opened the door for him.

"Trust?" Gabriel shook his head. "What the hell is that?"

Luciano tossed a nod toward the limo driver. Gabriel pulled out his Glock, and the driver flicked her gaze to the weapon.

"This isn't going to get ugly, is it?" she asked.

"That's up to you," Luciano replied.

"I'm being paid a lot of money for this job," she said. "I was told not to ask questions, no chit chat, just drive. I can do that if you put the damn gun away."

Gabriel glanced at Luciano, who nodded once. His brother returned the weapon to its holster, and the men ducked into the vehicle. The driver said nothing en route to Heathrow. At Departures, Luciano hugged his brother goodbye, waited until he disappeared into the main terminal.

Minutes later, Luciano was seated in his jet, the pilots waiting for clearance to taxi. He retrieved his bags, got comfortable in a leather chair, and stared out the window. While his heart should have felt heavy, it didn't.

That's because I don't have a heart. Not anymore.

If the Bomb Maker was already in the US, how many steps ahead of law enforcement was he?

On the flight back, he texted his cousin, Carrera Santini, a senior exec at the FBI and Sinclair Develin, the man known for being Washington, DC's Fixer.

> We need to talk

Seconds passed, then a response from Carrera.

> Come to the house for dinner Monday

Followed by a response from Sin.

> In Miami. Back Monday afternoon. Talk then.

Monday couldn't come soon enough for Luciano. In the meantime, he'd occupy his thoughts with something much more arousing.

Simone Redding.

SIMONE

Sunday late afternoon, Simone was working at her kitchen table when the doorbell rang. She checked the app.

No way.

She swung open her front door to the largest bouquet she'd ever seen.

"Simone Redding?" asked the courier.

"You got her." After taking the bouquet, she returned to the kitchen and set it on the table.

There's no way it's from him.

As she plucked out the card, she admitted that getting flowers from Luciano Santini wouldn't be the end of the world. It's not like her boss would find out. As far as Simone knew, she wasn't sure what her new boss knew or didn't know, but that was all going to get cleared up on Monday.

She read the card...

Next time, ladies first

...and warmth spread from her chest up to her neck while her lips tugged up in a smile.

There was no signature, but she didn't need to call the florist.

The bouquet was lavish. Leaning close, she inhaled a heavily-scented pink rose, then a yellow one with bright orange tips. Her eyes fluttered closed and she breathed them in again.

So beautiful.

The five Birds of Paradise alone were stunning, but paired with the dozen roses, the baby's breath, and the greenery, made for a breathtaking arrangement.

He knows how to get my attention.

She moved the vase to the center island, then cleaned up her brunch dishes and pans from hours earlier. Back at the kitchen table, she continued working, pausing to appreciate the stunning bouquet.

As a watcher for Z—real name: Philip Skye—she'd been left to do her own thing. It was an easy gig that had served its purpose, but as of late, she'd grown bored.

Maybe that's a good sign. Maybe I'm ready to go back.

Years earlier, when an ALPHA Operative had gone off the rails and killed another Op, Z had created the watcher. These top-secret positions ensured that the people hired to serve and protect at the highest level, were doing their jobs and not engaged in any activities that would compromise their positions or the organizations they served.

Over the past two years, she'd watched plenty of ALPHA Ops, FBI Special Agents, Secret Service Agents, high-ranking military officers, and Navy SEALS. Every gig was different. After a designated period of time, she'd write up a report and forward it to Z. Sometimes Simone would observe an ALPHA Op after a mission, especially when the mission didn't go as expected.

Pain shot through her chest. She knew, firsthand, how that felt.

Now that Z had retired, she'd been readying her reports for her new boss, Carrera Santini. Reading through the file on Luciano Santini, she wondered what Carrera would say about her watching his cousin. One thing she had gleaned from Z's off-the-books gig was that Luciano conducted a lot of work in person at his mansion in Great Falls.

Though Z was convinced Luciano was still involved in his family's crime business, she had seen nothing that would lead her to believe he was doing anything illegal. Admittedly, she hadn't been able to learn very much about him at all. Once his guests were behind the massive gates and fence surrounding his estate, they vanished from sight.

Where Luciano lived was very special to her. He had purchased the property from Colton Mitus, whose home had been her refuge for three years while she patched together the shattered pieces of her broken life.

A shudder had her pushing out of her chair. While she'd loved working for Colton and appreciated that he'd afforded her a safe place to live, she hated thinking about *why* she'd gone there in the first place.

The aroma of freshly-cut flowers wafted in her direction and she ran her fingertip over the velvety petals of a yellow rose. One more inhale before she filled her mug and sat back down. She opened the dossier she'd created on Luciano Santini, skimmed the report until she found what she needed —his personal cell phone number. With phone in hand, she typed out a simple text.

> The flowers are beautiful. Thank you. I don't think we should get together again.

Her finger hovered over the up arrow. Instead of sending the message, she re-read the card.

Next time, ladies first

Her thoughts drifted to his hard, sculpted body, his hungry mouth on hers, the sensuality in his touch, and the possessive way he held her. Her insides quivered with desire.

Why say no to sex with a handsome, powerful man? It's just a hookup... for the fun of it.

She deleted the last sentence.

> The flowers are beautiful. Thank you

Before she could change her mind or analyze it further, she sent it, then turned her attention back to work.

Her phone buzzed with a text from her close friend, Frederica.

> Yo, I'm leaving the gym. Should I swing by?

Since day one at Quantico, she and Frederica—Fred for short—had become fast friends. Though they were very different, both physically and how they approached a challenge, they worked well together and they got along great.

A short time later, her doorbell rang. Simone hurried to open it.

"Safe to enter?" Fred asked.

"Come back later. I'm busy with my harem of men."

Laughing, they entered her kitchen. After Fred dropped her workout bag in the corner, she filled her water bottle. Her short, blonde hair was plastered to her head and her workout clothes were damp with sweat.

"Are you trying to kill yourself?" Simone asked.

Fred eased down at the kitchen island and swiveled toward

Simone. "I've got a mission this week, so I pushed myself super hard."

A pang of envy shot through her, but she squashed it down. "Tell me about it."

As an ALPHA Operative, Fred chased down the worst of the worst. Serial rapists, serial killers, and terrorists who escaped prison or got off on a technicality or a botched police investigation, then went right back to doing whatever heinous crime had gotten them arrested in the first place. Most times, ALPHA arrested them, but sometimes their missions would call for more drastic measures.

Elimination.

It was a dangerous job that could go wrong more ways than it could go right.

Fred stood there gawking at the bouquet. "What the— okay, so you *gotta* spill. Who is this from? What kind of wild sex happened to get a bouquet *that* big?"

Simone emptied her coffee in the sink and filled a glass with water. "You won't believe me."

After inhaling the beautiful scent of the flowers, Fred said, "These are not grocery store roses. This is *the* real deal here, like, from a high-end florist."

"I know. My kitchen has never smelled so good."

"I'm starving." Fred opened the refrigerator door. "You made brunch!" A squeal of delight had her pulling out plastic containers.

She slid an English muffin into the toaster, popped a plate of scrambled eggs with chopped mushrooms and onions, and three pieces of bacon, into the microwave.

"You missed your true calling," Fred said. "Chef."

A flicker of melancholy washed over Simone. She knew her true calling, but she'd walked from it years ago. Being an Op had been the best job Simone had ever had.

As if sensing her sadness, Fred put her arm around Simone,

gave her a quick hug. "ALPHA would welcome you back just like *that*." She snapped her fingers.

Shorter than Simone, Fred was more muscular, and someone who lived for work. At thirty-five, she was three years older than Simone. She'd never married, but had been engaged twice. No kids, no pets. She was a phenomenal ALPHA Operative who gave one-hundred percent on every single mission.

"You know the secret to my cooking," Simone said.

"Yup. Butter." Fred slathered some on the English muffin, pulled the plate of bacon and eggs from the microwave, and sat catty-corner at the table. After taking a bite, she said, "I'm still waiting."

"For what?"

"Who sent you the flowers, Red?"

She loved the nickname Fred had given her during their training at Quantico.

Simone chugged some water. "I went to Burke's last night. I hadn't been in a while, but I got myself on the list."

"Nice."

"Turns out, I was being stalked."

Fred furrowed her brow. "For real?"

"By one of the men I've been watching."

"No shit. Turned the table on you, huh? So, what, you hooked up with him? Must've been someone pretty hot for you to do that. Good thing Z is gone. He woulda canned your ass for sure. Okay, drumroll...hit me with it."

"Luciano Santini."

Fred's eyes widened, her eyebrows crowding her forehead. She opened her mouth, but said nothing.

"Yeah, so you're speechless," Simone said. "That's not something I see very often."

"How did that even happen?"

"He said, and I quote, 'You've been watching me from a distance for over a month. Time for a closer look-see.'"

"I love that. He's definitely my kind of man. Went on the offense and cornered you at your secret hideout."

"I know, right? Pretty slick."

"Sooo, how was it?"

"He's sexy as hell, very smooth, and sick handsome. So get this, I took care of him, but when he was about to return the favor, he got called away—"

Fred's belly laugh made Simone chuckle. "That is too perfect." She continued laughing. "You've been watching him for weeks, he stalks you, you give him a blowjob. That man has the most charmed life. Did you get any dirt on him?"

"Not a damn thing. If he's doing anything illegal, he flies well below the radar. He's taken his private jet a few times, but I can't find out where he goes and he's never gone for more than twenty-four hours."

Fred rubbed her hands together. "Ooooh, a man of mystery." She plucked the card from the bouquet. "He wants an encore. Go for it. I mean, the man owes you one. Who would turn down sex with *him*?"

"I got caught up in the party," Simone said. "Hard not to when everyone's screwing."

"Don't overthink this. Let him take care of you. It's an orgasm, not a marriage proposal. Seriously, just go with it."

"I won't overthink it," Simone said. "Sex for the sake of it."

"Exactly. Isn't that why you went to Burke's? To hook up with some stranger?"

"I went to Burke's because I'm a sexual pervert," Simone replied, and the women laughed.

"Right, my voyeur friend. I forgot you're into watching." She pulled Simone's laptop over. "Unlock this for me." After Simone did, Fred logged into their website.

"Our site is crap," Fred said. "Totally outdated. I have ideas. If you like them, I'll ask for the changes."

When they'd both moved from FBI Special Agents to Operatives at ALPHA, Z had suggested their cover—personal shoppers for a fictitious group of high-end clients.

Fred turned the laptop toward her.

Red & Fred
Personal Shoppers with an Eye for Design

Then, pointed out all the places where they could make improvements.

"This needs new verbiage," Fred said. "The graphics are, like, five years old. We need a complete overhaul."

The doorbell rang.

Simone checked her doorbell app and her heart skipped a beat. "No way." Standing there dressed in all black was Luciano Santini. She spun her phone toward Fred.

"Oh, wow, it's him." Grinning from ear to ear, Fred took off toward the front door. After opening it, she said, "Here to see Red?"

Excitement fluttered through her.

Here we go.

"Who?" Luciano asked.

"Oh, sorry. Simone."

"Yes, Simone. Is she home?"

"Sure is. Who can I say is calling?"

"Luciano Santini."

Simone wondered how many house calls he made. She doubted many.

"I'm her business partner, Frederica. C'mon in."

Unlike the previous evening, Simone wore no makeup. She'd dressed in a pair of shorts and a worn sweatshirt from her alma mater, Boston University. The urge to flee upstairs had her foot moving in a frenetic rhythm beneath the kitchen table. Rather than sit there bouncing, she pushed out of the chair.

Fred strolled into the kitchen, a smug smile covering her face. "I should probably take off."

"You don't have to—" Simone's attention was hijacked the second Luciano entered her kitchen.

Instead of the air getting sucked from her lungs, she breathed deep. Her shoulders relaxed while her gaze floated over him. Not one strand of his beautiful, thick hair was out of place, his perfectly sculpted face had her biting back a moan, until her attention dropped to the rest of him. And that damn moan ripped from her, but she cleared her throat, hoping to cover.

"Mr. Santini, hello... again." She extended her hand. She needed to do *something* and she sure as hell wasn't going to hug him.

Maul him, yes. But hug him, no.

"Ms. Redding." He took her hand, pulled her toward him, then pressed his luscious mouth to her cheek and kissed her. Slow, purposeful, and utterly captivating.

"Oh, mama," Fred whispered.

On impulse, Simone palmed his chest. The soft cashmere sweater warmed her skin, but his naked skin would feel so much better. He kissed her other cheek, this time letting his lips linger an extra beat.

When he stepped away, she wanted to pull him close again and give him a *real* kiss hello.

Stop. Get it together.

"Did I catch you at a bad time?" he asked, the intensity in his eyes turning up the heat.

"Frederica and I are just having a business meeting," Simone replied, as Fred displayed their barebones website.

Though it could have been cringy, Simone just went with it. She'd stopped apologizing and making excuses for herself a long time ago.

"Red and Fred," Luciano read before he regarded Simone.

"You're personal shoppers?" His lips twitched, but the smile he was biting back shone in his eyes.

He wasn't buying it, but she wouldn't expect him to. He was one of the most successful businessmen in the world. His clothing lines were legendary... and expensive as hell.

"We have a small client base," Fred said before addressing Simone. "I'll go ahead and ask our website designer to make those changes." After a brief pause, she asked, "Red, are we still on for dinner this week?"

"When is that again?" Simone asked, blanking on pretty much everything.

"Tuesday. If you're too...um... *busy* to cook, I'll pick up something. Love you, babe." Collecting her gym bag, Fred tossed a nod at Luciano. "You two kids have fun."

And she was gone.

Alone with Luciano Santini.

Simone shifted toward him and his hungry gaze devoured her alive.

Ohgod, what am I getting myself into?

3

THE OMEGA

LUCIANO

Luciano didn't stop by a woman's home, *ever*. For reasons that were completely foreign to him, he had to see Simone. After landing at Dulles, he'd instructed Stuart to drive him to her house in Alexandria.

Beyond her obvious beauty, grace, and *talents*, he needed to know why she'd been tailing him. That's what he kept telling himself, but that wasn't the real reason. In a word, intrigue had him swinging by her house. She was different... and he liked that.

He found himself staring into her eyes while the energy swirled around them. "I wanted to apologize for leaving so abruptly."

"I found someone else to finish the job."

Of course she did.

Then, she smiled.

A shot of adrenaline surged through him. He arched an eyebrow, then walked right up to her. "I started something I have every intention of finishing."

Her breath hitched and her lips parted. She did a quick glance at his mouth before pinning him with her bright green eyes. "What did you have in mind?"

"Have dinner with me."

"Why would I do that?"

"We both know the answer."

"Because I'll be hungry?" She opened her refrigerator. "And I don't have anything to eat?"

He glanced inside. Looked stocked to him, but he wasn't there to inventory her food supply.

"What won't you eat?" he asked.

"Red meat. I used to be a vegetarian, but now I eat chicken and fish."

"Do you get seasick?"

Up went her eyebrows. "If I say yes, will that get me out of this?"

He smiled. "We'll dine on my boat."

"Planning to throw me overboard?"

"Come hungry." The urge to touch her had him pressing his lips to her soft cheek. One lingering kiss, then a second to her other cheek. Her flowery aroma soothed him, and he inhaled deep.

Rather than step away, he stared into her eyes. Her pupils expanded, blanketing her irises in a sea of blackness. The intensity in her gaze kept him cemented in place, but the second she stroked his arm, he pulled her close and kissed her.

"Fuck," she murmured as she snaked her arms around him and pressed flush against him.

It would be easy to succumb to the desire. Take her in her kitchen, or in her bed, but he was better than that. She wasn't going to get fucked now.

She'd have to wait until later.

"One dinner, that's it," she said taking a step toward her front door.

"Because you're eager to get back to spying on me?" She tried biting back a smile, but failed. He liked the effect he was having on her. "As a personal shopper," he continued, "you can take our training programs and become a verified shopper for us."

He was calling her bluff.

She said nothing.

Once outside, he peered down at her. "Addio bella."

As he stepped off the porch, her moan caught his ear. She was having the same effect on him. A powerful—and dangerous—mix of emotions. He shouldn't be *engaging* her. He should be cutting her off, punishing her for snooping.

But he wasn't afraid. Fear was an emotion that *never* came into play.

Stuart opened the back door of the Rolls Royce. After slipping inside, Luciano glanced up at her front porch, but she was gone. As the sedan drove away, he pulled up her background check on his phone.

Who are you Simone Redding, and why can't I find out anything about you?

His phone buzzed with an incoming text from his cousin Willie—known to fhe family as Willie Boy.

> A biz associate asked for an intro. Tomorrow good?

Luciano gritted his teeth. His cousin was high maintenance, but he was family, so Luciano accepted him. It was born out of a promise to Willie Boy's father before he went to prison.

Rather than get into it by text, he called his cousin.

"Heyo, Lulu," Willie boy answered. "When you comin' by?"

"Who is he and what does he want?" Luciano asked as the car gained speed on the beltway toward Great Falls.

"His name is Dante. Known the dude for years. He's lookin' to grow his business."

Luciano slid his gaze out the window. "How?"

"Lulu, he asked for a meeting. Come by the restaurant. Spend ten minutes with him. Decide for yourself."

"So, you don't know?" Luciano shook his head in frustration.

"He didn't get into deets."

"Monday at six. Ten minutes."

"Thanks, bud." The line went dead.

Luciano called his chef.

"Yes, sir," Louis answered.

"Dinner for two on my yacht tonight. No red meat. I'll take the meal with me."

"What time?"

"Six-thirty," Luciano replied.

"It'll be ready."

"Thank you, Louis."

"Of course, sir."

As Stuart drove him to Great Falls, Luciano worked. There was always something that needed his approval, a new clothing line to review, a virtual meeting to jump in on. In such a creative industry, the only one he was competing against was himself. What could he improve upon? How many new collections could he add in the coming year? And how could he hone his work environment so his employees *loved* their jobs?

He returned home, headed into the kitchen.

"I was already preparing Coq au Vin with mushrooms," said his chef. "One of your favorites."

"Perfect, Louis."

"I'm pairing it with roasted baby potatoes and my kale salad."

"Very nice," Luciano said before trotting up the winding staircase and down the long hall to his bedroom.

The house was too large for one person, but it was a perfect place to seek refuge when his life had blown up around him.

Over time, he'd hired Chef Louis, who lived there with his wife, Therese, an in-house attorney at Santini International. Luciano had the lower level redesigned into their living space. Mitus had used it for kink shows, but when Luciano moved in, sex was the last thing on his mind.

After showering, he dressed in black pants, a tailored white shirt, and a black sport coat. All his clothes were handmade by his personal tailor at Santini International.

Forty-five minutes later, he was back in the sedan, being driven toward Simone's. This time darkness blanketed the evening sky.

As he was climbing the steps to her porch, the front door opened. She exited wearing a black, pleated jumpsuit with V-neck. An ordinary garment that hugged her like a second skin. She would look stunning in one of *his* jumpsuits from their newly-developed ladies' collection.

A surge of testosterone made his heart pound faster. "You look beautiful, Ms. Redding."

"Mr. Santini."

"Call me Luciano."

She stepped outside, locked her front door.

"You can call me Ms. Redding." She arched a perfectly sculpted eyebrow before dropping her gaze to check him out. Slowly. And he loved every second of her eye-fuck.

"You clean up well," she said.

That constant pull to touch her had him stroking her back. Once. Twice. Then, he removed his hand. This wasn't a date. This was a one-off meeting. He wanted information. He owed her physical gratification. It sounded cold, but he didn't want to read too much into their evening. He didn't trust her, and he knew nothing about her. Most likely, she had her own agenda.

Stuart opened the back door of the Rolls Royce. She slid in, he followed. Seconds later, the sedan pulled onto the street.

"Something smells good," she said.

"Coq au Vin."

"If you're doing this to get me to talk, it's not happening," she said.

"At all?" he asked. "I'm not talking about myself all evening."

"Most men love talking about themselves."

"Not me." After a beat, he said, "I won't ask you why you've been following me if you don't hide surveillance devices on my yacht."

She opened her small clutch and showed him. "Beyond lip gloss, my cell phone, and my driver's license—so they can ID my body when it washes up on shore—there's nothing."

He ran the back of his fingers over her soft cheek. "Only pleasure. No pain."

"Death isn't always painful."

His heart squeezed. All death was painful. If not to the victims, then to the survivors.

Forcing himself to stay in the moment, he said, "Ms. Redding, I'm going to make you writhe in ecstasy until you surrender to the pleasure again and again."

"Ohgod." Her breathy whisper floated in the air between them.

Their undeniable connection had him peering into her eyes, the pull to kiss her impossible to ignore. It was like nothing he'd experienced, and he couldn't tear his gaze away.

"What excites you?" he murmured.

"I'm a voyeur," she said. "That's why I went to Burke's. I don't like hookups, so I wouldn't have had sex with a stranger."

"Why did you have sex with me?"

"I've been watching you for weeks. You didn't feel like a stranger."

Same.

She crossed her legs and the slit in her jumpsuit revealed

her toned thigh. Like a magnet, he was drawn to her shapely leg.

With a gleam in her eyes, she took his hand, pressed his palm against her thigh. In that split second, everything jumped to Mach speed. Her breathing changed, a moan shot out of him. The air turned electric. When she slicked her tongue over her lower lip and glanced at his mouth, he captured her face in his hands, leaned over, and kissed her.

"Mmm," she purred as she pressed her tongue inside.

He kissed her slowly, relishing the way their tongues tangled, the seductive, growly sounds she made every time he caressed her bare thigh. She curled her long fingers around his biceps and squeezed, then intensified their kiss. Ignoring his trapped boner, he ran his fingers through her soft hair, letting the strands tickle his fingers. Then, he slowed the kiss, dropped a soft one on her lips before breaking away.

She heaved in a breath. "Nice."

"Wait until I put my mouth on your pussy," he murmured.

"And your brother barges in with another emergency."

He chuckled. "No interruptions tonight."

Her throaty moan sent a jolt to his cock, now straining to escape the confines of his pants. While he ran his fingertips over her thigh, she stared into his eyes.

"What're your fetishes?" she asked.

"Feet," he replied.

"Legs too?"

"Yours."

"I did see a few women going into the mansion. They were all tall."

"Next time you're outside my home, let my guard know. We'll make sure you get better pics."

Her smile sent another wave of excitement traversing through him. This was becoming addictive... and annoying. She had too much control over his emotions.

"Why feet?" she asked.

"They can be very erotic, especially with a toe ring or ankle bracelet. I like rubbing them. I like them on my cock. Blood red or black toenail polish is key."

"I like it rough sometimes," she confessed. "I also like consent non-consent, but I haven't done that in a long time."

"Do you like to be tied up?" he asked his cock now throbbing.

"As part of the CNC, I do. And I like it from behind."

He pulled her to him, his mouth against hers while she pushed out of the seat and straddled him. Her fingers dove into his hair as she ground against him. He grabbed her ass with one hand, wrapped his other around her neck. Despite her being on top of him, he was controlling her movement... or trying to, but she was grinding on him pretty good.

"Fuck," she bit out. "I'm out of control around you." She kissed him hard, then backed away, but she didn't climb off him.

The car stopped, Stuart exited the vehicle, and opened the back door.

Simone smirked at Luciano. "Busted." Pushing off him, she collected her clutch and got out.

Luciano raked his hands through his mussed hair and followed.

"Thank you, Stuart," Luciano said. "Take the night off. I'll call for an Uber."

"I'll wait," Stuart replied. "If I fall asleep and don't hear your text, call me. I'll be parked in your spot, sir." With the insulated travel bag of food in hand, Stuart headed down a pier.

Luciano clasped Simone's hand and led her toward his vessel. He liked touching her, liked how the warmth from her hand traveled up his arm.

"I'm not a hand holder," she said, "but I'm making an exception, just this once."

He squeezed her hand in acknowledgment.

"Which one is yours?" she asked.

"The last on the right. This is my cousin Carrera's marina. He runs Carrera Cruises, but I dock here."

"That's a lot of boat."

"It's a sixty-foot Princess Skybridge," he said.

"She's a beauty."

After Luciano helped her aboard the Omega, she removed her shoes, and waited on the sofa in the stern while he flipped on the blower, checked the engine compartment for bilge water, and disconnected the shore power. Once he'd fired up the engines, he and Stuart untied the ropes securing the yacht to the slip.

"Enjoy your evening, ma'am, Mr. Santini," Stuart said before walking back down the pier.

Luciano opened the door to the interior and Simone stepped inside.

"This is fancy."

He led her to the bridge, waited for her to climb into the plush leather co-captain's chair before he sat in his. "Time for fun, Ms. Redding."

He steered the yacht out of the marina, then through the No Wake zone. Once on the Potomac River, he increased the speed and the yacht glided effortlessly over the water. If there was anything that helped calm his tormented soul, it was boating. As he glanced over at his dinner companion, guilt slithered around his soul. He shouldn't be having fun, ever. He should be hunting down the monster who shredded his life.

As if sensing his struggles, she appeared by his side. "Call me Simone," she murmured, plucking him from his maddening thoughts.

In the darkness, his gaze found hers. She looked so much more relaxed on the water. Like she could leave her own demons on shore and drift happily downstream.

"I didn't learn anything about you," she whispered. "Not one damn thing."

"That's because there's nothing to learn," he lied.

She smiled. "I know who your friends are, so I'm sure you're up to something evil. I gotta say, though, you wear it very, very well."

"No one wears evil like I do," he said with a smile.

They passed a Carrera Cruise ship and then another. This part of the Potomac was a hot spot for evening boating, especially in the fall when the nights turned crisp. He captained the yacht until he found his favorite spot on the river. An alcove tucked out of the way. And he dropped anchor.

"Are you hungry?" he asked.

She slipped her hand under his sport coat and caressed his back, then dropped her hand to his ass and squeezed. "I'm starving. Absolutely starving."

The sultry look in her eyes was his green light. Then, she reached over and ran her hand over his crotch. "Are you hungry?"

"Yes," he replied. "I'm fucking famished."

∾

SIMONE

SIMONE COULD NOT REGULATE her breathing. Desire thrummed through her at a frenetic pace. From the intensity in Luciano's eyes to the way his designer duds hugged his perfectly sculpted body, she was primed for a release. It would take very little effort to push her over the edge.

But it was more than a physical attraction. He was the epitome of power. There was a strength in the way he carried himself, the way he spoke, and how he commanded the space. He demanded respect simply by existing. She'd never been around anyone like him. It was a heady combination that left her hungry for more.

He wrapped his hand around her arm, guided her from the bridge to the cabin. She admired the exquisite sofas, chairs, and artwork. She was floating, like she was having an out of body experience. Being on his private yacht didn't feel real. Was this a trap? Did he bring her here to force her to tell him who'd hired her?

Her insides were throbbing, and she shoved out any thoughts about her job, about her being a watcher, about his alleged white-collar crimes. In this moment, all that mattered was his mouth on hers, his body on hers, his cock inside her. That was it. She didn't care about anything else except this Adonis of a man standing inches away.

With a strong hand around her waist, he guided her down the stairs and into his private quarters at the end of the hallway, furnished with a beautifully appointed king-sized bed.

"My stateroom," was all he had to say.

She could tell him no, but that was the last thing she wanted to utter. Alone with Luciano Santini seemed like a bad decision she'd regret later. Now, it was absolutely necessary, like breathing. She *had* to have him. For her, there was no other option.

Standing behind her, he slowly unzipped her jumpsuit. When he pressed his lips to her skin and kissed her shoulder, a shiver of excitement raced down her back.

"Yes," she whispered dropping the clothes off her shoulders.

Once again, she'd skipped the bra and panties.

As if he governed time, he slowly circled around to face her. His attention dropped to her chest, her tits, then back into her eyes. Desire poured from them and she trembled with anticipation. Never before had she felt this kind of raw power. He removed her belt, the jumpsuit dropped to the floor. He stepped back, his ravenous gaze devouring her with an intensity that left her breathless.

His eyes turned black as coal. But it was the groan that ripped from his soul that made her knees weak.

She slipped off her sandals while he draped her outfit over a chair. With a grace that held her complete attention, he removed his sport coat and unbuttoned his shirt enough to tug it over his head in one smooth move. The desire to touch him had her moving close, but she didn't kiss him. She wanted him to kiss her.

With her attention pinned on him, she unbuckled and loosened his pants. Before they dropped, he pulled out a packet of condoms, tossed it on the bed. His pants hit the floor, his rock-hard erection rivaling the hard slab of his abdomen.

All man. All muscle. All hers.

Her pulse clamored in her ears, her pussy swollen with anticipation.

"I need you inside me," she murmured.

"Not until I make you come with my mouth, *Simone*."

She loved the way he said her name, the way his wicked-hot mouth formed the word, *Seemone*. Never before had it sounded so exotic. Never before had she needed a man to utter it over and over, again and again.

If he was evil, she was being romanced by the devil himself.

And she was all-in.

Flinging back the comforter and sheet, she crawled in and laid on her back. She was done waiting. It was time and she was ready.

"I love the way you taste," he murmured as he stalked over to her, then placed a pillow under her head. "Watch me ravage you."

"Ohmygod," she bleated.

How could one man undo her so easily? Was it his power?

His wealth? His looks? Was it that he was the most secretive man she'd ever met?

Whatever the answer, she was mesmerized by his every move.

Planking over her, he stared into her eyes. His mouth found hers and she groaned into him while her arms and legs wrapped him like a blanket. The kiss was wild and intense. Their tongues pulsed against each other while she raked her fingernails down his back. Their sounds reminded her of animals in the wild, the rawness of their embrace making her squirm and undulate beneath him.

He broke the kiss, his breath now coming faster, his eyes wild with need. He found her nipple, sucked it hard while pinching and teasing the other. Mini explosions of euphoria shot through her. But, when his slipped two fingers inside her, she rose off the bed, crying out from the pleasure.

"Luciano, oh, fuck, yessssss."

"You're soaked for me, Simone."

In and out he finger-fucked her, teasing her, taking her to the edge, but not over. Her senses were on fire, every part of her coiled for a release.

"If this is my punishment for spying on you, I accept."

He stopped. "Are you ready?"

His voice was deep, dark, even a little scary. To her, however, it was filled with so much promise. So much desire.

"Yes," she gasped. "I'm dying for you."

He put his gloriously handsome face between her legs and breathed deep. "So good." Then, he licked her opening, ran his tongue over her clit.

Shocks of pleasure charged through her. She sank her fingers into his thick, luscious hair while he massaged her pearl with his talented tongue. An assault of the absolute best kind. When he slipped three fingers inside her, she roared with pleasure.

"Harder, more, faster," she cried out. "Give me everything."

But he did just the opposite. He slowed down his licking, slowed his fingers too.

"You're killing me," she protested, her body shaking with anticipation.

"You want the pleasure to last, so let it build."

He moved away from her pussy altogether and collected her foot in his large hand. And he placed her big toe into his mouth and sucked. Tingles flew up her leg to her aching clit. He caressed the arch of her foot, sucked her second toe.

"I can't wait to fuck you," he said.

She bent her knees, spread her legs wide.

The fire in his eyes burned into her soul as he returned his face to her swollen pussy. With his hands positioned on the inside of her thighs, he tongued her with a ferocity that had her mewling. Over and over and over.

She started thrashing on the bed, then bucking. When he slid his fingers back inside her, the orgasm shot out of her so hard, she felt it in the back of her throat.

"Ohmygod," she blathered while she shook and convulsed through the orgasm. "Luciano, ohhhhh."

Streams of ecstasy washed over her while she stared down at him. When she grew still, he lifted his face. Her wetness covered his mustache, his mouth, his stubbled chin, but it was the smile on his face that sent her flying to the moon.

Simone Redding was a naughty, naughty girl... and she couldn't be happier.

∼

LUCIANO

Feasting on Simone had turned him into a savage beast. Desperate to thrust inside her, he wanted to fuck her until she screamed his name in ecstasy again and again. He wanted her boneless, sated, and curled in his arms.

She pulled him onto her, kissed him with a ferocity that had him growling like a cornered animal. Her ravenous sounds made him want to fuck her so hard, she wouldn't remember her own name.

She tore open the condom packet, handed it to him.

After covering himself, he planked over her. "First, we fuck my way. Then, we fuck yours."

"What is mine?" she asked, her breath coming fast.

"From behind with you trapped."

"Get in me," she commanded.

He leaned against the propped pillows. "Sit on me."

She straddled him, collected his shaft in her hand, and sunk down on him. One effortless glide and he was rooted inside her. So fucking deep. So fucking good.

She kissed him, he fondled her tits, ran his tongue over her big areolas and engorged nipples. So fucking erotic. The more he sucked, the bigger they plumped. She glided off, then sank down, taking him all the way in. Again and again while streams of pleasure pounded him.

"Lay down," she said.

Still rooted inside her, he slid them down on the bed. Now sitting on him, she started riding him, hard. Up and down over his cock. Pleasure turned to euphoria. None of it he deserved, but all of it he needed. So fucking badly.

Fucking helped. Fucking Simone helped more.

He was captivated by her beauty, by her guttural sounds, by the aggressive way she rode him.

"I'm gonna come again." Gliding faster, she raised her arms over her head, her moans turning to cries.

He squeezed her nipples, teased them with his thumbs.

He liked the way she fucked.

He liked it a lot.

He ran his thumb over her clit and she cried out as her core clamped down on his steely shaft. But it was the way she pinned him with her half-hooded eyes, the look of ecstasy washing over her face that pushed him over. And he unloaded into her, shooting his come so hard, he almost blacked out.

"Fanculo a mi," he said when he stilled.

She collapsed on him, breathing hard. "What does that mean?"

"Fuck me," he said on a growl.

Lifting her face to his, a smile tugged on her lips. "That was some serious fucking."

It sure as hell was.

4

THE ABRUPT EXIT

LUCIANO

"You zhuzhed me up," Simone said rolling off him. "Serious Zhuzhing with a capital Z."

He chuffed out a laugh. "My designers use that word. You put a whole new spin on it."

"You fuck good... too good."

"It's you. I'm just along for the ride."

That made her smile. "I'm not buying that. I think it's *your* world and everyone else lives in it."

He leaned over to kiss her, and she stilled. "What are you doing?"

"Kissing you."

She pushed out of bed, opened the closet, and pulled out his robe. After covering herself, she turned back to him. "Yeah, so this was fun. I give you props... you're a man of your word." She paused, her penetrating gaze anchored on him. "That means a lot to me."

She looked adorable in his bathrobe. Instead of feeling joy, another pang of sadness flitted through him.

"Don't go."

He did not want to be alone.

She sat on the edge of the bed, ran her fingers through her mussed hair and stroked his chest. Her soothing touch had him breathing deep while her tender caresses kept the demons at bay just a little longer.

"Don't go?" she crooned. "Is Mr. Santini a romantic?"

"I have no heart."

"Neither do I."

He propped up on his elbows. Now, inches away, the pull to kiss her overpowered him. Again, he leaned toward her. This time, she didn't back away. Their lips met in a tender kiss.

After pushing out of bed, she vanished into the bathroom, returning shortly after. "Sex, then food."

"Then more sex."

While she dressed, he cleaned himself up in the bathroom. Seconds later, he was back in his stateroom. As he pulled on his pants, she eyed him like she was going to devour him alive.

"If you continue eye-fucking me, we won't get to the food," he said.

She shook her head, blinked several times. "Those are very nice pants."

"As a personal shopper, you would be an expert on that, yes?"

Pursing her lips, she slinked out of the room with a sway in her hips that had him following close on her heels. In his spacious galley, he pulled out the dinner containers, then a Santini Chianti from his private collection.

"Yes?" he asked, holding out the bottle.

"I'll have a glass." She pulled out two stemless wine glasses, tapped one with her fingernail. "Acrylic."

"Unbreakable," he replied.

She pulled silverware from a drawer. He collected cloth napkins, suggested they eat on the stern. With their heated plates of food in hand, he gestured toward the back of the yacht. Once outside, he waited for her to sit before easing onto the leather bench across from her.

He was well aware she was the enemy, sent by someone to flush out his illegal activities. Illegal activities that had to do with his crime family, *not* his assassinations.

Regardless of what they'd sent her to find, she would find nothing.

She raised her glass.

"Salud," he said.

After tapping their goblets, they sipped. The wine ignited his taste buds, and he savored his private label before swallowing it down.

"Nothing better than a glass of wine on my boat with a beautiful woman."

"Especially after you've been zhuzhed," she replied before slicing into the chicken. "Mmm," she murmured as she chewed. "Delicious."

"My chef is very talented." He forked the kale, slid the crisp vegetable into his mouth.

She leaned back, glanced around. "Do you entertain here often?"

With a slice of chicken poised at his mouth, he said, "Are you asking as Simone the spy, Simone the personal shopper, or Simone my dinner companion?" He tried the chicken. As expected, cooked to perfection.

"Just Simone," she replied. "I'm not trying to trick you into giving anything away."

"I'll take you at your word." *That's not happening.* "I entertain friends, family, and business associates on the Omega. She's very special to me, so I don't invite just anyone."

"She's stunning."

"She's a well-crafted vessel that affords me the luxury I've earned." He collected her hand, kissed her soft skin. "*You're stunning.*"

Though composed, she appeared a little uneasy.

"Never slept with a mark before, have you?" he asked.

"No."

"Tell me what you do when you're *not* working."

"I like to cook, but nothing like this," she said. "My parents live in South Carolina and I visit when I can. My brother and his husband are in Tysons. I like hanging with them."

"What does your brother do?"

"He runs a computer software company in McLean. He and his husband used to breed German Shepherds."

"Beautiful dogs. We had them as kids, for protection."

"Why?"

"Because my dad and uncle ran the Santini syndicate, but you already knew that, didn't you?"

"I did." She sipped the wine. "Now, my brother breeds French Bulldogs. When they moved to their Tysons' condo, they decided a smaller dog would work better."

He appreciated that she asked nothing about the Santini crime family.

"What do you do besides cook and visit family?" he asked.

"I love listening to classical music when I work out, but I don't like it otherwise." She shrugged a shoulder. "One of my many quirks."

He moved beside her on the bench, pulled his plate and wine glass over. Then, he collected her hand in his. "You're very intriguing," he said before pressing his lips to her hand and kissing it.

Her fingers were trembling. "Are you cold?" he asked.

She shook her head.

"Do I scare you?"

"No." Then a playfulness brightened her eyes. "But when

you tie me up and take me against my will, I'm going to act like I'm scared to death."

Energy surged through him, landing between his legs. "I can't wait." After a pause, he asked, "Why are you shaking?"

She tugged her hand away. "Truth?"

"It'll be a first."

"You're—" She stared into his eyes for several seconds.

SIMONE

SHE COULDN'T TELL him the truth. That would be way too revealing. She was having dinner with Luciano Santini on his sixty-foot yacht... after having crazy-hot sex with him. That was beyond insane. Yes, she'd dated handsome men, a few had some bucks too, but no one like Luciano.

Not even close.

She was a regular girl. Wouldn't he date a princess from some foreign country or an actor worth millions?

He was studying her so hard, he'd furrowed his brows. "Tell me," he coaxed.

She broke eye contact, lifted the stemless wine glass and swallowed down a hearty gulp. Not the most suave move, but she needed a stall so she could come up with something to say.

Then, it hit her, and the sharp sting of truth snapped her back to reality.

She was just someone to fuck. Someone he wanted to confront, someone he wanted information from. He'd spotted her watching him, so he'd tracked her down, then moved in for the kill.

Only he'd used sex as a tool. Was he expecting her to open up about who sent her? Was he expecting a late-night confession? Did he actually think she'd be that gullible and naïve?

Yes, he was a *god* in bed. Yes, he was *very* handsome with a shit-ton of money, but he wasn't interested in *her*. He was interested in who she was working for.

The sex high she'd been enjoying fell out from under her and she plummeted back to reality. Her reality where people have jobs—not an empire—and people have money, just *not* boatloads of it.

She moved off the bench. "This was fun, but I gotta take off."

Surprise flashed in his eyes. "Finish your dinner, then I'll take you back."

"I'm out."

She hated being a bitch. He'd been nothing but nice... and so damn talented, but she didn't live in a fantasy world. She lived in the real world where she didn't date billionaires.

Before she blurted out anything else she'd regret, she hurried down the stairs to his stateroom. Moving as fast as she could, she dressed, opened the door, and crashed into him.

"This is definitely one for my journal, but I'm out," she said.

"Are you swimming back?" he asked.

"What?"

"We're anchored in the Potomac, Simone."

Like every other time, her name came out like a purr, but she had to push forward. "Nothing like making a total ass of myself," she mumbled.

"Come." He extended his hand. "We'll finish eating, then we'll return to the marina."

"I... um..." She couldn't come up with a strong enough counterargument.

He clasped her hand, the heat from his radiating through her. "No more questions."

They returned to the table on the stern. Normally, she was a very even-keeled, composed woman. Being around him was a little intimidating.

It just was.

She forked the kale salad into her mouth and enjoyed a delicious medley of flavors. A touch of olive oil, the bite of lemon, and the crunch of almond slivers.

They ate in silence for a moment, the gentle breeze floating through her hair. She'd glance around, but within seconds, she'd find herself peering over at him. He was easy on the eyes and possessed an over-abundance of sex appeal and charisma.

He slid his attention to her before sipping his wine.

"Tell me about you," she said.

"What did you learn?" he asked.

She shook her head, slid a piece of chicken into her mouth. As she chewed, her attention stayed anchored on his. "You talk."

"I work seven days a week," he said. "I adore my grandmother, my father's mother. Elsa had a big hand in raising me. My father was too focused on the business, so he didn't spend time with us. I'm close with my brothers Teddy, and Gabriel—who lives in Italy. My cousin, Carrera Santini is like a brother to me as well."

She nodded in acknowledgment.

"After my father was murdered, my mother moved to Las Vegas. We aren't close, but I keep in touch."

Words were coming out of his mouth, but he was revealing nothing. She'd placed a wedge between them, and he'd left it there.

When they finished dinner, he said, "I'll take you back." Rather than invite her to join him on the bridge, he retreated inside. She sat alone on the stern, peering out at the black water. Within seconds, the anchor was raised into the vessel, then he motored toward the marina.

She liked being around him. He exuded power. And there was an undeniable connection that was constantly pulling her toward him. But she'd crossed a line and she didn't want to cross it again. Her career meant everything to her and she didn't want to get caught up in something that had no future.

There was no universe where Simone Redding ended up with Luciano Santini. That reality kept her grounded and she was determined to stay that way.

He pulled into the marina and backed into his slip. She grabbed one of the ropes from the pier and tied it to a cleat on the yacht. As she was tying another, he pulled up alongside her.

With a light touch, he collected the rope from her. "This is how you tie it." He showed her, then untied it, and handed her the rope. She mimicked what he'd shown her. "You're a fast learner."

They stood. "Help me tie the rest of them." Together, they worked to secure the vessel.

"Tonight was unexpected and fun." She extended her hand.

He pulled her close, kissed her. "Simone, thank you for spending the evening with me."

She melted from the way he held her so securely. She'd never felt so safe, so protected. His baseline scent was drawing her in. Her wildly fluttering heart was betraying her at every turn. Even so, she had to shut this down.

Breaking away, she said. "I'll call for a ride—"

"No." His abrupt tone caught her ear. "You are *not* getting into a car with a stranger in the middle of the night."

Gone was the charming lilt. Gone was the sparkle in his beautiful hazel eyes. This was a serious Luciano. But she didn't work for him. She didn't take orders from him either.

"I'll be fine." She grabbed her phone and toggled to a rideshare app.

"You are *not* getting into some random vehicle and letting some random man drive you away. If you won't allow me to escort you home, let Stuart take you. I trust him. He's a trained Army Ranger and he'll ensure your safety."

Seriously?

This was a little extreme.

"It's a twenty-minute car ride. What could possibly happen to me?"

A shadow fell over his eyes, then a flash of something. Was it anger? Sadness?

He sent a text, then said to her, "Stuart will meet you at the end of the pier." The bite in his voice caught her ear. He stepped onto the pier, extended his hand.

She'd insulted him. After chugging in a deep breath, she collected her shoes, then placed her hand in his and was lifted off his yacht.

She'd ruined her fairytale evening and she had no one to blame but herself. "The Omega is lovely and I enjoyed your company."

He stayed silent.

"We come from very different worlds," she continued. "This was a magical night, but I've got a pumpkin to catch. Your driver can take me home."

"As you wish," he replied, devoid of all emotion.

She'd had amazing sex with Luciano Santini, then she'd insulted him.

"Yeah, so I'm the dumbest woman on the planet. I get that." She kissed his cheek. "You deserve better."

"I don't deserve *anyone*," he replied.

In the nearby parking lot, Stuart flashed the car's headlights.

"Goodnight, Simone."

She melted from the sexy way he pronounced her name.

"Goodbye, Luciano."

As she hurried toward the waiting car, she mumbled, "I'm too stupid to live."

Yet, she was doing the right thing. She'd slept with her target, then had dinner with him on his yacht, and had sex with him *again*. Those were grounds for termination. If Z had been her boss, and he'd found out, he would have let her go without a second thought.

But Z's not your boss. Not anymore.

Stuart opened the back door and she got inside. Relieved the privacy screen was still up, she leaned against the leather seat. As he pulled away, she glanced back down the pier, but Luciano's yacht was too far down to see him.

Carrera Santini is my boss now, which is probably worse than having Z. Maybe I got myself fired anyway.

Normally composed, a shudder skirted through her. *Did I overreact?* She stared out the window as streetlights whizzed by. By the time they pulled up to her home, she concluded that the hookup was bad enough, joining him on his yacht was worse, the sex—while phenomenal—was a mistake—and she did the right thing by leaving.

Stuart opened the car door for her.

"Thank you for driving me home."

"Yes, ma'am," he replied.

At her front door, she punched in the entry code on the keypad. Her lock slid open and she disappeared inside, turned off her house alarm, and crumpled to the floor in her foyer.

A few seconds passed before she pulled out her phone. It was almost midnight. She texted her brother.

> I did a stupid thing. Can you talk?

Seconds later, her phone rang.

"Hey," she answered. "Thanks for calling me back."

"What's going on?"

Her older brother, Gary Redding, had been her rock for as long as she could remember. But, she had been his too.

"I had sex with one of my targets," she said.

"Good for you," he replied.

"Not helping."

"Did he know you'd been watching him?" Gary asked.

"It was Luciano Santini, so yes, he did."

"Good Lord, you did not."

She chuckled. "I did, and it was better than anything I could've imagined."

"Then, what's the problem?"

"Seriously, Gare, you're not helping."

"It was a one-off, well, maybe not. How many times did you climax?" He laughed.

"How can you make light of this?"

"How can you not?" he asked. "It's not like you committed a crime. It's not like you're adding *that* to your report."

He had a point.

"I'm surprised you got yourself worked up at all. Just chalk it up to living dangerously and move on."

After thanking him for walking her off the ledge, she hung up. As she sat in her foyer, she wished she'd never had sex with Luciano.

How do you go from Luciano Santini to any other man?

The only place to go now... is down.

On her way upstairs, her phone buzzed with a text.

Sognami, Simone

She pulled up the translator on her phone, typed in the Italian word, and read the English translation—*Dream of me.*

Her heart skipped a beat.

Damn that man.

5

RECONNECTING

SIMONE

Monday, just before two in the afternoon, Simone walked down 10th Street toward the J. Edgar Hoover building in Northwest DC. Her first meeting with Carrera since Z had left the Bureau.

Rather than upload the twenty-seven reports to ALPHA's secure website, she wanted to get a feel for Carrera's management style. This was more of a meet-and-greet from ten-thousand feet than a get-in-the-weeds review for each of her targets.

That morning, Carrera had emailed her that they'd meet in Z's basement office. While it was creepy as hell in the lower level, it was absolutely necessary. As a watcher, she had to stay in the shadows. No one at the Bureau knew she worked there.

Being a watcher was her way of staying connected to ALPHA without actually being in ALPHA. When she'd taken a leave of absence, she'd walked from a job she loved. A safe choice for a vulnerable time in her life.

After entering the FBI building, she held her badge under the scanner, the light flashed green, and she proceeded through to the first guard. After placing her computer satchel on the conveyer belt, she walked through the metal detector, then collected her bag on the other end. As she made her way through the lobby, she spotted her old boss and mentor, Peter Hirzog, chatting with several people in a small group.

Dammit.

She spun around, beelined toward the exit. Since only Z knew the watchers existed, she had no reason to be there, especially unescorted.

Peter Hirzog had been her first supervisor after her training in Quantico and her favorite during her five years as a Special Agent. He spent a lot of time with all his agents helping them navigate their way through a sea of bureaucracy and hierarchies.

Relax. He didn't see me.

She hurried outside, called Carrera.

"Hey, Simone. Do you need an escort?"

"I've got my badge. I almost ran into my old boss, Peter Hirzog. I'll chill in the coffee shop next door. Can I bring you something?"

"I'm good," he replied.

Simone hung up, entered the busy eatery. After ordering a coffee, she waited in the pick-up area.

Her phone buzzed with a text from Fred.

> I swung by the Bureau to speak with a legend builder about updating our website. Did I just see you in the lobby?????

"Simone!" the barista called out.

I knew the universe would punish me for sleeping with Luciano.

Simone glanced up to see Peter Hirzog holding out her coffee, a big smile plastered on his face. "I think this is yours, Red."

"Peter," she said trying to sound surprised.

Hirzog was average height with a fit build and a head of graying hair, parted on the side and held in place with gel. He always wore a dark suit, a white shirt, and a brightly-colored tie. Never without a smile or a positive word, he was highly respected by his peers and subordinates.

"What a great surprise!" he said handing her the hot beverage. "What are you doing here? Tell me you're thinking of coming back to the Bureau." Still smiling big, he crossed his fingers.

She forced a chuckle. "I was in the neighborhood, had to grab a cup."

"You always did like this place," he said. "If you have a minute, let's catch up."

What could she say?

"Sounds great," she replied.

After they found a table in the corner, he excused himself to collect his drink. Seconds later, he returned, another man by his side.

"Red!" Jerod exclaimed.

"No way." She pushed out of the chair, extended her hand toward the familiar face.

Former colleague and ATF agent Jerod De Clerq stood there grinning from ear to ear. Ignoring her outstretched hand, he leaned in and hugged her.

Jerod looked more muscular than she'd remembered, maybe even dropped a few pounds. His military-short, light hair was slicked back with gel, his brilliant white teeth popped against his tanned skin.

"Damn, it's good to see you," Jerod said.

"It sure is," Peter agreed.

The two men sat beside each other, Simone sat across from Peter.

"It's been a while," Simone said.

"Too long," Jerod added.

She and Jerod had worked a handful of cases together during her five years as a Special Agent. He was a total team player, a hard worker, and someone Simone had always liked.

"What have you been up to, both of you?" Simone asked.

"Working," Peter said.

"Peter's a muckety-muck at the Bureau now," Jerod said, and both men laughed.

"A few years back, I took a job in Philadelphia," Peter replied. "It was a great opportunity. I came back to HQ last year."

"He's a Deputy Director," Jerod said.

"Nice," Simone replied.

Peter leaned close. "I've got the Director's ear."

She smiled. "I'm not surprised." Pausing, she sipped the drink before regarding Jerod. "Are you still with ATF?"

"Jerod is Deputy Director of Field Ops," Peter said.

"Congratulations," Simone said. "You've done well for yourself."

"I got promoted, moved to Atlanta," Jerod explained. "Recently, a position at HQ opened up, and I applied, never thinking I'd get it." He broke into a smile. "Crazy bat-shit world. Here I am running my own department."

"Well deserved," Simone said.

"Are you still a kick-ass Special Agent?" Jerod asked. "No, wait, you're a supervisor now, right?"

"I left years ago," Simone replied, sadness swirling through her.

Jerod furrowed his brow. "Really? I thought you'd be a lifer."

"I did too," Peter agreed.

So did I.

"What are you doing with yourself?" Jerod asked.

She glanced from Jerod to Peter. "I'm a personal shopper."

Jerod's eyebrows shot up. "Really?" He pointed to his clothes. "I could use your help."

"Nah. You look great, but I'll add you to my wait-list." Eager to change the subject, she said, "Are you two working on something together?"

"I have a meeting nearby," Jerod said. "I texted Peter to see if he had time for coffee."

"I remarried," Peter volunteered. "My first wife had an affair—"

"Peter, let it go," Jerod murmured.

"I met my new wife, Lucy, in Philadelphia," Peter explained. "We're throwing a dinner party this Friday night to celebrate our one-year anniversary."

"Congratulations," she said.

"I want you to be there," Peter said.

"What? Oh, no, I couldn't—"

"Please," Jerod piped in. "I won't know anyone—"

"You'll know me," Peter interjected, and the men laughed. "I insist," Peter continued. "It's at my house in Chevy Chase." After pulling out his phone, he asked, "Do you still have the same number?"

"I do."

He scrolled, then got busy typing. Seconds later, her phone buzzed. "I texted you the address." He put his hands in prayer. "Please, it would mean so much to me."

She nodded. "I'll be there."

"Great! Cocktails at seven. Dinner at eight." His phone rang and he stepped away to answer.

"How's life on the outside?" Jerod asked.

"Peachy," she replied, her sarcasm front and center.

Jerod laughed. "We had a lot of fun working together."

"Made some arrests too."

"Those were the good ole days," Jerod said. "Years back, I got assigned the biggest damn case of my career, then it got yanked."

ALPHA probably took it.

"Bummer," she said. "Which one was it?"

"The Bomb Maker," he replied.

Simone's stomach dropped while bitter bile rose in her throat. "That was a big one."

"A career changer if I'd gotten to work it," Jerod replied. "The Bomb Maker obliterated the hell out of several government buildings in major cities. What a cluster fuck."

Goosebumps covered her arms, hair on the back of her neck stood on end, and a shiver traveled down her spine. The memories came crashing back into her thoughts like a locomotive thundering down the tracks. The destruction caused by The Bomb Maker was etched into her soul.

Peter returned to the table. "I've got to head back."

"Same," Jerod added.

The three made their way out of the crowded coffee shop. On the street, she heaved in a breath. Just thinking about The Bomb Maker made her sick to her stomach.

"Let's do lunch," Jerod said to her. "I loved going to Rudy's with you." He scrolled on his phone, then showed her the display. "Same number?"

She viewed her contact info. "You got me."

"Red, it's great to reconnect," Jerod said. "I'll text you about lunch."

"See you Friday night," Peter said.

The men took off toward the federal building. But they got no more than twenty feet before Peter stopped to speak to someone. Jerod put a hand on Peter's shoulder, whispered something into his ear, and continued walking.

She waited several seconds, then decided to go for it. Head down, she strode past Peter. Just as she was about to veer toward the building, Peter called her name.

"Simone, wait up!"

Ah, dammit.

"Where're you headed?" he asked.

"I'm meeting a client," she lied.

"You know, I couldn't understand why you left the Bureau," he said. "It never made sense to me. You were an excellent agent." He gestured to the building. "I assumed you'd make a career here. Wondered if you went undercover, but when I asked around, I was told you left." He stepped close. "Did you move to ALPHA?"

What the hell?

Simone had a great poker face. "What's ALPHA?"

The color from Peter's face drained. "It's nothing." He glanced at his watch. "I'm late for a meeting. See you Friday." He strode toward the entrance and vanished inside.

She had no idea he even knew about ALPHA, but he should never have asked her about that, especially in public.

What happened to having some damn discretion?

Her guts churned. She might not work for ALPHA, but her allegiance was still with that organization, if for no other reason than to protect its secrecy. She tossed her coffee into the trash, and hastened inside. Hirzog stood near the elevators talking to several people.

I gotta call this.

She exited the building, got Carrera on the phone. "Sorry, Peter Hirzog cornered me in the coffeeshop."

"Lucky you."

"Not a fan?"

"No," Carrera replied.

"He thought I'd gone undercover, then asked if I'd joined ALPHA."

"That's not good," Carrera said.

"Peter's still in the lobby, so we'll have to reschedule."

Carrera pulled up beside her on the sidewalk. "I just got called to an offsite meeting."

"Hey." She hung up, extended her hand. "Good to see you."

He shook it. "Slash has been asking about you. Come by tonight for dinner, and we'll talk after."

"I'd love to," she replied. "Slash has wanted me to meet Elsa for a while now."

A black Range Rover pulled up to the curb. The back door opened and Luciano exited. Hit- after-glorious-hit of adrenaline powered through her. His impeccable blue-gray suit accentuated his muscular form to perfection. His bulging biceps pressed against the sleeves, while his white dress shirt made his beautiful olive skin tone pop.

She gave him a once-over. Approved. Then, did it again.

A gust of wind blew his hair every which way, but he combed his fingers through it and it yielded to his touch.

Just like me.

"You got out. You never get out." Carrera followed his cousin's gaze, which was pinned on her.

Luciano's muscles ticked in his chiseled jaw. "Simone."

"Luciano," she replied.

Silence, while they drilled each other with their searing gazes.

"Okay, so this isn't weird or anything. I'm gonna wait in the car." Carrera vanished inside the Range Rover.

Despite being on a busy sidewalk, her attention was laser-focused on Luciano.

Someone sidled over, but she couldn't break eye contact. She was consumed, the energy swirling at a frenzying pace around them like an invisible tornado.

"Is *this* your client?" asked a familiar voice.

Simone dragged her attention from Luciano. Peter Hirzog stood there glaring up at Luciano. Within seconds, Carrera rejoined them.

The energy shifted, the pleasant October afternoon turning frigid cold. As expected, Luciano stood there, a pillar of strength and fortitude. He was brimming with confidence, yet he wore his brand of sophistication like armor. If these two men were enemies, Luciano was keeping those feelings close to the chest.

Peter regarded her. "Do you know him?" The bite in his tone surprised her.

Simone stayed silent. It was none of his damn business.

To her surprise, Luciano's lips split into a sinister smile. "What do you want, Hirzog?"

"Stay away from him," Peter warned her. "He'll ruin your life."

"It's *your* fault your ex went looking elsewhere," Luciano bit out.

Whoa.

Hirzog swung at Luciano, but he grabbed Hirzog's wrist, twisted it behind his back, forcing Peter to spin around. Wincing in pain, Peter, said, "You're a motherfucking cocksucker, Santini."

Luciano's driver, Stuart, appeared. "I need to get you off the street, Mr. Santini."

Simone had had enough. She had no idea what kind of bad blood had passed between them and she didn't care. "I need to leave."

Luciano released Peter, then turned to her. "Do you need a ride?"

While his composure remained intact, the fire in his eyes burned brightly. And she was drawn to that flame like a magnet. The connection between them made her shiver with delight. Never before had a man made her feel so alive.

Peter tugged down his suit jacket, glared at both Santinis. "I told you two to watch your backs, and I meant it." Then, his angry eyes jumped to her. "This man is poison."

On a growl, Peter bolted down the sidewalk, taking his fury with him.

"That was intense," she murmured.

"Ride?" Luciano asked.

"I'm gonna walk this one off," she replied before eyeing Carrera. "Later." Then, she shot Luciano a smile.

As she walked down the street, she turned to look back. He stood on the sidewalk oozing power and determination while people bustled past him.

For reasons she couldn't explain or begin to understand, he had drawn her into his web and she liked it.

She liked it a lot.

∼

LUCIANO

LUCIANO SEETHED AS they plodded through heavy DC traffic en route to Sin's office in Georgetown. Seeing Hirzog did that to him.

Once on M Street, Stuart drove around the corner and parked in Sin's private lot tucked behind his building. Inside, a man and two women waited at the elevators. One of the women checked him out, then offered a smile. He tossed her a nod, but said nothing.

His thoughts drifted to Simone. Smart, beautiful, and strong-willed was a combination he found captivating.

The elevator doors opened. He and Carrera waited for the others to step inside, then followed. On the top floor, everyone exited. Behind reception a large sign hung on the wall.

DEVELIN AND ASSOCIATES

While the man and other woman spoke with the receptionist, the woman who'd checked him out, marched over. "You look familiar. Have we met?"

"No," Luciano replied.

She stared at up him for several seconds, then said, "Well, we're meeting now. I'm Sheila."

"Luciano." His smile made her cheeks flush.

"Mr. Santini and Mr. Santini," said the receptionist, "Mr. Develin will see you now. Go on back."

"Can I get your number?" Sheila asked. "Maybe we can have coffee sometime."

Luciano whispered in her ear. "Not a good idea. I'm a very bad man." He winked before he and Carrera headed through the expansive office.

As they passed the bullpen, several employees popped up from their cubicles like prairie dogs. They stopped in front of Sin's closed office door and knocked.

The door opened and Evangeline Develin smiled at them. "Good to see you guys." She hugged Carrera, then Luciano. "Luciano, why do you always look like you just got back from vacation on the Amalfi Coast?"

Luciano flashed a smile. "Ciao, bella. That color looks great on you."

She was wearing a burgundy pantsuit from his WorkSmart collection and had paired it with a black camisole.

Sin appeared in the doorway. "Boys."

"How was Miami?" Luciano asked.

"Fun," Evangeline replied.

"We had a good weekend," Sin said before addressing his wife. "Are you joining us?"

"Not for this meeting," she replied.

Sin stepped aside so the men could enter. After shutting the door, he pulled a bottle of Santini whiskey from his credenza.

"It's five o'clock somewhere," Carrera said.

Luciano and Carrera sat on the sofa while Sin poured a finger's worth in three lowball glasses, then eased into an upholstered chair. After tapping their glasses together, they tossed back the top-shelf liquor.

"Thanks for meeting in person." Luciano set down the glass.

"What's going on?" Sin asked.

"Gabriel and I flew to London and met with three men from Haqazzii's terror cell. They were on their way here."

"How'd that go?" Sin asked.

"As expected," Luciano replied.

"Learn anything?" Carrera asked.

Luciano pulled the folded map from his breast pocket, opened it, and set it on the coffee table. "They worked for The Bomb Maker. These buildings could be his next targets—"

"The White House, the Capitol, FBI, Justice, State, Supreme Court, the Pentagon, and the CIA." A growl shot from Carrera. "This is bad."

"Jesus," Sin bit out.

"They had legit US passports and believable aliases," Luciano said. "The Bomb Maker is here and they said he'll kill us all."

"He struck five years ago, then vanished," Carrera explained. "Targeted buildings in LA, Chicago, New York, San Francisco, and DC. His base of operation for his terrorist team was in Arlington."

"Government or civilian buildings?" Luciano asked.

"Both," Carrera replied. "The larger the building, the better. He likes killing, and he likes wreaking havoc on a city."

Sin poured more whiskey. "Once his house in Arlington had been located, Z and Luther sent ALPHA in to take them out, but the mission went sideways. The Bomb Maker had wired the house. Every Op—but one—was killed in a massive explosion. He even took out his own men."

Luciano leaned back on the sofa. "Brutal."

"What happened to him?" Carrera tossed back a mouthful of liquor.

"Vanished," Sin answered.

A smile split Luciano's face. "I'm going to like hunting this one down."

Sin retrieved his laptop, got busy, then turned the computer around. "This is the only pic ALPHA has of him."

Luciano and Carrera eyed the blurry photo of a light-skinned man dressed in dark clothes with shoulder-length brown hair and sunglasses.

"Could be anyone," Luciano said.

"Average height, average build," Sin said. "No tats, no piercings, nothing to help ID him."

Carrera pulled the map off the table, studied it. "I *don't* think this is a job for ALPHA." He eyed both men. "Weigh in."

"I agree and disagree," Sin said. "Luciano takes the lead, but he can't work this alone."

"I'll work it with my team," Luciano said before folding up the map and tucking it back into his breast pocket.

"You need an investigator," Carrera said. "Someone trained and experienced in tracking."

Luciano's phone rang with a call from his cousin Willie Boy. He silenced it, then checked the time. It was after six.

"Devo andare. I have to go." Luciano stood. "No one from ALPHA knows about our *business* arrangement. Once your team finds him, mine will go in and finish the job."

Sin shook Luciano's hand. "I'll talk to you," Sin said.

"I'll see you later," Carrera said.

Luciano didn't know what he was talking about. "Later?"

"You said you'd come for dinner," Carrera replied. "G-ma's probably been in the kitchen all afternoon."

"Sounds like Elsa has a favorite," Sin said.

"Definitely," Carrera replied.

Luciano smiled. He adored his grandmother. "I'll be there." He tossed Sin a nod. "Ciao."

On the elevator ride down, Luciano read the text from his cousin, Willie Boy.

> Dante's here. Where are you ????

He can fucking wait.

Luciano slid his phone into his pocket, exited the building, and strode toward the sedan, parked out back. Luciano ducked inside.

"Stuart, I need to stop at Willie Boy's."

"I'll join you." Stuart glanced in the rearview mirror, and Luciano replied with a nod.

Stuart wasn't just his driver, he was Luciano's security detail.

En route to Old Town, Alexandria, Luciano asked, "How's your sister?"

"Much better," Stuart replied. "Changing her doc at the hospital made a difference. Thank you for taking care of that."

"Keep me posted on her health," Luciano said. "I'll arrange for in-home nursing care once she's discharged."

"Sir, you don't—"

"Stuart, let me do this for your family. Take off any time you need."

Luciano's phone buzzed with another text from Willie Boy.

> Are you coming ????

> On my way

He was doing this to honor his uncle. Unfortunately, Willie Boy didn't know the difference between his ass and his elbow, but he was family. Family mattered to a Santini.

Stuart parked at Willie Boy's restaurant in Old Town. The exterior looked like hell, but Willie Boy had told Luciano to butt out, so he had. Inside, Luciano glanced around. Willie Boy hadn't done a damn thing to update the eatery. It was like stepping back in time thirty years. The place needed a complete overhaul. But the food was good, so customers kept coming back.

Luciano slid his sunglasses into his pocket. Stuart kept his on.

The hostess beamed at them. "Hello, Luciano. Hi, Stuart."

"Ma'am," Stuart said.

"How've you been, Tara?" Luciano asked.

"No complaints." She led them through the busy neighborhood restaurant, stopping in front of a closed door in the back.

Knock-knock.

"Yeah," Willie Boy called out.

Tara opened the door. "Your cousin and his bodyguard."

Luciano and Stuart entered. The stench of lager and cheese was undeniably the trademark odor of Willie Boy's private room. The low-lit space consisted of four round tables and several framed family photos hanging on the walls. At the back, a swinging door separated the kitchen.

Willie Boy and another man were seated at one of the tables. His cousin glanced over, then grinned. After pushing out of the chair, he swung his arms wide. "There he is!"

Luciano kissed both his cousin's cheeks, then patted his face. "You look like crap, Willie Boy."

"Jeez. That's how you greet me?"

Thirty-four-year-old Willie Boy stood at five-nine. Dark circles shadowed his eyes. His stomach hung over his belt, but his Santini Original suit jacket hid the flab. Though Willie Boy didn't care about clothes, Luciano made sure his cousin dressed like a Santini. Willie Boy's dark wavy hair had grown to his jawline, and he tucked both sides behind his ears. He had a strong Italian nose, a mouthful of crooked teeth, and diamond studs in his ears.

"Thanks for showing up," Willie Boy said before acknowledging Stuart. "How you doin' Mr. Fletcher?"

"Good, sir."

Willie Boy smiled. "Mr. Fletcher calls me sir. I like him." Then, he turned toward the man seated at the table. "This is Dante."

The man stood, extended his hand. "Mr. Santini." They shook. As Dante extended his hand to Stuart, Stuart crossed his arms.

Willie Boy dragged a chair over, gestured to Luciano. "Sit."

As Luciano eased down, he spied Stuart pulling out his phone. Luciano trusted very few, but those he did trust—Stuart being one of them—he trusted completely.

"Dante is interested in doing business with you," Willie Boy said.

Inwardly, Luciano cringed. His cousin was so fucking stupid. "Are you a clothing designer?"

"No," Dante replied.

"An apparel distributor?"

Dante fiddled with his large diamond pinky ring. "Also, a no."

"Are you in the spirits business?"

"Like ghosts?" Dante blurted.

"Whiskey." Luciano bit back a growl.

"No, I'm not," Dante said.

"Mr.—?" Luciano asked Dante.

Dante stared at him.

For fuck's sake. "What's your last name?"

"It's Dante, just Dante."

Luciano glared at his cousin. "Non farmi perdere tempo."

Willie Boy raked his hands through his hair. "You know I don't understand Italian."

"You're wasting my time, Willie Boy."

"Mr. Santini," Dante said, "I need a million counterfeit. When I told your cousin, he thought you could help me."

Stupido idiota del cazzo. Stupid fucking idiot.

Luciano's pulse didn't jump, his blood pressure never

wavered, but a growl ripped from his throat. He rested his ankle over his thigh, paused for a few seconds while he eyed the stranger across the table.

Dante parted his dark hair on the side and slicked it back with product. He'd made the bonehead move of wearing Luciano's competition, but he'd come dressed to do business. The suit cost several thousand. While Luciano wasn't impressed with Dante's flashy pavé ring or matching diamond-stud earrings, he'd noted that Dante concealed his eyes behind rose-tinted glasses.

Luciano never trusted anyone who kept their eyes in perpetual shadow.

He regarded his cousin. "Willie Boy, how do you and Dante know each other?"

"Old friends," Willie Boy replied. "We've known each other for—what—a few years now?"

"Yeah," Dante replied, fiddling with his ring. "Sounds 'bout right."

Luciano exhaled a huff. He was getting nowhere with these two. "Have you done business together?"

"Have we done business together?" Willie Boy parroted back.

When Willie Boy repeated back a question, he was stalling. Yes, the two had done business. Maybe this Dante guy ran a money laundering business. Could have been any number of illegal activities. Or he could be undercover FBI, hoping to arrest Luciano for the white-collar crimes they could never pin on him. Whatever the hell it was, Luciano wasn't taking the bait... and he was done with this bullshit meeting.

"Dante, I run Santini International. I can't help you."

Dante shot Willie Boy a cold stare. "Your cousin said you had money I could use."

Luciano's phone rang, he silenced it. "What would you use the money for?"

"My mother has hundreds of thousands of dollars' worth of medical bills," Dante said. "She's well now, but the debt has stressed her out. I want to help her."

Not buying that.

"Drugs? Prostitution? Human trafficking?" Luciano asked.

"It's for my mother, Mr. Santini."

Luciano rose, checked his phone. His personal assistant had called. "Like I said, I can't help you." Then, he glared at Willie Boy. "Don't waste my time again."

On the way out, he called Dominic.

"Mr. Santini, the initial shipment of couture holiday gowns arrived. The colors are all wrong and the design team is struggling with the mistake."

"Get Ezra on the phone and call me back." Luciano hung up.

Outside, Luciano slid on his sunglasses.

"Where to?" Stuart asked.

"Home," Luciano replied. "Did you get his picture?"

"Yes, sir," Stuart said. "I uploaded all of them to Truman CyberSecurity's IDWare, but got no hits. I'll forward you the photos."

They got in the sedan. Before Stuart left the parking lot, Luciano's phone dinged with a text from him. He scrolled through the pics of Dante, forwarded one to Sin and Carrera.

> Recognize him?

Sin replied.

> No. Should I?

> He hit me up for a mil in C$

Carrera texted.

> How'd he find you?

> WB

Sin texted.

> For what?

> Mom's med bills. I couldn't help him. I don't have C$

Of course he had counterfeit money. He had easy access to several million, with the ability to print more, if necessary. But every text, every phone call was traceable, which meant Luciano was always covering his ass.

Luciano's phone rang. "Santini," he answered.

"Luciano," purred his head designer, Ezra. "The colors are terrible. I'm sending you pics."

His phone binged. He tapped, then scrolled. "I've seen worse. Do they need to be redone or do we rethink the colors?"

"You mean go with these?" Ezra asked.

"Muted might work," he said. "Instead of fuchsia, I see dusty rose. Have a courier send over a few—this one, the pale green, and the charcoal—to Carrera Santini's. I'll review them there. How many were delivered?"

"Twenty-five thousand," she replied.

"That's a small run. Put through another run with the corrected colors. I'll let you know about the muted dresses after I see them." Luciano hung up.

"Lemonade," he said under his breath. The couture gowns weren't a problem.

His cousin blabbing that he could supply some shady *business associate* with a million in boodle?

That was a problem.

6

HELLO, AGAIN

SIMONE

Simone loved hanging with Slash. Years earlier, when they worked together at ALPHA, the two had become close friends. After Simone left, she'd let those relationships go.

She needed time to heal.

Over time, and with the help of a skilled therapist, Simone learned coping skills for her survivor guilt and PTSD. As she reemerged, she reached out to the ALPHA Ops she'd once been close with. Slash was at the top of that list and they picked right up where they'd left off.

Simone and Slash chatted on the porch while Carrera's grandmother put the finishing touches on dinner. Simone glanced into the kitchen. "We should be helping."

"Carrera's got Elsa," Slash said before topping off Simone's wine glass. "Plus, it gives us time to catch up."

"I like this chianti," Simone said.

"It's Santini Chianti," Slash said. "Carrera's cousin, Luciano, sends it over by the case."

Just hearing his name sent a thrill thrumming through her.

"A perk of being a Santini." Simone sipped the wine.

After a beat, Slash said, "Red, I need to talk shop with you."

The French door opened and Carrera's grandmother walked into the room. "Room for one more?"

Slash patted the sofa cushion next to her. "I'm glad you're taking a break." She glanced inside. "Did you leave Carrera in charge?"

"Of course not," Elsa replied, and she and Slash laughed.

Slash poured Elsa a glass before turning her attention back to Red. "Come with me to rescue training."

Simone glanced over at Elsa.

"I went with Amanda May," Elsa said. "Watching the team work was an absolute thrill."

"Elsa knows about the rescue team?" Simone asked.

"I don't know anything," Elsa said with a sly smile.

"She came with me once," Slash explained. "I didn't want to leave her alone. It's a long story, but someone tried to burn her house down—"

Carrera walked onto the porch.

Elsa put her arm around Slash. "Amanda May rescued me. Carrera too."

"It was all Slash," Carrera said.

"Team effort." Slash smiled at her husband. "Red, you should come to training. You'd love it."

"I *left* the group," Simone reminded her.

"It's time to come back," Slash said. "At least, check out our training."

Excitement pounded through her. *I would love that.*

"Don't you need to clear that with someone?" Simone asked.

"If I could bring Elsa, I'm sure Rebel would have no prob if you joined us. Even if you just did target practice, it would be great shooting alongside you."

"I'll let you know," Simone replied.

"Simone, let's chat before dinner," Carrera said.

"Absolutely," Simone replied.

In the kitchen, Simone collected her computer bag, followed Carrera down the hall to his home office. He sat behind his desk, she eased into a guest chair.

She eyed the framed photos on the shelves behind him. Two snagged her attention. One of him and Slash at their wedding, sharing cake and laughing. She loved that Slash had found her person. The second was of Luciano, Carrera, Teddy, and Gabriel on the Omega, big smiles on their handsome faces.

They're living their best lives.

"Do you go by Simone or Red?" he asked.

"At work, I've always been Red, but either works."

"Alright, Red. I reviewed your history with the Bureau and with ALPHA. Impressive."

"I had a good run."

"Ever consider returning?"

"It's crossed my mind," she replied.

"Have you been keeping up with target practice?"

"No."

"Tucker Henninger built a training town at Henninger Security. If you check it out, flash your badge and there's no charge. The Bureau has an account with him."

"Gotcha."

"Let's talk about your accounts."

She set her laptop on the edge of his desk. "I tap out around thirty jobs at a time."

His eyebrows jutted up. "That's twice what the other watchers can manage."

"I like staying busy, plus I work a lot of gigs at night. People get crazy when the sun goes down. I was reviewing a Baltimore detective for an Op position. On paper, he was perfect. I was about to send my report to Z, but decided to follow him one night." She leaned back. "My squeaky-clean cop was in tight with a drug dealer, and I'm not talking about someone working the streets."

"Nice work."

"Z was pretty hands off," she continued. "He sent me cases, I'd upload my reports to the portal. On occasion, I'd meet with him in the dungeon." A smile flitted across her face. "That basement office is one creepy place. Did you meet Ralph?"

"Who?"

"Ralph the rat. Fattest damn rodent I've ever seen. Talk about a wide-load."

Carrera laughed. "Thanks for the heads up."

"It's good to meet in person," she said. "The job can get lonely."

"For some, it's a great gig, but for someone like you, it served a purpose." He paused. "What does your therapist say?"

"I've been cleared to return."

"Consider coming back, okay?"

Simone nodded. "Who would I talk to about that?"

"Do you know Cooper Grant or Providence Luck?"

"No."

"They run ALPHA now. Slash or I can introduce you."

"Gotcha," she replied. "I'll upload my files to the portal. Of the thirty I've been working, I'm sending you seventeen." She logged into ALPHA, sent him her assessments.

"What about returning to the Bureau?" he asked.

"Why the push?"

Carrera stroked his beard. "Sometimes we have to confront our fears in order to get past them. From what Slash told me, you were a great Op. I'm concerned you're using this job as a crutch."

A myriad of emotions—sadness, guilt, anger—rushed over her. "Thanks for being direct."

"I want what's best for my employees," he said. "Any questions or concerns for me?"

"Nothing." She closed her laptop, slid it into her satchel.

"Thanks for your flexibility," he said. "Appreciate you coming to the house."

She smiled. "This is a much better deal for me. I get to hang with Slash."

His warm smile touched his eyes. "Come over anytime."

Tell him.

After a beat, she said, "There is one thing... Z had me watching Luciano."

The lines between his brows deepened. "How long?"

"Six weeks."

"Did you include that report?"

"No, it was off-the-books."

"Whad'ya learn?" he asked trying to sound casual. But she was good at reading people. Carrera didn't like that she'd been spying on his cousin.

Luciano's strong, hard body flashed in her mind. The passion in his kiss, the way he tasted, how he undid her with very little effort. She *wanted* to say, "He's erotic, he's intense, and he's a god in bed."

"Red?" Carrera asked, snapping her from her arousing thoughts.

"Nothing," she replied. "I got nothing."

The knot between Carrera's brows relaxed.

What are you hiding Carrera? Is there more to your frequent visits to the mansion beyond visiting a blood relative?

"Is there anything in ALPHAnet about Luciano?" he asked. "Notes on your phone or at your house?"

That had her arching an eyebrow. "Nothing."

She was being honest. No reason to jot anything down because everything associated with Luciano Santini was tattooed in her brain.

"Did you notice anything unusual?" he asked.

"Unusual?"

"Anything that would make you think he's doing something illegal?"

Interesting, coming from his cousin.

"No."

"Glad to hear it." He stood.

She shouldered her laptop and rose. *Be transparent. He's one of the good guys.*

"He knew I was tailing him."

Carrera smiled. "I'm not surprised. Did he confront you?" He opened the French door to his office, waited for her to exit.

"He did," she replied as they walked down the short hallway.

"You can stop surveilling him." After entering the kitchen, he said, "Consider my job proposal with ALPHA."

"I will."

"Going forward, we can meet here or at the Bureau—"

"And risk running into that asshole Hirzog?" asked a man, his deep, raspy voice thundering through her.

Simone stopped short, her gaze seeking and finding the source.

Luciano.

The seconds passed while their heated stares made her heart pound hard and fast in her chest.

Him... again.

He stood alone near the cooktop, a wooden spoon with pasta sauce poised near his seductive-as-sin mouth, those insanely kissable lips beckoning.

"Ciao, Simone," he said.

"Luciano."

"I heard no introductions are needed," Carrera said.

"We've met." Luciano's heated gaze stripped her bare.

And she fucking loved it.

He placed the spoon to his mouth, tasted the pasta sauce. "Simone, try this. It's gotta be Elsa's best batch."

A beaming Elsa walked into the kitchen. "You always say that, Lulu."

Lulu?

"There's gotta be a story with that nickname," Simone said.

Elsa patted Luciano's back. "He's always been my Lulu."

After kissing his grandmothers' cheek, Luciano held out the spoon to her. "Simone."

No way would she let him feed her in front of his family, but resisting Luciano? That was impossible.

Slash entered wearing a stunning dusty-rose gown, hijacking everyone's attention.

"*Wow*," Carrera said. "You look amazing."

Slash did a slow three-sixty, modeling the couture formalwear. "It's a Santini Original. What do you think?"

"That's an interesting color, Lulu," Elsa said. "It's soft, very feminine. I like it."

"My astute grandmother." Luciano walked over to Slash, eyeing the fabric. "It was a mistake. Rather than discard the shipment, I needed them modeled."

Simone moved closer. The dress was full-on couture. An off-the-shoulder gown with a chiffon bodice that showed off Slash's figure, without looking slutty.

"What do you think, Simone?" Luciano asked.

"It's beautiful. I love the hourglass fit."

Luciano walked over to a garment bag hanging over the French door and pulled out two gowns—a pale green and a charcoal.

"This should have been a vibrant green and this ebony." Luciano walked over to Simone, held each one up to her, then offered her the charcoal one. "Please."

She stilled.

Slash took the dress, then Simone's hand. "We got this."

Up the stairs they went. Behind the closed door of Slash and Carrera's bedroom, Slash removed the dress from the hanger. "This'll look great on you."

"I'm not trying that on," Simone said.

"Why not?" Slash replied. "Luciano needs our help."

Simone removed her shirt and pants, then slipped into the gown. After Slash zipped her, she stood in front of their full-length mirror. As she eyed the dress, Simone ran her fingers down the silky material. This one had a high collar and a halter back.

This is the most beautiful thing I've ever worn.

"Wow," Slash said. "It's a perfect fit. Great color on you." She stood beside Simone and stared at herself. "I'm not a dusty-pink person, but it's a pretty color for someone else."

"The color works with your light eyes and blonde hair," Simone said eyeing her friend in the mirror. After a beat, she said, "Carrera thinks I should return to ALPHA."

Slash beamed at her. "Yes!"

"He mentioned a training town—"

"Yeah, at Tucker's shooting range. I'll schedule something." She opened the bedroom door. "Time to model a Santini Original."

Together, they returned to the kitchen.

The second Luciano saw her, everything went into slo-mo. The intensity in his bedroom eyes pierced her soul. As he made his way over to her, she felt like the luckiest woman on the planet. She was wearing a Santini Original and the man himself was coming over to examine the goods.

A foot away, he stopped, his complete attention focused on her in his dress. "Turn."

She turned slowly until she was facing him once again.

"Bellisima," he murmured. "It was made for you. What do you think?"

"It fits perfectly, it feels sensational, and I love the color," she replied. "What do *you* think?"

He lifted his phone, dialed. "It's different... I like it."

"Hello, darling," a man answered. "Tell me you love them."

He had been studying the dress on her, the dress on Slash, and glancing over at the green dress, still on the hanger.

"Limited run." His gaze slid to Simone. "We'll call it the Dreamy Collection."

"Brilliant. I'll place an order."

He hung up, flashed Simone a smile, sending her heart tripping into the stratosphere.

Take it down a few.

"I appreciate your help," he said to her and to Slash.

"Of course," she replied. "I'm going to change."

"Same," Slash said.

Simone forced herself to walk toward the stairs. She could stare at him for hours, but she'd had her fun, then she'd rejected him. Time to move on.

She thought about Carrera's questions about Luciano. Had she made any notes? Did she notice anything unusual? Anything that would make her think he's doing something illegal?

What are you up to, Luciano Santini? And how much does Carrera know?

The women returned to Slash's bedroom.

"Luciano's been checking you out pretty good," Slash said.

"Not me, the gown." Simone turned and Slash unzipped her, then Simone returned the favor.

"Nope, it's you," Slash said. "Did you two just meet?"

"We met at a party last weekend." Simone slid the dress onto the hanger.

"Luciano doesn't go to parties." Slash laid the dress on the bed, pulled on her jeans.

"It was a private party, and he was there stalking me."

Simone shouldered into her shirt. "I'm sure Carrera will tell you later. Z had me watching him."

Slash's eyes widened. "Why?"

"We're talking about Z." Simone started buttoning her shirt. "He's very secretive. He just asked me to tail him."

"What did you see?" Slash pulled on a T-shirt, tucked it into her jeans.

Simone tugged on her pants. "I saw nothing, but the way Carrera was questioning me, I think I totally missed the elephant in the room. Anyway, he told me to stand down."

"So, Luciano went to the party for *you*?"

"To confront me."

"Was he angry?"

Giving Luciano a blowjob popped into her thoughts. "Angry? No. More like charming, but I denied watching him. I couldn't tell him."

Simone draped the dresses over her arm.

"Of course." Slash opened the bedroom door.

As they walked down the hall, Slash asked, "Are you thinking of coming back to ALPHA?"

"Maybe. I miss it... a lot."

"I miss working with you."

Back in the kitchen, as Simone hung the gowns in the garment bag, she spotted Luciano on the porch alone, staring into the darkness.

"Dinner," Elsa said as she pulled plates from the cupboard.

"I'll let Luciano know." Simone walked onto the screened porch.

Luciano turned. Their connection was immediate and intense. She felt pulled to him, like a magnet. She couldn't have stopped herself even if she'd wanted.

Only she didn't want.

Halting inches away, she peered into his eyes. "Dinner."

"Are you hungry?" he murmured, his deep voice rumbling through her.

"I am," she replied, passion igniting her insides. "You?"

"I'm starving." The gritty need in his voice halted her breath. "Wait until you taste Elsa's skillet chicken. "Deliziosa." Then, he cupped her cheek, stepped so close his warm breath heated her skin. "Like you."

"Ohgod." She couldn't breathe, couldn't look away. In that moment Luciano Santini became her entire universe.

"Kiss me," he whispered.

That made her smile... until she realized she'd wrapped her arms around his back, and was clinging to him like a vine. She started to untangle herself when he kissed her.

Powerful, yet gentle, and overflowing with sinful promise. A moan floated into the air.

Her moan.

Her body and her brain had separated.

"Bene, no?" he asked.

He could speak Italian to her all day, every day. It didn't matter whether she understood. His gravelly, commanding timbre rumbled through her, captivating her completely.

"Your turn," he said. "Kiss me."

She pressed her lips to his, only this time, she lingered. The air crackled around them while heat flowed through her like lava.

"You shouldn't have left me the other night," he whispered. "Don't make that mistake again."

She'd defied him, something no one did. *Ever*. But she didn't give a damn how the world kowtowed to the magnificent Mr. Santini. She would never fall in line.

"I left because it was the smart thing to do," she pushed back.

"You left because you're afraid of getting hurt. Maybe you thought I was using you."

"Maybe I'm *not* attracted to you."

"Instead of the back and forth, tell me. Why did you leave?"

She could lie, she could walk away from him... or she could answer his question. As she mulled her answer, the fire in his eyes burned brightly. Being seared by Luciano was the best punishment she could ever imagine.

"You wanted answers. And you figured you could fuck them out of me. I wasn't going to tell you and I didn't want to be manipulated. We had fun—"

"Simone," he growled, the bite in his voice catching her ear. "I invited you to dinner on my yacht for your company, and because we had unfinished business."

Carrera walked outside. "You two can eat out here if you want privacy."

Simone severed their cozy connection, missing the warmth of his body and the desire in his eyes. "No privacy needed."

Being around him was addictive. Plus, she was curious. Why did Z tell her to watch him, and why did Carrera ask her all those questions about him? Where did he go on those late-night flights beyond running his billion-dollar empire?

"Excuse me." Simone hurried inside.

The delicious aroma of chicken, red sauce, oregano and garlic made her stomach growl.

Slash was pulling the garlic bread from the oven. Elsa was busy adding extra-virgin olive oil to the large salad. Then, she sprinkled in organic balsamic vinegar. When finished, Elsa wrapped her fingers around Slash's long hair and gave it a loving tug.

"Love you, Elsa," Slash said.

"Love you more," Elsa replied as she handed Slash a plate.

"You go first," Slash said.

"After my babies."

Slash selected a chicken cutlet, then scooped risotto from the large skillet. With a plate in hand, Simone sidled over.

"I've *never* seen Luciano kiss anyone," Slash said. "You've put a spell on him. Don't you think, Elsa?"

Elsa smiled at Simone. "He liked you in his gown. You wore it so well. I've always wished I'd been taller. How tall are you?"

"Five ten," Simone replied.

"Whew, that is tall," Slash said.

"Not when you're a gangly teen, but I've learned to be more accepting of myself. The good and the bad."

Simone took a chicken thigh, a scoop of risotto, and a slice of garlic bread. "Honestly, I could eat the entire loaf. This smells amazing."

"My models don't eat bread," Luciano said as he forked chicken onto his plate. "I tell them bread is okay. Moderation, right?"

"Sometimes abstinence, sometimes going all-in." With a playful smile, Slash waggled her eyebrows at Simone. "Depends on what it is."

Simone loved spending time with the Santinis. She loved how comfortable they were with each other, how easy the conversation came.

Elsa left her post at the stove and dished out their salads, handing each of them one as they made their way toward the table. Once everyone was seated, Carrera took Slash's hand. Luciano clasped her hand, and both men clasped their grandmother's hands.

"Heavenly Father," Carrera began, "Thank you for this food, for our family, and for our good health. Please watch over us, watch over those in need, and thank you for bringing Red—*Simone*—back into our lives. Amen."

"Amen," everyone said, but all she felt was the squeeze of Luciano's hand against her own.

Their eyes met and he winked.

I'm a goner. He's gonna take me on a wild ride, then dump me at the end, but I'm gonna enjoy the hell out of it.

Everyone dug in, pausing to praise Elsa for the meal.

"Elsa, this is so good," Simone said. "Is your secret butter?"

"EVOO," she replied, "and a mix of spices that ignite the taste buds."

"Ignite the taste buds?" Carrera asked. "You should write a cookbook with those killer words."

Everyone laughed.

Luciano pushed away from the table, retrieved a bottle of white wine and a bottle of Chianti. "The Chianti is a Santini wine, the white wine is not."

Chianti all around. As he walked back to his chair, he brushed his hand over her shoulder and across her upper back. Tingles of delight had her turning to acknowledge him as he eased onto the cushioned chair.

"Elsa, Simone is a personal shopper," Luciano said.

"That's wonderful," Elsa replied. "You two must know a lot of the same people."

∼

LUCIANO

LUCIANO SIPPED the Chianti before regarding Simone. She was waiting, her intense green eyes blazing with light.

"Yes, several," Simone replied. "Someone who comes to mind is a *terrific* man named Philip Skye. He goes by Z. It's kind of a fashion thing."

Carrera chuffed out a laugh. "Okay, wow."

"You've met your match, Luciano Santini," Slash said.

"I have a small client base," Simone continued. "Loyal people who have been with me for a while now. My area of expertise is home furnishings, some fashion. I've even helped my clients with their houseware needs." She shot Luciano a hard stare. "You know, blenders, toasters. Common-folk items."

"Toasters?" Luciano asked. "What're they for?"

Everyone laughed.

Luciano had wanted to ruffle Simone, but she'd run with it. As she chatted away about the art of selecting a sideboard or a coffee table, he couldn't take his eyes off her. She carried herself with a confidence he found refreshing, but it was her inner beauty that intrigued him.

"If you've worked with Z, then you must know home-furnishing icon, Schezan," he continued.

No such person existed.

"Schezan? Oh, I heard he left the biz," she quipped, "*and* he left the country."

Slash's right. I've met my match. She's calling me on my bullshit.

With an arched eyebrow, she slid her gaze from him to Elsa. "Elsa, were you married for a long time?"

Elsa's smile brightened her face. She and his grandfather had been close. When he died, Luciano had been concerned for her.

"I was married for over fifty years," Elsa replied.

"What a blessing," Simone said.

Years earlier, Elsa had told him, "I miss G-Pa every day, but I feel his presence. Life is different without him, but he knew how much I loved him. We have an unbreakable bond for eternity."

Those words had stayed with him. That sounded like a once-in-a-lifetime love. Something he'd had... and lost.

Pain gripped his chest. It followed him wherever he went, keeping his life in a constant state of gray.

"I mentioned to Luciano that he should consider a home furnishings line," Simone said. "Why stop at fashion and spirits? Maybe Schezan could return and help with that."

She plucked him from his sadness, spurring a flicker of hope. Simone Redding was a firecracker who was taunting him for the fun of it. Would this game of cat and mouse never end?

For the first time in a long time, he hoped not.

When they'd finished dinner, Simone helped clean up. "Thank you for having me. Elsa, you're an amazing cook who *should* write a cookbook. I'm sure Luciano could help you get it published. The Santini name alone would make it a bestseller."

Elsa clasped her hand and patted it. "Thank you. It was lovely meeting you, Simone. I love meeting Amanda May's friends. Please come back."

"I'll book us some time at Tucker's," Slash said, "and I'll text you the date."

"Sound great," Simone said. "Carrera, thanks for talking shop."

"I'll walk you out," Luciano offered.

He took her computer bag from her, slung it over his shoulder. Together, they walked toward the foyer. Their evening wasn't over. She just didn't know it yet.

"Plans tonight?" He opened the front door.

"No. You?" As she walked past him, her baseline scent caught his attention and he breathed her in.

They walked down the driveway toward her car, parked curbside. "I have a meeting tonight, around eleven."

"Well, no worries that I'll be following you." She opened the back door of her vehicle and he stashed her satchel on the floor behind her seat.

"Why's that?" he asked.

"Gig's over." She turned to face him. "Of all the people I've been tasked with tailing these past two years, you were the highlight."

He appreciated her honesty. "I'm going to miss you skulking around, but I like you better without the binos." He stepped close, but he stopped short of kissing her.

"When do you ask for permission?" she whispered.

"I loved our sparring in there," he murmured.

"Schezan?" Her lips curved. "I almost fell for it."

"Almost?" he whispered before his lips brushed against hers.

Her whimper urged him on. He pulled her flush against him while she sunk her fingers into his hair at the nape of his neck. The pressure of her mouth on his was a direct hit to his cock, now firming in his pants. Though he wanted to deepen their embrace, he ended it. His goal? Leave her frustrated and eager for more.

"Drive safely, Simone."

Without a word, she got behind the wheel of her SUV, started the vehicle. She didn't unroll the window, didn't say another word, but she didn't have to. He could feel her energy pouring into him. She put the car in gear, seared him with a sultry gaze, before driving into the night.

Back inside, he found Elsa in her family room chair, busy with her crossword puzzle. Carrera and Slash were finishing up in the kitchen while the Keurig churned out a coffee.

"I'm having a cup," Slash said. "Coffee for you, Luciano?"

He slid onto a barstool at the island. "Sí."

She set the mug of freshly brewed java in front of him, then got busy making another. "What do you want to know about her?"

Luciano chuckled. "Who?"

Carrera pulled up a chair beside him. "Schezan?" He barked out a laugh. "What the hell was that?"

Slash laughed. "I can't believe she mentioned Z."

"Tell me about her." Luciano sipped the hot drink, appreciating the robust taste. Carrera and Slash exchanged glances.

"No point in lying," Slash said.

"Agreed," Carrera said.

Slash collected her mug of coffee, stood across the island from them. "Do you want to sit babe?" Carrera asked her.

"I'm good." She slid her gaze to Luciano. "Red used to be an ALPHA Op."

I wasn't expecting that.

"Okay," Luciano said.

"She came from the Bureau," Slash continued.

"Who does she work for now?" Luciano asked.

"Me. She's a watcher," Carrera pulled his wife's mug over, drank down a mouthful, and slid it back. "She worked for Z."

Frustration slithered down his spine. "Fratello, did you know she's been watching me?"

"Not until tonight," Carrera replied. "She came to the Bureau to meet with me, but bolted when she saw Hirzog in the lobby."

A growl rolled out of him.

"Did you guys get into it?" Slash asked.

"Yeah," Luciano replied. "Hirzog's scum."

"He was Red's old boss," Slash explained, "and he's well liked at the Bureau."

A snarl curled his lip. "Figlio di puttana."

"Translate," Slash said.

"Motherfucker," Carrera clarified. "Z had her watching you, but it wasn't on any of the reports he gave me. If she hadn't told me, I wouldn't have known."

"And?" Luciano sipped the beverage.

"She said she saw nothing, and I told her to stand down." Carrera's phone rang. "It's Cooper. I'm putting him on speaker."

"Elsa—" Slash called out.

"I won't say anything," Elsa replied.

Carrera answered. "Hey, Coop, what's going on?"

"We got a tip on a bomb maker's possible location," Cooper explained. "We think it might be *The* Bomb Maker, so we're sending in a team this week."

"Arrest or hit?" Carrera asked.

"We can't take him out," Cooper explained. "We don't have positive confirmation it's him, and we've got little to go on from five years ago."

"Where?" Carrera asked.

"Silver Spring."

"When's the mission?"

"Wednesday, three A.M.," Cooper replied. "We're watching on a live feed. I'll let you know the details."

Carrera thanked him and hung up. "I'm gonna watch this one go down."

"Why's that?" Slash asked.

"The last time ALPHA went after The Bomb Maker, the mission was an epic fail. This time, there can be no mistakes." He regarded Luciano. "Watch with me."

"I'll be there." Luciano finished the coffee, rinsed the mug, set it in the dish drainer.

"Look at you," Slash teased. "Red doesn't think you can do menial labor, but here you are cleaning up after yourself."

On a laugh, he kissed Slash on both cheeks. "Smart ass." Before zipping the garment bag of couture gowns, he offered one to Slash.

"I'm not much of a pastel girl," she replied. "You designed a *black* wedding gown for me."

"And you looked amazing," Carrera replied.

"She did," Luciano agreed before pulling out the charcoal dress. "Take this one."

"No way," she replied. "That's for Red."

"I hadn't thought of that," he replied with a flicker of a smile.

"Headed there now?" Carrera asked.

"A gentleman never kisses and tells." Luciano said goodbye to his grandmother. "Ti amo, Elsa. La cena era perfetta." He leaned down, kissed each of her cheeks.

"Ti amo, mio Lulu," his grandmother replied. "I like Simone. Do you?"

"I like Simone too," he replied.

"You're a good boy, Luciano."
"I'm many things, Elsa. *Good* isn't one of them."

7

IRRESISTIBLE

LUCIANO

Luciano parked his jet-black McLaren Bespoke in Simone's driveway. No way in hell was he street-parking this baby. With the garment bag draped over his arm, he made his way to Simone's front porch. It was almost eleven.

After sitting on the wooden bench, he texted her.

> Simone

A few seconds passed and she replied.

> Luciano

> Are you busy?

No response.

Well, this would be more of a challenge than he thought.

The front door opened. Still no Simone, but he would take the open door as the green light he needed. Into the home he went. After he closed the door, he snapped the dead bolt in place.

She slinked over from the dark living room, her sublime body wrapped in a silky robe.

"Plan on staying?" Even in the darkened foyer, he couldn't miss the heat in her luminous eyes. In true form, she brushed past him, sashayed over to the stairs, walked up a few, and glanced over her shoulder.

Then, she smiled at him before continuing on.

Another green light he couldn't ignore.

Up the stairs he went, a maddening desire driving him onward. This wasn't just about sex. He didn't just *want* to see her. She was becoming his obsession. A raging, infuriating, ravenous need had sent him there, had forced him to send that text, to enter her home.

"You're taking me off my game," he growled.

Down the dark hall she continued, stopping in front of an open bedroom door. Turning to face him, she said, "Enter at your own risk."

"Is that a threat?" His voice came out in a husky groan, the need to ravage her taking control.

"It's a dare." Her words came out as a whisper, but they sounded like a promise to him.

She vanished into the room and he followed. He opened the door to her walk-in closet, hung the garment bag on the rod. When he exited, she'd dropped her robe.

A nude Simone was an intoxicating invitation of everything right... and everything wrong. He shouldn't be this interested, but he was. In the silence of the night, he would take care of her. And then, he would leave her because that's what he had to do.

To protect himself, but more so, to protect her.

She slinked close, helped him strip off his clothes. The only sound was their breathing, already in sync. To his surprise, she was in control. Maybe because she was home. Maybe because she wanted this. Whatever the reason, he was ready to give her all the pleasure for as long as she wanted him.

He stood naked before her.

She trailed the back of her soft fingers down one cheek, then his other. Despite the dark room, her blazing eyes sent him flying high. With a delicate touch, she ran her fingernails down his chest, slowing on each defined mogul of his eight-pack before her fingers curled around his saluting hard-on.

"I brought you something," he rasped.

She ran delicate fingers over the head, wetness sprang out. "I can tell."

"The gowns, Simone. I brought you the Santini Originals."

She stilled, surprise widening her eyes. "All of them?"

"Yes."

She was lightly running his hard shaft back and forth in the tunnel of her hand. Streams of pleasure streaked through him, his cock aching for a release. But he had tremendous control. He would wait until she'd been fully sated.

"I'm not here for a late-night fuck," he said.

She leaned close, pressed her mouth to his cheek and kissed him. As she broke away, she whispered, "Then, why are you here?"

"To watch you come undone when I make you writhe with pleasure," he said, his voice strained with desire.

"I'll let you suck my toes—" a groan shot out of him—"and I'll rub my feet on your cock if you tie me up and take me."

Naughty, naughty Simone Redding.

She started to break away, but he snaked his arms around her, drawing her against him. Skin against skin, her warm breath coming faster now.

"Are you wet for me, Simone?" A moan ripped from her chest, the vibration landing in his.

They came together in a kiss that surprised him. Light and lingering, she dug her fingers into his hair, slipped her tongue into his mouth, and arched her back, pushing her breasts against him.

He dropped one hand to her ass and squeezed while their tongues tangled, their moans coming faster. She ended the kiss, nibbled his jawline all the way up to his earlobe, then she bit it.

The harsh sting of pain sent a jolt through him. He liked her aggression.

"I'm drenched," she whispered. "But you shouldn't take my word on that."

Stepping back, she guided his hand between her legs. He palmed her pussy, the heat from her core warming his hand. Time to tease and torture.

Moving slowly, he slipped a finger between her folds, caressed her dripping sex. The pull to taste her sweet, sweet juices had him dropping down in front of her. She widened her stance and he paused to stare into her eyes.

"I'm shaking so hard," she purred. "I could pass out."

"I'll catch you." He placed his face into her shaven pussy and ran his tongue over her opening. Her throaty cry sent a shock of energy pounding through him.

She pulled back the hood of her clit, exposing the most tender flesh and he polished it with precision. Light flicks back and forth, around and around until her moans turned to mewls. He palmed her ass, pressed her flush against his mouth, and devoured her with a ravenous intensity.

"Ohmygod," she cried out. "Luciano, fuck, I'm gonna come." She started bucking and shaking, the orgasm shooting through her, while fisted fingers clung to his hair.

When she stilled, he licked her gently, then stood. "Taste

yourself. Taste your sweet pussy that I can't fucking get enough of."

She threw herself into him, kissing him, biting him, clawing his back while her guttural groans ripped through him. "So good," she rasped out. "More, I want more."

Panting, her chest rose and fell as she stared into his eyes. Without another word, she opened her closet door, returning with black ropes.

Unexpected, and extremely hot.

After handing him the soft ties, she seared him with a kiss that teased and tantalized every cell in his body. Electricity shot through him at a maddening pace.

"I can't wait for you to punish me with your cock," she murmured as she caressed his erection.

"Jesus," he bit out.

She was on fire, the swirling energy taking him higher and higher. The anticipation of being with her had turned him into a beast. He wanted her, wanted to drive himself inside her. Wanted to take pleasure, give pleasure, and get lost in everything Simone.

She pulled an unopened pack of condoms from her night table. After opening the box, she set one on the bed.

"Lie on the bed, in child's pose, so you're on your knees and forearms, with your arms over your head," Luciano commanded.

She did as told. Seconds later, he'd secured her wrists together, shoved the rope under the mattress to hold it in place. "Ass up, spread your legs." She obeyed him. He looped the rope around one ankle and tucked the rope under the mattress, then repeated it on her other.

He covered himself with a condom. His balls had already drawn up, his throbbing cock ready to release inside her heat. But he was addicted to her sounds, to the way she squirmed and bucked, and the way she screamed his name from the ecstasy he could bring her.

Bringing her pleasure helped keep his demons at bay.

She tugged at the rope around her wrists, but she was trapped. Then, she tried moving her feet. He'd secured those as well.

"Simone, what's your safe word?" he asked.

"I'll use yellow if I need you to back off and red to stop you. Black is if I'm spiraling."

"Spiraling to where?"

Her lips curved into a smile. "To hell, of course."

"Should I stop?"

"No, you should go harder and faster," she replied.

I won't last two minutes with her.

He climbed on the bed, ran his hand down her long, lovely back, then slipped a hand beneath her and fondled her breast, teased her already hard nip with his finger. Back and forth, back and forth before he pinched it.

She whimpered.

"You've been a bad girl," he said, "and you need to be punished."

"I'm sorry, sir." He was surprised at how different her voice was. Her dry sarcasm had been replaced with a soft innocence, like a submissive.

He cupped her other tit, massaged it harder, then teased the nipple until it too turned to stone. On his knees behind her, he ran the head of his now sheathed cock over her pussy and up to her anus. Slowly, he teased her with his erection, but she stayed silent.

"How does that feel?" he asked.

"Not good. I don't want you to touch me. You're a bad man. An evil man."

A smile tugged at his lips. He *was* all of those things.

"I'm going to fuck you to remind you that when you disobey me, you will get punished. Hard and fast and very, very deep."

"Please no," she whispered.

"Simone," he said checking in.

"Green, green, get me to black."

He loved the eager desperation in her voice, the begging that only he could appease. He positioned at her opening, pressed inside, her wet pussy widening to accommodate his thickness. Pleasure slithered through him, igniting every muscle, every cell, every atom. He felt alive, he felt like he could fuck her to the moon, but he didn't deserve the pleasure.

She was right. He was a bad man, an evil man.

The deeper he tunneled inside, the more garbled her sounds. When he was all the way inside her, he paused. Then, he withdrew. He held her hips in place and he started fucking her. In and out, again and again, while hit after hit of dopamine drowned him in pleasure.

Pleasure he didn't deserve. Not now, not ever.

"Yes," she cried out, snapping him back to now. "I'm a very bad girl and you should fuck me harder. So much harder."

He thrust to her end and did it again. Her groans and grunts sliced through the night while he fucked her hard and fast.

"Black." Her insides clenched around him, she started bucking against his shaft, and then she cried out shaking through her drenching release.

Her orgasm triggered his and he climaxed inside her, groaning through the ecstasy.

And then, they stilled. The calm after the storm.

After several seconds, she said. "I'm going to get you off with my feet."

I've found the perfect angel, even in the depths of hell.

SIMONE

SIMONE LOVED FUCKING. Wild, ravaging, hard fucking. She loved being tied up, loved being punished. It had been years since she'd allowed someone to restrain her, and she never wanted their fun to end. But it would end. He'd find another plaything and move on. Rather than scold herself, or kick him out, she was all-in.

He withdrew, but he didn't head to the bathroom. He stayed. Kissed her back, dropped a trail of worshipful kisses from one shoulder to the other. Then, he untied her wrists, rubbed the skin, kissed each palm.

Why is he being so tender? He doesn't have to romance me. This is about screwing, nothing more.

With nimble fingers he untied her ankles. "Roll over."

He placed a pillow under her head, sat on the edge and lifted her leg.

"Such shapely legs," he murmured as he stroked her calf, kissed the crown of her foot.

His touch quieted her mind, the gentle caresses a remedy for everything that ailed her. His calming effect quenched her like a crystal-clear lake in the middle of the scorching desert.

She didn't know she needed this, but as he ran his long fingers over her toes, a peace came over her. He had this magical way of whisking her away to his own private sanctuary.

When he finished, she sat on his lap, wrapped herself around him, and kissed him. One soft kiss turned into another while the passion swirled around them, their connection an undeniable magnet. The build was slow, luxurious, and all-consuming.

"You zhuzhed me up *again*," she murmured. "I'm out of control around you."

His smile—his perfectly evil, breathtakingly beautiful smile—sent her rocketing into the night sky. Hurtling through space, she felt like she would get sucked into the black hole that was forever Luciano Santini.

Look away.

But she could not.

Get out of bed.

She didn't move.

I can't keep doing this with him.

Yet, she couldn't think of a single reason to stop.

Confidence rolled off him in tsunami-style waves. His gaze never left hers... and hers stayed anchored on him. Nothing else mattered but the way she felt in his strong embrace, the way his fingers combed through her hair, then sent electricity whizzing through her when his fingers brushed over her heated skin. The air sizzled with untamed energy, their eager bodies and their minds hooked on the rush of endorphins.

Everyone woman deserves to have sex with an Adonis. Even if it's only once. Mine just happens to be Luciano Santini.

"You've turned me into a beast," he said.

She inhaled another deep breath, hoping to calm her palpitating heart, but it was pounding out a maddening rhythm in her chest. She placed two fingers on his carotid.

"Your heart rate is slow and steady. Mine's gotta be over a hundred."

"Let's slow you down, belleza." He captured her face in his hand, kissed her, softly. She melted at the gentle way he pressed his lips to hers. Tender touches and soft kisses while she floated on a silver cloud.

His phone rang, piercing their intimate moment. He disentangled himself from her, retrieved it from his pants pocket, looked at the screen, and silenced it. Then, he returned and kissed her forehead. "I have to go."

Her heart fell. Their fairytale moment was over.

She wasn't going to ask him to stay. She wasn't going to

bring up the foot job. That would make her sound needy. If nothing else, she had her dignity.

Into her bathroom she walked, him close on her heels. She wasn't hurt. She wasn't angry either. She was a realist and, despite the couture gown delivery, this was a booty call.

And she'd been the booty.

Truth was, his speedy exit stung a little. Rather than attempt to make small talk or to stand there like a lost puppy, she turned on the shower. Steeling her spine, she said, "Lock the front door on your way out."

Surprise flashed in his eyes. Had she not been full-on staring at him, she would have missed it.

"Of course," he replied.

She pulled her hair up, secured it with a giant clip, then stepped under the hot spray. Time to move on. As she was lathering up, he pulled open the shower door. "Dinner sometime?"

The obligatory question.

She didn't want to reject his offer, but she didn't want to pin him for a date and time. Better to play this one chill. "Sure."

Rather than lean in to kiss her, he took one of her hands, kissed it. "I'll be in touch."

"Thanks for the gowns."

Again, less was more.

He left the bathroom and her guts knotted. Maybe hooking up again with him wasn't a brilliant idea, but she didn't have to do it again.

And I won't.

She washed off. While rinsing, she turned up the heat, let it scald her back. Off went the faucet and she dried off, moisturized her skin, and slipped into her silky robe.

Sex energized her, so there was no way she'd be able to sleep. Rather than crawl into bed, she made her way downstairs. In the foyer, as she rounded the corner, movement caught her eye and she startled.

Luciano sat on the sofa in the living room, looking damn near perfect in his suit and white dress shirt. As expected, his just-sexed hair had fallen back into place. The front porch lights streamed through the windows, bathing him in a soft glow. When he turned, the sadness in his eyes surprised her.

"I wanted to thank you for tonight," he said.

She walked into the front room. "No need. It was fun."

"I'm talking about the entire evening. I liked that you met Elsa, that you know Slash. My life is very compartmentalized. The overlap is different."

She offered nothing more than a simple nod.

He rose. "I want you to know something about me." He walked to her, clasped her hand in his. "I meant it when I asked you to dinner."

Did he feel guilty that he was leaving? He didn't strike her as someone who would.

Ahh, I know.

"This doesn't have to be awkward if we run into each other's at Carrera's." She tucked her hair behind one ear. "I'm a grown woman who invited you into my house, into my bedroom, and into my body. I have no expectations, especially when it comes to you."

He furrowed his brow. "What does that mean?"

"Look, you're a playboy. A no-strings man. I'm good with that, but I'm not gonna repeat this."

"I understand," he replied. "That's why I asked you to dinner."

"Like a date?"

He kissed her cheek. "Yes."

"I don't date," she blurted.

"Why not?"

"I'm not on any dating sites and I don't go to bars. I work a lot—"

"I would imagine that your spy job *and* your personal shopper career take up all your time." He smiled.

Her lips tugged upward, but she wouldn't give him the satisfaction of a full-blown smile. She had every confidence Slash and Carrera had told him about her *actual* career, but she wasn't saying a word. Not one damn word.

"Do *you* date?" she asked.

"No," he replied.

He was stroking her hand with his thumb sending delicious sparks soaring up her arm. He kissed her, leaving his lips on hers for several glorious seconds.

His phone rang.

To her surprise, he silenced it, kissed her again.

She ended the kiss, but she did kiss his cheek, then his other cheek. That made him smile. "Let me walk you out."

She started to pull her hand away, but he kept a firm hold on it. Together, they walked to the front door.

"Goodbye, Luciano."

"Buona notte, Simone."

She waited on the front porch while he walked toward his car, the cold night air swirling around her thin robe. His confident swagger kept her glued to his every move. He glanced at his phone, slipped inside his very expensive sports car. It roared to life and he backed out of her driveway. On the street, he turned on the headlights, tapped the horn, and sped away.

"Wow," she murmured.

Luciano Santini was the most compelling, complicated man she'd ever met.

LUCIANO

Luciano returned Teddy's call.

"Yo," Teddy answered. "I got a hit on the Fuller brothers."

"Nice," Luciano drove out of Simone's neighborhood, her beautiful scent still surrounding him.

"They've been flying below the radar for months," Teddy continued. "One of them made the bonehead move of stealing a wallet and using a credit card at his favorite strip club. The card got flagged and I found 'em."

"Where?"

"DC apartment." After a beat, Teddy said, "The credit card got turned off. I'm concerned they're gonna bolt."

"Neighborhood surveillance?" Luciano asked.

"Everything is cued up to turn off."

It was one-thirty in the morning.

Luciano accelerated, and the McLaren flew down the road. "I can be home in twenty."

"Twenty at your house, another thirty to DC," Teddy said. "That puts us there around three."

"What about building surveillance?" Luciano asked.

"I turned off the exterior cameras," Teddy replied. "I'll take down the power in the building."

"Let's do it." Luciano hung up.

Twenty minutes later, he pulled up to the gates of his mansion, acknowledged the night guard in the booth, and drove inside. Up the tree-lined driveway he flew, parking at the fountain out front.

Dressed in all black, Teddy waited on the front steps. As he rose, Luciano extended his hand. Teddy clasped it, pulled him in for a hug.

"Who were you with?" Teddy asked.

"What makes you think—"

"Why don't you ever just answer my question, you know, like direct?"

"Simone Redding," he said. "She was at Carrera's."

"How does she know Carrera?"

Luciano plugged in his six-digit code on the electronic lock, then stood in front of the retina scanner. The light turned green, the lock slid open, and he walked into his home.

"Z had her watching me, but Carrera pulled her." Luciano walked down the hallway, stopping in front of a closed door. Again, he paused in front of a retina scanner, then stepped away so Teddy could move close. The light flashed green and Luciano opened the door.

Once inside, movement tripped the light sensor. Both men walked over to the back closet. Luciano plugged in a ten-digit code in the electronic lock, the door opened, revealing over twenty weapons of various sizes.

"I have to change." Luciano exited the room, rode the elevator to his bedroom. There he changed into skintight black pants and a black pullover sweater. On went his Kevlar vest, a black knit cap, and his leather boots. In his walk-in closet, he left his wallet and phone on the marble table, pulled the burner from its charger, confirmed it was on silent, and slipped it into his pocket. He shouldered into a double holster before grabbing his black leather gloves.

Down the stairs he went, returning to find Teddy admiring his gun collection.

"Do you like her?" Teddy asked as Luciano handed him a double shoulder harness. Teddy pulled his Glock from behind his pants. "I'm good."

Luciano shook his head. "Two weapons."

On a grunt, Teddy shouldered into the harness, tucked his Glock into the right one and slid one of Luciano's SIG SAUERs into the left.

"Well?" Teddy asked as he pulled on his black gloves.

"Well, what?"

"For fuck's sake," Teddy bit out. "Why has talking to you become so damn difficult. Do you like Simone?"

"I do. She's different, but it's complicated."

"What have you told her?"

"Nothing," Luciano replied. "I wanted to, but I took off instead."

"That's not good," Teddy said.

"I fucked up."

"Maybe if she knew—"

"Her knowing won't change anything."

"Maybe it will," Teddy pushed back.

"I don't deserve to be happy—"

"Lulu, you gotta forgive yourself. I mean, hell, it wasn't your fault."

"Enough," Luciano murmured.

"I'm here if you wanna talk."

Luciano draped his arm around Teddy's shoulder. "You're a good brother."

"If you're gonna get all mushy on me, go back to *not* answering my questions."

Luciano slid a Glock into one holster, a SIG SAUER into the second. Then, he attached an ankle holster and slid a third weapon into that. After shoving a mini lock pick set into his pocket, he said, "Time to take out two monsters, Santini style."

They grabbed their night goggles, left the weapons room. From there, they took the elevator to his underground garage.

"Do you have on body armor?" Luciano asked.

"Hell, yeah."

"Range Rover," Luciano said.

They slid into the vehicle, buckled up. As Luciano was pulling out of the garage, Teddy said, "maybe it's time you forgave yourself."

Searing pain sliced through his heart. "Never."

"What about loving again. Can you do that?"

"I love them physically."

"No, Luciano," Teddy said. "With your heart."

"I don't have a heart. That's why I'm an assassin."

"It's a job, like any other."

"Is that how you see it?" Luciano drove down his long driveway, pausing to wait for the gates to open.

"Someone has to thin the herd. We're like lions chasing gazelle."

"They hunt to eat."

"We do it to protect the innocent," Teddy replied. "We do it so that good people can live their lives. We do it to stop these monsters because law enforcement can't."

"Well said, Theodore." In the darkened car, he glanced over at his brother. "Are you ready to take out two serial rapists?"

"Every damn time." Teddy gave him the address and Luciano sped toward DC.

At three-thirty in the morning, Luciano stopped a block away from the DC apartment building. Teddy got busy on his phone and the entire block went black.

"That's gonna cause a shit-ton of problems," Luciano bit out.

"I can't take out just the one building. They're all on the same grid."

They exited the car. "Silence your ringer," Luciano instructed.

"Yeah, yeah, I do that now *without* having to be told."

They pulled on their night goggles, exited the SUV. Luciano opened the hatch, handed Teddy a silencer from the duffle bag. He took one for himself, attached it to his Glock. With stealth, they strode toward the back of the DC apartment building. The door was locked. Teddy aimed his weapon, but Luciano pulled out the lock pick set.

He couldn't get the bar to release, and Teddy kept grumbling under his breath. Over a minute later, the bar gave way and Luciano opened the door. They bolted up the back stairs to the third floor.

To his relief, the hallway was dead quiet. With his weapon

at the ready, Teddy led him to the apartment, located in the middle of the hall. This had to be the worst location. They weren't near an exit and they were surrounded by tenants.

Teddy tried the door handle. It turned, and they slipped inside the apartment. They had to be swift and they had to be exact.

"Please, no," a woman whimpered from one of the bedrooms. "You're hurting me. I'm begging you to stop."

Bile rose in Luciano's throat while hatred filled his soul. He swept the living room. No one was there. The kitchenette was also empty.

"STOP!" screamed the woman.

Luciano pointed to the second bedroom and Teddy took off past the first. Luciano strode to the doorway. A woman was shackled to the bed, her bruised, bloodied body the evidence Luciano needed to take down the monster.

One of the brothers stood nearby. He whipped his head toward Luciano, but the room was pitch black.

"You have too much power." Luciano raised his weapon, fired a single shot.

POP!

The bullet pierced him between the eyes, the man dropped to the floor.

The woman screamed.

Ah, fuck.

"Shh," he said to her. "Police are on their way."

"Please don't hurt me," she murmured.

He covered her with a blanket. "I'll get you help."

She started sobbing. "Thank you."

BANG!

POP! POP! POP!

Luciano bolted into the other bedroom. The other Fuller brother lay crumpled on the floor. Teddy stood there like a statue. Luciano strode over.

"Jesus, no."

The brother had shot the woman he had chained to the bed. She was bleeding out, a gaping hole in her chest.

Luciano grabbed Teddy by the arm. "Let's go."

As they passed the first bedroom, Luciano paused to speak to the surviving victim. "Help is coming."

They exited the apartment and were blinded by phone flashlights from people in the hallway. The sound of the gunshot had caused tenants to scurry out of their homes. He and Teddy flipped up their goggles, kept their heads down, and strode down the hall toward the back entrance.

"Grab those guys!" someone shouted.

Teddy bolted, Luciano close on his heels. They flew down the stairs and out into the night, not stopping until they'd returned to the vehicle, parked on the street. Breathing hard, they got in, Luciano started the engine, and they left.

On the main road, he turned on the headlights, hit the gas. After he removed his night goggles, Luciano extracted the burner phone from his pocket. With the exception of a few at ALPHA, Luciano couldn't stand law enforcement. And he trusted them even less.

But he needed to ensure the victim got the help she needed, so he made the call.

"Hey," Carrera answered. "You okay?"

"Fuller brothers had prisoners," Luciano said. "One living, one murdered by one of the brothers."

Teddy rattled off the address.

Luciano normally didn't do business over the phone, but in this case, he had no choice.

"I'm on it." Carrera hung up.

Luciano glanced over at his brother. "How you doing?"

"I couldn't save her," Teddy murmured. "I fucking couldn't do it."

His heart broke for his younger brother. He would hold on

to this for a long time and blame himself for even longer. No matter what Luciano said, it wouldn't make a difference. Teddy was very hard on himself. Always had been.

"What can I say to help alleviate your pain?"

"Nothing, brother," Teddy replied. "It is what it is. We went in to take out the monsters. We got it done, but there was collateral damage."

Luciano knew about collateral damage better than anyone. Those most precious to him had been just that.

8

THE CATASTROPHE

SIMONE

Simone had spent the last two days trying to forget about Luciano. And she'd failed. Over and over and over again. Thinking about him during the day was bad enough, but he'd managed to slither his way into her dreams. Even there, his charm, charisma, and consummate power kept her anchored to his side and focused on his every damn word.

At just after noon, she pulled open the squeaky door to Rudy's, stepped inside, and inhaled the familiar aromas of Washington's favorite greasy spoon. She hadn't been back in years, but from the looks of things, nothing had changed.

Metal tables, red cushioned chairs. Small, dirty windows that sat high on the walls. She'd been a regular until she'd stopped coming. In a split second, her entire life had forever changed. But here she was, stepping back in time.

Or... maybe I'm walking toward my new life.

Rudy bustled over. "Welcome to Rudy's." Then, a smiled brightened his weathered face. "I never forget a pretty face. I forget names—"

"Red," she said.

"Yes! Welcome back, Red. It's been a while. Table for one?"

Movement caught her eye. Jerod—seated at a corner table—was waving his arms. She laughed, then tossed her lunch companion a nod. "My friend's already here."

Rudy escorted her. After she sat, he handed her a menu. "I remember you two used to come in pretty regularly. It's good to see you again. Do you need a minute to order?"

"One Coke, one iced tea, unsweetened," Jerod said. "Did I remember that right?"

Simone smiled. "You got it. Can you remember what we ate?"

"Of course." Jerod handed Rudy his menu. "Two burgers, everything on 'em with a giant fry to share." Then, he regarded Simone. "How does that sound?"

"Perfect," she replied.

Rudy grinned. "Be right back with those drinks."

After collecting her menu, Rudy whizzed off, and Simone took a few seconds to take in the restaurant.

"I don't think anything has changed," she said.

"You've changed," he said. "And you broke my heart."

Simone stared at him. She had no idea he felt that way. "You had a thing—"

"Wait, that came out wrong. We were good friends, but there was no—"

"Romance, sparks, sexual chemistry," Simone said, her thoughts jumping to Luciano. "Then, how did I break your heart?"

"You left law enforcement," Jerod said. "I've been pretty surprised about that. Peter thinks you went undercover, which makes total sense."

Rudy returned with a chilled tea for her and a soda for Jerod. He set a small plate of lemons on the table between them. "I remembered."

"I'm impressed, Rudy," she said.

"You're the man, Rudy," Jerod echoed.

Rudy offered a little bow before moving on to the next table.

"Why did you leave, Red?" Jerod asked while squeezing lemon into his drink.

She squeezed two lemon chunks into the chilled tea. "I had an arrest go sideways. It messed me up pretty good."

"I'm sorry, honey," Jerod said. "I wish you'd called me. We always shared the stress of our jobs."

"Yeah, well, I didn't talk to anyone but a therapist," Simone confided.

"PTSD?" he asked.

While sipping the drink, she nodded.

"Peter is convinced you're undercover," Jerod pressed again. *Talk to him. He was a good friend.*

"He's not wrong," she said, "but it's not something I talk about."

ALPHA Operatives were given badges for several federal agencies—FBI, ATF, State, DEA, and DHS, to name a few. Since they couldn't come clean that they were with ALPHA, they used their aliases when making an arrest, interfacing with other LEOs, or interviewing witnesses.

"We always did keep each other's secrets," he said. "Do you remember what you said when you met Alice?"

Alice had been his girlfriend.

"Not really."

"You didn't think we were right for each other."

"Ouch. Sorry."

"No, I loved it, and wished I'd broken it off sooner. When Alice went out of town for six months, I started man-whoring around." Jerod shook his head. "Not my proudest moment."

Simone nodded. "I remember that."

"You gave me great advice. You said that if I couldn't be

faithful to her, I should break it off and find someone I could be faithful with." He showed her a photo of his girlfriend. "Becca and I are talking about her moving here so we can be together. I'd love for you to meet her."

"Where does she live?"

"Atlanta," he replied. "So, what case were you working that messed you up?"

She leaned forward. "The Bomb Maker."

His eyebrows jutted up. "Wow. That was my case. How'd you get it?"

Despite the uneasiness in talking about it, she couldn't help but crack a smile. "Jerod, not even *you* could work *every* case."

"Of all the cases I got assigned, I *hated* losing that one."

"It was good you didn't end up working it. It was a total fail. I left, went into private industry."

"Whatever happened to The BM?"

She chuckled. "Leave it to you to say something totally inappropriate about one of the worst mass murderers of our time."

Rudy returned with their food. "Enjoy, my friends." He set down their plates, put the French Fries and Ketchup between them. "I'll be back with refills."

After he left, Jerod asked, "Did The BM get arrested?"

Simone's stomach lurched as she bit into the greasy burger. Maybe talking about The Bomb Maker wasn't so smart after all.

"He was never found," she replied.

"Maybe he blew himself up," Jerod added.

"Why would you say that?"

"He blows up a bunch of buildings, then just vanishes?" Jerod shook his head. "There was never a manifesto, never even a suspect to question. I'm guessing The BM is dead."

She glanced around the crowded restaurant.

I can't talk about this here.

Needing to change the subject, she asked Jerod about his work.

"I oversee all of ATF's cases and direct field agents in what investigations they should or shouldn't follow," Jerod explained. "As much as we want to put the same number of people-hours into everything, we don't have it."

"So, your real title is Czar," Simone said playfully.

"That's me," Jerod replied. "Ruler of all things at ATF."

Their conversation came easy... always did. He talked about his friendship with Peter Hirzog and how Peter had written a great letter of recommendation for his current job.

"I owe him a debt of gratitude," Jerod said. "It's great to be back in the DMV, especially connecting with wonderful friends like you."

She felt the same.

They finished up. Jerod insisted on paying, then suggested they get together again.

"Are you returning to the Bureau?" he asked outside on the sidewalk.

"I don't think so," she replied.

"If you change your mind, consider ATF. You'd make a great agent and I would definitely fast-track you for management. You know, paying it forward."

She thanked him and hurried off. She had four clients she needed to follow up on that afternoon. Two with Secret Service, one with the CIA, and a final check on an employee at the Pentagon.

As the afternoon wore on, her thoughts floated back to Luciano. She missed tailing him, missed staring through her binos at him, and she missed catching glimpses of him as he entered his office building at CityCenter in DC. Just seeing him made her heart flutter.

But their last hookup had ended awkwardly. He'd done the

deed, gotten a call, then bolted. Except he'd waited downstairs to ask her out.

He's hella complicated. Let it go and move on.

Still, she couldn't stop thinking about him.

It was almost six in the evening when she returned home. She hurried to get the homemade meatballs in the oven before boiling water for pasta. Short on time, she heated a jar of her favorite red sauce on the stovetop. Then, she got busy making Alfredo sauce.

With the broccolini rinsed, she placed it in the steamer. "Broccoli's tasty little cousin," she said to herself.

Twenty minutes later, dinner was ready.

Knock-knock. Then, the doorbell chimed.

Simone's phone buzzed with an incoming text. While pouring the cooked pasta into the colander, she glanced over. It was a text from Luciano.

> Can't stop thinking about you. Dinner Saturday?

Adrenaline powered through her while she hurried to open the front door. After confirming Frederica was outside, she swung open the door.

"Hey, babe. Perfect timing."

As they walked toward the kitchen, Fred said, "Yeah, mama. Smells goooood!"

Simone eyed the pastry box Fred set on the counter. "Whatcha bring?"

"Six little surprises." Fred lifted both saucepan lids. "Mmm, red sauce *and* Alfredo sauce. Homemade?"

"The Alfredo is," Simone replied. "I got slammed at work. Carrera sent me a bunch of new clients."

Fred washed her hands, pulled out two plates, got busy setting out silverware.

After filling glasses with water, Simone opened the pastry

box. "These look amazing." Fred had bought six different mini cakes. Red velvet, chocolate, pistachio swirl, tiramisu, white chocolate, and a cheesecake. "We're going to get fat."

"We're not eating them *all* tonight."

The next few minutes was a flurry of activity as they filled their plates and sat down at the table.

"Broccolini?" Fred asked as she mixed the Alfredo sauce through the pasta. "Why ruin a perfect meal."

"It's good for you."

Fred held up a stalk and bit into the florets. "I feel like a giant eating a tree."

Simone laughed.

They lifted their water goblets, clinked glasses. "BFFs forever," Fred said.

"Amen," Simone replied.

Simone's phone buzzed, but she'd left it on the counter. "Meatballs came out pretty good."

"So good," Fred echoed. "Did I tell you I have a mission starting at one this morning? Well, actually tomorrow morning."

"Tell me about it." Simone forked a piece of meatball into her mouth.

The color drained from her friend's cheeks and she broke eye contact. "Nah, it's nothing. Same 'ol thang."

Even though Simone was no longer a part of ALPHA, the two friends kept no secrets. Normally, Fred shared details about her missions.

Simone swirled the pasta with red sauce around her fork, slid it into her mouth, and chewed. After swallowing, she eyed Fred, who looked downright uncomfortable, something Simone wasn't used to seeing.

"What's going on with you?" Simone asked.

Fred sighed. "I shouldn't have told you because I don't want to spin you up."

"I'm good, really."

"We got the location of a master bomb maker, but there's no confirmation it's *him*."

Simone's heart slammed against her chest. "*Him* being The Bomb Maker?"

With her mouth full of food, Fred nodded.

"What *do* you know?"

"He's been making explosives for terror cells."

Simone's guts knotted, and she set down her fork. "Are you dropping him?"

"We can't without confirmation it's *him*, so we gotta arrest him."

A growl shot out of her. "If I were there, I'd open fire, ask questions later."

"Yeah, I hear ya, but we don't have much to go on."

"Are the terror cells here or abroad?" Simone asked.

"Both," Fred explained. "Several shipments of raw materials were tracked to a house in Silver Spring."

Excitement coursed through Simone. For the first time in a long time, she missed her old life and wished *she* was going on that mission.

"How many on the team?"

"Six of us." Fred shot her a smarmy smile. "I got lead."

"I'm not sure if that makes me feel better or worse," Simone said.

"Red, we got this. ALPHAs beta-testing bodycams and I'm the guinea pig."

"Nice."

Just thinking about The Bomb Maker spun her up in the absolute worst way. While she wanted to tell Fred *not* to go, she would never. Her friend was a trained ALPHA Op, an excellent markswoman, and she'd be surrounded by other well-qualified people.

"Be careful," Simone murmured.

"Babe, it's me," Fred replied with a cocky smile. "Once he's arrested, I hope they find evidence it's *The* Bomb Maker."

"He killed thousands, injured so many others, and destroyed too many lives." Anger made her flush and she chugged down her chilled water.

Fred twirled pasta on her fork. "It'll be freakin' awesome to get him off the streets. But I am curious... where's he been the past five years, and why resurface now?"

"I think about him ghosting every single day. I'll be sending you good vibes."

"We're gonna rock the mission. HQ meeting at one in the morning to review the plan, head out by two, latest. I'll call you tomorrow and let you know if we got him."

Simone's phone buzzed again.

Fred eyed her empty plate. "I want more, but I don't want to be stuffed. Plus... dessert." She carried their empty dinner dishes to the sink.

Simone pulled two dessert dishes and two forks.

"Check this out." Fred held out Simone's phone. "You've got texts from Luciano Santini. Is Mr. Big Bucks interested in my girl?"

Simone read each of his texts.

> Sorry I bolted the other night. Can't stop thinking about you. Dinner Saturday?

> Carole Jeans in Tysons?

> After dinner, a ride on my yacht or dancing at a private club?

Excitement permeated her entire being. He was pursuing her. Plus, he'd apologized. She had to give him props for that.

Fred chuckled. "You look like you're in heat."

"I do not."

"Your cheeks are flushed."

"From the spice I added to the red sauce."

"You're talking to *me*," Fred said. "I see right through your BS." She leaned over, read the messages, then grinned at Simone. "Holy hell, mama. He likes you." She waggled her eyebrows. "You gotta lock this one down."

Simone laughed. "Lock him down? And that's coming from Ms. Independent?"

"Lemme tell you something sister... if I had a gorgeous billionaire asking me out, I'd be closing him on the big M."

"Big M?"

"Marriage, baby. The big ring, the big house, the whole shebang."

Simone laughed. Hard. "That's your advice? What if he's a jerk? Or he's crazy? Or he's a workaholic and he's never around? Wait, he could be a total tool who can't keep his dick in his pants."

"With you? Don't you wanna get boned by your man?"

Simone chuckled. "With *other* women."

"I would screw him so often, he wouldn't even think of doing it with anyone else."

"I'll keep your sage advice in mind." Simone held up a mug. "Coffee before your mission?"

"Full-throttle."

Simone made Fred a bold java, a decaf for herself.

Fred slid Simone's phone toward her. "Reply to him."

"He can wait."

"Ugh, you're playing hard to get. You should be all over that."

Simone shook her head. "Cake now, texting later."

They selected red velvet and white chocolate, split the mini-cakes in two, and returned to the table with their plates and mugs. The conversation resumed, but Simone couldn't help but worry about Fred. She hoped this was a different bomb maker and not *The* Bomb Maker. The last time anyone had tried to arrest him, the mission had gone horribly wrong.

A shiver skirted through her.

As they dug into their delicious desserts, Simone said, "Why don't you swing by tomorrow night? We can finish off the leftovers and share two more slices of cake?"

Fred offered an encouraging smile. "No worries about the mission. I got this."

Am I that transparent?

"I invited you over because you're my friend and I'm sure as hell not eating all those desserts by myself," Simone said.

"Hey, I'm not gonna say no to having dinner with you, but I'm gonna be fine. Really. It'll be like every ALPHA mission I've ever been on. You'll see."

They finished eating. Fred offered to clean up, but Simone ushered her out. After a hug goodbye, she waited on the porch as Fred jumped in her Jeep and drove away.

"Please, Lord, keep her safe," Simone whispered as she retreated inside.

After cleaning up from dinner, she opened her laptop. Carrera had given her twenty-eight new cases. Before diving in, she thought about going out with Luciano.

Do it. But don't read anything into it.

With phone in hand, she replied.

> Sat works. Club sounds fun. I'll wear one of my Santini Originals

Seconds later came his reply.

> I look forward to seeing you, Simone

So do I.

Then, she thought about Fred's advice—"You gotta lock this one down"—and chuckled.

"I'm not locking anyone down, most of all Luciano Santini... but he might be just what I need to kickstart my life."

LUCIANO

LUCIANO PARKED in Carrera's driveway, exited his Range Rover. It was almost two o'clock Wednesday morning and the upscale Alexandria neighborhood was dead quiet. As he made his way toward his cousin's front door, Sin parked beside him.

He emerged from his black SUV, walked over. Together, they entered the dark house, a light in the kitchen illuminating their way. Luciano spied his cousin in his office, wrangling with temporary blinds.

Carrera eyed them through the glass and opened one of the French doors. "I need to cover this."

"It's two in the morning," Sin said. "No one's awake."

"My grandmother sleeps down the hall," Carrera explained. "She already knows more than she should." As he taped the paper blind over the glass, Luciano pulled another from the box and attached it to the other door.

Both large displays on Carrera's wall and the one on his desk were dark.

"When does the stream go live?" Luciano asked.

"As soon as I click in," Carrera said. "They should be on their way to the target's house now."

Rather than relax on the sofa, the men sat in guest chairs. Carrera locked the door. Once he sat, he hopped on his laptop. Seconds later, all three displays lit up.

"Frederica Salgado, longtime ALPHA Op, is lead," Carrera explained. "We're watching through her BWV—Body Worn Video."

"Just the one camera?" Luciano asked.

"Yeah," Carrera replied. "Livestream only."

"Is Dakota watching?" Luciano asked.

"Yeah," Sin replied. "He and Providence are watching from their safe room at home, so the kids don't wander in."

"Rebel's watching at home too," Carrera said. "Cooper's with him."

The men grew silent as the vehicle Frederica was driving came to a stop, the engine went dead. In silence, she exited, walked around to the back hatch and opened it. The three Ops who rode with her pulled on their night goggles. One quick check of their comms before they joined up with the other two Operatives who'd parked next to them.

"We go in together, we come out together," Frederica said, then paused. "Questions?"

There were none.

"Is everyone up for the mission?" she asked.

One by one, the five Ops confirmed they were.

"This is an arrest-priority mission," Frederica reminded them. "The suspect lives alone. Doesn't mean he is alone."

"If he opens fire?" asked an Op.

"Like we discussed, we return fire," Frederica said, her voice calm and steady. "Let's fall in line."

"They're at a small neighborhood park two blocks from the target site," Carrera explained.

Pairing off in twos, they made their way to the street. Down the block the ALPHA SWAT team walked in silent formation.

Frederica signaled, and three of the Ops veered toward the backyard. The street was quiet, the small house dark. The body cam was equipped with the same lens as the night goggles, filling the screen with a greenish hue.

Frederica led two Ops to the front door. She tried the handle. It was unlocked.

"That never happens for me," Luciano said.

"Same," Sin added.

"Is the back door locked?" Frederica whispered, the comm catching her words.

They couldn't hear the response.

"On three," Frederica said.

She counted them down, and they entered the house. Frederica and her team cleared the first floor. It was empty.

"Report in," she murmured.

"Copy," she replied.

"We're heading upstairs," Frederica whispered before leading them up the stairs.

Midway, she paused.

Either she heard something or the stairs creaked. Moving with stealth, she led the team to the second floor. There, she directed them to split up, each clearing one of the bedrooms. She went into the room straight ahead, scanned the area.

Someone was lying under the blankets. She approached, pulled off the linens. And stilled.

"It's a blowup doll," Frederica muttered. "For the remote team, we've got blowup dolls positioned in the basement and in the other beds."

"Team, the dolls are a set-up." Frederica hurried out of the bedroom and into the hallway. "Abort, abort, abort! Team, GET OUT!"

Luciano's guts twisted. "Jesus, no."

"Ohgod, it's an ambush," Carrera said.

A flash of bright white light exploded onto the screen.

KABOOM!!!

Frederica's camera went dark.

An eerie silence filled the room.

Luciano's heart dropped.

"Jesus." Carrera grabbed his phone, made a call. "Rebel—"

"My team's suiting up," Rebel said through the speaker.

Sin also made a call. "Are you watching?" He listened, then said, "Agreed." He hung up.

Luciano pushed out of his chair, the anger flowing through him. They'd been baited to the house by someone who'd planned to take them out.

"How the hell did he know?" Sin bit out.

"Someone on the inside," Luciano said. "That's the only way."

His thoughts floated to Frederica. Though he'd only just met her, his heart broke for her, for all the Ops and their loved ones.

"Simone," he murmured.

"First responders are on the way," Sin said.

"It's gotta be The Bomb Maker," Carrera said. "That's exactly what happened to ALPHA five years ago."

"ALPHA Ops aren't safe," Luciano said.

"No one at ALPHA is," Carrera replied.

"What a cluster fuck," Sin bit out. "If we couldn't find him then, how the hell are we going to now?"

Luciano tapped his fingers on the desk. "We're smart. We'll figure it out."

"We?" Carrera asked. "You're not law enforcement."

A smile ghosted Luciano's face. "How perfect is that? He won't see me coming, but he'll feel my wrath when I find him." After a beat, he continued. "If this is The Bomb Maker, we can't feed his ego. That will only fuel him."

"Good point," Carrera said. "What are you thinking?"

"Sin runs damage control with the media." Luciano regarded Sin. "Tell them a gas leak caused the explosion."

"Aren't we putting the public at risk?" Sin asked.

"We're trying to stave mass chaos," Luciano insisted. "And we can't give him the satisfaction of being the center of attention. The media will go berserk with this story. They'll dig into his past and that will spread to every city in the country."

"He's got a point," Carrera agreed.

"The Bomb Maker is excellent at his job," Luciano continued, "and he knew ALPHA was coming to arrest him, so he's got an inside track—"

"That makes him even more dangerous," Sin said.

"Right now, he'd got *all* the power," Luciano bit out. "Once I get a handle on this, I'll take that away."

Carrera nodded. "If there's anyone who can take the power—"

Sin's lips split into a smile. "It's Luciano."

Knock-knock.

Luciano opened the French door.

Slash stood there, dressed in camo, her Glock in the shoulder holster, her helmet in her hand, her go-bag over her shoulder. "Rebel called the team. I'm out."

Carrera pushed past him. "Be safe."

"Do you think they're alive?" Luciano asked.

"We won't know until we get there," Slash replied before tossing a nod at Luciano and Sin. "This is a cluster." She regarded all three men. "Fix this."

She kissed her husband goodbye before bolting toward the garage as Elsa loomed into view.

His grandmother was small in stature, but height mattered not to the strong-willed Elsa Santini. With her hands on her hips, and dressed in what looked like a bathrobe from the 70s, she smiled up at him.

"What's going on?" Elsa asked. "Where is Amanda May going in the middle of the night?"

"She's got a rescue mission," Carrera replied.

Luciano stepped into the hall.

"Lulu! What a wonderful surprise." Elsa hugged him and he held her close. If there was anyone in the world he adored, it was her.

"Elsa, what are you doing up?" Luciano asked.

"I heard voices." She peeked around him. "Sinclair, is that you?"

Sin slid his phone in his pocket and joined them.

"Good to see you, Elsa," Sin said. "Is your robe a Santini Original?"

"No," Elsa replied. "Lulu hasn't created anything like this."

"That's an idea. Bring the past into the present," Luciano said, but his thoughts jumped to Frederica and the five others who probably just died, and a thirst for revenge overtook his tortured soul.

Elsa broke from him, padded toward the kitchen. "I'll make coffee," she called, over her shoulder.

"I'm gonna take off and get a jump on the media," Sin said. "So, we're going with house explosion, but what about ALPHA's Rescue team at the scene?"

"Rebel's got it covered," Carrera explained.

Sin's phone buzzed with an incoming text. "Dakota's headed to the explosion site."

After Sin left, Luciano asked Carrera, "Can you do something for me?"

"Name it," Carrera replied.

"Simone and Frederica are best friends," Luciano said. "She needs to hear about this from you and Slash."

Carrera squeezed Luciano's shoulder. "You got it. We'll tell her today."

"Let's go check in with the *real* boss," Luciano said.

The cousins walked into the kitchen.

"Why are you here, Lulu?" Elsa asked. "What's going on?"

Luciano shifted his attention from his grandmother to Carrera, then back to Elsa. "Why can't I have coffee with my family?"

"In the middle of the night?" Elsa swatted his arm. "Please be safe."

"When has playing it safe ever gotten me anywhere?" he asked.

Carrera's phone rang. He answered, took if off speaker. After a brief conversation, he hung up. "ALPHA missions have been suspended until further notice."

"Like I said, he won't see me coming," Luciano bit out. "But he'll know I'm there when I play my hand."

SIMONE

AT SIX-THIRTY IN THE MORNING, Simone stopped peddling her stationary bike, closed the training app, and stepped off. She completed a few reps with her hand weights before making her way upstairs. After a quick shower, she dressed in yoga pants and an oversized shirt.

She'd take the morning to familiarize herself with the new cases Carrera had dropped into her ALPHA inbox, then spend the afternoon tailing her existing clients. She had three reports to finalize that evening before she uploaded her findings into the portal for Carrera to review.

I gotta text Slash about target practice.

She pulled the box of cereal from her cupboard, pausing to eye the box of mini cakes stashed on the counter.

Don't do it.

Ignoring her warning, she opened the lid and stared at the desserts.

"Not for breakfast."

Guilt whizzed through her and she closed the lid. *What kind of a friend am I? Fred brought these to share and I'm thinking about scarfing them down. Shame on you Simone Redding.*

She poured cereal into a bowl, dropped in a handful of almonds and a heaping spoonful of raw sunflower seeds, added some blueberries, then milk. With her bowl in hand, she ate at her small kitchen island.

She had a lot of work to do on her newest targets before she could start tailing them. Most were LEOs, several were military. Two were being considered for Secret Service, a few for the Bureau, one for ALPHA. Rebel was considering an ALPHA Op for his BLACK OPS rescue team. A civilian being was being considered for a presidential appointment. After logging into ALPHA, she reviewed their files, requested background checks on them, and started mapping out a strategy. Some of the gigs were short—two weeks—while others were a month or longer. The next two hours were a blur of work.

At just before nine, her phone rang. It was Slash.

"Hey, babe," Simone answered. "Are you calling about target practice?"

"Carrera and I are in your neighborhood. Any chance you're home?"

Slash's tight voice caught Simone's ear. "I'm here."

"Be there shortly." The line went dead.

Simone closed her laptop, made her way to the front door. She stepped into the chilly October morning. A black SUV drove down the street and parked in front of her house. Every ALPHA Op drove a bullet-proof vehicle.

They made their way up the driveway.

As they got closer, she said to Carrera, "You work for the Bureau. How'd you wrangle an SUV?"

Slash's smile was tight. "It's my SUV."

Simone slid her gaze from her to Carrera.

He mustered a rueful smile. "Thanks for letting us swing by."

Simone retreated inside, held the door open for them. "I just made a pot of coffee."

Silence as she poured the coffee, handed them each a mug. When they sat at her kitchen table, she couldn't miss the angst in Slash's eyes.

"I was just reviewing the new accounts you gave me, Carrera."

"Those'll keep you plenty busy," he said.

"There was a mission this morning," Slash began.

Simone's stomach dropped. Though she wasn't supposed to know, she did. "Ohgod, Frederica."

Slash shuddered in a breath. "There was an explosion."

Everything went into slow motion. Deafening silence thundered in Simone's ears. The pit in her stomach turned into a boulder, the tightness in her chest made breathing impossible.

"Please, no," she whimpered.

"I'm sorry," Carrera said.

Excruciating agony ripped through her soul. A wail exploded out of her, then a searing pain sliced through her heart. She collapsed on the table, like a ton of bricks, unable to move. Her arms and legs nothing more than dead weights.

"Breathe," Slash said as she grabbed Simone.

Then, she heard Slash and Carrera talking, but she couldn't understand them. Little yellow stars were closing in. They guided her into the family room, helped her lay down on the carpet. A numbness came over her, yet she'd broken into a cold sweat. And she couldn't stop shaking.

She had so many questions, yet she couldn't speak, too overwhelmed with shock.

Carrera left the room, returning with a glass of water and an icepack. On auto-pilot, she took a few sips. Slash pressed the frozen block against her forehead for a few seconds. The tiny yellow stars faded away, leaving only the harshest of realities.

Fred was gone.

"How many?" she whispered.

"All six," Carrera replied.

The fury and loss powered into her like a freight train. Heat and freezing cold whipped through her bones. She thought she was going to pass out again. Sucking down a breath, she pressed the ice pack to her chest. The cold chilled her skin until it started hurting. She set the pack on the carpet, then forced herself to sit up.

Slash left, returning a few seconds later with a paper towel. She wrapped the cold pack and offered it to Simone. Simone took it, pressed it to her cheek.

"Was it The Bomb Maker?" Simone asked, the feeling returning to her limbs.

"We don't know," Carrera said.

Flashes of scenes from five years ago sped through her mind like a living nightmare. A blinding bright light, a monumental explosion. Five dead, one survivor. The images still so fresh, it was as if no time had passed at all.

"We want you to stay with us for a few days," Slash said.

Simone stared at Slash for the longest time. Slash ran a comforting hand down her arm, clasped her hand. "We got you."

Tears pricked Simone's eyes. She hated showing weakness, but she couldn't stop them. They flowed down her cheeks, and she wiped them away.

Grief constricted her throat. She didn't want her new boss to see her this way. It was unprofessional. Forcing herself up, she excused herself to the powder room. There, she blew her nose, forced down the mountain of sorrow that threatened to burst from the depths of her soul. She would cry later, when she was alone.

Knock-knock.

She cleared her throat, wiped her wet eyes and tear-streaked cheeks, then opened the door. Slash pulled her in for a hug. "You aren't going through this alone."

The warmth from Slash's embrace triggered an overwhelming tightness in her heart, like her soul had been shattered into a million pieces. She hugged Slash, grateful for her friendship.

"Carrera's gonna take off and give us a little time," Slash said. "I can drive your SUV over to our house after you pack."

"I can't intrude," Simone pushed back. "I'm fine here."

Slash led her into the kitchen. Simone eyed the box of cakes—the ones she was going to devour with Frederica that evening. *Ohmygod, no. No, this can't be happening. She's going to walk through that door and everything's going to be okay.*

Despair was destroying her as she chugged in a shaky breath.

Carrera gave her a hug. "I'll see you back at the house later." Then, he dropped a light kiss on Slash's lips. "I'm heading to ALPHA."

"Wait," Simone said to him. "What are you going to do about this?"

"We're going to annihilate him," Carrera bit out before he let himself out.

After the front door closed, Simone asked, "What more can you tell me?"

Though still numb, and in shock, she needed to hear everything. Sitting next to Slash at the kitchen table, she steeled her spine. "Frederica confided that she was wearing a body cam. Did you see what happened?"

"No," Slash replied. "I was sleeping, but Carrera watched. He said there were decoys in the beds. They looked like mannequins, but Frederica reported in that they were blowup dolls. She realized it was a trap, but too late."

Simone choked back a sob while her heart squeezed so hard, she rubbed her chest. "Ohgod. It must've been so terrifying for them. "Where's Frederica? Where are the other Ops?"

"Providence is handling everything."

Simone couldn't believe what she was hearing. She needed to wake up from this horrific nightmare. More tears clouded her eyes, the loss impossible to comprehend.

"I need to confide in you," Slash began. "There might be a mole in ALPHA. How else would the bomber know the team was coming to his house?"

"Frederica said someone had been providing explosives to terror cells. Do you know which group?"

"No," Slash replied. "ALPHA got a hit when shipments of raw materials were tracked to a house in Silver Spring."

"If it's the Haqazzii terror cell, it's The Bomb Maker." A fury long buried burbled to the surface. "He's in tight with that group, but he would have had to turn someone at ALPHA in order to learn about the mission." Simone shook her head. "I'm having a hard time believing someone at ALPHA *could* be turned..."

"Come back to ALPHA," Slash said.

"What?"

"You can't help if you're a watcher," Slash insisted. "You won't get access to the case."

"I don't know..."

Slash stood, offered an encouraging smile. "Baby steps. Let's get you packed and over to our house."

"I don't—"

"Carrera knows a lot more than I do."

I won't learn anything here.

Do it. Do it for Fred.

Simone stood on wobbly knees.

"You've been working solo for a while now," Slash continued. "I remember when you were at ALPHA, I used to call you kick-ass Red."

"Feels like a lifetime ago."

"I remember how wrecked you were when you left," Slash said. "I begged you to stay, but you had to go into hiding—"

"Luther and Z were worried The Bomb Maker knew I'd survived."

"Well, if The Bomb Maker *is* back, don't you want to be the one to eliminate him?"

The hatred, revenge, and fury she'd pushed down came roaring out of her so hard, she staggered backward.

"Whoa," Slash said grabbing her arm. "Let's sit down."

"I'm okay," Simone said. "You're right, if anyone is driven to drop that son of a bitch, it's me. He stole my life."

"Ready to take it back?"

A determination she hadn't felt in years burst through her. In spite of the pain, she felt energized, she felt alive. She needed to do this... for herself. More than that, she needed to do this for the ALPHA Ops he killed and the havoc he wreaked on a country she deeply loved.

An unexpected streak of confidence raced through her. "Yes. I. Am."

"Hell, yeah!" Slash exclaimed.

Twenty-minutes later, Simone's suitcase was packed, and the women hurried out. Slash loaded the suitcase into Simone's SUV and got behind the wheel.

"Thank you," Simone said.

"I got you," Slash replied.

Five years ago, she'd been forced into hiding. She'd walked away from a career she loved in order to stay safe... and to heal. Though she'd been cleared to return to work months ago, she'd stayed in the shadows, watching others live their best lives.

Fred had died doing something she loved. Simone owed her friend—and the other victims—her absolute best. And her best was returning to a job she was good at—damn good at—and hunting down a monster who'd risen from the dead.

For you, Fred.
I'm doing this for you.

9

THE DECISION

LUCIANO

Luciano had a full day at Santini International, but his thoughts kept ping-ponging from Simone to the deadly ALPHA mission. Another bout of seething fury rumbled through him and he growled.

He'd been up most of the night searching the dark web for chatter about the explosion. There had been one comment, buried in a group of supporters and sympathizers of the Haqazzii terror cell. Written by Inferno531, it read, "The Bomb Maker is back!"

While Luciano couldn't confirm its validity or its origin, he wasn't going to dismiss it either.

"So, is that a no?" Ezra asked, plucking him from his thoughts.

Luciano slid his gaze from the small group of models to his head designer. "It's good."

"Good isn't good enough," Ezra said. "That's what you tell us. What's missing? What does it need?"

Luciano eyed the clothes.

"The pants aren't wide enough. I want *bell* bottoms, and the scarves are boring." Luciano walked over to the models, studied the garments up close. "The shirts and sweaters work."

One of the models smiled at him. He flashed her a smile before turning to Ezra. "Tweak it."

Ezra tucked his long hair behind his ears. "It needs zhuzhing, doesn't it?"

Luciano thought of Simone, their sex-crazed evening, and the lust pouring from her eyes. He smiled. "That's exactly what it needs."

"You got it," Ezra replied.

Luciano thanked his team before leaving the design center. He paused in front of the exit door to the stairs. It would be faster, but he wouldn't be visible. Whenever he could, he made his presence known. He brought his energy into every room, every conversation, and every interaction.

Instead, he strode to the elevator bank. He said hello to everyone, offering a friendly smile or handshake. Being "the boss" was a full-time job and a full-time responsibility. How he acted, how he carried himself, what he said, even the way he looked at his work family mattered. He was scrutinized, criticized, and dissected on a minute-by-minute basis. While he didn't give a damn, he didn't want the Santini brand to suffer.

Milan housed his European headquarters and, while it would have made more sense to work in New York City, his US operations were located in the fashion district of DC... and DC loved him for it. He occupied a five-story building in CityCenter, on Palmer Alley in Northwest.

"Luciano!" His Sales and Marketing VP flagged him down. "Did you get a chance to read the results from last quarter?"

"I did. Our numbers look great, but we can do better."

The Veep rolled his eyes. "Are you never satisfied?"

"I just said our numbers look great." Luciano's phone buzzed with a text. "And we can do better. We can always do better." Then, he winked. "I'll swing by and congratulate your team."

His employee smiled. "Now, that's what I'm talking about."

They rode the elevator, along with several others. Luciano said hello to all of them, asking what projects each of them were working on. One by one, the elevator thinned, leaving him to exit the top floor alone.

He read the text from Carrera.

> Four, off the grid

Meeting that afternoon, four o'clock, ALPHA's Black Site.

After slipping his phone into his pocket, Luciano took the stairs down one flight to sales and marketing. En route to his VPs office, he said hello to several managers and account reps. Without sales and marketing, he was nothing. These people got the word out, followed up with their clients, introduced his new product lines, told them about upcoming sales, and managed to increase sales in the US, year over year.

"Suzie, good to see you," Luciano said. "How's the baby?"

Suzie grinned. "He's almost nine months old."

"Where are the pics?"

Beaming with parental pride, she showed him a few adorable baby pictures. Though he smiled, the pain tore through him.

"Children are life's greatest joy," he said. "God bless him."

Her eyes grew moist. "Thank you, Mr. Santini."

Luciano continued on. Being the boss could be intimidating, so he went out of his way to let his employees know they were appreciated.

The VPs office door was open. "Henry, ciao."

Henry pushed out of his chair, shook Luciano's hand. "Thank you for coming down. Did you want to make a speech?"

Luciano did not. He wanted to find the monster who was terrorizing ALPHA, but he painted on a smile. "Of course."

"It's gonna make their day."

The men walked into the bullpen—rows of cubicles filled the large room. Luciano waited while Henry gathered the team.

"Whose desk can I stand on?" Luciano asked.

"Mine," offered up an employee.

"Grazie." Luciano removed his shoes, climbed on the desk, shot the group a friendly smile.

"Ciao," he began. "I want to congratulate you on an outstanding quarter. Your achievements are a direct result of your efforts, working smart, and fostering lasting relationships with our customers. You are the front line. Without your hard work, the beautiful clothing lines we create would gather dust. Grazie e il mio sincero apprezzamento. Thank you and my sincere appreciation."

Several employees thanked him. He acknowledged them with a nod before stepping down. He slipped into his Santini Italian leather loafers, shook a few hands, kissed a few women on their cheeks—ignored their breathy sighs—shook Henry's hand again, and headed toward the elevator.

He hadn't been back in his office two minutes when his assistant appeared in the doorway. "Mr. Santini, you have a visitor. Allaya, one of our models, wants a word."

He had no idea who Allaya was. "Stay," he told Dominic.

"Of course."

His assistant retrieved the young woman, the model who'd smiled at him in the design center.

He gestured to the guest chairs. "Please."

Over the years, his personal assistant had been through this with him dozens of times. Anytime anyone requested a one-on-one, Dominic was right there.

Power was a strong aphrodisiac. That, along with wealth, was like catnip. He wasn't interested in bedding *anyone* at his company. His only focus was on fostering a professional environment where his employees felt appreciated and respected. He wanted their best during working hours, not their bodies.

"Could I have a word alone?" Allaya asked as she flicked her long, dark hair off her shoulder.

She wore a low-cut dress, but Luciano did *not* look, he didn't sneak a peek, and he didn't glance. His attention stayed focused on her face.

"What can we assist with, Allaya?" he asked.

"I... um..." She cleared her throat. "I'm going to Milan for a show next week. I was curious if you ever go there."

"I visit my Milan headquarters several times a year, but not next week."

"Perhaps coffee when I return?" Allaya asked.

He gave her props for persistence. "We'll see if we can schedule something with the team. Are you headed there on your own or with Santini International?"

"The in-house team." Her gaze darkened. "I was interested in coffee with you, you know, outside of work."

His assistant shifted in his chair.

"Thank you, but no." Luciano stood. "Safe travels."

After walking them out, he shut his door, returned to his desk.

He wanted to find out how Simone was doing. While he didn't want to reveal his relationship with Carrera and Sin, he didn't need to disclose anything beyond his sincere condolences.

Rather than text, he started to call her, but his thoughts jumped to his own loss. A text was nothing. A phone call was better. But showing up in person to console someone was a more sincere gesture.

He left his office, pausing at Dominic's desk. "I'm leaving."

His assistant jumped on his computer. "I'm sorry, Mr. Santini, I'm not seeing an off-site meeting."

"A friend of mine had a death in the family."

"I'm sorry," Dominic said. "Do you want me to send flowers?"

"No. Let Stuart know I'm on my way down." Luciano powered down the hall toward the elevator. As it slugged its way down, it stopped on every floor. Luciano offered a smile, asked every employee how they were doing. Making them feel seen and heard was vital to his success. His leadership style demanded respect at every turn.

His sedan pulled up in front of the building. Stuart exited, opened the back door, and Luciano slipped inside. He instructed him to drive to Simone's home.

When the car pulled up, he exited, rang the doorbell. No answer. He wondered if she was too distraught to answer, so he called her.

After a few rings, she answered, "Hello, Luciano."

"Simone, I'm very sorry about your loss," he said. "I stopped by to see how you're doing."

"I appreciate that. I'm staying with Slash and Carrera for a few days."

"I'm glad you're not alone."

"Thanks for stopping by," she said. "It means a lot."

The call ended and Luciano returned to the vehicle.

Death fucked with his head... and his heart. "I want to visit my family, Stuart."

"Yes, sir," Stuart replied.

While they snaked their way through heavy traffic, Luciano made a call. He needed information, and he needed it fast. After a few rings, the familiar, scratchy voice answered.

"It's been a while, Lulu. How you doin'?"

Carlo Garibaldi was head of the Garibaldi Family. Once fierce rivals, Luciano now considered him an ally.

"How are you, Papà?"

Bene," Carlo replied. "Vecchio da morire."

Luciano chuckled. "You're not old as fuck."

"When are you comin' to see me and bring me somethin'?"

"What would you like?"

"A woman," he said. "Bring me a woman."

"How 'bout a suit? And some shoes."

"Not as good, but I'll take 'em."

"I need to talk to Franky."

"I don't talk to him no more. He can't be trusted. He takes money from those dannazione terrorists."

"Where can I find him?"

"You don't see him at Willie Boy's? He plays pool there. Lazy bum."

"Grazie, Papà. I'll send over something nice for you."

Luciano hung up, shifted his gaze out the tinted window.

I don't miss that life.

Luciano called his assistant. "Put together a gift bag for Carlo Garibaldi. Include a black suit from my Infinity collection, black loafers, and a pair of slippers."

"Two black dress shirts?"

"Yes. Have I sent him a gold chain with a crucifix?"

"I'll check. Please hold."

Luciano appreciated that Dominic kept excellent records.

"No crucifix. You sent him a gold Rolex two years ago."

"When can you send everything?"

"Tomorrow, Saturday latest."

"Take the weekend off," Luciano said. "If not tomorrow, Monday. Have it couriered to his restaurant."

"Yes, sir. Anything else?"

Stuart pulled in to the cemetery, and the noose tightened around Luciano's neck.

"No," Luciano replied. "Thank you, Dominic. Enjoy your weekend."

"Thank you, sir."

Stuart stopped the sedan at the top of the hill. Luciano

exited, walked over to the Santini family plots and stared out over the well-kept lawns. The location was perfect. His great-grandfather had seen to that. First, he paid his respects to his G-pa, Elsa's beloved husband. The name SANTINI was carved into the black granite headstone.

"G-pa, I'm looking after Elsa for you," Luciano said. "We all are. She misses you, but I entertain her with my stories... most of 'em true." He glanced out at the errant hawk flying overhead. "I met a woman." He shook his head, but the image of Simone wouldn't leave. "What should I do?"

Seconds passed. No answer came, so he moved on to the next grave, also with the name SANTINI engraved into the headstone.

Luciano dropped to one knee, brushed away a few errant leaves. "I miss you, Linda." Thoughts of his beloved wife filled him with sadness. Though the memories should have comforted him, he felt alone, the best part of his life taken from him.

"I'm so sorry, my love."

After a long moment, he moved to the next grave. "Hello, my angel. Are you playing in heaven today?" He kissed his finger, pressed it to the headstone. "Daddy loves you so much. I miss our story time. I miss our father-daughter dancing. You were the best little dancer." Tears pricked his eyes. The emotion churned in him, the loss gutting him. It never got any easier. Never. "I love you Caterina."

He shifted to the next gravesite.

"Hey, big guy." Luciano ran a hand over the headstone. "Are you taking care of your mama and your baby sister? I feel your presence, Marco. I feel you with me. Always. I love you, son."

Agonizing sorrow ripped through him.

A tear slid down his cheek as he moved back to his wife's

headstone. "Linda, I can't find him, but I'll never stop looking. Ti amo."

He bowed his head. "Heavenly Father, thank you for the blessing of my family. They were my entire world. I miss them, but I know your plan is bigger than my insignificant one. They were my greatest joy." He paused. "Please watch over my living family, especially Elsa, and even Willie Boy. Help Simone through this difficult time. Forgive me for committing the ultimate sin. In Jesus' name. Amen." He crossed himself and rose.

A gust blew the swirling leaves past him. He shoved his windblown hair into place as he made his way back to the sedan, parked on the side of the cemetery road.

It never gets any easier.

SIMONE

THE SHOCK of losing Fred and the ambush against the ALPHA team had morphed into a fury that engulfed Simone. Just one day after learning of the massacre, she was a woman with a purpose. When her own team had died, she'd been devastated and overwhelmed with grief, survivor guilt, and fear.

This time, she felt only hatred and a desire to avenge her friend. A sense of loyalty rose from the depths of her being and she had stayed up scouring the dark web until she fell asleep on Carrera and Slash's family room sofa after four in the morning.

She'd found nothing.

At six, Elsa padded into the kitchen to make coffee. When Simone pushed off the sofa, Elsa's startled scream woke Slash and Carrera. The excitement was the perfect way for Simone to jumpstart her day. No caffeine needed.

At a little past noon, she arrived at Liv Savage's beautiful

McLean estate she shared with her husband, Jericho Savage, their three children, and Jericho's grandmother.

She rang the doorbell.

"Simone, come in," Liv said through the intercom.

She entered their home, made her way through the grand foyer. Unsure where Liv was, she stopped.

Liv walked out of the kitchen, a warm smile on her pretty face. After embracing Simone in a hug that filled her with love, Liv invited her into the kitchen.

"I hope you're hungry," Liv said.

Simone eyed the take-out food from her husband's popular restaurant, Jericho Road. "That's a lot of food."

"The kids will love this when they get home from preschool," Liv explained. "Even though it's from Jericho Road, it's more of a treat then a staple."

Simone smiled. "I'm guessing you feed them vegetables."

"As many as I can sneak into their tiny tummies." Liv pulled out two sparkling waters.

In addition to racks of ribs and burgers, there were more French fries than Simone had ever seen in her life, along with coleslaw and baked beans.

After plating their food, they sat at the kitchen table.

"I'm so sorry for your loss," Liv said. "Whatever you need, I'm here."

"Thank you for seeing me on such short notice," Simone said after nibbling on a fry.

"This isn't a professional visit," Liv said. "I cleared you to return to work months ago. This is two friends having lunch."

Liv was the therapist who'd helped Simone navigate through her PTSD after The Bomb Maker had eviscerated her life.

"I know," Simone said, "but I *also* know your schedule is booked solid weeks ahead."

"I appreciate your saying that. I did juggle a few things, but it's all good. I'm working tonight and Jericho has the kids." She smiled. "Those three little ones will be completely exhausted when I get home. Jericho is such a great dad."

Seeing the love in Liv's eyes reminded her that there was good in the world.

"Are you still a watcher?" Simone asked.

"No, when Z left, I resigned. I started seeing patients again, so I'm enjoying that." Liv bit into the burger.

"So, Dr. Blackstone," Simone said, "I'm going to ask you to put on your professional hat for a minute."

Liv nodded.

"After my team and I got ambushed, I was a mess. This time, I'm filled with rage. I want revenge. I spent hours on the dark web searching for The Bomb Maker. I'm consumed with hatred."

"I'm not surprised," Liv said.

"I don't want this feeling to go away. I want to use my anger to hunt him down."

Liv's eyebrows shot up, but she stayed silent.

"You cleared me to return to ALPHA, but I didn't request an interview. I wasn't confident I could do it," Simone said. "I'm thinking your recommendation could go a long way toward reinstating me."

Liv finished chewing, put down her fork. "I uploaded my recommendation months ago. Providence, Cooper, and I talked about you returning to ALPHA."

"I never heard from them."

"Cooper wanted to reach out, but Providence didn't want to pounce."

"I wasn't ready, but I am now."

Liv smiled. "I'm glad to hear that." Then, her smile fell away. "In order to remain objective—"

"When I find that monster, I'm gonna kill him."

"You sound like Jericho," Liv murmured.

"Then you can understand how I feel."

"I understand completely, but I don't condone it."

"I'm glad we talked," Simone said. "I needed to get some insight into how you summarized my situation after you released me."

"I told them you'd know when you were ready. I'm sorry it's under these circumstances."

Simone's heart fell. "So am I. I can't even process what's happened. All I feel is rage. He got away with murdering thousands, then he kills my team and vanishes into thin air. Now, he's back with a bang, starting with ALPHA. He's got all the power. All of it."

"For now," Liv said, "but I'm confident once ALPHA puts together a plan, he won't have the power for long."

"Thank you for rearranging your schedule, and for lunch," Simone said. "I needed to talk with you because you were there for me."

"And I'm here for you now."

Simone walked over to the sideboard and admired the family photos. "Liam is getting so big. How are things going with Owen and Layla?"

Liv and Jericho had fostered, then adopted Owen and Layla after Carrera and Slash had removed them from a dangerous living situation.

Liv beamed, and love filled Simone's heart. "My babies are like a pod. They're very close. Jericho and I are talking about, maybe, having another."

"That's wonderful," Simone said.

The women finished eating. Simone helped Liv clean up, then she left. As she jumped into her SUV, she made a call.

"Providence Luck," answered the woman.

"Providence, it's Simone—Red—Redding. I know things are chaotic at work, but I'd love to swing by and talk with you and Cooper. How's tomorrow?"

"Did you get my text?" Providence asked.

Simone glanced at her phone which she'd silenced while lunching with Liv.

> We need to talk

"I was in a meeting and missed it." Simone said.

"When can you come by?"

"I can be there in twenty."

"Looking forward to it." Providence hung up.

As she drove out of Liv's driveway, determination spurred her onward. She would work the case for Fred. She'd return to ALPHA for the Ops who'd been murdered, and she'd do it for herself. A shiver skirted through her, but she wasn't backing down.

It's time... time to face the devil.

∽

LUCIANO

LUCIANO WALKED into Willie Boy's restaurant, pausing at the hostess stand. "Tara, is Willie Boy in the back?"

"Hello, Mr. Santini," Tara replied. "He's there. I can bring you—"

"I got this." He flashed her a quick smile, took off into the busy eatery.

Willie Boy didn't know how to run a business to save his ass, but he was surrounded by people who did. Seven days a week, from eleven in the morning until midnight, locals looking for authentic Italian cuisine dined there. Nothing fancy, just damn good food.

He passed the closed door to Willie Boy's private salon and

entered the billiard room. Two pool tables took up most of the dingy room, a handful of chairs lined one of the walls.

What a dump.

Two people he didn't recognize were playing a game of pool.

"I'm looking for Frankie," Luciano said. "Have you seen him?"

They both shook their heads.

Luciano retraced his steps, stopping at Willie Boy's private salon. Not bothering to knock, Luciano walked in. He swept the room in search of his target and found his cousin sitting at his regular table in the back, surrounded by his usual group of kiss-ass associates. Luciano was there for information and he was not leaving until he got it.

As he approached the table, the lowlifes scattered. Only Willie Boy and the nobody who wanted a mil in boodle stayed.

Willie Boy glanced over and grinned. "Heyo, Lulu! We was just talking 'bout cha. You remember my friend, Dante."

Luciano kept his attention glued to his cousin. "You seen Frankie?"

"Frankie hasn't been 'round," Willie Boy said. "I heard he left town."

Luciano approached the table. Willie Boy kicked out the wooden chair with his foot. "Sit, have a beer with us."

Refusing to sit, Luciano said, "I need Frankie's number."

Dante shot him a cool stare. "Mr. Santini, I was hoping you'd changed your mind. Willie Boy is convinced you can help me."

"Help you with what?" Luciano snapped.

"That mil in counterfeit," he said fiddling with his diamond pinky ring. "Like yourself, I'm not used to refusals."

Luciano didn't give a fuck about Dante. Shifting his attention back to Willie Boy, he said, "You got a number for Frankie?"

Willie Boy scrolled through his phone, rattled off the number, then dialed. The number had been disconnected. Per usual, his cousin was of no help to him. Most likely, Frankie was dead.

What a fucking waste of time.

"I'm gone," Luciano said.

Dante stood. "I'll walk you out."

"I don't need an escort." Luciano tossed a nod at Willie Boy before leaving the salon.

Outside the restaurant, Luciano slid on his sunglasses while Stuart brought the vehicle around.

Dante pulled up beside him, pointed to a Lamborghini. "See that sweet ride over there. She's mine. I have money, Mr. Santini. I'm a successful businessman, just like you."

Stuart pulled the sedan over to the curb, got out, and opened the back door. Luciano glanced in Dante's direction. "If you're so successful, why the hell are you hanging out with Willie Boy?"

Dante's mouth dropped open.

"Crawl back under whatever fucking rock you escaped from," Luciano murmured before ducking into the vehicle. Stuart shut the door, got behind the wheel.

"Where to, sir?" Stuart asked.

Knock-knock.

Dante rapped on the window with his diamond pinky ring. Luciano rolled it down.

"You're gonna regret not doing business with me."

Despite the threat, Luciano wasn't scared. While he could have had the last word, he didn't need to. In this situation, his silence held more power.

Luciano tapped the button and the window closed. "Drive."

Back at his office, he gave Stuart the rest of the day off. Rather than head inside, Luciano entered the garage beneath the building and got behind the wheel of his black SUV, parked in his spot.

As he headed out, he called his brother.

"Yo," Teddy answered.

"I need a check run on someone using an alias. I've got photos."

"Send over what you've got."

"Are you working?"

"Recon," Teddy replied. "What's his name?"

"Dante."

"What's his story?"

"He's hanging out with Willie Boy—"

"So he's a loser douche—"

Luciano chuckled. "He wants a mil in boodle. Willie Boy told him I could help."

"Willie Boy's an idiot. I could never understand how you two were friends."

"We were kids."

"Gotta bolt," Teddy said. "Here he comes." The line went dead.

After texting Teddy the photos of Dante, he continued on Route 7, then turned onto a quiet side street. A few more turns until he drove down a dirt road, then past the NO TRESPASSING sign. The woods cleared, he turned into a parking lot, continued to the back of the unmarked warehouse, and pulled up an app on his phone. He entered the passcode, the hangar door opened, and Luciano parked behind a black SUV, one of several in ALPHA's fleet.

He'd arrived at ALPHA's Black Site.

He exited the vehicle, made his way toward the door. The scanner flashed green, the door slid open, and he entered. Down the hall he strode toward the break room. The closer he got, the louder the voices.

There he found Carrera, Sin, and Sin's twin, Dakota Luck,

head of BLACK OPS. Also in the group was Cooper Grant, ALPHA co-lead, Rebel Dillinger, head of the rescue team, and Jericho Savage, ALPHA's sharpshooter.

"Looks like I found the party," Luciano said as he shook their hands.

"Good to see you, brother," Jericho said. "How you been?"

"Ruthless, power-hungry, ready to take this monster down." Then, Luciano smiled. "How 'bout you, Savage?"

"I don't have a comeback for that," Jericho replied, and the guys laughed.

"No one ever does," Sin added before shifting toward Luciano. "Why didn't you include arrogant and wealthy?"

"We're all arrogant and wealthy," Luciano replied.

Another round of laughter filled the room.

Despite the hardship they were facing, he appreciated that these men stayed true to who they were. Powerful, driven individuals who were loyal to their tight-knit group, to their families, and to their organization.

The men made their way toward the conference room.

The Black Site was ALPHA's secure location, tucked into a wooded area of Great Falls. In addition to offering conference rooms with state-of-the-art surveillance monitoring, it also offered a safe haven for up to thirty Ops and their families, something Dakota knew about firsthand.

The place was void of any warmth or personality. Should the location be breached, there could be nothing that tied the building to its occupants or the organization that owned it.

When Rebel started the rescue team, the woods provided a secluded location to train his team. Whether they were using live rounds or rappelling from a helo, it was the perfect spot to run and gun. Nothing but privacy for miles and miles.

They entered the conference room, sat around the table.

"Thanks for meeting on such short notice," Dakota began. "This is a tough day for us, for our organization, and for the families and friends of the victims. Coop, how's the team doing?"

"Not good," Cooper replied. "We told everyone not to come in, but the Ops are there en force. They've got Danielle combing the dark web for chatter, for anything—"

"I found something," Luciano said.

All eyes on him.

"It was buried in a random group for supporters and sympathizers of Haqazzii's terror cell," Luciano explained. "Inferno531 wrote, 'The Bomb Maker is back', but I couldn't confirm the validity of the comment."

"Nice work," Dakota replied.

"He had the upper hand when he left," Sin said, "and he picked right back up where he left off."

"Cooper, what about your recent hires?" Luciano asked. "Were they well vetted?"

"Yes, but we have no direct control over who they share information with," Cooper replied. "Most of them have families. A friend or family member could get access to our site."

"So... not one-hundred-percent secure?" Luciano asked.

"In theory, yes," Cooper replied. "In reality, no."

"The rescue team is ready to go," Rebel said, "but I told them to stand down."

Dakota got busy on his laptop. A blurry photo appeared on the display behind him of a white guy with shoulder-length brown hair. "This is all we have of The Bomb Maker."

"Could be anyone," Jericho said.

"ALPHA was the last group he hit before he went missing," Dakota said. "It was his 'fuck you' to law enforcement."

"Even if we had a lead, I can't assign a team," Cooper said, "It's too dangerous."

"That's gotta piss off your Operatives," Luciano said.

Cooper nodded. "They're furious with me. I wouldn't be surprised if some of them work the case anyway. We're concerned there's a mole in the group. How else would The Bomb Maker have known we were coming?"

Jericho's phone buzzed with a text. He read it, pushed out of the chair. "It's Liv. Normally, I wouldn't—"

"Family comes first," Dakota said.

Jericho strode out.

"We can't do nothing," Sin said.

"The investigation on the home explosion will close," Carrera said.

"Why is that?" Jericho asked.

"I told the press it was a gas leak that caused the explosion," Sin explained. "I also called in a favor or two. The arson detective got himself into a mess a few years ago. He owed me one."

"And we got the bodies out fast," Rebel added.

Jericho strode back in. "Liv has an idea." He sat, set his phone on the table. "Babe, you're on speaker."

"Hi guys," Liv said.

The men acknowledged her.

"I just spent some time with Simone Redding," Liv said. "She's ready to return to ALPHA and she could work the case."

Simone?

Luciano flicked his gaze to Carrera.

"Did you clear her to return?" Dakota asked.

"Months ago," Liv replied.

"PTSD?" Sin asked.

"Not anymore," Liv replied. "I thought she'd be a mess, you know, because she and Frederica were such good friends."

"Since Quantico," Dakota added.

"Don't get me wrong," Liv said. "She's grieving, but she's definitely angry. It's a controlled rage. In the right environment, with the right people, that fury could be channeled into finding the suspect."

"Thanks, Liv," Sin said. "Very helpful."

"Jericho—" Liv said.

"Yeah, babe," Jericho replied.

"I had Jericho Road delivered for Simone and me, and there's a ton left. Will you be home for dinner?"

"Absolutely. I'll pick up the kids on my way. Love you."

"Love you, babe." The line went dead.

Without question, Luciano knew what he had to do. "I'll go after The Bomb Maker."

All eyes on him.

"I'm not law enforcement," Luciano continued. "I'm not ALPHA. I'm an assassin who plays by my own set of rules."

"And those are?" Cooper asked.

"Kill or be killed." A smile tugged at the corners of his mouth. "As you can see, I'm good at what I do."

"You can't work alone," Cooper said

"I have a crew," Luciano said.

"You need someone on the inside," Dakota said. "Someone with access to ALPHA and other law enforcement sites."

He *did* have access to ALPHA, but he wasn't divulging that. He slid his gaze to Carrera and a knowing look passed between them.

"Reinstate Simone," Carrera said.

"She's hasn't worked a case in a while," Dakota said.

"For the past two years, she's been a watcher," Carrera said. "Her caseload is twice everyone else's. She's smart, she's a hard worker, and she's thorough."

"She just lost her best friend," Sin added. "Is she in the right headspace?"

"You heard Liv," Jericho said. "She's ready and she wants the case."

Silence.

"I'm not sure," Dakota said.

"I am," Luciano said. "I'm one-hundred-percent confident she'll get the job done and I'll finish him off. And just to cover our asses, we'll use Jericho's sniper skills if we need him."

"I'm in," Jericho said.

"If we want it done right, we do it ourselves," Cooper said. "This job needs to stay tight. Nothing outside our circle."

The men agreed.

"We vote," Dakota said.

"No," Luciano pushed back. "I don't want to know if any of you *don't* think she can do it. I know she can. Schedule a meeting here. Let me talk to her."

"You?" Sin asked. "She can't know you're gonna take The Bomb Maker out."

"She can't work this alone," Cooper said. "That's unreasonable and unfair."

"One meeting," Luciano asked. "She'll either agree to work with me or she won't."

"I'm in," Sin said.

"I've been in," Jericho said, and the guys laughed.

"Same," Cooper echoed.

"Simone will get it done," Carrera said.

"What about me?" Luciano asked his cousin.

"You? As far as you're concerned, The Bomb Maker is already dead."

"It's a go," Dakota said. "This meeting never happened."

"And nothing we said gets repeated," Sin said.

"There isn't a single one of you who won't tell your wives," Luciano said.

Silence, then laughter.

"He knows us better than I thought," Dakota said.

"I know everything I need to know—" Luciano said.

"And a hell of a lot more," Carrera muttered.

Luciano winked at Carrera. "Grazie, cugino."

"Providence and I will talk to Simone," Cooper said. "We'll keep everyone posted."

Luciano wanted to speak with Simone directly. He didn't need these middlemen when it came to teaming. He would go to the source, present his offer. She was either all-in or she wasn't.

When it came to a job like this, there was no in-between. People were going to die. There could even be collateral damage. This hunt wasn't going to be easy, but it was absolutely necessary. If they didn't take out The Bomb Maker, he would eliminate ALPHA, then unleash a maelstrom of terror on the nation.

Luciano would *not* let that happen.

I'm coming for you, you son of a bitch... with everything I've got.

10

THE PARTNERSHIP

SIMONE

Simone drove down Route 7 in Tysons with a mix of emotions. Her heart had been shredded, the grief gaining momentum like a locomotive roaring down the tracks. Yet, the anger could not be stopped, the hatred turning her heart to stone.

After heading down the familiar road, she pulled over, her gaze trained on the rearview mirror. Though she hadn't seen anyone tailing her, she had to be sure. Five minutes later, when she felt certain she was alone, she drove down the street. The last time she'd been at ALPHA HQ, the facility was located in Middletown, Maryland, near Camp David.

When Luther retired, and Providence and Dakota took over, they relocated to a nondescript building in Tysons. She drove to the end of the street. There stood a lone, warehouse-like structure with bars over the reflective-glass windows and a sign over the front door.

ALPHA MEAT PACKING

There it is.

Her heart took off in her chest, the excitement coursing through her veins. Her entire body tingling with anticipation. Her pain and her anger would fuel her. Yes, she was scared, but a *healthy* dose of fear would keep her on high alert. And she would need every ounce of it if she was going after The Bomb Maker.

But who's gonna take him out?

Simone was the first to admit she was rusty at firing a gun. Once a strong markswoman, she hadn't been to target practice in a while.

She killed the engine, walked to the front door, and pressed the buzzer. A voice through the intercom instructed her to drive around back. Seconds later, as she exited her vehicle, Providence opened the back door and welcomed her inside.

She crossed the threshold and an unexpected calmness settled into her soul.

I'm home.

"Red, it's good to finally meet you." Providence shook her hand.

"You too," Simone replied.

Also tall, Providence kept her hair short and her makeup light. She exuded warmth, yet had an air of professionalism about her that reminded Simone she was working at the pinnacle of law enforcement.

She was led into a break room where Providence topped off her water bottle, pulled a bottle from the fridge, and offered it to Simone. With waters in hand, they walked down the hallway, voices bursting from every office.

"Everyone was told to stand down," Providence said as she entered her office and closed her door. "Everyone on the research team is working from home. But our problem children —" Her warm smile touched her eyes— "our Operatives, they all came in. Every last one of them. I've been a wreck all day, checking the surveillance cameras for anyone driving into the parking lot."

"Has anyone?"

"No." Providence paused to drink. "It's been quiet, but I'm wondering if we've got a mole on the inside."

"I hope not," Simone said.

"I'm very sorry for your loss. For all our losses."

"Thank you." Simone sipped the cold water. "I'm sorry for you as well. You lost an entire team."

Providence nodded. "I've been on the phone with the families. It's been a rough day. Frederica's mom and dad requested her remains be returned home to Wisconsin." She cleared her throat. "Tell me what's been going on with you."

Simone's heart ached, but she pushed on.

"After I left ALPHA, I worked for Mitus Conglomerate for three years, and I've been a watcher for the past two. It's been a great experience."

"I read Z's notes on you," Providence said. "He was very impressed with your work ethic, and he trusted you, which is very unusual for him."

Simone smiled. "I liked working for Z."

"I also re-read Liv Savage's clinical analysis," Providence continued. "You've been cleared to return for several months. How do you feel about returning now?"

"I'm very interested."

"In what capacity?"

"As an Operative. Fred—Frederica—told me that there's a ninety-day trial. That's perfect. Slash offered to take me to Henninger's for target practice. I'd make that a priority, going a few times a week on my own."

"You're saying all the right things."

"I'm not sure I'd be here if Frederica wasn't killed," Simone confessed. "That affected me to my core. It brought back what happened to me—to my team. The first time, I was afraid he'd come after me because I was the lone survivor." She steeled her spine. "I'm not afraid anymore."

"I appreciate your honesty," Providence said as her phone rang again. "I'm sorry." She glanced at it. "It's my husband." She answered. "Hey, honey. I'm meeting with Red." Silence. "Understood. Okay, thanks for the call." She smiled. "I love you too."

Providence hung up, shifted her attention back to Simone.

"I'd like to work The Bomb Maker case," Simone said.

She wasn't sure she was the most qualified to take the case, but she was, without question, the most motivated.

"You can't work it alone," Providence said.

"What about working with an experienced Op?"

Tap-tap-tap.

"Come in," Providence said.

A man walked in, his gaze jumping from Providence to Simone. Providence made the introduction. Simone stood, shook Cooper Grant's hand, then Providence suggested they all sit at her table.

"You've got this," Cooper said. "We'll talk offline." He addressed Simone. "Good meeting you, Red."

"Same," Simone replied.

"Let me know when you're finished," Cooper said.

After Providence acknowledged him with a nod, he left, closing the door behind him.

Providence leaned back in her chair. "Like I mentioned, you can't work the case alone. It's too dangerous. We'd pair you with a seasoned vet, certainly a good marksman."

"Understood. Whatever you need."

"Should we decide to bring you back, when can you start?"

Excitement and determination powered through her. "As soon as Carrera accepts my resignation."

"What questions do you have of me?" Providence asked.

"No questions, just one comment. I will do whatever it takes to find the person or persons responsible for these explosions and I will remove the threat in whatever fashion ALPHA deems best."

If that didn't put a button on their meeting, she had no idea what would.

Feeling empowered, she thanked Providence and left the building. As she drove onto the main road, she called Frederica to let her know the good news. She dialed, the phone rang, then reality crashed into her moment of bliss.

Ohgod, she's gone. She's never gonna answer her phone.

A wail shot out of her, tears welled, and her throat tightened with emotion.

Shuddering in a breath, she forced herself to stay composed. Rather than head back to Slash and Carrera's, she drove toward home. She needed time, alone, to grieve.

Once inside, she walked into the kitchen, saw the box of mini cakes waiting on the counter.

And she lost it.

LUCIANO

Luciano needed to see Simone. She was hurting, he could offer his support and encouragement. Though he expected she'd be at Carrera's, he tapped the app tracker, selected her, and zoomed in. To his surprise, she was at home.

Being alone in grief was the worst, yet he'd pushed everyone away too. Maybe he wouldn't have turned into a cold-blooded killer if he'd allowed his family and friends to help him heal.

He rerouted his course, hit the gas.

Not long after, he pulled up to her Alexandria home. Her car was in the driveway. He cut the engine, hastened up the walkway to her front door.

He rang the doorbell. A couple of minutes passed.

Nothing.

He was about to call her when she cracked open the door.

"Now's not a good time, Luciano."

"Let me in."

She opened the door a little wider. Her eyes were bloodshot, her nose red, her cheeks wet with tears. He nudged it open, pulled her into his arms.

"I got you."

She started sobbing. He moved her into the foyer, shut the door behind them, then he held her.

No words, just support.

Her sobs turned to wails, then she quieted. He didn't feel the need to move her. He didn't need to say anything. He was there for her and that was it. When her sobbing subsided, she pulled away.

"I ruined your suit."

He offered an encouraging smile. "I've got more."

The knot between her brows relaxed. She retreated into the bathroom, blew her nose. Rather than wait in the foyer, he stood in the bathroom doorway, caressed her back.

"I must look terrible," she murmured.

"You look beautiful," he replied.

He could never understand why women were so obsessed with their looks. Yes, his wife had been pretty, but it was her warmth, her personality that had first attracted him to her.

Beauty was eye-catching, but substance mattered more. He'd wanted the whole package, beauty, brains, and backbone. Something strong enough to last a lifetime.

Nothing lasts forever.

She was studying him so hard, he wondered if he'd said something out loud. "Why are you here?"

"To offer my condolences."

"How'd you know I was here?"

He could lie or he could come clean and tell her Teddy had put a tracker on her vehicle when she'd been stalking him. If they were going to work together, he had to fess up... but was now the right time?

Wait.

"I didn't think you should be alone," he said. "Your grief is so raw."

"Can I get you something to drink?" She went to squeeze past him, but he was blocking her way.

He ran the back of his fingers down her cheek, replacing his hand with his lips. Then, another light kiss on her other cheek. Her musky smell drew him in. "Let's sit."

He stepped out of the doorway and waited for her to lead the way. To his surprise, she curled her fingers around his bicep, walked into her kitchen. There, she opened a pastry box and stared at the contents.

Inside were four pieces of cake, all different.

"Frederica brought these over." Sad eyes peered up at him. "We shared two. She was coming back tonight and we were going to eat two more. That was the plan." More tears welled up in her eyes, spilling down her cheeks.

With a light touch, he brushed away the streaks with his thumb. "Tell me about your friend."

"Do you want coffee?"

He clasped her hands in his. "Simone, I'm here for you. Just you."

A little smile tipped one side of her mouth. "But I came here to be alone."

"I'll go, if you want."

His comment was met with silence.

Don't send me away.

"You can stay," she whispered.

"How 'bout I make us coffee?"

"You know how?"

Appreciating her sense of humor, he smiled. "You can walk me through it."

While he made coffee—without instruction—she eased onto a counter chair, rested her head on her arms. Her hair flowed over the Quartz and he paused to appreciate her. But his heart broke for her loss. Turning away, he pulled two mugs, a plain white one and one with the words, BADASS BABE.

When the coffee finished brewing, he filled the mugs, sat beside her. She lifted her head. Grief-stricken eyes met his. Then, she spied the mug and choked back a sob.

"That was a gift from Frederica."

Feeling compelled to comfort her, he caressed her back. "How did you meet?"

"We used to work together."

"Where?"

She regarded him for several seconds. Though her beauty held his attention, he was more fascinated with what she'd say. Would she come clean about her *real* career or continue the personal shopper charade?

"We were both junior buyers at a major department store," she said.

He bit back a smile. "Right, personal shoppers."

So, we're back to make believe.

He pulled the cake box over. "Which cake would you choose? What about Frederica?"

"The tiramisu was her favorite." A rueful smile touched her eyes.

"She has excellent taste."

"Had. She *had* excellent taste." A shadow fell over her eyes. "She's not here."

"She's not here physically, but her spirit is with you."

"I'm not sure I believe that."

"Frederica will always have excellent taste." After a beat, he asked her which cake she'd pick.

"Cheesecake. So, on the third night, we'd share the chocolate and pistachio swirl."

"Would you feel better eating this now or should we freeze them?"

Her phone rang. She glanced over, perked up. "Excuse me." She answered. "Simone Redding."

"Red, it's Providence Luck."

"Let me take you off speaker." She tapped the button, pressed the phone to her ear. "I'm here."

He knew Providence was offering her the job. He sipped the hot drink, took another mouthful, and set down the mug.

After listening for a moment, Simone said, "A partner? That makes sense." More listening. "Outside the organization? You mean, like, at the Bureau?" She furrowed her brow. "Monday? Absolutely." She grew silent. "I'll ride in with Slash. Thank you for this opportunity." She hung up, heaved in a deep breath.

This was Luciano's moment.

Tell her.

"Congratulations on your new job," he said.

"How did you... I mean... that wasn't—"

"I'm your new partner, Simone. Welcome to the dark side."

SIMONE

SIMONE WASN'T OKAY. That much she knew on her own, but she was hearing things. Strange words were coming out of his mouth.

Is he trying to mess with me? Is this a joke?

Luciano collected her hands in his, caressed her soft skin.

"I know the explosion wasn't from a gas leak," he began. "I know Frederica was on a mission to arrest someone making bombs. Maybe The Bomb Maker."

"How do you know this? Is my phone tapped?"

"I know this because I have access to powerful people in high places. I've been able to take care of business for them, when they can't do it."

She tugged her hands away, steeled her spine. "This has been a really tough day. You walked in on a moment when I needed to be alone. I appreciate that you're here, but you're not making any sense. Is it me? Is it you?" She moved off the counter stool, stood on the other side of the island. There, she folded her arms and glared at him.

"I thought you ran Santini International," she continued. "Clearly, Z was on to something. Did you just tell me you're my partner? How is that even possible, and why didn't Providence say anything?"

"She's going to, on Monday. Where's your meeting?"

"No idea. She said Slash would drive me."

"To the Black Site, where Rebel trains his rescue team."

"Ohmygod, you're with ALPHA." Pausing, she furrowed her brow. "Why would Z—"

"Not ALPHA—"

"I shouldn't have said that."

"Relax. Everything stays between us."

She inhaled a deep breath. It marginally helped.

"First, I hate law enforcement, but there are people who straddle the line of good and evil that I'm tight with," Luciano continued. "ALPHA goes after the worst of the worst, yes?"

"Right." Now, he was starting to make sense.

"When criminals get off on a technicality or escape prison, ALPHA might be tasked with re-arresting them... or taking them out."

She nodded.

He knows as much as I do... maybe more.

"Sometimes they can't take someone out, despite the evidence. They have to arrest them. And that person might not get charged." A devilish smiled brightened his handsome face. "That's where my team and I come in—"

"You don't work alone?"

He shook his head. "We take out the monsters ALPHA can't."

"You're a contract killer?"

"It's my volunteer job."

Strangely, that made her laugh. "You're a sick fuck."

"I run Santini International and take out thugs on the side."

"This has gotta be a nightmare," she murmured. "Are you for real?"

"ALPHA doesn't know if there's a mole on the team—"

"Providence mentioned that."

"The first time The Bomb Maker struck—"

"Five years ago," she said.

"Right. He took out his own men along with ALPHA."

Muscles running the length of her back turned to steel. *That* she knew, all too well. He paused to study her for a long moment before continuing. Though she could have told him— *more like bare my soul*—she stayed silent.

"Frederica's mission was also an ambush," he said. "He was expecting them."

"How do you know?" she asked.

"I was watching the live feed with Carrera and Sin."

Her heart plummeted, her guts twisted. "You saw?"

"I did."

She shook her head. "I'm not ready to hear about it."

"Not up for discussion," he replied. "ALPHA Ops have to stand down. The entire organization is at risk, but no one needs to know you're a part of the group, especially since you won't be going there."

"I was there today."

"We'll work at the Black Site or at my home. Both are secure."

Though elated she'd been brought back into ALPHA, she wasn't sure how she felt about working with Luciano. As it turned out, Z had been right about him. He *was* up to no good.

"Now I understand why Z had me watching you."

He smiled. "Not a personal shopper?"

Despite her grief, she couldn't help but appreciate his handsome face, the way his eyes gleamed with mischief.

He lives for danger.

She gestured to her home. "I have no real fashion sense and I've never taken much interest in home furnishings either. I can appreciate beautiful décor or a stunning couture gown, but I don't seek them out."

"You could wear a burlap bag and look phenomenal." After a breath, he said, "Z thought I was still involved in organized crime, specifically counterfeit money."

She wanted to ask him if he was, but opted not to. At this moment, not knowing seemed like a better way to start their professional relationship.

Less is more.

She extended her hand. "I look forward to partnering with you, Luciano. It's a relief not to pretend to be in the home furnishings and apparel industries any longer."

He lifted her hand, pressed her skin to his lips, and kissed it. "We're gonna have a lot of fun catching The Bomb Maker." Another sly smile blanketed his handsome face. "When we're finished with him, he's going to regret his actions."

"Which ones? He's been killing people for years."

"Every single one of them," Luciano replied. "And he'll regret them for all eternity."

Feeling like she wanted to do something to solidify their newly formed partnership, she slid over the piece of tiramisu. "Let's share this."

He forked off a small piece, held it out to her. She opened

her mouth and accepted it. Sweetened cream, espresso, and savory chocolate filled her with everything good.

Though her life without Fred would never be the same, staying focused on Luciano helped. His presence soothed her in ways she couldn't begin to understand.

"In honor of Frederica." Luciano paused to take a small bite of the decadent dessert. "If you're having a bad day or if you're overwhelmed with grief, tell me."

"Thank you," she said. "What about you? Will you tell me if you're having a bad day?"

His gaze hovered on hers for longer than she expected, then he set down the fork and leaned back in the chair. "All my days are the same."

"Seriously?" She sipped the coffee.

"They're filled with anger and a need for revenge. My world is dark and ugly."

"You love Elsa. You run a successful business." Then, she grew quiet for a few beats before she forked off a piece and offered it to him.

When he opened his mouth, she slid the treat inside and slowly extracted the utensil, her gaze locked on his luscious mouth. Mesmerized by him, she stilled.

He lifted the mug, sipped. "What do you know about me?"

He murmured the words, a secret only meant for her to hear.

"Nothing from watching you," she replied. "I couldn't find anything about you beyond the basic information online. You're the founder and CEO of Santini International. Your European headquarters is in Milan. Your US HQ is in the fashion district of DC. Beyond a few articles I read online, there's nothing. Why is that?"

"Nothing to know."

"What are your demons, Luciano?"

Pain flashed in his eyes before a shadow darkened them. The anger masking his true feelings. Sadness.

"Life is full of surprises," he murmured. "Not all of them are good."

She took no issue with his need for privacy, so rather than press him, she said, "I'm a good listener, if you ever feel like talking."

"Grazie, Simone."

Her heart fluttered at the sexy way he pronounced her name. Seemone.

Just because they were going to be working together—if indeed that was true—didn't mean they had to spill every little thing about themselves. He had stopped by to comfort her. Mission accomplished. That was enough for one day.

They finished the tiramisu in silence, their gazes locked on each other. She could have looked away, but his beauty, his power, and his intensity kept her riveted on his every move. And for reasons she couldn't begin to fathom, he stayed anchored on her as well.

When they finished, she stood. "Let me walk you out."

"I'm not leaving you alone. Not today. I can wait outside or I can follow you to Carrera's."

"I'm okay, really," she insisted. "I mean, I'm not okay, but I feel better."

"Grief comes in waves," he said with conviction. "Now, it's like a tsunami, engulfing you in water. You feel like you're drowning in pain."

The need to touch him had her slipping her hand around his bicep and guiding him toward the front door. "Who have you lost?"

"My entire life," he replied.

Before she could question him further, he opened the front door. "Are you ready to head back to my cousin's or do you need me to wait for you?"

"You're right. I shouldn't be here alone." She hugged him, relishing his hard body, the delicious scent of his skin, and the perfect way their bodies fit together. One light kiss on his cheek. "Thank you for being here for me." She broke away, offered a little smile. "I owe you one, partner."

"Anytime."

After she locked her front door behind them, he walked her to her car, waited while she got in. She watched him walk to his SUV. Beyond his obvious good looks and the swagger in his step, there was an energy that surrounded him. If she stared hard enough, she could almost see it.

Is that what pure power looks like?

She started her vehicle, backed out of the driveway. As she made her way toward Slash and Carrera's, he stayed behind her, like a guard. For the first time in a long time, she felt protected. Like someone had her back in every way that mattered.

11

THE DINNER PARTY

LUCIANO

The following afternoon at four-thirty, Luciano opened his front door. Teddy walked in dressed in a tattered shirt, torn jeans, and his leather jacket. His worn satchel hung over his shoulder, his motorcycle helmet clutched in his gloved hand.

He shot his brother a smile. "I'm starving. I hope Chef has made a lot of food."

"Appetizers now. We'll work before dinner."

The brothers entered the kitchen. "Yo, Chef, how's it hangin', baby?"

Chef Louis laughed. "I'm good, Teddy. How's by you?"

"Can't complain." Teddy set the computer bag on the kitchen island, paused to check out the array of small plates Louis was prepping.

"I love you, Chef," Teddy said. "I gotta get me a chef, like, for real."

"I have several friends I can recommend," Louis replied.

Luciano poured them each a glass of sparkling water.

Teddy guzzled his, refilled the glass.

Louis set a large plate in front of Teddy and an appetizer-sized plate in front of Luciano. Teddy set four sliders on his, along with a large portion of shoestring fries, two mozzarella sticks, and a handful of fried pickles. Silence while Teddy inhaled the food.

Luciano had eaten a late lunch, so he chose a slider, a Caprese skewer, and a sampling of the vegetable crudités with onion dip.

After Teddy had wolfed down half the plate, he leaned back and smiled. "I didn't eat all day."

"What time would you like dinner, sir?" Louis asked.

"Teddy, seven?" Luciano asked.

"That'll work."

When they finished eating, Luciano topped their glasses, and the brothers took off toward his home office. When Luciano moved in, he had the dark paneled walls replaced with white paint. A large piece of abstract art occupied most of one wall, several small prints hung behind his desk. The French doors faced the back of the property. Those were open. He'd screened in the patio, allowing the afternoon breeze to flow through.

At the conference table, Teddy pulled out his laptop, logged in while Luciano stared outside at the spacious backyard and the Olympic-sized swimming pool. The home had been his sanctuary, but lately, it felt more like a prison.

"Good news or bad news first?" Teddy asked.

Luciano smiled. Teddy always started his debriefings the same, and Luciano always responded in kind.

Luciano joined him at the table. "You decide."

"I'll start with the bad," Teddy began. "I reached out to everyone I know. There's chatter in the Haqazzii cell that The Bomb Maker's back, but when I talked to a reliable source, he said he hadn't heard anything."

Luciano knew his way around the dark web, but Teddy was a master at knowing which chat groups were in-the-know, how to hunt for coded messages. He was an asset to Luciano and to his clandestine—and very illegal—organization.

Most of their hits were because Teddy had gotten the intel he needed and tracked the thug down.

"The good news—although it's not good, but more like informative—" Teddy continued.

"Theodore," Luciano said.

"What? I'm telling you what I found out."

Teddy had a long-winded way of providing data.

"The ALPHA hit was definitely him, so as I see it, he either had surveillance on the house, and he got out in time—"

"It was an ambush," Luciano interrupted. "He staged blowup dolls in the basement and in the beds."

"Gotcha." Teddy started typing, then got busy reading, his eyes sliding back and forth at a rapid rate.

When Teddy was young, his teacher said he wasn't smart enough to learn how to read. Between Luciano and Elsa, they spent a lot of time teaching him. And when he finally got it, he never stopped. Nowadays, Teddy read everything he could get his hands on.

"I'm watching the explosion," Teddy said.

Teddy shouldn't have access to ALPHA, but he did... and not because Luciano had given it to him.

When finished, Teddy growled. "That was brutal. What does he have against ALPHA?"

"No one knows," Luciano explained. "They think he found out the organization existed and he wants to make a stand. Show them who's boss."

"Alpha the ALPHAs," Teddy said.

"They think he might be an Op."

Teddy got busy on his computer. "Yeah, so that doesn't

make sense. Why strike years ago, do nothing, then hit them again now?"

"They don't know." Luciano took a few swigs of the sparkling water. "If you have access, maybe he does too."

"As far as I can see, I'm the only one outside the organization who's in." He spun the laptop around. "Check it out."

Luciano skimmed the page. Most everyone who worked for ALPHA was logged into the system.

"They're all working remote, which could make it easier for him to access the site. He logs in as an employee, cloaking his real IP address."

Luciano pulled the map he'd taken from the terrorist in London, opened it, and set it on the table. "This is what I took from the Haqazzii terrorist."

Teddy tapped each of the circled targets. "This is good. I can target my search better. Does the FBI know?"

"Only ALPHA."

"I'll ask around. Did the terrorists give you a time frame?"

Luciano smiled. "No, they weren't very cooperative."

"You didn't beat it out of them?"

"That's your specialty, not mine."

"I'm meeting a contact in Turkey." Teddy raked his hands through his long hair. "I'll be going dark for a few days."

"Is Gabriel going?"

"That's the plan."

Luciano shifted toward his brother. "What does your gut say, Teddy?"

Teddy slid his gaze to the laptop for a long moment. "I'd be surprised if The BM is in ALPHA." He waggled his eyebrows. "It's fitting, don'tcha think?

Luciano smiled. Leave it to Teddy to give The Bomb Maker that nickname. "It's a good pun."

"I'll keep digging," Teddy said. "I'm surprised no one's bragging over this. It was a targeted hit, especially since the team was going to arrest him."

"I'm working the case with someone," Luciano explained. "Well, she's working the case and I'm going to take him out."

Teddy furrowed his brow. "Who?"

"Simone Redding."

Teddy chuffed out a laugh. "The one who was watching you? Talk about irony."

The conversation moved to other topics, but Luciano's thoughts kept jumping back to Simone. He knew the power of anger and loss. It had driven him to become a killing machine. He would hate for that to happen to her.

∽

SIMONE

FRIDAY AFTERNOON, Simone was in *no* condition to attend Peter Hirzog's dinner party. Being festive and making conversation was the last thing she wanted to do.

She and Slash were stretching in the lower level of Slash's home after going for a hard run. Training wasn't just limited to target practice. If she was going after The Bomb Maker, she needed to be at the top of her game.

Carrera walked around the corner dressed in a T-shirt and shorts.

"You're coming with me to one of Rebel's trainings," Slash said. "They're fun."

"My wife's a beast," Carrera said as he walked over to the weights.

"Can I get both your thoughts on something?" Simone asked.

"Go for it," Carrera said.

"My old boss, Peter Hirzog, invited me to his house for a dinner party tonight," Simone said. "I can't go."

"I wouldn't cancel," Carrera said.

"I want to curl up in a ball, not go to a dinner party," Simone pushed back.

"Hirzog has the ear of the Director," Carrera explained. "Might be good to find out what he knows."

"But I'm in mourning."

"Exactly," Slash said. "He could be the perfect person to talk to. Did he know Frederica?"

"Yeah, we both worked for him."

"We're flying blind here," Carrera said. "I'm in a position of power at the Bureau, but I don't have the Director's ear. Does Hirzog know you and Frederica stayed close friends?"

"No. I lost touch with him after I left."

"Does he know you moved to ALPHA?" Slash asked.

"He thought I went undercover." Simone started stretching her calf muscle. "And he asked me if I jumped to ALPHA."

"If you can do it, go," Slash said. "The more you know—"

"The more you know," Carrera said finishing her sentence. They laughed.

An inside joke or couple speak.

Despite her sorrow, watching them interact brought her joy.

"Seriously," Slash said. "If he asked you about ALPHA, maybe he's willing to share things with you."

"Can't argue with that," Simone said.

As she stretched, she thought about how she'd play things if she went. "I'll have to ask him if he knew Frederica died in a gas explosion?"

"Exactly," Carrera replied. "Bait him. See if he tells you anything."

"How would he know something that ALPHA doesn't?" Simone asked.

"Good question," Carrera replied.

"How does he even know about ALPHA?" Slash asked.

"Another good question," Carrera replied. "Maybe he'll confide in you since you two were close."

Elsa came downstairs. "I made a big pot of my homemade chicken soup." Her smile crinkled her eyes. "For Simone."

"Thank you, Elsa," Simone replied, before eyeing Slash.

"Elsa, Simone has to go out—" Slash said.

"I'll have a big bowl when I return," Simone added. "I'm going to get ready. I don't want to go, but I'll see what I can find out."

Whatever it takes, Fred. I will get to the truth.

AT SEVEN-FIFTEEN THAT EVENING, Simone street parked at Peter Hirzog's upscale estate in Chevy Chase. She collected the bottle of wine in a gift bag that Slash had given her and made her way toward the front door.

The crispness in the air reminded her that autumn had replaced the warm days of summer. She pulled her long, cable sweater close, climbed the front stairs, and rang the doorbell. She didn't want to be there, so she'd see what she could learn, then bolt.

Peter answered the door. "You made it," he said with a warm smile. "Come on in."

"I almost canceled. It's been a rough couple of days. I'm not sure if you heard—"

He raised his eyebrows. "Heard?"

"Frederica Salgado died in a home gas explosion." Her heart broke.

"Oh, no. I'm so sorry." He enveloped her in a warm hug.

When she broke away, he asked if they'd stayed friends.

"We had."

"I'm sorry for your loss," he said. "I lost touch with her when I left town. Is she still with the Bureau?"

"No."

A middle-aged woman with shoulder-length hair and a friendly smile walked toward them. "You must be Simone. I'm Lucy, Peter's wife."

Simone offered her the gift bag. "Happy anniversary."

"How thoughtful." Lucy pulled out the bottle. "Oh, it's a Santini Chianti. I'll serve it with dinner."

She glanced at Peter, but he didn't seem fazed. Simone hadn't checked the bottle Slash had given her. The last thing she wanted to do was tick him off.

"Come in and meet our guests," Lucy said.

They made their way through the two-story foyer and into the spacious kitchen with dark cabinets and soft pendant lighting. The delightful aroma of spices filled the air. There were several people chatting in the kitchen, and Peter made introductions. Two from the Bureau whom Simone didn't know, three neighbors, and two longtime friends of Lucy.

Jerod sauntered in, spotted her, and broke into a smile. "Hey, Red. It's good to see you again."

She forced a smile. "Hi, Jerod."

I shouldn't have come.

Being there made her head hurt. She wanted to feel the pain, the loss, the emptiness in her soul, not make small talk at some dinner party.

As if sensing her pain, Peter said, "Let's move into the family room."

Once there, Jerod said, "Being around you two feels like old times."

Only it didn't. Fred was dead, Simone was paired with an assassin to work the case, and The Bomb Maker was back.

"Jerod, do you remember Frederica Salgado?" Peter asked.

Pain sliced through her.

Jerod shook his head. "Name doesn't sound familiar."

"Years back, she was a Special Agent on my team," Peter

said. "And Simone's close friend. Unfortunately, she passed away in a home gas explosion."

"Ohgod, that's tragic," Jerod said. "I'm sorry."

"Thank you." Simone forced down the lump in her throat. She couldn't talk about Fred. If she did, she'd lose it. Glancing around, she saw Lucy alone in the kitchen.

"I'm going to see if Lucy needs some help," she said.

"I should go," Peter said.

"I got this." Simone returned to the kitchen. "Lucy, can I help you?"

Lucy had just pulled a skillet of sautéed chicken breasts from the oven, her cheeks red from the blast of heat. "I would love some."

"What can I do?"

Lucy handed her a water pitcher from the refrigerator. "The dining room table's already set. The goblets are in there."

Grateful to be of use, Simone filled the glasses.

When she returned to the kitchen, Lucy handed her a serving spoon. "Help me get the chicken onto the platter."

As the women worked, Lucy said, "I don't think Peter's mentioned you, but he doesn't bring his work home with him." She smiled. "Correction. He *does* bring his work home with him. He's a workaholic. But he doesn't talk about his job."

"I worked for him several years ago when I was a Special Agent. He was a great mentor."

"I hear that a lot," Lucy said. "His career means everything to him."

Lucy called the guests in, they served themselves, then sat around the large oak table in the dining room. Before joining them, Lucy dimmed the chandelier.

Peter raised his wine glass. "Happy anniversary to my Lucy. It's been a busy, crazy, fun first year." He glanced over at Jerod then back at his wife. "Love you."

"I love you, Peter." Lucy raised her glass to him across the table. Everyone toasted them, then sipped the wine.

"Delicious," commented one of the guests. "What is this, Lucy?"

"Simone brought it," Lucy replied. "I thought it would be fun for everyone to sample. It's a Santini Chianti."

"Out of my price range," one of the guests said. "I like to keep my wine purchases under twenty."

Simone was sitting to the right of Peter, who was positioned at the head of the table. She slid her gaze to him. If he was angry she'd brought a Santini wine, he didn't show it. In fact, he was having a side conversation with Jerod, and wasn't paying them any attention.

The meal was delicious, but Simone's guts were in knots. She managed to eat enough that it didn't draw attention. After dinner, while Peter was making coffee, she decided to call it. It wasn't the right environment to talk to him in private, plus, she wasn't about to pummel him with questions.

She wandered in to find him placing coffee mugs on the counter while Jerod relaxed on a counter stool at the island, his attention glued to his phone.

"Peter, thank you for inviting me," Simone said.

"You're not leaving, are you?" Peter asked.

"I am," she replied.

"Let's chat on the porch," he said. "Let me tell the guests the coffee is ready."

Jerod put his arm around Simone. "You look so sad. It breaks my heart. What can I do to help?"

"That's sweet, but I'm okay," she said. "It's not the right time to be social."

"I understand." He gave her shoulder a little squeeze before removing his hand. "The power of death is life-changing."

Peter returned, poured a cup of coffee, offered it to Simone. She declined.

He set it on the counter, slid it over to Jerod, then poured one for himself. Then, he held up a bottle of amaretto and a bottle of Grand Marnier.

Jerod took the cognac, poured in a healthy amount while Peter added amaretto to his.

Onto the porch they went. Surrounded by darkness, Peter turned on the light hanging over the sofa.

"I appreciate your being here, Simone," Peter said, after they got comfortable.

She glanced at Jerod, then back to Peter. "It's good being around you guys. Reminds me of when we used to work together."

"If you want to return to Justice, I would hire you in a heartbeat," Jerod said.

"Same," Peter added. "You were an outstanding agent." He sipped the drink. "I could use your help with something... something personal."

"I'm not taking on any new clients right now," Simone said.

"Are you talking about being a personal shopper?" Peter chuckled. "I'm not buying that. Did you move over to the Agency?"

"No, Peter," she replied, her patience worn thin. "I'm not with the CIA."

"My money's on you going undercover, but I can't get confirmation on that."

"Not undercover, Peter."

A hit of adrenaline punched through her. In a way, she *was* going UC. Not for the Bureau, but for ALPHA. Pride filled her heart. That, and determination. She was doing something to help an organization that had once brought her tremendous joy.

And she was doing it for Fred.

"Like I said, I need your help," he said. "Like a side gig, just between us."

This oughta be interesting.

"What would I be doing?"

"Surveilling Luciano Santini."

Not this... again. What is law enforcement's obsession with him? Rather than dismiss him, she leaned back, crossed her legs. "Why would I do that?"

"He's very close with Carrera Santini—"

"They're cousins—"

"And Sinclair Develin."

"I'm not following, Peter. What do you suspect him of?"

"I'm convinced Carrera and Sin have formed some kind of alliance. And if Luciano Santini is involved, it's hella illegal. He ran—or still runs—the Santini crime family."

As her agitation grew, she tapped her fingernails on the arm of the wrought iron sofa, letting the *rap-rap-rap* fill the silence.

"Years ago, we had a conversation that stayed with me," Peter continued. "I'd recommended you for a promotion, which you got. You told me you appreciated that I was the epitome of professionalism. I was very touched by that."

She nodded. "I remember."

"You said that in a work environment where women aren't always welcome, I made you, and all the women on the team, feel like equals. You told me I never said or did anything inappropriate."

"Still holds true."

He smiled. "You told me you'd be there for me, if the time came when you could return the favor."

"I did."

A coldness hardened his eyes. "I need to call in that favor, Red."

She grew silent while the bass pounding in her head grew louder. Megaphone loud. She couldn't believe this was happening. Why call in that favor now? And why her?

"I need to know what he's up to," Peter said.

Look who's doing something illegal now.

"I'm not comfortable doing that, Peter," she said. "I'm sorry."

"You don't have a choice, Red."

Anger slithered around her heart. "I don't work for you."

"You do know how favors work, don't you?"

She nodded, once.

"I'm calling mine in."

Glaring at Peter, she stood. "Not happening."

If he was trying to intimidate her, it *wasn't* working. Her frustration grew with each passing second.

"Peter, you can't ask Red to do that," Jerod said. "It's wrong on so many levels. I get that you hate the guy because of what happened with your first wife, but you're with Lucy now. You've got the Director's ear for fuck's sake. Let it go with Santini."

Peter's face turned beet red. "I was a goddamn cuckold and made to look like an ass."

"Be pissed at your ex and don't drag Red into this," Jerod said. "She's suffering enough. Her friend is dead, Peter. Dead!"

"You and I both know Santini is up to no good," Peter insisted.

"Enough." Jerod pushed off the sofa and regarded her. "I'll walk you out."

"Red, I'm sorry," Peter said. "Jerod's right. You just lost a good friend and here I am being a total jackass."

"I'm gonna head out." A myriad of emotions—frustration, anguish, and disappointment—followed her inside. After thanking Lucy, she made her way toward the front door, eager to leave. Jerod caught up with her as she opened it.

"Let me walk you to your car." Outside, he said, "I'm sure this dinner party was the last place you wanted to be."

"It was fine."

"I'm here if you want to talk," he said. "Death is the *ultimate* loss. It messes with people in a way that nothing else does."

"It sure as hell does." At her SUV, she opened the door and climbed in.

"And no worries, when you're up to getting together again, I won't talk about Luciano Santini and I won't ask you to spy on him either. Just two *old* friends getting together. Well... *I'm* old."

"You're not old, Jerod."

"I just turned forty-nine. Fifty is looming." He fake-gasped.

She smiled. "You look terrific. What's your secret?"

"Tanning spray and I've started coloring my hair. I refuse to let gravity win, so I'm chasing away the wrinkles too."

She started her vehicle. "Thanks for the save tonight."

"I'll text you." He shut her car door, shot her a smile before heading back inside.

As she drove to Slash and Carrera's, disappointment tinged her thoughts. Tonight, she'd seen a different side of Peter. Until now, she'd held him in such high esteem.

Cut him some slack.

But she couldn't. He was obsessed with taking down Luciano.

She'd never known any man who could create this kind of buzz. Surely, there were plenty of *other* people in the nation's capital worthy of surveillance. On a personal level, she got it. One-hundred percent. Luciano was a top-tier DC power player. He was sick wealthy, total eye candy, and an international superstar.

By the time she returned to Slash's, muscles running along her shoulders had turned to granite. She was used to working with the good guys to catch the bad ones. At the moment, she wasn't sure who the good ones were.

"Oh, Fred," she sighed. "I wish you were here. We'd sort through everything and figure it out together. I'm sure of it."

I've been thrown into the deep end... with the sharks. This time, I'll have to figure it out for myself.

12

THE SECRET

SIMONE

Simone hadn't slept well. She'd stayed up until after one in the morning scouring the dark web, only to come up short *again*. No one in the Haqazzii terror cell chat rooms was talking about The Bomb Maker, and Inferno531 had gone silent. If there *was* online chatting, she wasn't skilled enough to find it. Around two in the morning, she'd started obsessing over Peter's request to spy on Luciano. Though she'd refused him, she couldn't ignore his ask.

When she woke, at half past six, she knew what she needed to do to alleviate her anxiety.

But first, target practice.

After a quick breakfast, she and Slash headed to Henninger Security. It had been years since she'd been there but, as she walked into the facility, the familiar sounds and smells filled her with hope. She'd once been an excellent markswoman.

I can do this.

While Slash signed in, Simone showed her FBI badge to the desk clerk, then signed in too.

"Lookee who came back to the mother ship," said a familiar voice.

Tucker Henninger's blond hair had grown past his shoulders. His grin was contagious, and his outstretched arms were welcoming. After a warm hug, he said, "It's been a while, girlie. Where you been?"

"I left the Bureau."

"That's a crying shame, darlin'," Tucker said. She'd always loved his southern accent and good-natured ribbing. "Well, welcome back to Henninger's. Check out my training town. Cost me a fortune, but it's used daily by LEOs."

"I will," she replied, "but I need to start with the basics... target practice."

"Alrighty, then. You ladies go have fun."

Upon entering the indoor firing range, they decided to stay together, rather than split off into different lanes.

"Day one," Simone said before covering her ears with protective muffs.

While she'd kept her go-bag, she no longer had a weapon. With their eyewear in place, Slash handed her one of her smaller Glocks. Simone eyed the weapon. It felt oddly familiar in her hand.

"Just like riding a bike," Slash said.

"You go first."

Slash stepped up to the line, got in position, relaxed her knees, raised the weapon, and fired at the target. The bullet pierced the center circle.

Nice.

Slash fired off a few more rounds before lowering her weapon. She offered an encouraging smile, and made room at the line. "Your turn."

With a mix of excitement and anxious butterflies, Simone moved into place. She raised her weapon, aimed, and fired off a shot. The bullet missed the target completely.

"Do you want pointers?" Slash asked. "Or do you want to feel your way back?"

"Pointers," Simone said.

"Ready your stance. Breathe in, relax your knees, release your breath slowly, softly squeeze the trigger."

Simone applied the coaching, and fired off three rounds. The bullets struck the target, moving closer to center with each shot.

"Nice," Slash said. "Again."

Simone did as instructed, getting more comfortable with the feel of the gun in her hand, her palm and fingers cradling the grip. Again and again, she fired, until the weapon no longer felt foreign to her.

She lowered the Glock. "Fire with me."

Slash stepped up. It took a few rounds before they were unloading in sync. Over and over and over. By the time they finished, the target was a shredded mess. Slash pressed a button that brought the target to them, attached a fresh one, and send it back out. When they'd decimated that one, they placed the guns in their cases, stepped out of the booth, and removed their protective wear.

Today had been a good first day.

"Tomorrow, we'll move the target farther back," Slash explained. "And we'll swing by here on Sunday too. That way you'll be ready to rock it out at Monday's training."

Simone raised her eyebrows.

"At training base camp," Slash said.

Code for the Black Site. Another flurry of anticipation flowed through her.

"Thank you for this," Simone said. "You're a great instructor."

"I help Rebel sometimes, so he gets firing time."

As they drove back, Simone said, "I was thinking of heading back home today. I don't want to—"

"Nope." Slash shot her a smile. "Stay the weekend. On Monday we'll drive to the site together."

"I like that," Simone replied.

"I've missed hanging with you."

"Same. I'd like to make dinner for everyone tonight, unless you have plans."

"Later today, Luciano, Teddy, and Gabriel—who's in from Italy—are coming over. Elsa will probably be cooking up a storm when we get home."

It was almost noon.

As Slash pulled into the garage, Simone shot off a text.

> Any chance you'll be home this afternoon? I was hoping to swing by

No dots appeared.

She and Slash went inside and laughter snagged her attention. Into the kitchen they went. Simone recognized Teddy Santini. He was with Luciano the night of Burke's party. The other man had olive skin, dark brown hair that fell to his shoulders, deep brown eyes, and a toothy smile.

Another handsome Santini.

"Hey, I recognize you," Teddy said. "You're the one tailing Lulu."

Silence while everyone stared at her.

"We kissed and made up, so it's all good," Simone replied.

Laughter erupted from the group.

"Haven't we met?" Teddy asked.

He remembers me from Burke and Morticia's.

"This is my good friend, Simone Redding," Slash said. "She's staying with us for a few days."

"Ciao, bella signora." Gabriel stepped right into her space, collected her hand in his, and kissed the backs of her fingers.

"That's Gabriel," Carrera said. "He's a lady-eater."

More laughter from the family.

Gabriel chomped his teeth together and winked at her before regarding Elsa. "G'ma, are you ready?"

"All ready," Elsa replied. "Teddy, are you driving?"

Teddy opened the fridge. "I'm gonna hang here and chow down. Gabriel can take my truck." He tossed his brother the keys.

Gabriel put his arm around Elsa. "Al mercato, mia nonna."

"Sì," Elsa replied.

"Grocery store," Slash translated.

Simone's phone buzzed and she read the text.

"I've gotta take off," Simone said.

"È un piacere, bella signora," Gabriel said.

Simone glanced around for help.

"It's a pleasure, beautiful lady," Gabriel translated.

"He's like a shark circling," Teddy said, and the family cracked up.

She excused herself, hurried upstairs to the guest room. After showering, she dressed in a tailored white shirt, form-fitting black pants, and black stilettos. After playing around with her hair, she pulled it into a French twist, but left strands framing her face. A little blush, a layer of mascara, and her favorite maroon lipstick.

Returning to the kitchen, she found Teddy and Carrera eating lunch at the island.

"Where's Slash?" Simone asked.

"She's taking a shower," Carrera replied.

"I'm heading out for a few."

"Dinner's gonna be a feast," Teddy said, his mouth full of food.

"I don't want to intrude on a family—"

Carrera held up his hand. "Don't even go there. Dinner's at seven."

Teddy raised his bottle of beer. "Happy hour starts now."

She laughed.

Pointing at her, Teddy blurted, "I remember where I've seen you before. Didn't I interrupt you and Lulu—"

"I'm out. See you guys later." Simone bit back a smile as she took off toward the front door. Once outside, she laughed out loud. She'd hoped Teddy *wouldn't* remember that he'd seen her buck naked and sprawled on a bed with Luciano's face planted between her legs.

She climbed in her SUV, drove out, and headed west on I-495 toward Great Falls. Thirty minutes later, she stopped in front of the iron gates, rolled down her window.

"Good afternoon, ma'am," said the guard.

"Simone Redding."

"You've been cleared to enter. Park at the fountain."

The giant gates swung open. As she drove past the beautiful oak trees lining the long driveway, wonderful memories flooded her thoughts. Jamming on the guitar while Chad pounded on his drums. Friday happy hours where she'd park herself on a kitchen stool and enjoy a glass of wine after a long week at work.

This home—once Mitus mansion—had been her sanctuary, her refuge for three years. She'd made lifelong friends and would remain forever grateful to Colton. There, she'd felt safe. Something she desperately needed.

She parked at the fountain and made her way toward the front door. Self-assurance followed her as she trotted up the steps and rang the doorbell. Last night, she hadn't known what to do, but in the light of day, she'd made the right decision.

The door opened and she swallowed down a moan. Luciano's wicked-hot smile lit up his face, but it was the heated look in his eyes that halted her breath. Unless she was fooling herself, he looked genuinely happy to see her.

"Simone, come in."

As she crossed the threshold, he wrapped his fingers around her arm, pulled her close. While he kissed her cheek, she savored his musky scent. Her heart skipped a beat when he pressed his lips to her other cheek and lingered an extra second before pulling away.

The second she peered into his eyes, the energy shifted. The desire to be close to him, to touch him, to be touched *by* him, had her heart pounding fast and her insides roaring to life.

His power consumed her and ignited her at the same time.

"You look beautiful," he murmured.

She wanted to tell him that he, too, looked beautiful. Too beautiful really. As she expected, he was dressed to impress in a pair of tight black pants and a black quarter-zip sweater. Lucky for her, he'd left it unzipped, and she checked out his sun-kissed skin.

In truth, everything about him captivated her. Even the evil. *Especially the evil.*

"A glass of wine with lunch?" he asked.

"Lunch?"

"Are you hungry?"

She wasn't, but the wine might help her get through this conversation.

"I'll take a glass of liquid courage."

He gestured toward the kitchen. On the way, she glanced into the living room, then the dining area. The furniture had been replaced with modern pieces that boasted soft curves and muted colors.

"I love the changes you've made," she said.

Up went his eyebrows.

"I used to live here," she said. "I was Colton Mitus's biz manager for three years. His employees lived here with him. It was an unusual arrangement, but everyone loved it."

They entered the kitchen, the familiar space making her smile. "I always loved this room."

Luciano had updated the decor—five sleek black counter stools, a striking black dining table with six cushioned chairs—off-white Quartz counters, bright white kitchen cabinets, and Bertazzoni appliances. She glanced out the French doors to the expansive backyard and perfectly-placed swimming pool.

As she got situated on a counter stool, Luciano reached for two bottles of wine. And that's when she glimpsed his ass.

Well, hello there.

Those tight pants hugged his backside and she locked in. Round, strong, muscular and so damn perfect. When he turned back, she was staring at his junk. Rather than panic, she gave him the once-over, slowly raking her gaze up and down, appreciating every physical thing about him.

"You're not subtle," he said.

"You dress well."

He's not buying that.

"You eye-fuck better." His fiery gaze sent a ripple of excitement through her.

Ohmygod.

She couldn't hold back her smile. "Touché."

He set the bottles on the island, retrieved two stemless wine goblets. As he eased on the chair beside her, he said, "I started a women's clothing line after designing Slash's wedding gown. I have something that would be perfect for you—"

"Not a wedding dress, I hope."

"You'd look *perfetta* in a wedding gown, but no. I have a pair of Santini black pants and a white shirt that would be beautiful on you."

She glanced down at herself. "I'm wearing a white shirt and black pants."

"But you're not wearing *Santini*." He held up a bottle of white and a Santini Chianti.

"I heard you make a luxury whiskey," she said. "Care to share?"

His smile set off a series of fireworks that sent her pulse racing. There was something completely addicting about seeing him smile. His bright, white teeth were almost perfect, save for a jutting left eye tooth. Somehow, that slight imperfection made him more human. As she homed in on that tooth, she fantasized about him standing behind her and biting her neck. She'd strip him naked, go down on him, then take him inside her. And she would get lost in everything Luciano. The bad would fade away, leaving only the sweet, sweet good.

"Mmm." The sound floated from her before she could smother it.

As he reached into a cupboard, he asked, "Everything okay?"

"All good."

Only my thoughts are very, very bad.

He poured them each a finger's worth of amber-colored liquid, then returned to sit beside her and raised his glass. "To my new partner."

They clinked glasses and drank. Simone rarely drank hard liquor, but as the whiskey wet her tongue, a medley of delicious tastes filled her mouth.

"That's amazing."

"Thank you." After a beat, he asked, "Are you here to confess your sins?"

She smiled. How could she not? Luciano Santini was the supreme puppet master. Everyone was living in his world... a world he'd created by amassing power.

"No, something else."

As she stared into his bright eyes, the need to kiss him overtook her. It came on like a lightning strike. Sudden, powerful, and intentional. She couldn't breathe, couldn't think. Her gaze jumped from his eyes to his mouth, those luscious lips tugging her toward him by an invisible force she couldn't resist.

STOP!

She pushed off the stool, walked around the expansive slab of quartz, and breathed.
Get it together.
"I have a problem," she began. "Well, not a problem exactly. More like a situation." She hated when she rambled, but this was unchartered territory. She'd never worked with an assassin, but she was certain she didn't want to get on his bad side.

That wouldn't end well for her. She also knew the definition of loyalty, and she coveted that.

"Talk to me," he murmured.

She wasn't sure if it was the rasp in his voice or the way his attention stayed glued on her, but she found herself sitting down beside him. His enigmatic presence made her feel safe... and alive, like she was super-charged with electricity.

"We're working together, and that means something to me. I value partnerships in the workplace."

He nodded. "Same."

"Okay, good." She took a mouthful of whiskey, swallowed it down. "I don't know you well, but I have to trust *someone*. I need to feel confident you'll have my back, especially if things go sideways. The Bomb Maker isn't like any other criminal, so I'm going into this with eyes wide open."

She broke eye contact, glanced outside.

"Simone. What do you want to tell me?"

She swiveled toward him, her gaze drilling into his. After shuddering in a breath, she released it in a sigh.

Then, silence.

LUCIANO

SIMONE WAS STRUGGLING. Luciano wanted to help, but he didn't want to rush her. The fact that she'd come to him spoke volumes. He knew she'd gone to Hirzog's for dinner. Carrera had seen to that.

As he stared into her eyes, he found himself hoping she would tell him the truth. Then, maybe, he could let his guard down. Distrusting everyone he met, until they proved themselves, was a tiresome way to live. Tiresome, but necessary. If he put trust in the wrong person, he was a dead man.

Luciano offered an encouraging smile. That helped, but not in the way he'd intended. Her pupils expanded, the black bleeding over the green, then she slickened her lower lip with her tongue. He loved how responsive she was to him. It was alluring as hell, but also distracting. He meant to calm her, not rile her. She was his partner now, not his lover.

She can be both.

No, she can't.

Normally the epitome of control, he had to touch her. His fingers tingled to stroke her soft skin. He swiveled toward her, scooped her hands in his, and her fingers braided around his. Touching each other felt natural... and unprofessional. Still, he didn't tug his away. Just the opposite. He gave her an encouraging squeeze.

"Several years ago, I worked for Peter Hirzog at the Bureau," she began. "We'd lost touch, but we ran into each other last week."

"I remember," he said.

"He invited me to his home last night for a dinner party. Turns out, he had an ulterior motive for asking me."

"What did he want?"

She pulled her warm hands away, leaving him missing her. "He asked me to spy on you." She tossed back another mouthful of whiskey. "I was surprised. First, Z, now him. I refused, but he put the pressure on me."

"Did you cave?"

"Hell, no. Someone else I worked with, Jerod De Clerq from

ATF, was there. He told Peter his issue should be with his ex, not you. Anyway, I wouldn't be surprised if he finds someone else to do his spying."

Hirzog wasn't letting go of something that had happened over two years ago, but Luciano didn't give a damn about him. Despite the power Hirzog wielded, he was like an annoying gnat.

As he peered into her eyes, he hoped she was being honest. Trust was the cornerstone to any healthy relationship, professional or personal.

"Thank you for telling me," he said.

For too long, she stared at her lap, then she murmured, "The *last* thing I want is to get on your bad side."

"Why's that?"

She lifted her face to his. The knot between her eyes was gone, replaced with a searing gaze. "I'm determined to find The Bomb Maker, and w*hen* I do, I'm confident you'll take him out. I've never straddled both sides of the law, but I get it. I would much rather have *you* in my court than Peter Hirzog. If I betray you, you'll eliminate me. What's he going to do? Not invite me to another dinner party?"

Her sweet smile touched his tortured soul.

Either she was telling the truth or she was playing him for a fool. And if that were the case... she was good. Very good.

"Hirzog is living in the past." A somberness came over Luciano. "He would be happier if he made peace with what his ex-wife did and let it go." He stared out the French doors. "Holding onto the past is preventing him from living his best life now."

Though their relationship had shifted to a professional one, he wanted her to know *why* Hirzog hated him so much.

"He blames me for his failed first marriage." Luciano sipped the whiskey. "His first wife arranged a lunch meeting through a mutual friend. She told me she was single. Back then, I didn't fact-check."

"Lessons are always learned the hard way."

"Unfortunately," he replied. "I found out two weeks after I'd started seeing her. She insisted her marriage was ending, but I broke it off. I don't know if she tried reconciling with Hirzog or if she left him, but I never saw her again. I might be a killer, but I'm not a cheat, and I want nothing to do with wrecking marriages."

"They say every criminal has his lane. I'm glad you found yours." Her seductive laugh strummed his heart like a stringed instrument.

She placed her hand on his leg, and heat shot through him. "My comedic timing needs work. I appreciate that you have marital morals. Finding our person is *everything*."

For the first time since losing Linda and the babies, pain didn't shred him. Instead, a sense of peace blanketed him.

She caressed his thigh. Her slow, sensual touch had his cock firming in the small space between his legs. Then, she jerked her hand away. "Sorry," she murmured.

With her empty glass in hand, she sauntered to the sink and set it down. Luciano rose as she walked back over to him. He couldn't miss the hunger in her eyes. All he wanted to do was devour her in a million different ways.

"I'm out," she said brushing past him, the clickety-click of her stilettos tapping across the marble floor.

"Don't. Go."

She stilled, then turned.

Two easy strides and she was inches away, her luminous eyes burning with an energy that rivaled his own. He was crazy attracted to her, but it was more than a physical connection. There was something intoxicating about her that kept him grounded, yet flying high at the same time.

"We haven't eaten," he said.

"I'm not hungry."

He curled one of her long, dark tendrils around his finger. "You sure about that?"

A shadow fell over her eyes. "We shouldn't," she rasped.

"No, we shouldn't," he agreed.

She leaned up, kissed his scruffy jawline. "We're going to, aren't we?"

Her breathing had changed, her chest rising and falling faster. She was working her lower lip pretty good, and the grit in her voice had turned him hard.

"Yes," he replied, his raspy voice rumbling through his chest. "We are."

They came together in a whoosh of explosive energy. His arms anchored her close and she clung to him like a lifeline in a raging sea. They were close, but not close enough.

"For the first time in my life, I hate clothing," he said.

She laughed, the joy in her eyes touching his broken, broken soul. Her mouth found his, her full lips sending him soaring, while the desire to root inside her took hold. She wrapped one leg around his, and he smiled.

She broke the kiss. "What?"

"You're a flamingo," he murmured.

"I'm poison ivy," she retorted.

"Even better." He clasped her hand, led her toward the foyer.

"I've never been naughty with a coworker."

"Same," he said as they began the long climb to the second floor.

"We're bad," she said as she quickened her pace.

"Very bad."

At the top of the stairs, he turned toward her. "Which room was yours?"

She pointed down the left hall. "Are these empty?"

"All but mine."

She tugged him on. "I've never had sex here."

"Didn't Colton host kink parties?"

"He liked to watch. That's what turned me into a voyeur. His live sex shows opened my eyes to a world of kink. He called them Fornication Nation."

Luciano laughed.

She pulled to a stop in front of a closed bedroom door. "Tuck me in. All this talking has tired me out. I need a nap."

"As you wish." He opened the bedroom door.

She grabbed him by the neck of his sweater and pulled him in. He shut and locked the door behind them.

"Why are you locking it?"

"My chef Louis and his wife live in the lower level."

Another mellifluous laugh floated from her. "They live in Fornication Nation."

He chuckled. "I'm not sure they'd want to know that."

She pushed onto her toes, stared into his eyes. "No regrets about this, and we work the case like the bosses we are."

"One-hundred percent."

He slipped his hand around the back of her neck, drew her close, and kissed her. One soft kiss that led to another, and another, and another. She opened her mouth, he deepened the kiss and was rewarded with her husky moan. Their bodies came together, the need to touch her had him snaking his arm around her back and sliding it under her shirt.

Her approving moan sent another zing of desire pounding through him. He stroked her beautiful back, unhooked her bra, then slowed the kiss until it ended.

Breathing hard, she fisted the bottom of his sweater and pulled it over his head. Her attention jumped from his eyes to his chest and she pressed her palms against his pecs.

"You're made of steel." She pressed her mouth to his chest and kissed him, then dragged her tongue down his chest and over his abs. Sexy Simone sent desire pounding through him.

Kneeling before him, she peered up. Her half-moon lids shaded her lustful eyes.

He had to have her, the need overtaking his every thought.

Slowly, she unzipped his pants. They dropped to the floor. Next, she pulled his boxer briefs over his erection. As she caressed his rock-hard shaft, she murmured, "I don't give blowjobs, but I can't *stop* with you. I need your cock in my mouth, filling me with your hot juices."

Jesus.

Excitement oozed out of him. "Taste me," he commanded.

She rolled her tongue over the head, the pleasure shooting through him like a cannon. She licked his shaft, placed her lips over the head, and devoured him with her mouth. And she sucked him slowly.

Agonizingly sweet torture ripped through him. On a low growl, he sank his fingers into her hair and surrendered to the pleasure, letting her work his cock with her talented mouth.

"You taste good," she said as she ran her finger over the glistening head.

"Do you want me to wait?"

She pulled him out, pierced him with her fiery gaze. "I want you to choke me with your big, hard cock."

Fuck me.

She cradled his balls with one hand, slid her finger between his ass and caressed his anus. Bolts of electricity charged through him as she started deep throating him.

All the way in and almost all the way out.

His cock throbbed, the pent-up energy begging to escape. When his balls tightened, she worked his shaft with her fingers while lashing the head with her tongue.

"Fuck, Simone," he roared as the orgasm shot out of him.

Wave after wave of ecstasy washed over him. In those glorious seconds, color brightened his dark world, and he was bathed in sweet, sweet euphoria.

She slowed down, then stilled before pulling off him and disappearing into the bathroom. Seconds later, she slunk out, her lustful gaze searing him with desire.

Floating on a sex high, he snaked his arms around her. "I love watching you squirm with pleasure, and I want to bring it all to you, until you beg me to stop."

Her lips parted, her throaty groan reverberating in his chest. His cock stirred.

While peering into her half-hooded eyes, he unbuttoned her shirt, pressed his mouth to her chest, then deposited a trail of kisses across the swell of her breasts. "All mine."

A growl shot out of her. "Suck my tits."

Pausing, he dropped a kiss on her mouth. "Patience and control." Moving slowly, he slid his hands under the shirt and shouldered it off her. Next, he pulled her bra away, exposing her fantastic breasts.

She cradled them in her hands, pushing them toward him. And he dipped down and covered her large areola with his mouth, teasing her nip with gentle tongue flicks until it hardened. Then, he sucked her tender flesh.

"Yessss," she hissed. "I like that."

He sucked her other nipple while she arched her back and urged him to suck harder. When he finished, her ruby red nips were hard as stone and twice as engorged.

As he unzipped her pants, she pinched her nipples while her gritty moans ripped through him. Off came her pants, then he slid his hands inside her thong, and tugged them down. She stepped out of it, then pushed up on her toes.

"Fuck me."

The grit in her voice turned him hard again. Around her, he was unstoppable and insatiable. Simone turned him into a beast and he couldn't get enough of her. She pressed her breasts against his chest and dragged them over his skin. Then, she curled her fingers around his semi and led him to the bed. She tugged back the duvet and the linens, then crawled in.

"I have condoms in my pants pocket," she said.

"Jesus."

"Premeditated," she replied as she spread her legs.

Her pussy glistened with her juices, and he couldn't roll on the condom fast enough.

"I'm a bad girl, daddy." She arched off the bed. "Can you help me?"

"Fuck, yes," he growled.

Planking over her, he kissed her, their tongues meeting in a torrent of greed, while he trapped her wrists about her head with one hand and held them down. The harder he kissed her, the deeper her groans, until she started gyrating beneath him.

He ran his fingers over her slickened core, then slid his wet fingers into his mouth. "Delicious, baby girl."

"Ohgod," she moaned. "Can you punish me with your cock, daddy?"

He positioned himself at her opening and dragged his cock over it, until he reached her clit. Again and again until he pierced her with it, sinking inside the tight juncture between her legs.

"Fuck," she cried out. "I'm a naughty girl." She raised her ass off the bed and he sunk in until he reached the end.

They started moving against each other, creating the intense friction they needed. Her heavy lids and flushed cheeks turned him into a savage. He couldn't get enough of her while she clawed his back wildly. Faster and faster he pounded into her as their kisses turned brutal. Her groans turned to mewls, then cries, as she raced toward an orgasm.

"You're punishing me so good," she rasped between breaths.

He massaged her breast, tugging on her nipple, but when he repositioned so he could grind on her clit, she started shaking beneath him.

"Coming so hard," she ground out. "Oh, fuck, yes."

She moaned and convulsed while her pussy trapped him inside her. The pure ecstasy on her face sent him over the edge and he climaxed inside her. Hard.

He'd crossed a line that should never have been crossed... and he couldn't wait for more.

Have I met my match or am I falling into a trap set by someone out for revenge?

13

THE CONFESSION

SIMONE

Simone lay panting on the bed, sated, yet still ravenous with desire. She was buzzing high on Luciano. He returned from the bathroom.

"I'm gonna lose my job," she murmured to herself.

"No, you won't." He laid next to her, pulled her onto his chest.

"First, you weren't supposed to hear that and, are we cuddling?"

"Intermission while I reload." She lifted her head. "Would you rather I sit across the room in the chair?" he asked.

Of course she wouldn't. She loved how their bodies melded together, loved his beautiful olive skin and hardened, defined muscles. She ran soft fingertips over his chest and shoulder, then down his arm.

She didn't want to admit she liked their closeness, but she didn't want to give him a smarmy answer that might cause him to move away from her. So, she said nothing.

He caressed her back with a tender touch. "I didn't think so."

"We can't do this again."

"You're right," he murmured.

Despite knowing it was for the best, her heart sank.

He ran his fingers over her shoulder, then gently nudged her onto her back. Rather than get out of bed, he rolled toward her, leaned up on his elbow, and peered into her eyes.

With a tender touch, he ran his fingers over her chest, then down her abs. As he made his way back up, he caressed one breast, then the other before winding his way back up her chest, her neck, and finally, cupping her face with his hand and turning her toward him.

Then, he leaned over and dropped a worshipful kiss on her lips. "You're taking on a difficult case and you're doing it out of loyalty to your friend. I respect you for that." He kissed her again. "Without much to go on, you're going to get frustrated."

"No doubt." With the pads of her fingers, she traced his strong, straight nose, then caressed his dark, rough stubble. When she stared into his beautiful hazel eyes, her heart skipped a beat.

She liked him, and that left her feeling unsettled and vulnerable.

"That's where I come in." He kissed her, this time dipping his talented tongue into her mouth.

And... just like that, the energy shifted.

Slow, gentle strokes with his tongue that sent a series of tingles flowing through her. He slowed the kiss, then ended it, leaving her desperate for more. When he moved over her, she felt the snare of his line, the way he hooked her with a simple touch or the intensity in his eyes.

One kiss on each cheek, then her chin before he worshiped her body with his mouth, leaving his scent, and marking her with his essence. He kissed her abs, her pelvic area, and the insides of her thighs, working his way closer and closer to the small, hidden pearl between her legs.

"When you're not making any headway," he said, "I will relax you."

She watched the most handsome man she'd ever known bury his face between her legs and devour her in a long, possessive lick. Once, twice, and on the third time, he rolled his tongue over her clit.

And her body bowed to his. Every action elicited a reaction. He stroked her thigh, she emitted a purr, he licked her core, she moaned, he slid three fingers inside her and she released a cry. The pleasure he brought her was unrelenting. He knew when to be intense, how to bring her to the edge, then ease her back down. She was a puppet and he the master, controlling the amount of pleasure he doled out.

She could not get enough.

As the passion continued to build, she promised herself she would protect her heart.

I'll be chill. I'll accept that his world and my world are different. He's a billionaire executioner and I'm... I'm...

"Coming," she cried out as the orgasm powered through her like a tornado shredding everything in its path.

I'm a goner.

She floated back to earth feeling completely at ease.

He lay beside her. "Ms. Redding, we're gonna have fun working this case."

She never wanted this blissful state to end, never wanted to return to reality where a madman was stepping back into the spotlight by taking out a group of highly trained, highly skilled Operatives.

Nothing like returning with a bang.

And here she was spending her Saturday in bed with a man who made more in a minute than she made all year. A man who could have any woman, but he chose her.

Is it because I showed up on his doorstep? Probably.

Despite the cold, harsh reality that was creeping in, she would focus on the positive. They'd work the case, have sex, she'd solve it, he'd eliminate the killer. They'd agree it had been fun and they'd move on.

Loss and loneliness settled into her bones.

On a shiver, she pushed out of bed. "I should take off. I came here to tell you about Peter."

After he rose from the bed, he flashed her a killer smile. "You look like you got sexed real good."

"You are some kind of cocky, you know that?"

"The best kind. We should get ready. It's time to head back to Carrera's for Elsa's feast."

There was no clock in the room, she'd left her phone in the car. "What time is it?"

"It's five-thirty," he replied.

"Wow, we've been at it for a while."

"Not long enough." He kissed her, then escorted her to the bathroom.

Her neat French twist had turned into an explosion of hair, but it was the happiness in her eyes that surprised her the most.

She was having fun with him. More fun than she'd had in a long, long time.

An hour later, she parked in front of Slash and Carrera's home. Up the walkway she went, then she tried the front door. It was locked, so she rang the doorbell.

Seconds later, Slash swung it wide. With a smile, she said, "There you are. Everything okay?"

Simone entered the house. "All good."

As they headed toward the kitchen, Slash murmured, "If you need to talk... about anything."

"Thank you for being there for me. I'm ready to start work on Monday."

"Training's gonna be fun."

They entered the kitchen. Gabriel and Teddy were seated at the counter. Carrera was helping his grandmother at the stove. Slash returned to the center island to finish cutting vegetables for a salad.

Gabriel turned. "I thought Luciano was with you."

Simone shot him a cool smile. "Why would you think that?"

Mischief danced in Gabriel's eyes. "Brotherly intuition."

He knows.

Simone had too much on her mind to care. She sidled next to Slash. "What can I do to help?"

Slash pulled out another cutting board and knife, then slid vegetables toward her. "Elsa said it isn't a salad unless there's ten different vegetables."

"Ten," Simone said as she rinsed a few mushrooms.

She glanced over at Gabriel and Teddy. "Gabriel, what do you do in Italy?"

"I own several wineries and I run Euro Operations at Santini International," he replied. "I've been in Italy for several years now."

Elsa put her arm around Gabriel. "I wish I could see you more."

"I'm here all the time, Elsa." He kissed the top of her head, and she smiled.

"You're a good boy."

"No, I'm not," Gabriel pushed back. "I'm a baddy." He winked at Simone.

"He is, G-ma," Teddy said as he swiped a celery stick and started munching on it.

"Luciano is approaching the front door," the surveillance system announced.

Simone's cheeks warmed, her pulse quickened. She flicked her attention toward the hallway, eager to see him again.

The front door opened, then shut.

Relax. He's just a guy.

Anticipation sent a tremble skirting through her.

No, he's not just a guy. He's a powerful, charming, and completely charismatic man.

When Luciano strode into the room, the air became electric, the swirling energy halting her breath. He skimmed the group. When he homed in on her, a shadow darkened his eyes. The desire to go to him, pull him close, and kiss him breathless had her leaning against the counter to stop herself.

In his hand, he held four large black shopping bags, the word SANTINI emblazoned in gold across each one.

Then, he flashed the group a movie-star smile and held up the bags. His family clamored around him, but she stayed cemented behind the large island, watching the scene unfold.

"Elsa, for you." He handed his grandmother a bag. With a childlike smile, she retreated to her lounge chair in the family room and peered inside.

"Lulu," she exclaimed as she extracted a garment, then another, and finally a third.

He'd gifted her a pastel pink blousy shirt, a pair of black cashmere gloves, and a matching cashmere scarf.

Next, he handed Slash a bag. She extracted a black halter shirt, black jeans, and a black cashmere scarf like the one he'd given his grandmother. Slash grinned. "I love you, Lulu. These rock." She wrapped the scarf around her neck.

Then, he pulled out three identical black cashmere sweaters for Carrera, Gabriel, and Teddy.

Carrera pulled his on over his T-shirt. "Nice."

As everyone was admiring their gifts, he turned his full attention on her. One step at a time, he stalked over to her and offered her the final bag. "Simone."

She could feel the pull, the invisible tug to touch him, to hold him close and run her fingers through his luscious hair or caress his chiseled face.

"Thank you." She lifted out an espresso-colored cashmere scarf. "It's beautiful."

He gently draped the plush garment around her neck. "It's perfect on you."

She started to set down the bag, when he said, "There's more."

To her surprise, a silky black garment lay neatly folded at the bottom of the bag. She lifted out a beautiful silk negligée. Though she could have been embarrassed by the intimate apparel, she was not.

Then, he reached inside the bag, pulled out a matching silk robe. "For the next time," he murmured. "When you *don't* have to leave."

She stared at him for the longest time, unsure she'd even heard him correctly.

"Yowza," Teddy blurted, his boisterous voice snapping her out of her Luciano trance. "That's some sexy-sexy."

"It's very zhuzhy," she said to Luciano. "Thank you."

He kissed her cheek. "I can't wait to see you in them." After kissing her other cheek, he whispered, "And out of them."

Her insides quivered while her heart galloped in her chest. He was slaying her with his words. The air crackled with fiery energy, but the room had grown eerily silent. All eyes on them. Breaking away, she tucked the items back in the bag and returned to reality.

Salad making.

Teddy held up a beer and a bottle of wine. "Who wants what?"

"Nothing for me." Luciano pulled a bottle of sparkling water from the refrigerator. "Any takers?"

As he twisted the lid, Simone said, "Water for me."

"Same," Slash added.

"Lulu," Teddy said, "why is everything a competition?"

"Here we go," Carrera mumbled.

"This has nothing to do with you, Teddy," Luciano answered while filling three glasses. "I'll have wine with dinner, fratello."

"Wine for me," Gabriel said, taking the bottle from Teddy.

Teddy glared at Luciano, but Luciano just chuckled.

"Whatever," Teddy grumbled before opening the beer and draining half the bottle.

After Gabriel poured Elsa a glass of chianti, she held it up. "Alla famiglia."

Everyone toasted, then drank.

"Boys, when are you going to stop competing?" Elsa asked.

"Everything is a competition," Teddy replied.

"Not here," Luciano said. "Not here, brother."

Someone is approaching the front door," the security system announced. "An unknown male."

The doorbell rang and Carrera headed toward the foyer.

Simone's phone buzzed and she read the incoming text from an unknown number. "If you take that case, you're a dead woman."

Ohgod.

She stared at the words, the threat filling her with dread.

"Heyyyyo!" a male voice called out, hijacking her attention.

"Ah, fuck," Luciano murmured under his breath.

LUCIANO

Luciano wasn't interested in spending time with Willie Boy, but he'd take full advantage. Just because he didn't respect his cousin didn't mean he'd be a total jackass. With his signature smile in place, he opened his arms, embraced the Santini in a two-cheeked kiss.

"How've you been?" Luciano asked.

But Willie Boy was too busy eyeing the designer shopping bags. "Where's *my* present?"

Elsa appeared, but Willie Boy didn't acknowledge her.

"Show some respect," Luciano said, trying to keep his annoyance in check.

Willie Boy smiled. "Where's my present, *please*?"

"I'm talking about Elsa," Luciano said.

"Hey, G-ma, how's it goin'?" Willie Boy asked, his eyes glued on Simone. "Who's the hot chick? She's gotta be—what—almost six feet. I'd like to climb her."

Luciano grabbed Willie Boy by the scruff of his ratty T-shirt. "Enough!" he roared.

Teddy appeared next to Luciano. "What's your problem, Willie Boy?"

"I'm joking." Willie Boy tucked his long hair behind one ear. "Why the hell is everyone so damn uptight?"

"Don't be a dick to the ladies and show them some damn manners," Teddy said. "And say hello to G-ma."

Willie Boy air-pecked his grandmother's cheek. "Mwah," he said. "What's for dinner, G-ma?"

Luciano slid his gaze to his grandmother.

"I invited him," Elsa said.

"I see a shit-ton of Santini designer bags," Willie Boy said.

"You can have mine." Teddy handed Willie Boy his cashmere sweater.

Willie Boy pulled it on, but he was swimming in it. Teddy was twice as muscular and several inches taller. Willie Boy stared down at the sweater, then yanked it off.

"This doesn't fit," Willie Boy said. "Swing by the restaurant and bring me something."

Luciano gritted his teeth. He took orders from no one, especially his lazy-ass cousin.

"La cena è pronta," Elsa said. "Mangiamo."

Luciano broke from the group, his gaze trained on Simone.

He was drawn to her in a way he couldn't comprehend. Might've been her composure. Maybe her cool aloofness. Definitely her beauty, poise, and possibly the best poker face he'd ever seen.

"Who's the class act?" she whispered.

He had to touch her, so he ran his hand over her back.

"Lower," she whispered.

He dropped his hand to the middle of her back.

"Almost," she urged him on.

When he ran his hand over her ass, a purr rolled out of her. And blood rushed through his veins.

"Better?" he murmured.

Her sly smile was her only reply.

With the large salad bowl in one hand, he placed his other hand on the small of her back and guided her to the table. He set the bowl in the center, pulled out a chair for her. When she sat, he eased down at the head, across from Carrera.

"Willie Boy, will you say grace?" Elsa asked.

"Nah, I'm no good at that," Willie Boy replied.

"I got this," Luciano replied.

Everyone bowed their heads, but he found himself anchored on Simone.

"Heavenly Father, please bless the food we are about to eat. Thank you for our time together as a family. In Jesus' name. Amen."

Her eyes fluttered open and she raised her head. When she turned in his direction, everything became crystal clear. Their relationship had potential to become something significant. Maybe even something worth fighting for.

Dishes got passed around and plates were loaded up with food. His grandmother was her happiest when her family was together, sharing conversations over a homemade meal.

Luciano made the introduction between Willie Boy and Simone.

"Who do you know here?" Willie Boy asked her.

"No one," Simone replied dryly. "I just wandered in."

The group laughed.

"She's funny," Willie Boy said. "Slash, is she your friend?"

"Yup," Slash confirmed.

"Come to my restaurant," Willie Boy said. "Ask for me."

"He owns Willie Boy's in Old Town," Luciano explained.

"How's Saturday?" Willie Boy guzzled his beer, then tried squelching his belch, but it exploded out of him anyway.

"I'm taking on a new client," Simone answered, "and I don't want to commit to anything until I get into a rhythm."

"Are you a dancer or somethin'?" Willie Boy asked.

"I'm a personal shopper," Simone replied. "I have a new client who's very demanding. From what I can tell, he'll be monopolizing all my time."

"I don't get the rhythm thing." Willie Boy shoved too much lasagna into his mouth. "Swing by anytime," he said, his mouth crammed with food. "I'm there every day."

While the chatter continued, Luciano found himself peering over at Simone throughout the meal. He expected she'd be quiet, but the crease between her brows had deepened. She didn't strike him as someone who would get unnerved about work, but The Bomb Maker case was personal to her.

Very personal.

After dinner, Luciano poured a small amount of Santini Whiskey into several lowball glasses. While the family started cleaning up, Luciano suggested he and Willie Boy talk outside on the screened porch.

Willie Boy sank onto the sofa, tipped the glass of top-shelf booze to his mouth, and tossed the alcohol back. Then, he relaxed back, clasped his hands behind his head and said, "She likes me, I can tell."

Luciano chuckled.

"What? You don't think someone as sophisticated as Simone is into me?"

No, I don't.

Luciano leaned against the chair rail, sipped the whiskey that bore his name.

"I promised your dad I'd watch out for you," Luciano began.

"Yeah, well I don't need no babysitter. We ran the business, fifty-fifty."

The *business* Willie Boy was referring to was his family's *illegal* business, the one Luciano got out of years ago. The same one that his father and his uncle co-ran before his father got murdered and his uncle was sent to prison. But what Willie Boy *didn't* know was that his uncle had told Luciano to manage the business solo.

He'd said, "I love my boy, but he doesn't have the business smarts you do, so give him somethin' to keep him busy, and you take care of things."

The Santini crime family was once the most revered and feared families on the east coast. Now, they were a bunch of disorganized hoodlums. Luciano didn't give a damn about any of that. That was Willie Boy's problem.

"I don't want you offering counterfeit money to strangers," Luciano said.

"He's an *associate* of mine and you got the bills," Willie Boy pushed back. "It's a legit business opportunity."

"Counterfeit money *isn't* legit, Willie Boy."

"If you're worried Dante's law enforcement, he's not."

"How do you know him?"

"We go back a-ways."

Luciano waited. It was always this way with Willie Boy. A simple question got him a simple answer. One that explained nothing.

Tedious didn't begin to describe this convo. He glanced into the house. The group had moved into the family room, but

Simone stood alone in the kitchen, staring at her phone. Her lips were slashed in a thin line, the divot between her brows still etched deep.

An urgent need to check on her had agitation streaking down his spine.

"I've done business with him," Willie Boy said.

"Doing what?"

While clucking his tongue, Willie Boy stroked his shaven cheeks. These two tells alerted Luciano that his cousin was anxious or about to lie.

"I hired him to do a job. Jesus! Why is everything the fucking inquisition with you? He's looking for boodle. You got it. It's a simple exchange of services—"

"What did we learn as kids?" Luciano asked.

"How to swindle people? I dunno. Whad we learn?"

"Family first, and never trust an outsider." Luciano sipped the whiskey. "Don't put me in that position again."

"I'll buy the boodle from you," Willie Boy said.

His cousin didn't have the finances to do a large deal like that. Moreover, Luciano still had no idea who Dante was.

"Take him to Papà," Luciano suggested.

Fear clouded Willie Boy's eyes. "Carlo Garibaldi won't do business with me."

Luciano glanced inside. Simone was gone. *Dammit.* As he made his way toward the door, he spotted her in the family room.

"Dante's puttin' the squeeze on me," Willie Boy blurted. "I kinda owe him."

"Well, I don't." Luciano strode inside as Simone vanished up the stairs.

"Goodnight, Simone," he said.

When she turned, he couldn't miss the concern in her eyes. "Goodnight, Luciano." She continued on.

Every muscle in his body urged him up the stairs, but he didn't want to hound her.

Fuck it.

He took the stairs two at a time. She was entering the guest bedroom.

"Wait," he said as he pulled alongside her.

Intensity radiated from her, but it was the worry in her eyes that had him stroking her cheek with the back of his fingers. "What's wrong?"

"It's been a long week."

The longer she held his gaze the stronger the desire to pull her close, but she opened the door, stepped into the room. "I'll see you Monday."

She shut the door, leaving him wondering what the hell had happened in the last hour and a half. She wasn't okay. Of that he was certain.

He would respect her need for privacy, but starting Monday, no more secrets.

14

COMING HOME

SIMONE

Early Monday morning, Simone woke refreshed and ready to work. Initially, the death-threat text had rattled her, but she refused to be intimidated or scared into submission. This time, she'd push through the fear, the concern, and the monsters lurking in the shadows.

She'd once been a beast. She'd find her inner beast again... or she'd die trying. That's how determined she was.

After a quick cup of coffee and a piece of toast, she said goodbye to Elsa. "I'm sorry to leave," Simone said. "I'm envious of Slash and Carrera."

Elsa smiled. "Sometimes I feel like a third wheel."

"Don't say that," Slash said as she put her arm around Elsa and kissed her cheek. "That's stupid talk."

Carrera chuckled. "We're a three-legged stool, G-ma."

Elsa laughed, then set her sights on Simone. "You better come back for our next family supper."

"I'm sure she will," Slash said. "If Luciano doesn't invite her, I will."

Simone thanked Carrera for his hospitality

"I'm sorry to lose you as a watcher, but you're back where you belong," Carrera said. "I'm here if you need anything."

Slash grabbed her handbag, slid on her sunglasses. "Love you, husband." She kissed Carrera goodbye.

"Love you more, babe."

"Where are you two headed?" Elsa asked.

"Simone is training with the rescue team today," Slash replied.

Elsa's eyes lit up. "You are going to have so much fun, Simone."

Simone smiled. "It's been a while, so we'll see how much *fun* I have."

"Will she be rappelling out of the helicopter?" Elsa asked Slash.

"No, she won't," Simone replied, and everyone laughed. "That's definitely not happening today."

Slash followed Simone home. She dropped her suitcase in the foyer, hurried back outside, and into Slash's ALPHA SUV.

Simone's phone buzzed with an incoming text and a shiver skirted down her spine. *Be a boss lady.* She glanced at the text from her brother, Gary, as Slash drove of the neighborhood.

> Sis, we haven't seen you in f-o-r-e-v-e-r. Come for dinner. You pick a night and I'll make it work.

Relief washed over her and she replied.

> Starting a new work project today. Let me get back to you.

Then, her relief was quickly replaced with dread. What if the person who sent the threatening text was watching her? She turned to check.

Slash pulled onto the main road. "Looking for a tail?"

"Yeah," Simone replied.

"Rebel's in the black SUV on our left," Slash explained. "His wife, Brit, is in the back seat with binos."

"Wow, okay."

"There's another black SUV in front of us," Slash continued. "That's Dakota and Providence. She's driving. He's lookout. Prescott—he's on the rescue team—is driving his SUV, and his sister-in-law, Addison, is his lookout. She's an ALPHA Op and also on the rescue team. They're behind us. And if that's not enough protection, Hawk is flying an ALPHA helo for aerial surveillance, and Cooper's with him. Hawk and Prescott are brothers, and Hawk is married to Addison."

"This is crazy."

"We're a much more sophisticated group than in the beginning," Slash continued, "and super tight. It's definitely fam. You'll fit right in."

Excitement swept away the last remnants of fear and anxiety. Yes, it might take her a hot minute to find her footing, but she would. An entire organization rested on her finding The Bomb Maker and she would not let them down.

The convoy veered off the main road, then made several turns, finally driving onto a dirt road. They stopped at a large NO TRESPASSING sign. Five minutes passed before Slash's phone rang.

She answered, put the call on speaker.

"We've been cleared by Hawk," Dakota said.

All four vehicles continued onward. The woodsy area cleared and the dirt road turned into a paved one that led to a warehouse-looking building similar to ALPHA HQ, sans windows. Slash followed Dakota around back and stopped in front of a large hangar door. When everyone had rolled in, the giant door rose, revealing an oversized garage with a fleet of black SUVs. One by one, the vehicles pulled into the empty left lane. The drivers killed their engines, and the ALPHA Ops exited.

This moment felt surreal. Simone had imagined returning to ALPHA dozens of times, but she wasn't sure she could muster enough inner strength.

But I did, and I'm back.

Despite feeling elated, sorrow tinged her heart. She wouldn't be there if Frederica and her team were still alive.

The team made their way toward the entrance. One by one, they stood in front of the scanner. Each time the light flicked from red to green.

When it was Simone's turn, Dakota extended his hand. "Welcome to BLACK OPS, Red. It's great to have you back."

As she shook his hand, a sense of allegiance filled her soul.

"We'll scan your retina," Dakota explained.

Simone stood in front of the scanner, the light flashed bright, then went dark. After Dakota keyed in information on his phone, the door swung open.

She stepped out of the way while the Ops filed past, pausing to introduce themselves or welcome her into the group. There was a brief second when she wished she'd returned sooner, so she could have worked with Fred again, but that wasn't her path.

My time to return is now. I'm going to hunt down the monster I was too terrified to search for then.

The group moved as a pod, surrounding her like a newborn. Their faith in her buoyed her spirits. If *they* believed in her... she had better believe in herself.

As Brit made a pot of coffee, Providence gave Simone an unexpected hug. "Welcome back. We'll do whatever we can to ensure your success."

"Thank you," she replied.

Cooper Grant joined them, welcomed Simone with a warm

handshake before addressing Providence. "Did you bring a chip?"

Providence unearthed a small plastic container and a hypodermic needle, and Simone's pulse shot up. She hated needles.

"Is that for me?" Simone squeaked out.

"We might have a rabbit," a man called out as he approached, and everyone laughed.

"Nicholas Hawk." He shook her hand. "We got you. It's not gonna hurt a bit."

Addison joined them. "Red, welcome back to ALPHA. We are *not* injecting you with a chip in the middle of the break room." She shot her husband a smarmy look. "Troublemaker. We need her to solve this case, not run screaming from the building."

The group laughed as Slash put a comforting arm around her. "Let's head to the locker room."

As she and Slash made their way down the quiet hallway, Slash said, "This is the Black Site, also known as the Safe House. Down that hall are several private suites with bathrooms. There's a fully-stocked working kitchen and a rec room. Offices and two conference rooms are housed on the opposite side of the building. You'll see those later."

Slash stopped in front of the women's locker room. "Let's suit up for practice."

"Was the needle a joke?" Simone asked as they walked in.

"ALPHA Ops have chips in their necks. It's for our protection in case we're taken. It became policy after Cooper got kidnapped."

Slash brought her over to a locker. "Your gear."

Simone's locker was stocked with two pairs of camouflage shirts and fatigues, a three-pack of black socks, two black ski masks, an ankle holster, and a single shoulder holster. There was a go-bag and a duffle bag as well. She knelt to check the combat boots.

"How are these the right size?"

Slash waggled her eyebrows. "ALPHA knows all."

Simone grew quiet as she changed into training gear. Minutes later, she pulled her hair into a ponytail, wound it into a neat bun, and secured it with clips.

With her boots in hand, she joined Slash on the bench.

"How are you doing?" Slash asked.

"I'm ready to get started."

Providence walked in, the needle down by her side, but Simone spotted it right away. Her heart kicked up speed and the desire to bolt took hold, but she stayed seated on the bench.

Providence sat next to her, held up the needle. A microchip was floating in a tiny amount of fluid. "I insert this in the back of your neck, between the layers of skin. If you have sensitive skin, it might itch a little, but that'll go away."

Slash took her hand and Providence chuckled. "It's an insertion, not an injection."

"I don't like needles," Simone murmured.

"Let me tell you about training this morning," Slash said.

As Slash chatted away, Providence stood behind Simone. With a tender touch, she inserted the chip. Simone felt the brief stick of the needle.

"All done," Providence said. "You did great." She handed her a small tube of cream. "Use this if you itch." She stood. "I'm a phone call or a text away, for anything. What questions do you have for me?"

"Will I be assigned a laptop?"

"Great question. I was going to give you everything after training, but we can do it now."

"I'm heading outside," Slash said.

"I'll bring Red out in a few," Providence said.

Simone grabbed her go-bag, slung the duffle over her shoulder, and left the locker room with Providence. The hall was quiet, but when they turned the corner, the collection of voices grew louder, reaching a feverish pitch as they passed the break room. She glanced in. The group was still nestled in there, like a family at a holiday gathering.

But this was no holiday. This was Simone's much-needed second chance. The woman once known as Red felt like she'd come home. A surge of confidence spurred her forward.

In the conference room, a laptop, a computer bag, two Kevlar vests, and a double shoulder holster waited on the table. After they sat, Providence opened the laptop, typed in a temporary password, then slid over the laptop so Simone could change it.

"You'll have a partner *and* a mentor," Providence explained. "They're your first points of contact, but you can also reach out to me or Cooper. Since we don't know if there's a mole, keep your guard up."

"Of course," Simone replied.

"Slash wants to be your mentor. We think it's a great fit, but you have the final say."

"Slash is perfect."

"You'll meet your partner after training." Providence gestured to the Kevlar vests. "One is kept at ALPHA, one at your home. Since ALPHA is closed for now, keep both with you."

Simone nodded.

"And definitely wear one for training today." Providence unearthed a black essentials pouch from the go-bag. She withdrew several badges—ATF, DEA, FBI, DHS, CIA, and State Department, all with her photo.

"Your alias stayed the same," Providence said.

Adrenaline surged through her. Things were getting real. Like *really* real. She stared at the name on the government badge and a myriad of memories came flooding back.

"Joelle James." She hadn't said that name out loud in years.

"You'll need these." Providence set two weapons on the table. A Glock and a SIG SAUER.

All I have to do is take them and it's game on.

Simone pulled the Kevlar vest on, then the double shoulder holster. After checking both weapons for ammo, she secured them. "Now, I'm ready."

Providence escorted her to the back door. "You've got ear and eye protection in your duffle. Put them on before you head outside. I'll be working here all morning if anything comes up. The team is right through that door. Are you ready to get started?"

"Absolutely."

Providence wished her luck before walking away. Simone fitted on the muffs and eyewear, pushed open the fire door and walked outside.

The muted sound of multiple rounds sent excitement racing through her. She waited near the door and watched as Rebel's highly-skilled Operatives fired live rounds at targets.

Rebel acknowledged her with a nod, then held up his hand. The team stopped shooting. Guns were lowered, ear protectors removed. As Simone jogged toward them, butterflies zoomed in her tummy while her heart pounded loud and strong in her ears.

This was her chance for a do-over. She couldn't be more grateful or more determined to right so many wrongs by flushing out a killer.

~

LUCIANO

As far as Luciano was concerned, Simone was killing it. Rusty, yes, but after twenty minutes of focused effort, the change was impressive. She'd taken direction from Rebel and from Slash, put their suggestions into play, and by the time they finished, she was hitting the target like a pro.

More than her ability to take direction, she appeared cool under fire. That was something he'd been concerned about. Time would help her confidence. As her abilities improved, so would her belief in herself.

Though her beauty shone through, it was her effort and determination that kept his attention anchored on her. When target practice ended, they set down their weapons and protective gear, and ran in formation. In this portion of the training, she had no problem keeping up. When it came to sit-ups and push-ups, she was a beast.

She struggled with pull-ups, but with an assist from Prescott, she finished the reps.

Sin exited the building. "How's she doing?"

"Great."

"Do you think she'll take the case?"

"I do. She's motivated by the death of her friend." Luciano's phone buzzed and he read the text from his assistant.

"Do you think she'll work with you?" Sin asked.

"No other option," Luciano replied.

"You'll have to trust her."

Luciano gritted his teeth. He'd been trained *not* to trust by his father, then after his world had imploded, he trusted no one. Even now, he struggled to believe that anyone had his back.

After he replied to his assistant, a wind gust blew his hair every which way. In one fluid move, he raked his fingers through, and tamped it down.

"Have you found any more chatter about Haqazzii's terror cell?" Sin asked.

"No. You?"

"Nothing. We're sitting on a ticking time bomb. At some point, Carrera will have to share intel with the Director."

"That's gonna spin everyone up," Luciano said.

"No shit," Sin replied. "What choice do we have? If the terror cell blows up those buildings, it's another 9/11 all over again."

"Let's see how Simone and I do before we trigger a national panic."

As the training session came to an end, the two men retreated inside. Down the hall they strode, stopping in the break room.

"I've got a meeting with Dakota." Sin extended his hand. "Use any office here, except his."

Luciano shook it. "We won't work here. It puts everyone at risk."

"Your place?" Sin poured coffee into a mug.

"It's secure."

In silence, the men headed toward the offices. Luciano stopped in front of the conference room. "I'll wait in here. Who's bringing her in to me?"

"I will," Sin replied. "She'll want to shower and change before your meeting. Expect push-back."

"Why?"

"You're an outsider and an assassin."

A sly smile filled Luciano's face. "She'll be fine working with me."

"I wouldn't be so sure about that," Sin said before continuing on to Dakota's office.

I got this... and I got her too.

Luciano set down his computer bag. Seconds later, he was logged into Santini International and calling his assistant.

"Mr. Santini," Dominic answered. "We have a problem."

After listening, he asked a few questions, directed Dominic on how to handle it, and ended the call. Then, he turned his attention to his laptop, cloaking his Internet footprint, and jumping on the dark web.

"Come out and face the devil."

Luciano went on the hunt for Inferno531. He couldn't find any new posts, but there were several *about* Inferno531. Normally, he'd ask Teddy to do the Internet hunting, but he wasn't playing the Teddy card without consulting Simone.

Twenty minutes later, Sin appeared in the conference room doorway. "Ready to meet your new partner?"

A rush of adrenaline powered through him.

He offered a tight nod. Sin stepped in, leaving Simone standing in the doorway. The air turned frenetic.

Her beauty captivated him, her can-do attitude excited him. The intensity in her eyes spoke volumes. He'd made the right decision by telling her in advance. Surprising her would have been a mistake.

Unable to ignore the pull, he made his way toward her. If she accepted this gig, and he had every confidence she would, they'd be equal partners going forward. Rather than shake her hand, he curled his fingers around her arms.

"Hello, Simone." He pecked one cheek.

"Luciano," she replied as he kissed the other.

He relished her soft skin, her familiar and intoxicating aroma. He heard Sin talking, but he couldn't engage. Staring into Simone's eyes was the best medicine for his suffering soul. His connection with her was unlike anything he'd ever experienced. A powerful, invisible force he couldn't deny.

"Red," Sin began.

"Yes," she replied, her attention still locked on Luciano.

Dakota, Providence, and Cooper entered the room, severing their connection.

After joining them at the table, Providence set a bottle of chilled water in front of Simone. "How was training?"

Simone's smile sent a burst of energy through him. "Great. I need target practice, I'm going to hit the gym harder, but I loved it."

"Good to hear," Dakota said.

"Red," Cooper said, "The Bomb Maker case is yours, if you're up to working it."

She glanced over at Luciano. "Absolutely."

"Normally, you'd have the full support of our internal Internet Team," Providence explained, "but we're concerned this could be an inside job, so we think it would be best if you partnered with someone *outside* the organization."

"That makes sense," Simone replied.

"Luciano is well connected," Sin said. "We think he's the best choice."

Simone slid her gaze to his. "Since he's here, I'll assume he has access to ALPHA."

I do.

"He has access to the Safe House but not to our website." Dakota said.

I've got that too.

"Only you have access to ALPHAnet," Providence explained.

"I'm in, one-hundred percent." Simone arched an eyebrow at him. "What do you think, Luciano?"

He appreciated that she wanted his input. The atmosphere was solemn, too solemn, so he shot her a smile. "I think we're gonna kick The Bomb Maker's ass and make his life a living hell."

She smiled back, and his world shifted a little. Never before had a lover been his work partner. New territory for him. But he had every confidence they'd find their way.

"Excellent," Dakota said.

"Luciano, can you drive Red home?" Providence asked.

"Of course." He shook their hands, waited for them to leave, and shut the door.

Alone with Simone.

Something that was fast-becoming his addiction.

He sat back down and their eyes met. So much energy passed between them. He wanted to kiss her hello, tell her how much he admired her inner strength, and how he couldn't wait to massage away her aches from training, and love her all night long.

Control, Luciano.

Instead, he said, "You killed it at training this morning."

"Nothing like jumping into the deep end." She extracted a small tube of cream from her handbag. "I'm being tracked." She set the item on the table. "Can you put this on my neck. I'm sure the spot is red. It's itching like crazy."

What the hell.

He stared at her. "Tracked by whom?"

"ALPHA. All Ops have chips in their necks. It's for our safety. That's what they tell us anyway."

With a tender touch, he moved her hair away, examined her neck. A circle of red surrounded a tiny pin prick. Resisting the urge to kiss her skin, he gently rubbed in the cream. While he *shouldn't* be having these types of thoughts, he was. And he wasn't going to fight himself on them. It had been years since he'd thought of another woman besides his beloved Linda.

"Does it look okay?" she asked.

"All good," he replied. "Are you still at Carrera's?"

"No, I'm back home." She tucked her hair behind her ear. "I don't think we should work here. It puts the group at risk. When we caravanned out, each driver had a lookout. It was crazy."

"They're in a tough spot because they don't know who they can trust."

"They can trust each other."

"Have you seen this group? They aren't individuals, they're a pod."

Her laughter touched his heart. "What's the plan?"

"We should work at my home," he replied. "It's secure—"

"We'll start there tomorrow." She opened her laptop. "Let's stay here today." She got busy typing, then glared at the screen. "I can't get into ALPHA's website."

"Maybe I can help," he said.

"I don't think you're supposed to see—"

He opened his laptop, logged in, and spun it around. "I'm already in."

Her eyes widened. "They said you don't have access—"

"Don't believe everything you hear." He shot her a smile, and damn if she didn't smile back.

She moved to the other side of the conference table, so she had her back against the wall, then pulled out the chair next to her.

"For me?" he asked.

She shot him a smarmy look. "You catch on fast."

He moved beside her, took her laptop, and did some troubleshooting. He isolated the problem, then asked her to try again. She got in.

"Nice." She toggled around. "This looks completely different from the last time I had access."

He laid out the map he'd taken from the terrorist in London. "A gift from a Haqazzii terrorist."

After reviewing the map, she said, "I hear they're very generous gift-givers. Did he give you his life too?"

"No. I took that."

Once again, she eyed the circled buildings, then shook her head. "This is bad... and a lot of pressure."

"We got this."

"Are you always this cocky?"

"Always," he replied.

She stayed focused on him for an extra beat before eyeing her laptop. "I'm running a report on all ALPHA employees who worked here five years ago when The Bomb Maker took out the first team, then I'll cross-check it against current employees."

She got busy, then glanced up. "How 'bout you?"

"I got accepted into a chat group with supporters and sympathizers of the Haqazzii terror cell." He toggled to the dark web, then over to the popular website.

She glanced over, did a double take. "That site sells illegal weapons."

He turned the laptop so she could see. "Firearms, explosives, bomb-making kits, training courses. It's a magnet for haters of democracy and capitalism." He logged into the account and a different screen populated. "This is where I found out The Bomb Maker is back."

"Show me."

He went searching for the thread, but couldn't find it. "Sometimes they're removed," he explained. "It was written by Inferno531."

She pulled the laptop closer, read several of the threads. "Such hate out there. Why can't we all get along?"

He pressed his mouth to her ear. "What would I do in my spare time if I'm not taking out the bad actors?"

Her breath hitched.

He loved how she responded to him, and he didn't give a damn that he wasn't being professional. He hadn't felt this way in a long, long time.

"Have dinner with me," he murmured.

"A working dinner?"

"If that gets you to a 'yes', then yes, a working dinner."

"I'll think about it."

He liked watching her work, her fingers flying over the keyboard, her attention laser-focused.

"Luciano, work," she scolded.

"Sì, signora capo," he said. "Yes, boss lady."

A smile lifted the corners of her mouth, but she said nothing more. They worked until someone knocked on the door.

"Come in," Luciano said.

Providence entered with a large, brown bag. "Lunch, courtesy of Mama Maria's."

"Thank you." Luciano pulled out his wallet.

"It's on ALPHA." Providence set down the bag. "Most of us are heading out and will be working from home. Red, I feel like the team's abandoning you on your first day. If you need anything, please call."

Simone nodded. "It hasn't sunk in yet, but it's great to be back."

"Are you finding your way around ALPHAnet okay?" Providence asked.

"No problem."

Providence regarded them. "I'm a phone call away, but I know you two are going to rock this."

"Absolutely," Simone replied. "I'll keep you posted."

In the doorway, Providence said, "Luciano, do you have an ALPHA SUV?"

"Hawk jacked up my Range Rover to ALPHA specs," he replied. "I'll make sure the hangar door is closed."

On a nod, she wished them luck and shut the door.

"We don't need luck," he said.

"No, we don't," Simone replied. "We need grit—"

"Cunning and ruthlessness," he bit out. "We need to flush out this monster and rip his heart out of his chest."

"Then, shove it down his throat," she replied.

"We're gonna have some fun, you and me."

She flashed him a smile. "We sure as hell are."

15

SIMONE'S BROTHER

SIMONE

Simone was ready to rock it out. She was fired up from training, but she'd be sore as hell tomorrow. Didn't matter. She'd push herself to ensure she was at the top of her game. ALPHA depended on her. Luciano was counting on her to deliver.

And she was *not* going to let them down.

There was a time when she lived for the challenge of the chase. She loved hunting down the monsters, forcing them out of hiding, and moving in for an arrest.

As she worked alongside Luciano, a different set of emotions took hold. Her body thrummed with energy. Though they were laser-focused, she was tuned in to his every move. And she found herself mirroring him.

He crossed his legs. She'd cross hers. He sipped the sparkling water. She'd drain her glass. Though she could have been annoyed with herself, she wasn't. She was drawn to him in every way that mattered... and even those that didn't. He cleared his throat and she fought the urge to clear hers.

He broke the silence with, "Not clearing yours?"

"Busted." She loved that he was as aware of her every action. "I'm *not* usually a copycat."

"I like that we're in sync," he murmured, then he pulled her hair aside and examined the back of her neck.

His tender touch ignited her passion and touched the deepest part of her heart.

"Does it hurt?"

"No," she whispered surprised by the ache in her voice.

"Did the itching stop?"

"Yes."

Streams of excitement flitted through her. He leaned close, pressed his lips to the back of her neck, and kissed her.

And her engine kicked on with a burst of adrenaline.

"Tutto meglio," he murmured. "All better."

"You shouldn't be kissing me," she whispered.

"Do you want me to stop?"

She *didn't* want him to stop. She loved his touch, craved his attention. But she had to ratchet it back.

"It's not professional."

"Do you want me to stop, Simone?" he repeated.

She melted from the way he pronounced her name. She imagined staring into his beautiful hazel eyes and kissing him. Heat spread from her chest to her neck, then settled in her cheeks. She never got flustered, but he was turning her inside out in the best of ways.

Of course she didn't want him to stop. She didn't want things to become complicated either. An office fling was the best way to ruin a great working relationship.

"I don't know," she murmured.

"Look at me."

She did. And the need to pull him into her arms took her breath away in a whoosh of anticipation.

"Are you playing with my emotions?" he asked.

His trust issues were beyond anything she could comprehend. Someone must've hurt him bad. Real bad.

"Of course not," she replied. "Why would you ask me that?"

"It's nothing."

"Are you playing with *my* emotions?" she asked.

"Never," he replied.

She peered into his eyes wondering what demons haunted him. Rather than push for answers, she dragged her gaze back to her laptop, refocusing her attention on the long list of ALPHA employees.

There were twelve people who had been with ALPHA during the first attack that were still working there today. She could eliminate Dakota and Slash, but she still needed to vet ten employees.

Throughout the afternoon, Luciano's phone buzzed with incoming texts or pinged with a never-ending string of emails. But he stayed focused on his search.

At six o'clock, as they were packing up, she asked, "Are all those messages from work?"

"I haven't looked."

"Aren't you concerned?"

"I'm concerned The Bomb Maker is going to take out those federal buildings and kill thousands of innocents. Santini International can't fall apart in a day. Most times, it's little fires. A million unexpected things. I've got smart, hard-working employees—"

"So you trust them?"

His eyebrow arched ever-so-slightly, then his cheek muscles ticked in his jaw.

Of course he doesn't.

"I expect them to do their jobs." He slid his laptop into his leather satchel. "Are you free for dinner?"

"I'm having dinner with my brother and his husband," she replied. When disappointment flashed in his eyes, she blurted, "Come with. My brother and his husband will love you."

"Another time."

For reasons she couldn't begin to understand, she didn't want him to spend his evening alone. "No, Luciano, you're coming with me."

"Grazie, Simone."

In the hallway, they were met with an eerie silence. Side by side, they made their way through the cavernous building and into the hangar where he led her to his Range Rover. After driving out, he tapped an app on his phone, then waited for the giant door to close before leaving.

The gray autumn day had bowed to dusk.

"What did you find out today?" he asked as he turned onto the main road.

"Don't you need directions?"

"I'm stopping at my house for wine," he replied. "Do you want to ask your brother—"

"It's fine, really," Simone insisted. Plus, she wanted to see the look on Gary's face when she introduced him to Luciano.

Within minutes, he pulled up to the iron gates of his property. The security guard greeted him, then asked for an eight-digit code, which Luciano gave him. The guard thanked him, then opened the gates.

As Luciano drove up the tree-lined driveway, she asked what the code was.

"If you're forcing me here at gunpoint, I use one code. If everything is good, I use a different one."

"Which did you use with me?"

"If four, armed security guards meet us at the fountain, you'll have your answer." In the darkening car, he flashed her a smile.

And damn if she didn't find herself smiling back.

As she expected, they were alone at the fountain. He

ushered her inside, then led her into the kitchen where Louis was working away, a pretty Black woman relaxing at the island with a glass of wine.

"Mr. Santini," Louis said. "I hadn't heard from you, so I'm making pan-roasted Halibut with a citrus beurre blanc, Inca red quinoa, and broccolini."

Simone's heart fell. Broccolini was the vegetable she'd served Frederica. The reminder felt like a sucker-punch to her gut and she flew out of the room. In the privacy of the bathroom, tears blurred her vision.

Get it together.

No matter how hard she tried, they flowed down her cheeks.

Tap-tap.

"Simone, you okay?" Luciano asked from the hallway.

She blotted her cheeks with a tissue, opened the door.

Concern filled his face. "What's going on?"

Feeling embarrassed, she said, "It's nothing."

He hitched a brow. "Simone."

"It's stupid."

He pulled her in his strong arms, held her close, and caressed her back. "Dimmi. Tell me."

Feeling safe in his embrace, she urged herself to tell him. Heaving in a breath, she peered into his eyes.

"Fred came over for dinner before her mission and I served broccolini." Another wave of sorrow hit. "It's stupid, I know."

"I got you." He cradled her in his arms for the longest moment while she clung to him. "Grief sneaks in like a monster under our bed." He dropped a loving kiss on her forehead. "Do you want to go upstairs and have yourself a good ugly-cry?"

She laughed. "Those are the worst... and the best." Standing on her toes, she dropped a light kiss on his lips. "Thank you. I feel like an idiot—"

"No. Never." His encouraging smile helped chase away the sorrow.

After chugging in a deep breath, she said, "I'm okay."

Back in the kitchen, he made introductions.

"Louis, Therese, this is Simone." Simone shook their hands. "Chef Louis is the best in the DMV and his wife, Therese, is my lead attorney at Santini International."

"It's a pleasure," Therese said.

"Good to meet you," Simone replied.

"I'm having dinner with Simone and her family," Luciano explained.

A smile danced in Louis's eyes as he glanced over at Simone. "Very good, Mr. Santini. The meal will keep for you."

"You and Therese enjoy," Luciano said before disappearing into the next room, returning with a Santini gift bag. "Do your brother and brother-in-law drink?" he asked Simone.

"Wine with dinner," she replied. "An occasional drink before."

"Perfect," he replied.

After saying their goodbyes, he escorted her to the foyer elevator. He tapped the down button, the single door slid open.

"Why are we going downstairs?" Simone asked.

"We're taking my McLaren."

When she worked at Mitus, the underground garage was packed with twenty cars. Tonight, she counted twelve.

"You're a collector," she said.

"I have a few," he replied.

His luxury collection included the Range Rover, a Mercedes-Maybach, a Rolls Royce, an Audi, a Porsche, a BMW, and a McLaren. He opened the passenger door of his sports car, then waited until she was tucked in.

After shutting her door, he slid behind the wheel, drove toward the exit.

"I'm in the Batmobile," she said.

"If you see the Batman logo in the sky, we've gotta change our plans."

She smiled, grateful for the playfulness.

As he sped down his private drive toward the gates, he asked, "Is this a date or are we two working professionals having dinner?"

"What about friends? Could we be two friends having dinner?"

He stopped the car. "Is that what you want?"

She stared into his eyes. Even in the darkened car, they burned like a million suns, the intensity of his gaze searing her.

"What would you do if we were just friends or coworkers?" she asked.

"Nothing," he replied. "But if we were on a date, I would do this." He wrapped his large hand around her thigh sending zings of desire shooting through her. "I would tell you how beautiful you look, and I would do this..." He cupped her cheek with his other hand, leaned close, and dropped a tender kiss on her lips. Then, another before he gripped the steering wheel with both hands.

The air turned volcano hot around her, the need to touch him, kiss him overwhelmed her thoughts. She *should* keep things professional, but she burned for him in a way that had her buzzing with hope.

She was waging war with herself.

My head or my heart? Or is this just a sexual fling?

"Let me know what you decide." He drove to the gates, they swung open, and he pulled through. He rolled down the window, said goodbye to his guard, and headed toward Tysons.

"Your brother lives in Monarch Towers," he said. "Is that where we're headed?"

"You did your homework."

"Of course." After a beat, he said, "Tell me what you learned today."

I learned I could be on a date with Luciano Santini.

"There are twelve employees who worked for ALPHA, then and now. Seven Ops, four from the Internet team, and one admin."

"What does the Internet team do?" He stopped for a red light.

"Research on perps, suspects, witnesses. We also have a Forensics team."

"What about people who interviewed for ALPHA, but didn't get offered the position or turned it down?"

"Z and Providence could help with that."

The light turned green, but he didn't move. Just then, someone flew through the intersection and almost T-boned the car in the other lane.

"That woulda hurt," she said. "How did you know to wait?"

"Elsa taught me to drive," he said as he hit the gas. "She'd tell me to wait, then she'd say, 'Look first, Lulu.' As a teen, I didn't listen to her, until I almost got hit. Now, I wait."

"Great advice." Simone's phone rang. It was her brother and she answered, put the phone on speaker. "Hey, I'm running late."

"Totally fine," Gary said. "I thought maybe you forgot."

"I'm bringing you a surprise."

"Wonderful," Gary said. "I hope it's something delicious to drink."

"We'll be there in ten."

"We?" Gary blurted. "Simone, who—"

"Love you." Simone hung up, and Luciano chuckled.

"If he wants to hang with his sis, you just sent him into a tailspin."

"He'll be fine." After a pause, she continued. "Given what I know from being a watcher, if I reported questionable behavior, the prospective employee *wouldn't* get called in to interview. I'm pretty sure they only bring in people they're excited about hiring."

"What about people who got fired from ALPHA?" he prodded.

"You ask good questions."

Luciano pulled into Monarch Towers and parked. They exited the sports car, he pulled the gift bag, and they made their way toward the brightly-lit lobby.

"For the people who got fired, I'll see if there's a report I can run," she replied. "If there isn't, I'll ask Z and Providence."

"Nice work."

"What did you learn today?" she asked him.

"I found a comment in a different chat room," he murmured. "It said, 'The Bomb Maker and Friends are unstoppable. Epic destruction on victory day.'"

"Friends?" she asked. They entered the building and she lowered her voice. "He's taunting law enforcement."

"Law enforcement doesn't know he's back," he murmured. "He's taunting ALPHA."

An older couple joined them at the elevator bank. "Hi, there," said the woman. "Do you live in the building?"

"I'm visiting my brother," Simone replied. "How 'bout you?"

"We're on the penthouse floor," said the man.

"That's where my brother lives. Gary Redding."

They broke into grins. "We're buying one of their puppies," said the woman. "Have you seen them?"

"We're about to," Luciano replied.

The elevator doors opened and the men waited while the women stepped into the cab.

The man regarded Luciano. "You look familiar. Are you a celebrity or a sports figure?"

"I'm not," Luciano replied.

Yes, you are.

If he wasn't going to mention his company or his top-shelf spirits, neither would she. Clearly, he liked his privacy.

The elevator doors opened, everyone filed out. The couple stopped at their home. "Enjoy those puppies," said the woman.

They continued on until Simone stopped in front of her brother's front door.

Seconds after ringing the doorbell, Gary swung the door open and grinned. "There's my baby!" When he saw Luciano, his eyes turned full-moon large, and he gasped. "Mr. Santini."

Bruce appeared cradling a puppy. "This is for you, Simone, honey." He regarded Luciano. "Would you like a puppy too?"

∽

LUCIANO

Luciano didn't like that Simone had gone silent about their evening. He *wanted* tonight to be a date. To make matters worse, the guilt he carried had only intensified as his interest in Simone grew. It made his head ache.

As he entered the two-story penthouse, the last thing he wanted to do was ask for an aspirin.

"This is Luciano Santini. This is my brother, Gary, and his husband, Bruce."

After exchanging handshakes, Bruce offered the pup to Simone. "This is little-no-name number four."

Simone's joyous laugh made Luciano smile.

As she cuddled the tiny black French bulldog, Bruce said, "I think someone has a new roommate."

"Please, Lord," Gary said to Luciano. "Let it be you."

Everyone laughed, the ice was broken, and Luciano relaxed. It had been years since he'd met a woman's family.

A lifetime ago.

While Gary stood there starry-eyed, Bruce welcomed them

into their home. Luciano admired the modern furniture, first-class all the way. The living room was furnished with opposing white sofas covered in light gray pillows. On the far wall hung a large, framed painting while a baby grand filled the corner near the floor-to-ceiling windows.

"Your home is beautiful," Luciano said.

"Thank you, Mr. Santini," Gary eked out.

"Luciano."

"Uh-huh," Gary said.

"Who wants a drink?" Bruce asked.

"Me, for sure," Gary replied.

"This is for you." Luciano held out the bag.

Gary took it, peaked inside, and pulled out a bottle of Santini Chianti. "Thank you. We love your Chianti and hope you come out with an entire line of reds."

"Or a chardonnay," Bruce interjected as he extracted the bottle of Santini Whiskey from the gift bag. "Much appreciated. You didn't have to."

With puppy number four in her arms, Simone hugged both men.

"Who wants a glass of something?" Bruce asked.

"Whiskey, please," Luciano said.

"I'd love a glass of wine," Simone said, "but you can save Luciano's chianti for a special occasion."

"This *is* a special occasion," Gary said. "You brought Mr. Santini home with you. I wish you'd told me. I would have put on a Santini Original."

Bruce laid a comforting hand on Gary's shoulder. "Honey, he's just a man."

"Oh, please," Gary said. "He's a designer god. An industry icon, and he's standing in my living room."

Bruce laughed.

"Where are all the puppies?" Simone asked when Bruce walked into the kitchen.

Luciano meandered toward the windows while Simone chatted with her brother. The living space was open and airy with a minimalist vibe. The panoramic view was stunning. Lights dotted the horizon toward the east and the north. As he stared into the night, he wondered what life would be like if he lived in a home like this. His had been a refuge, but also a self-imposed hell.

Simone sidled over, the adorable dog still in her arms, and smiled up at him. "Thanks for being here. I didn't think my brother would be so weird."

"He's fine," Luciano replied.

Wasn't the first time someone had reacted like that to him. Wouldn't be the last. People got tongue-tied around him, so he did his best to dispel their nerves.

Bruce appeared with a stemless wine glass for Simone and a lowball glass of whiskey for him. Gary joined them.

"Welcome to our home," Gary said. They clinked glasses, sipped their beverages.

"We're having filet mignon," Bruce said.

Luciano slid his gaze to Simone who remained silent. He was surprised they didn't remember she didn't eat red meat.

"Let's go visit the babies." Bruce led the way up the stairs to the second floor.

Gary opened a closed door to puppy mayhem. They were wrestling while Mom watched. One of the dogs raced over, yapping, its tail whipping back and forth.

Luciano's phone hadn't stopped buzzing. While he didn't want to be rude, he needed to see what was going on.

"Excuse me," he said. "I need to check on something at work."

"You're welcome to step out," Bruce said.

Luciano scanned his work emails, then read the text from Sin.

> Call me when you can

> Later

He pocketed his phone, glanced up to find Simone sitting on the floor, the rowdy pups crawling all over her. Gary was beside her while Bruce sat in a chair. He paused to appreciate the joy on her face, the way her smile touched her eyes, and how something so simple as animals could bring her such joy. In that moment, he envied her.

"Luciano, come sit with us," Simone said.

He crouched down and the dogs pounced on him, the mom too. They were small balls of energy, and he wondered if he would have caved and bought a dog for his children. While the moment should have been filled with laughter and joy, his heart felt heavy.

As if sensing his pain, she nudged him back. "Sit on your butt, Luciano."

"Oh, dear Lord, don't talk to him like that," Gary blurted.

She picked up two frisky puppies, placed them in his lap. One climbed up him and stared into his eyes, barked once, then bounded off to get a toy. As he played with them, he couldn't help but smile. They were adorable, naïve, and filled with boundless energy. When puppy-time ended, they returned to the first floor.

Back in the kitchen, Gary and Bruce got busy. The filets were removed from the sous vide, then Bruce seared them in a buttered cast iron skillet. The sautéed green beans were dished out along with the twice baked garlic potatoes.

He liked that they didn't re-route them into the dining room simply because he was there. After slicing into the steak, which was cooked to perfection, he complimented them. They beamed like they'd painted the Sistine Chapel.

"Simone, don't you like the filet?" Gary asked.

"I don't eat red meat."

Bruce opened the fridge and pulled out a glass container. "I made breaded chicken breasts last night." Two minutes later, he traded the red meat for the warmed chicken.

"This is delicious," she said. "Thank you."

The conversation moved from the puppies to Gary's software company, then Bruce asked how long he and Simone had been going out."

"We... um... so, it's—" Simone stuttered. "Complicated."

"This is our second date," Luciano said. "Our first date was on my yacht, the Omega." He said it like it was fact, like speaking his intention would turn it into a reality.

All eyes on him.

Is that what I want? A relationship with Simone?

As he and Simone connected across the table, they shared a smile.

I do want that, and I'll deal with the guilt later.

"Mom and Dad invited us to South Carolina for Thanksgiving," Gary said.

"Are you going?" she asked.

"We can't," Bruce explained. "We're spending Thanksgiving with my sister and her family in New York."

"Frenchie too," Gary added. "All her pups, but number four, are spoken for."

"We're gonna keep him," Bruce added. "Unless you want her."

"No to the puppy," Simone replied, "and I'm not spending Thanksgiving in South Carolina."

That's great. I'm spending Thanksgiving alone.

"Simone, spend the holiday with me," Luciano said. "It's at Carrera's this year."

Silence.

Her eyebrows jutted into her head. "What was that?" she murmured.

"How wonderful!" Bruce exclaimed.

More silence, until Gary said, "Simone, honey, what do you say?"

"To whom?"

"To Luciano for the invitation."

"Okayyyyy," Simone replied. "Sure."

"Thank you for inviting her," Gary said.

But Luciano couldn't miss the subtle curve in her lips and the smile in her eyes. No denying she liked his invitation. Now, if only he could get her to admit her feelings. That would help him in more ways than she could ever know.

When they finished dinner, they thanked their hosts, and left.

As they rode the elevator down to the first floor, she said, "You don't have to spend Thanksgiving with—"

He snaked his arms around her waist, pulled her flush against him, and kissed the hell out of her. A kiss that let her know *exactly* what he thought of her. She hugged him tight, slid delicate fingers into his hair, and kissed him back with so much passion his cock took notice.

A lot of notice.

When the doors slid open, she broke away, and released a sigh. "Damn, you can kiss."

He clasped her hand—because it was the *most* professional thing he could do to—and strode to his car. Once there, he opened her door, sandwiched her face in his hands, and kissed her again. Only, this time, he kept his touch light, his kiss gentle.

And she groaned into him, but she didn't deepen their embrace. After several tender pecks, she pulled away.

"This is breaking so many rules," she said.

"ALPHA has rules?" he murmured while nibbling her ear.

"Ohgod, you're making me crazy." She moaned. "My rules. I don't date men I work with."

"Well, Simone Redding, it's time to try something different."

"Why's that?"

"You're a smart, determined, beautiful, hard-working woman. Have you ever been married?"

"No."

"Are you on any dating sites?"

"No."

"Do you date?"

"Not much."

"Maybe you should take advantage of the low-hanging fruit." He pointed to himself. "I'm interested, and I'm the only man standing here. You could do worse, you know?"

Her smile split her face, then she laughed. "You're an assassin. What's worse than that?"

"An asshole."

She laughed. Hard.

They got in the SUV and he returned Sin's call.

"Simone is with me. You're on speaker."

"Someone came to my office today," Sin began. "He wasn't sure he needed a fixer, but he didn't want to go to the police. You both need to hear his story. Come to my office tomorrow at four."

Luciano glanced at Simone. She nodded.

"We'll be there." Luciano hung up, headed out.

Once again, he wrapped a possessive hand around her thigh. If she didn't like it, she could remove it or cut if off. Either would get her message across. Fortunately, for him, she did neither. To his surprise, she covered his hand with hers and wove her fingers between his.

Baby steps worked for him. This was all new territory for him.

All new territory.

He pulled into her driveway, killed the engine, and walked her to the front door.

"I want to invite you in," she whispered as she leaned up and kissed him goodbye, "but my first day back at ALPHA can't include sex with my new partner."

He kissed her cheek and murmured, "As you wish," then kissed her other. "I'll pick you up tomorrow at three-thirty."

"I can meet you—"

"Let's do this my way. Yes?"

She offered him a little smile. "Yes."

"Sognami, bella Simone. Dream of me, beautiful Simone."

One small step at a time.

This wasn't a sprint. This was his life. And hers.

Maybe even... ours.

16

ALPHA 2.0

SIMONE

At six in the morning, Simone woke with a start. Her heart was racing, her thoughts hazy. Someone was trying to kill Luciano, but she couldn't help him. He was being held by his ankles from a building rooftop. Burning up, she threw back the covers and stared at the ceiling.

That was terrifying.

Pushing out of bed, she dragged herself into the bathroom to get ready. Forty minutes later, she was sitting in her home office sipping coffee. After logging into ALPHA, she picked the first name on her list of possible suspects.

Time to do a deep dive.

Nowadays, most people posted their lives on social media. While an ALPHA Op wouldn't post how much they hated their top-secret job or their coworkers, they might post something about their views on the government, politics, or even law enforcement that could offer up a clue. It was like trudging through sludge without the luxury of time.

As she worked, she drained her coffee mug, refilled it, then drained it again. Her stomach growled and she glanced at the clock.

It was eleven-thirty.

That felt like ten minutes.

She made herself oatmeal with blueberries and walnuts, then returned to her office where a text from Cooper waited.

> Check email. Call if you want to discuss

She opened her email, skimmed, then clicked on the one from forensics. As she read the report, anger burned its way to her guts. The bomb-making materials that killed Frederica and her team were the same ones that took out Simone's team. This confirmed The Bomb Maker was back.

Her phone buzzed with an incoming call. "Good morning, Cooper."

"I see you're in ALPHAnet."

She ran her fingertip over the tracker in her neck. "How?"

"The system is much more sophisticated than it used to be," he explained. "I can see who's logged in and what they're working on."

Seemed like Big Brother was watching a little too closely for her liking, but she was not about to push back on day two. On day one, she'd barely avoided sleeping with her partner. She wasn't going to get into it with her new boss.

"I know it's intrusive," Cooper said. "It's designed to create a teaming environment. You can see others in the system too."

After he explained how to do it, she went looking for Luciano, but there was nothing.

"I've got several updates," Cooper continued.

"Great," she replied.

"The Bomb Maker rented a furnished house. The arson detective told me there was nothing personal in the home beyond the blowup dolls and some bomb-making supplies.

Like the first time, he set a trap, knowing we'd track him there."

"I need to follow up with the homeowner," she said.

"I spoke with her. I'll read you my notes. Hold a minute." After a pause, he returned. "She said she rented it to a person named Pat Smith. The homeowner knew nothing about him or her."

"How did she get the rent money?"

"Cash through the mail."

"Fingerprints? A return address"

"Neither. She deposited the money, tossed the envelope."

Simone's hope fizzled. *Another dead end.*

"There are ten ALPHA employees who've been with the group for the past five years," Simone said. "I'm vetting everyone but Dakota and Slash, but I'm having trouble believing this is an inside job."

"Same," Cooper replied, "but both times, The Bomb Maker knew we were moving in for an arrest."

"What about someone who got fired from ALPHA?" Simone pressed. "Someone with a grudge?"

"That makes more sense. Continue investigating current employees while I ask around."

"Would Z know?" Simone asked.

"Who?" Cooper asked.

Oh, crap.

"What did I say?" she covered.

"It sounded like Zee."

"I meant Dakota. Would Dakota know?"

"I'll check." Cooper ended the call.

Cooper doesn't know about Z?

Rather than berate herself for mentioning him, she jumped back into work.

At three-thirty, her doorbell rang. She'd eliminated a

female Op who'd been with ALPHA since its inception, a male Operative, and a woman on the Internet team.

Seven to go.

Back on the first floor, she glanced through the living room window. Luciano's Rolls Royce was parked out front. Excitement flitted through her. She opened the door and her heart skipped a beat. Luciano stood there with his hand in his pants pocket looking runway-ready.

"Hello, Simone."

His husky voice, paired with the irresistible way he said her name, hummed through her. How could one man undo her so easily? She steeled her spine.

Get real. This is work.

"Time got away from me. Come in while I change."

He stepped inside, shut the door.

Everything Luciano magnified a thousand-fold. His scent—a mix of soap and coffee—had her breathing deep. He looked phenomenal in his dark suit, white shirt, no tie. Like every other time, she peeked at his chest while her fingers tingled to caress his tanned skin.

But it was the intensity in his gaze, his sophisticated demeanor, and the power he wielded that had her biting back a moan.

"I left my laptop open if you want to read my notes." She headed upstairs.

"Can I watch?"

She turned. "Watch?"

"You change."

Her smile stayed with her until she entered her bedroom. Off came her shirt and yoga pants. As she stood in her walk-in closet staring at her suits, she imagined him coming in, kissing her shoulder, turning her toward him. They'd kiss, fall into bed, make love for hours—

Blinking away the fantasy, she slipped into a white shirt,

dressed in a black pantsuit, then pulled on her holster. In the bathroom, she freshened her blush and lipstick, ran her fingers through her hair, and hurried out.

As she passed her home office, she spied him at her desk, a mug in his hand. He looked like he belonged there.

I've lost it.

A billionaire who lives in a multi-million-dollar mansion does not belong in Normalville.

His gaze found hers and she smiled.

"Nice," he said.

"Slow progress on the case, but—"

"I'm talking about our clothes."

Since he'd given her permission to check him out, she raked her gaze over him. He wore his designer clothing like a second skin. He tossed her a nod and she glanced down.

"Ohgod, what is wrong with me?" She'd dressed in black and white, just like him. "I'll change."

"You look perfect. We need to go."

She sidled close and his musky scent filled her, his intense energy rolling off him in thunderous waves, sending a shiver of delight cascading through her. She logged out of ALPHA, closed her laptop. Down the stairs to the first floor they went, his power seeping into her every pore, touching the depths of her soul.

Outside, at the Rolls Royce, Luciano said, "Simone Redding, Stuart Fletcher."

"Mr. Fletcher."

"Ma'am."

Into the car they went. As Stuart pulled away, Luciano said, "Develin and Associates."

"Yes, sir." Stuart raised the privacy screen.

"You've been busy," Luciano said.

"I'm examining every Op," she said. "So far, nothing stands out. I asked Cooper for a list of people who got fired from

ALPHA and I made the mistake of suggesting he check with Z—"

"Mistake?"

"Cooper doesn't know about Z, which surprised me. He manages the Ops."

"Can you contact Z directly?"

Simone pulled out her phone, typed out a text to Z.

> I need your help

> ...

> See you in ten

She showed the text to Luciano. "Did you know?"

"No," he said. "I expect the worst, so I'm never surprised when it happens."

Interesting.

"You don't like him?" she asked.

"He sent you to spy on me, so, no, he's not my favorite person."

"You should be thanking him," Simone said dryly.

"Why's that?"

"The night we met, you got yourself a sweet blowjob."

A rumbling growl shot out of him. "I'll be sure to mention that."

She bit back a smile.

Stuart parked in Sin's private lot behind his building in Georgetown. They went inside, rode upstairs to Develin & Associates. Sin's assistant, Erica, escorted them to Sin's office.

Knock-knock.

"Come in," said Sin.

Erica opened the door and they entered his spacious office. "Can I get anyone a beverage?"

"Sparkling waters," Sin said, and Erica hurried out.

Sin and Z rose from the conference room table. Simone shook their hands.

"Good to see you again, Z," she said.

"Congratulations on your promotion," he replied. "ALPHA is where you need to be."

Z extended his hand to Luciano. "No hard feelings, Mr. Santini."

Luciano accepted the handshake. "It's only business, no?"

Sin's wife, Evangeline, joined them.

Sin's gaze softened. A look passed between husband and wife. It was quick, but Simone caught it. Like a silent language between soulmates.

"I asked Evangeline to join us," Sin said as his wife eased down at the conference table. "Evan, please."

"Simone," Evangeline began, "if The Bomb Maker has access to ALPHAnet, he's watching to see who's working the case. That makes you vulnerable. I want to help. Whatever you need. Our site is secure, and I'm available twenty-four-seven."

"Thank you. I appreciate that. Just to be safe, I'll keep my notes offline."

"Can you manage the case without writing anything down?" Z asked.

"No," Simone replied. "I'm not you, Z."

Luciano and Sin laughed.

"No, you're not," Luciano said under his breath.

"I'll get you access here," Evangeline said, "and I'll create a text thread where we can talk securely."

Erica returned with a rolling cart carrying small bottles of sparkling water, a coffee carafe, glasses, mugs, cream and sugar. She left the cart nearby, shut the door behind her.

Evangeline rose, poured coffee into two mugs, added a trickle of cream to one, and returned to the table. She placed the black coffee in front of Sin and kept the other for herself.

Simone loved their secret language. Evangeline didn't need to ask. She just knew.

"Inferno531 posted again," Luciano said, snapping her out of her romantic thoughts. "He wrote, 'The Bomb Maker and Friends are unstoppable. Epic destruction on victory day.' The friends he's referring to are members of the Haqazzii terror cell."

"Show Z the map," Sin said.

Luciano opened the map on the conference table. "I got this from a Haqazzii terrorist."

"Where?" Z asked.

"Heathrow, on his way to DC," Luciano explained.

"Where is he now?" Z asked.

Luciano's gaze darkened. He hitched his eyebrow ever so slightly, but said nothing.

"How many?" Simone asked.

"Three," Luciano replied. "A fourth arrived late to the party."

Z studied the map. "This is massive."

"Despite the size of the potential attack, there's no chatter out there," Luciano explained. "They're not talking on the Dark Web."

"The Bomb Maker must be making the weapons and selling them to the terrorists." Simone said.

"He's gotta be making a fortune," Z said. "Haqazzii has deep pockets."

"If we find the terrorists, we can stop this," Simone said.

"But we have to find The Bomb Maker," Luciano said. "If we don't, he'll sell to another terror cell. America has a long list of enemies."

The weight of the case felt like a boulder on Simone's shoulders. But, as she eyed the people around the table, a sense of duty filled her bones. She wasn't alone. She had powerful allies in her corner. People who made decisions that protected the nation.

I can do this.

What choice did she have? She'd stayed hidden for years. She owed it to herself, to Frederica, and to a country she loved to find the son of a bitch and turn him over to these hungry wolves. Her gaze fell on Luciano. As they regarded each other across the table, she believed they could get the job done.

"Z, I need to know who got fired from ALPHA or left with a chip on their shoulder," Simone said. "Anyone who might have a reason to hate the organization."

Z broke eye contact for a few seconds. "There were several, but only one stands out."

"Who?" Luciano asked.

"Peter Hirzog," Z replied.

What the hell. "Peter was in ALPHA?"

"He was one of our first hires," Z said. "And he was *not* happy when I let him go."

"How long was he on board?" Simone asked.

Z paused. "A year."

"What happened?" Luciano asked.

"I couldn't work with him. His ego needed too much stroking, so I sent him back to the Bureau."

"There's no way he's behind these attacks," Simone said. "I don't believe for a minute that he's working with terrorists."

"Don't rule him out," Z said.

Her mouth fell open. "He's a Deputy Director at the Bureau." Refusing to believe Peter was behind the explosions or the terror plot, she shook her head. "I'll check him out, but I'd like that list."

Z stood. "I'll get it to you." At the door, he turned back. "Mr. Santini, I have a job for you."

Silence... for several beats.

"I run Santini International," Luciano replied. "I can't help you."

"Oh, I think you can." Z left, shutting the door behind him.

"What the hell was that?" Luciano asked. "One minute he's spying on me, the next, he wants to hire me?"

"Just when I think I've got him figured out, he goes off the rails," Sin added.

"He'll never retire," Luciano said. "What would he do?"

"Have fun," Simone replied.

A smile filled Luciano's face, then Sin flashed a grin.

"He *is* having fun," Luciano said.

LUCIANO

LUCIANO ROSE from the conference table in Sin's office. "There's a lot of pressure to find The Bomb Maker before he blows up these buildings."

"We've got nothing to go on and, now, this bogus lead that Hirzog could be behind this," Simone bit out.

"I wasn't expecting Z this afternoon," Sin said. "I called you both in for something else."

Evangeline rose. "I've got an off-site meeting, but let's take a two-minute break so I can show Simone how to access our site."

While the women huddled around the laptop at the conference table, Sin and Luciano moved across the room.

"Do you think Hirzog is working with The Bomb Maker?" Sin asked.

"We can't rule anyone out," Luciano replied.

"I never dismiss Z," Sin said. "He's credible."

When Evangeline walked past, she rested her hand on Sin's

back "We're all set. Good to see you, Luciano." She winked at her husband, then left.

Sin stood there grinning like an idiot. Luciano chuckled. He knew the power of a woman's love. He'd felt that once himself. A touch, a glance could undo him. As he redirected his attention to Simone, his hardened heart softened a little.

Is she my second great love, or am I destined to spend my life alone in a living hell?

As if sensing his thoughts, her gaze found his. She offered a small smile before walking to the cart and opening a bottle of mineral water. There, she poured two glasses, offered one to him. Their fingers brushed when he took the glass, the spark traveling up his arm.

After swallowing down a few mouthfuls, she eased onto the sofa. "What's going on?"

Sin sat in the leather chair. Luciano sat on the sofa beside her.

"Yesterday, a man named Guy Chenkus came to see me," Sin began. "He got involved in something illegal, didn't know where to go, and ended up here." Sin flashed a smile. "All roads end here."

"I'll remember that," Simone said.

"I wanted you guys to hear his story, so I asked him back." Sin checked his watch, pushed out of the chair. At his desk, his hit a button on his phone. "Erica, is Mr. Chenkus here?"

"Yes," she replied. "I'll bring him back."

A moment later, Erica brought in a large man wearing a light suit, dark shirt, and striped tie. "Mr. Develin, good to see you again."

"Mr. Chenkus, these are my associates."

After Luciano and Simone shook Chenkus' clammy hand, Sin gestured to the table.

"A bottle of sparkling water?" Sin asked.

"Regular water would be great, thanks," Chenkus replied.

Sin called his assistant as they got comfortable around the table. Erica brought in a tray with a chilled spring water and a crystal glass. Chenkus cracked the lid and guzzled half the bottle.

"Go ahead, Mr. Chenkus," Sin said. "Tell them what you told me."

"I work at the State Department," Chenkus said. "Been there for seventeen years. I work in the Bureau of Consular Affairs where we process passport applications. About ten months ago, my boss hands me a few applications personally. Now, he's never done that before and I've worked for him for twelve years. He tells me they get priority status."

Chenkus swigged another gulp of water.

"Anyways, I created the passports and hoped that was the end, but he tells me to bring them to this drop-off point. A parking garage in Shirlington at eleven-thirty at night. I do it, but I'm nervous as heck. I hand them to some guy and he gives me an envelope with a grand in it. I 'bout shit myself." He glanced at Simone. "Sorry."

"You're fine," Simone replied. "Then what?"

"I've gotten several more requests over the months to make passports."

"How many?" Sin asked.

"No more than twenty total. The last time I met the dude in the parking garage, he tells me he's cutting my take in half." Chenkus's shoulders slumped. "I know this is illegal, but I got kids in college. I've been paying down credit card debt with this money and now I'm being squeezed."

"Why tell Sin?" Luciano asked.

"I can't go to the police. The police would question my boss and I'll get fired. I told the guy in the parking garage to find another patsy. I'm done. He threatened to kill me if I stopped." Chenkus patted his glistening forehead with the napkin. "Mr. Develin fixes things and I need this fixed."

"You did the right thing coming to me," Sin said.

"When the dude threatened me, I decided to do a little investigating, you know, on my own. I had a few applications to process so I looked 'em up on the FBI's Most Wanted. They weren't there, but I found 'em on the No-Fly list." Chenkus shuddered in a breath. "These are men with the Haqazzii terror cell and I'm helping them get into the country." He shuddered in a shaky breath.

There it is.

Luciano glanced over at Simone who met his gaze.

"Can we get a copy of those applications?" Sin asked.

"Sure, but we gotta keep this on the down-low." Chenkus's nervous chuckle filled the room. "But I don't need to tell you that. You're the Fixer."

"Who's your boss?" Luciano asked.

"Cary Newburg. He's actually my boss's boss. He runs the department. He's an SES."

"SES?" Luciano asked.

"Senior Executive Service," Sin clarified.

"Is he still your go-between or do you have the mule's contact info?" Simone asked.

"Mr. Newburg tells me when to meet the dude. It's that same parking garage at eleven-thirty."

"When's your next drop?" Sin asked.

"Tonight," Chenkus replied. "That's why I came to see you yesterday. I don't know what to do."

"Do you know the mule's name?" Simone asked.

"Nope."

"Where's the parking garage?" Simone asked.

"Randolph Street in Shirlington. I drive to the far corner of the top floor and he meets me. I don't even get out of my car."

"What does he look like?" Simone asked.

Chenkus wrung his hands. "I'm always so nervous."

"Take your time," she said.

"He's a white dude, dark hair. He might wear eyeglasses." Chenkus shook his head. "I'm not sure about that."

"Is he tall?" Simone asked.

"He looks about my height—I'm five-eight—but I've never stood next to him. I'm sorry I'm not good at this. It happens fast and I'm freaked someone's gonna see us."

"Does he dress a certain way?" Simone prodded.

Chenkus paused. "I don't remember anything about his clothes."

"Does he say anything?" Luciano asked.

"The only time we talked was when he cut my pay."

"Does he have an accent?" Simone pressed.

"I don't remember one." He glanced furtively at Sin. "What should I do?"

"Are you going tonight?" Sin asked.

"I mean, yeah. I kinda don't have a choice."

Sin pulled a pair of eyeglasses from his credenza, set them on the table in front of Chenkus. "Try these on."

Chenkus slid them on.

Sin got busy on his laptop, then spun it around so the group could see. "There's a tiny camera built into the frame. If you wear these tonight, we can get video. Can you get him to talk?"

Guy set the glasses on the table and blotted his face with the napkin again. "I can try, but he's there for, like, five seconds."

"Do your best," Sin said. "I'll send someone from my team to take pictures. If we can, we'll put a tracker on his car."

Luciano bit back a growl. *Take pictures? Track the car? I don't fucking think so.*

"Okay," Chenkus said. "I was hoping you could scare him, you know, threaten him. I mean, you are the Fixer."

"I can't ask someone on my team to approach a stranger in a dark parking garage at midnight," Sin explained.

"I thought you'd do it yourself," Chenkus pushed back.

"Everyone knows who you are. I thought, maybe, you could rough him up a bit."

"I have no idea who you're dealing with, Mr. Chenkus. Let's find out who he is, first." Sin stood.

Meeting over.

He shook Sin's hand. "Thanks for your time."

Sin walked him out. Seconds later, he returned and shut the door. "We need this mule."

"We sure as hell do," Luciano replied. "Are you thinking what I'm thinking?"

"We set up a team and grab him tonight," Sin said.

Luciano smiled. "È perfetto. That's perfect."

17

THE TRUTH

SIMONE

"Kidnap him?" Simone blurted. "Are you two *crazy*?"

Luciano and Sin exchanged glances. "Yes," Luciano replied.

"We are," Sin said.

"We need to bring him in for questioning," Simone said.

"Questioning, not kidnapping."

"He won't talk," Luciano replied.

"You don't have enough to hold him," Sin added.

"If we witness the exchange of money for illegal passports, I will." Simone's attention shifted from the men to the conference table. "Chenkus forgot the surveillance glasses."

Sin slipped them into his pocket. "Maybe we can catch him in the parking lot."

They made their way through the office toward reception. Down the elevator they rode and into Sin's private parking lot. A tall white privacy fence provided a natural deterrent to freeloaders who wanted to park there. That, along with the towing signs, helped keep the public out.

The brisk, sunny day had been replaced by a cold, dark evening. Simone buttoned her suit jacket. As she scanned for Chenkus, a car drove to the exit. "Is that him?"

Someone wearing a hoodie walked up to the driver's side of the vehicle, pulled a gun, and opened fire.

BANG! BANG! BANG!

The shooter bolted.

Luciano pulled a gun from inside his suit jacket.

Simone grabbed her Glock. "Shots fired!"

"I'm calling for an ambulance," Sin said.

Stuart burst out of the Rolls Royce and ran over. "Mr. Santini, I need to get you inside the vehicle."

"Stuart, we need to help him," Luciano said.

"Clearing the area." Simone took off toward the vehicle.

As she approached the car, Luciano and Stuart pulled up alongside her. With her weapon drawn, she peered around the white security fence. The nearby sidewalk was void of foot traffic, the gunshots frightening everyone away. The cars on the street had vacated the immediate area, the drivers fearing for their own lives.

Stuart opened the driver's side door while Simone scanned the area for someone in a hoodie. He was gone.

On auto-pilot, she turned her attention to the victim. And her heart sank. Guy Chenkus was gone, his lifeless eyes staring straight ahead. He hadn't even seen his killer coming. He'd been shot in the head, in the neck, and in the chest.

Luciano appeared by her side. "Any sign of him?"

"No," she replied. "That was the mule, wasn't it?"

"Yes, or someone who worked for him," Luciano bit out.

Sin joined them. "We don't disclose what we know."

"Agreed," Luciano said.

"What's your story?" Sin asked.

"We came to see you," Simone replied. "You walked us out. We heard gunshots."

"Put your weapons away," Sin said.

She and Luciano re-holstered their Glocks, but Stuart did not. "Mr. Santini, I'd really like to get you inside the vehicle."

"Go," Sin said. "I'll handle the police."

The wailing sirens grew louder as she and Luciano slipped inside the Rolls Royce. Seconds later, Stuart pulled onto the deserted street. As they passed the police cars, Simone turned around and stared out the back window.

"How am I going to find this monster when he's always one step ahead of us?"

LUCIANO

IN THE DARKENED CAR, Luciano peered over at her. The poker face Simone wore so well had been replaced with a melancholy that singed his soul. He knew that look. It was the look of grief and heartache and loss.

Despite what had just happened, she'd managed through the situation like a pro. First and foremost, she was an ALPHA Op. An elite group of LEOs who ran *toward* danger. Her courage, paired with her nerves of steel, impressed him the most.

"You did a great job tonight," he murmured. "I know you don't want to hear that—"

"Thank you. If only I'd seen the eyeglasses a minute sooner."

"If you had, we could all be dead."

"I'm blaming myself—"

"I get that, but this isn't on you."

"Are you wearing Kevlar?" she asked.

"What?"

"Body armor." She pressed his chest. "You're not."

"Are you?"

"No," she replied. "New rule. Body armor every day."

"It's a pain in the—"

Simone lowered the privacy screen. "Mr. Fletcher—"

"Stuart, please."

"Call me Simone."

"Yes, ma'am."

"Or that," she replied. "Stuart, Luciano and I need to wear body armor daily, wouldn't you agree?"

"Absolutely, ma'am. Mr. Santini, you told me you'd wear it months ago."

Silence.

"He'll do it," Simone said, "if I have to dress him myself."

Luciano leaned over, kissed her cheek. "I'll wear it."

As Stuart drove them out of Georgetown, holiday lights and wreaths on the lampposts lining M Street bathed the city in a festive spirit. Christmas used to be his favorite time of year. Now, it reminded him how fragile life was... how alone he felt, even when surrounded by family.

A pang of loneliness pierced his heart and he clasped her hand. He didn't give a damn how unprofessional it was. They were facing the monumental challenge of finding a killer who loved taunting them. Even though this enemy wielded significant power, Luciano wasn't deterred. If anything, he was more determined than ever to root him out.

"We need to find that mule and, when we do, we're doing it my way," Luciano ground out. "He cooperates, he lives. If not, we take him out."

Her gaze met his. "What happened that turned you into a killing machine?"

"I lost everything," he replied. "Everything that mattered."

The vehicle stopped. They'd arrived back at Simone's. Stuart opened the rear door, Luciano waited for her to exit before he pushed into the night.

In truth, he was furious. Flat-out furious.

A family had just lost their husband and dad. Now, they would join the group of walking dead.

Like me.

He needed to go for a hard run or punch his boxing bag until his taped knuckles bled, but as his gaze found Simone's, he knew only *one* thing could calm his angry soul.

Her.

"Thank you, Stuart," she said.

"My pleasure, ma'am."

She stared into Luciano's eyes, but she stayed silent.

"Mr. Santini, please don't linger outside." Stuart retreated inside the vehicle.

"Stay," she murmured.

This time, staying meant he would take the next step with her. A relationship... if she wanted that. Not a work fling, not another meaningless hookup.

As he soaked up her beauty, her essence, he knew his answer.

"Yes."

By doing this, was he abandoning his past? Never. Was he walking toward his future? He didn't know.

Her outstretched hand surprised him.

Was that a lifeline?

Take it.

He clasped her hand. "Stuart."

Stuart exited the vehicle. "Sir."

"Take the Rolls Royce home and pick me up here at eight tomorrow morning."

"Where's your vest, Mr. Santini?"

"Office and home."

"I'll bring you one of mine," Stuart said.

"Thank you for doing such an outstanding job, Stuart."

A prideful smile filled Stuart's face before he ducked inside the vehicle and drove away.

Luciano glanced around Simone's quiet neighborhood before they headed for the front door. Once inside, she closed the living room blinds while he bolted the front door.

"C'mon in," she said. "Are you hungry?"

He couldn't stomach food. "I'm good. Can I make you something?"

Her sad smile cut through him. "I can't eat. How 'bout a Santini whiskey?"

"That'll work."

In the kitchen, she flipped on the pendant lights over the center island and dimmed their brightness. He sat on a counter stool, his gaze cemented on her. She was composed, but he sensed that angst lurked below her cool exterior. After she dropped her suit jacket over a chair, then removed her Glock and shoulder holster, she poured two glasses from a brand new bottle.

"Did you buy that for me?" he asked.

"Guilty," she replied.

He walked over to her and pulled her into his arms. "I don't care how fucking unprofessional this is. I need to know you're okay."

She hugged him hard and he held her close. A calmness washed over him. Something he hadn't felt in a long time. After a moment, he kissed her forehead, broke away.

"Are you okay?" he asked.

Big green eyes peered up at him. "Hell, no. Are you?"

I'm never okay.

"I care about you, Simone."

"I'm scared."

"I'll protect you."

"I'm scared of how I feel about you," she whispered.

"How *do* you feel?"

She stiffened, then broke away. He wanted to pull her back, force her to answer, but that behavior worked with monsters, not angels. There was a vulnerability in her eyes and in her touch that made him want to protect her and always, always, keep her safe.

~

SIMONE

Yes, Simone did have feelings for Luciano, but now was *not* the time to talk about them. She'd been brought back to ALPHA to hunt down a mass murderer, not discuss her emotional state regarding her partner.

Chenkus's murder was top of mind. She was being honest when she said she wasn't okay. Death messed with her head. Even though his death wasn't her fault, she'd been berating herself for not getting outside sooner.

"Let's sit in the family room," she suggested.

With drinks in hand, they got comfortable on the sofa, pausing to sip the whiskey.

"Chenkus's death has got me spun up." She repositioned toward him and got trapped in his beautiful bedroom eyes. "I can't get into my feelings. We've gotta focus on the case."

"Whatever you need."

She melted. He didn't push her to talk, didn't insist she explain. He just let the words hang out there... for another day.

Focus up.

"Are we in over our heads with The Bomb Maker?" she asked.

He steeled his spine as a growl rumbled from his chest. The anger in his eyes was the most powerful thing she'd ever seen. It was like staring into the eyes of the devil himself.

"No," he replied. "I will unleash my fury on the mule, The Bomb Maker, and anyone else who gets in our way."

"Ohmygod," she whispered.

"I'm not the man you think I am."

Dread slithered into her soul. "Who are you then?"

"I'm a shell of a man with enough vengeance to last me a thousand lifetimes."

She wasn't scared *of* him, but she was terrified of what he would do when he came face-to-face with the enemy. Of one thing she was certain... it would be swift, it would be violent, and it would be intense.

He sipped the whiskey, set the glass on her coffee table. "When you've had it all and you lose it, what is there to fear when you have nothing?"

"What did you lose?" she asked.

Pain ghosted across his face, the divot between his eyes deepening.

"I lost my family," he murmured.

What family?

"You mean like your parents or a sibling?"

"My wife and my children," he replied. "My entire world."

She stilled, her entire self focused on him while his heavy words sank in. She'd run two background checks on him, but there was nothing about them in either report. He truly had lost everything, and her heart broke for him.

"Ohgod, I'm so sorry. I had no idea," she murmured. The pain in his eyes tore at her heart. She clasped his hand, held it in her own. "Luciano, I'm so sorry for your loss."

He acknowledged her with a nod. "I don't talk about it."

"I respect your privacy."

"I have feelings for you." He caressed her cheek with the back of his hand. "I never expected this would happen. I don't deserve love. I deserve to feel pain and loss."

"Why would you say that?"

"Because it's my fault they're gone."

LUCIANO

LUCIANO NEEDED Simone to know everything. Then, she would recognize the monster he'd become and let him go. It had to be now... before he told her how he felt.

"How did they die?" she asked.

He could see that she was holding her breath, probably terrified he'd killed them himself.

"They were killed during an assassination attempt. Someone wanted me dead, and they were collateral damage." Tears threatened to spill, but he didn't care. He felt no shame. It was impossible to talk about them and *not* feel.

Even he wasn't that callous.

She kissed his cheek. "I'm sorry." She draped her arms around him and held him close, then broke away to sit beside him. When she draped her legs over his lap, he placed a possessive hand around her bare foot and caressed her skin.

"I'm filled with guilt," he said. "Guilt that I survived. Guilt that, five years later, the killer is still out there. Guilt that I have feelings for another woman. It's killing me."

Her eyes grew large. "Me? I'm that woman?"

He smiled. How could he not? She had no idea what she brought to his life.

"I've never met anyone like you. You followed me around for weeks. You didn't give up, you did everything you could to learn about my illegal activities. I was impressed by your perseverance." He massaged her foot. "You're very beautiful. You're smart. You have grit *and* grace. You push past your fears, and I appreciate that about you."

"God, Luciano, you say all the right things."

"It's the truth. We haven't known each other long, but I'm thirty-three-years-old. I know myself, especially after having gone through so much. I know what I like, what I need in a partner. You challenge me, you push back. I like that. But I'm struggling with the commitment I made to my late wife."

"Tell me about her."

"Linda was a friend's sister. We met when I worked for the Santini family business." He winked. "She knew what I did, but she didn't care. We married, had a son, then a daughter. My life was very different. *I* was very different."

"Your life sounds perfect."

"I adored my family."

Talking to Simone helped. He'd hoped it would, but he couldn't know for sure... until he did it.

"They were killed when my car exploded." He put it out there in its rawest form. No point glossing it over. It was what it was.

Compassion poured from her eyes. "Ohgod, that's awful."

"My wife's car needed repairs, so I told her I'd take it in for her." Pain sliced through him like a thousand knives to his heart. "She worked part-time and, on those days, the kids went to pre-school."

"How old were they?"

"My son was four. My daughter two."

She kissed his cheek, clasped his hand. "I'm so sorry."

Emotion clogged his throat, but he pushed on. He needed her to understand the weight he carried around. He needed her to appreciate the reason for his deep-seated vengeance. "I left before she did, so I only know what the arson detective told me. She put the kids in the car, and when she started the engine, the car exploded. They were killed instantly."

Anguish poured into every crevice of his being, but he pushed on.

"I thought it was a hit by another family, but it wasn't. I

wasn't sleeping. I couldn't eat. The grief consumed me... until it turned to anger. I was determined to find the killer, but I couldn't. My brother, Gabriel, who owns several vineyards in Italy, insisted I come live with him. Elsa and Carrera made me go. When I got there, Gabriel had this crazy idea that we should start our own winery. I was numb and barely hanging on. I went along with it because I didn't care."

Her soft caresses on the back of his neck grounded him. "How long were you there?"

"A year. During that time, I left the family business to my cousin, Willie Boy, and I threw myself into the winery to escape the constant pain. We started Santini Chianti, then through connections I started a men's clothing line. That turned into Santini International. Santini Whiskey came later."

"You've done a lot in five years," she said.

"But I haven't done the *one* thing that matters. I haven't found my family's killer."

She sipped the whiskey. "Are you still searching?"

"That's why I started the assassin group," he explained. "After I met Sin, we formed a partnership. He introduced me to Dakota and we decided to take out the bad actors ALPHA can't."

"Thank you for telling me about your family," she said. "Thank you for trusting me, especially with how we met."

"I trust very few people, but the guys vouched for you. Slash adores you and I value her opinion." He kissed her hand. "Why did you leave ALPHA?"

"I was leading a mission that went horribly wrong. Everyone on my team was killed and I was terrified he'd come after me."

"Who?"

"The Bomb Maker," she replied. "Ever since he killed Frederica and her team, I feel like I'm living the nightmare all over again."

Desperate to touch her, he caressed her cheek with the back of his hand. "I'm sorry to hear that. Are you still afraid?"

"Not anymore. Now, I'm consumed with vengeance."

He smiled. "That's what I needed to hear."

SIMONE

SIMONE SHIVERED, but not from the cool temperature in her home. She was baring her soul to him, leaving herself open to getting hurt.

Luciano draped a throw blanket over her lap. "I knew about the earlier attack on ALPHA, but I didn't know you were the lone survivor."

"There were six of us," she began. "We'd gotten intel that The Bomb Maker and his employees had set up their operation in a deserted house outside Leesburg. When we went to make the arrests, the house exploded." Another shudder ripped through her. "Same as what happened to Frederica."

"Were you injured?" he asked, stroking her leg.

His gentle caresses, paired with the concern in his eyes, helped assuage her anxiety.

"Just as my team approached the house, Luther called me," she said. "Back then, he and Z ran ALPHA together. He'd never called during an arrest mission, so I took it." Another shudder whipped through her. "He was screaming for us to get out. His words still haunt my dreams. I was yelling for my team, but they were already inside. I ran toward the building and the explosion knocked me back. The Bomb Maker killed my team along with his own."

He put his arm around her. The strength from his touch filled her with encouragement... and love.

"That's rough," he murmured.

"I blamed myself and I had survivor guilt. ALPHA was concerned that if the killer knew I was alive, he'd come after me."

"Is that why you worked for Mitus?"

She nodded. "I was there for three years. It was like being in witness protection. I was me, but with a fictitious past. Only Colton knew the truth. I had PTSD, but I felt safer behind the gates. After I got the mental help I needed, I improved. I was cleared to return to ALPHA, but I wasn't ready, so I worked for Z. When Frederica was killed, I knew I had to take the case."

"We *will* find him," Luciano said, his voice velvety and low, yet brimming with his signature brand of confidence.

"We have to," she replied. "He's taken so much already."

His loving smile touched her heart. "Thank you for being vulnerable with me. I will have your back, Simone."

"I know that, and I'm grateful." Then, she offered a little smile. "I've got yours too. You know that, right?"

He kissed her. One kiss filled with so much love, she melted.

"Yes," he murmured before kissing her again. "I do."

He broke eye contact to stare at their clasped hands, resting on the throw blanket. "I told you I'm struggling with the commitment I made to my late wife." He fixed his eyes on hers. "I'm falling in love with you, Simone."

Her heart rejoiced. She captured his beautiful, chiseled face in her hands, and she kissed him.

Tell him.

"I'm falling in love with you too." She breathed deeply, hoping to slow her rapidly beating heart.

They came together in a powerful embrace. When it ended, he said, "Love isn't stagnant. It grows stronger or it fades away. If we are each other's person, nothing and no one can stop it."

She kissed him again, then murmured, "I could love you for a long, long time."

His smile filled her with hope. But she didn't want to get ahead of herself.

"We have a killer to catch and The Bomb Maker to hunt down," she said. "I need to start working *now*."

He rose with her in his arms and carried her up the stairs. "I'm going to love you first, then we work."

∿

LUCIANO

IN HER BEDROOM, she snaked her arms around him and pressed her lips to his. Desire spread through him. He was ready to lose himself in her passion, her beauty, and her soul-filling strength.

The bedside table lamp was on, bathing the room in diffused light, but his attention was solely focused on the woman in his arms.

"I need you, Luciano. Fury-filled you. Broken you. Loving you. I don't need you to comfort me and protect me. I need you to remind me that we're alive. That we've got what it takes to hunt down these monsters and eliminate them."

He framed her face in his hands and he kissed her. A wild, deep, biting kiss powered by greed and passion. She slowed it, ending it with a soft peck. Off came her shirt. She stepped out of her heels, removed her dress pants. Simone in a black bra and black thong was a perfect vision and the best escape.

"We don't deserve to feel good," he said, the guilt creeping back in.

She placed a finger over his lips. "One hour."

He collected her hand in his, dotted her warm skin with kisses before he married his lips to hers. Her throaty moan ripped through him, kicking up the heat. She ended the kiss and helped him out of his jacket and shirt.

With her attention cemented on his pecs, she pressed her

mouth to his chest and kissed him. As he toed off his shoe boots, she sauntered over to her queen-sized bed, tossed the throw pillows onto the floor, and threw back the linens.

"I know the demons that chase you," she murmured, "and I'm going to help you escape them... for a little while."

He removed his pants and boxer briefs, his jutting erection at-the-ready. She caressed his shoulders, scraped her fingernails down his chest and his abs until her hands came to rest around his shaft. While she fondled his balls, she massaged his shaft sending pleasure skyrocketing through him. When he stroked her bare ass, a groan shot out of him.

"I need you, Simone," he bit out.

"I'm gonna take good care of you."

She released her hold and collected a pillow. "Lie on the floor facing the bench," she commanded.

Unexpected, but he'd go with it.

"I've never done this, but I'm going to give it a try," she said as he lay down.

After tucking the pillow under his head, she collected a bottle of massage oil and eased onto the bench. She removed her bra and his attention dropped to her breasts, her pert nipples beckoning.

She trickled oil into her hands and rubbed it all over her tits until they glistened. His cock bobbed up and down in approval. A barely-there smile tugged at the corners of her mouth as she caressed her thigh, then her calf, and finally her foot. Jolts of energy powered through him as she ran her long fingers over her provocative toes.

After covering her feet in oil, she laid them on his chest. Then, she dragged her toes down his torso until she'd sandwiched his cock between the soles of her feet.

"Yes," he rasped.

Her feet on his throbbing cock was driving him wild with need. He couldn't wait to see what she'd do next. Moving slowly, she began to rub his cock with her feet. Back and forth, up and down, she glided over his hardness with her talented toes.

"Fuck, that feels good." The mounting pleasure turned his cock hard as steel.

Then, she caressed his balls with one foot while rubbing the underside of his cock with the other. Again and again while the pressure continued building.

A raspy groan rumbled out of him and he grabbed her feet, put her soles together, and began thrusting through the arch.

"You are so fucking hot," he ground out.

She retook control, placing the head between her long seductive toes while gliding on his cock with her other foot. Euphoria had him grunting through the pleasure.

"Come for me," she commanded, the grittiness in her voice pushing him closer to the edge.

She worked the head with her toes, faster and faster until the orgasm exploded out of him.

His groan thundered through his chest, the ecstasy lifting him from the depths of hell.

She slowed, then stilled, their searing connection taking him higher still. Then, she retreated into the bathroom, returning with a towel. After cleaning him up, she held out her hand.

He stood, threaded his arms around her, pressed his lips to hers. The intensity of their kiss had her grinding against him while her hungry moans sliced through the quiet night. They tumbled into bed, their mouths ravenous, their tongues eager. The second they connected, he knew.

She's the one.

The one he would never have. Being alone was his punishment for—

She stopped kissing him. "Come back to me," she whispered. "Don't go there. Not yet."

He pulled her close, kissed her softly, and breathed her in. She was dealing with her own demons, yet she was there for him.

And she wanted nothing in return.

He planked over her, kissed her. "You're an amazing woman. Thank you for the gift."

"Mama's gonna need some foot practice," she murmured.

"You're a fantastic lover."

Her smile told him everything he needed to know. She'd done that for him because his needs mattered to her.

Their kiss was filled with love, their gazes still locked on each other. He moved from her mouth to her nipple and was rewarded with a moan. She arched into him, ran delicate fingers through his hair.

"I love when you suck my tits," she murmured, urging him on. When he bit her nipple, she cried out. "Yessssss"

He ran his fingers over her pussy, appreciating how soaked she was, then slipped his fingers inside. She spread her legs, welcoming him to probe, to stroke, to tease.

The faster he went, the more intense her sounds, but when she pushed into his fingers, he gently removed them.

Her sad face made him smile. "I'm hard again. Condom?"

"No condom. I'm on the pill. I want nothing between us. But if you're seeing other women—which is none of my—"

He kissed her. "Just you, Simone."

She guided his penis to her core. "Mmmm, yes."

He pressed inside, withdrew, pressed in farther, withdrew. Just skin on skin. She rolled them sideways, lifted her thigh, and he sunk in farther. They moved slowly, but the fire in her eyes ravaged him like a wildfire burning across an open prairie.

On her side, she raised her arm over her head and ground into him. The oil on her breasts let her glide easily. Faster and faster they moved, the intensity of their lovemaking taking him to another crescendo.

"I love how good you fuck me," she ground out. "I'm gonna come."

She kissed him, then started bucking while she cried out through the release. When her insides clamped down around his cock, he exploded inside her.

Their mutual groans filled his ears with the sweetest sound while they surrendered to the intoxicating passion.

Staring into her eyes, he knew. For a ruthless assassin who had a *strong* dislike for the law, he was falling in love with a top-secret law enforcement agent ... and he was powerless to stop it.

18

MORE TRUTHS

LUCIANO

As Stuart drove him to Baltimore in his bullet-proof Range Rover, while wearing one of Stuart's Kevlar vests, Luciano's phone buzzed with a text from Simone.

> Thanks for the zhuzhing this morning and for the *strong* urging to contact Peter Hirzog

> You're easy to love, Simone

That text said it all. She *was* easy to love.

He spent the hour-long car ride on three video meetings regarding his spring clothing lines, he made eight phone calls, participated in a video meeting with his distillery, and fired off too many texts to count. He squeezed every moment out of his workday, in part, because he ran a global empire, but also because downtime gave him time to think about the one who got away.

The killer who shredded my life.

In Baltimore's Little Italy, Stuart drove past the popular tourist restaurants, and into the heart of the district. Three more turns and Stuart parked in front of an upscale restaurant that served genuine Italian cuisine. More importantly, it was the epicenter for the Garibaldi family, still run by Carlo Sr.

As expected, the front door was locked. He knocked and Benita opened the small window in the old, wooden door.

"Sì?" asked Benita.

"Benita, it's Luciano Santini and Stuart Fletcher."

She smiled. "I don't have my glasses on." She slammed the little window shut, opened the door. "Good to see you, Lulu."

He stepped inside and was enveloped in a warm hug. She eyed his chest. "What are you wearing. You got somethin' on under your suit?"

Luciano glanced over at Stuart. "My security detail insists I wear body armor."

"What's that?" Benita asked.

"A bullet-proof vest," Stuart replied.

"Stuart, you take good care of our Lulu." She smiled up at him. "And you're such a good eater."

"Thank you, ma'am."

In addition to running the restaurant, Benita was Carlo's wife and gatekeeper. Luciano handed her a Santini gift bag and she peered inside. "Grazie, hon."

"He's meeting with someone. Lemme get you boys something to eat."

If Luciano had just finished a five-course meal, he wouldn't have refused her. She seated them at a table in the back. A server set down a basket of warm bread. Within minutes, he and Stuart were enjoying bowls of homemade spaghetti, each with a giant meatball. His favorite comfort food. Twenty minutes later, he was ushered into the back room while Stuart waited at the table.

Papà was almost eighty, but he wasn't ready to relinquish

his power to Carlo Jr. After Luciano kissed each of his cheeks, he waited for Carlo to offer him a seat. Sitting without being invited was presumptive and disrespectful. Luciano might not be running the Santini family business anymore, but he still followed the expected customs.

Carlo tapped the chair catty corner. "Sit, Lulu."

Luciano eased down. "You look good, Papà. You're wearing the suit I sent you."

"You make nice things. I appreciate the gifts. I liked the crucifix, but Benita took it. Did you find Frankie?"

"I didn't find him. I trust you Papà, and I need your help."

"You did good for yourself, Lulu."

"Grazie."

"Di che cosa hai bisogno?" What do you need?

"The main supplier of bomb making materials in the area."

Papà's eyes widened. "You gotta let that go, figliolo."

"It's not for me."

Pausing to sip his wine, Papà's bony hand trembled. "That's a dirty business."

"It's important."

Carlo smiled, his wrinkled face creasing like an accordion. "You're a good boy. I'll help you."

"Grazie, Papà." Luciano paused. "Willie Boy ran the business into the ground."

"È una vergogna."

"He *is* a disgrace." Luciano pulled out his phone, tapped on the photo of Dante that Stuart had taken at Willie Boy's. "Do you recognize him?"

"No. Who is he?"

"A nobody who wants a mil in boodle."

"Never trust an outsider. *Never.*"

"I'll send you another crucifix," Luciano said.

Carlo smiled. "Igor Stachko. He's in Springfield, Virginia."

"What's his front?"

"He runs a chemical supply company." Carlo pulled out his phone, then his glasses.

Though Carlo was painfully slow, Luciano stayed silent.

"My eyes don't work like they used to." Carlo handed him his phone. "You find him."

As Luciano scrolled through his address book, he said, "When was the last time you got your eyes checked?"

"I don't trust doctors."

Luciano found Igor's contact info and sent it to himself, then showed Carlo what he'd done. Another sign of respect.

He set Carlo's phone on the table. "Grazie, Papà."

"You should take over your family's business."

"Not me."

"What's Theodore doing?"

"He works for me."

"Gabriel?"

"He runs the wineries and Santini International in Italy."

"Have you heard from —"

"Don't say his name," Luciano pushed back.

"He's your brother," Carlo said. "Lui è famiglia."

He's not family to me.

"Papà, grazie. Sempre un piacere." Always a pleasure.

"I know our families were rivals, but I always liked you, Lulu."

After kissing Carlo's craggily cheeks, he left. Luciano had one objective when he went to speak with Carlo. Goal achieved.

On the drive back to DC, he called his assistant, requested another crucifix and a case of Chianti for Carlo. "Include something for Benita."

"What did you have in mind?" Dominic asked.

"Send her a dress and a cashmere coat from our Ladies collection. What's the latest work emergency?"

"If I say none, I'm scared I'll jinx things," Dominic replied.

"It's the calm before the storm." Luciano hung up, slid his focus out the window as they drove south on I-95.

He couldn't deny that The Bomb Maker was holding all the power. The terrorists were making their way into the country without resistance. Guy Chenkus was dead, at the hand of some mule. Was it the same man who did the money-for-passports trade or someone else?

Luciano had no idea how many people were involved in this deadly operation. What he did know was that he and Simone would get the upper hand... and the shift of power would begin.

That's when he would strike.

Fast and deadly.

∼

SIMONE

S<small>IMONE HADN'T SLEPT WELL</small>, despite how much she loved being in Luciano's arms. She'd suspected him of being involved in his family's crime syndicate, but she never imagined he'd been married with young children. Her heart squeezed.

He lost his babies.

She'd been devastated over the loss of her team. Yes, the Ops were like family, but it wasn't like losing your *actual* family.

Thirty-minutes later, Simone was sitting at her kitchen island, sipping hot coffee while reading a secure email from Z. He'd fired three from ALPHA while heading up the organization, one of them Peter Hirzog.

Providence called. "How's it going?"

She thought of Guy Chenkus. "Working it like a boss lady."

"That's what we want to hear," Providence replied. "I sent over a list. Cooper and I fired four ALPHA employees. One—

Karen Woodside—is currently serving time. While she hates ALPHA, my gut says she's not behind these bombings."

Simone clicked on the email. "Got it."

"I'm sorry you have to work from home. If you need any help, let me know."

"I need to use my Joelle James alias," Simone said. "A man named Guy Chenkus was gunned down in Georgetown last night, and I need to talk with a homicide detective at Metropolitan Police Department."

"I might be able to help. Hang two seconds."

While Simone waited, she reviewed Providence's list of potential suspects. Her attention was diverted when her phone buzzed with a text from Peter Hirzog.

> Call me

"Thanks for waiting," Providence said. "Call Nikki Cardoso. She's a branch commander in homicide with the MDP. She and Emerson worked together at Arlington Homicide. Emerson's texting you her number."

"Perfect. Thanks for your help." Simone hung up as her phone buzzed with a text from Emerson with Nikki's number.

> Thanks for the help. When I call Nikki, I'm Joelle James, FBI

> No worries. I texted her that a LEO I've worked with would be following up on a DC homicide

She returned Peter Hirzog's call, and he answered right away.

"Red, thanks for calling me back. Any chance I can take you to lunch today?"

Though she doubted he was behind the bombings, she had to pursue the lead. Z had fired him. He had a long-standing grudge against Luciano. Did he have one against ALPHA too?

"Sure," she replied.

He suggested a restaurant, and she agreed to meet him. After hanging up, she called Nikki Cardoso with the Metropolitan Police Department.

"Homicide, Commander Cardoso," Nikki answered.

"Commander Cardoso, this is Joelle James, FBI." Simone said.

"Emerson just texted me and told me to be nice." Nikki laughed. "Please call me Nikki. What can I help with?"

"I'm following up on the murder of Guy Chenkus in Georgetown. I'm hoping there was something your detectives found at the scene."

"I'm curious," Nikki said. "What's the Bureau doing with this?"

"I can't discuss the case. I'm sorry."

"Playing hardball."

Dammit.

"I'm just messing with you," Nikki said. "My detective doesn't have much to go on. He was shot in his vehicle leaving the parking lot at Develin and Associates. Mr. Develin can't disclose the purpose of his visit. There were no eye witnesses. My detective talked to his wife, but I don't know the details. If we learn anything, I'll let you know."

Simone thanked her, provided her contact info, and hung up.

She spent the next two hours doing a high-level search on Z and Providence's potential suspects. Of the seven, one had died, three had moved out of state. Former Op Karen Woodside was in prison. That left Nina Roy, a former ALPHA OP now with ATF, and Peter Hirzog.

After spending a few minutes coming up with a believable reason to talk with Nina Roy, she called her.

"Good morning, Nina Roy."

"Ms. Roy, this is Joelle James, Special Agent, FBI. I got your name from a few agents I know at the Bureau. I'm considering a position with ATF and was hoping you'd have ten minutes for an informational interview."

"I've got a short break between meetings in an hour. Can you call me back then?"

"Any chance we could chat in person?"

"Sure. Call me when you're in the lobby."

Simone thanked her and hung up. She slipped her FBI badge into her handbag, shouldered into her jacket, and left through her garage.

The brisk November air meant winter was fast approaching, but she loved the crispness so she opened the sunroof and slid on her shades.

En route to ATF in NE DC, she thought about Luciano. She'd fallen fast and she'd fallen hard. Easy to do with Luciano Santini. But he had a dark side. In his free time, he took out bad actors. The ones that even ALPHA couldn't touch. But her heart wanted who it wanted, so for now, she'd enjoy the newness of their relationship, try to keep it under wraps, and stay focused on the reason she'd returned to ALPHA.

I can't believe I'm back.

After searching for street parking and coming up short, she parked in a lot. As she walked toward ATF's headquarters on New York Ave, her phone buzzed. She lifted it from her jacket pocket and read the text.

> I warned you not to take the job. Now, I have to kill you. I will win. I always do. Mass destruction and chaos will be mine

"Fuck you," she blurted as a chill streaked down her spine.

But she couldn't operate in a vacuum. She had to tell Luciano.

She hurried into the lobby of ATF. Once through security, she called Nina Roy. A few minutes later, a middle-aged Black woman approached her.

The two shook hands. "Thank you for seeing me," Simone said.

"We'll chat in private," Nina said.

They rode the elevator, and Nina escorted her to a nearby office. After sitting behind her desk, Nina asked, "Why are you thinking of leaving the FBI?"

Simone eased into a guest chair. "A change of pace, new faces, different kind of cases. How long have you worked here?"

"Seven years. I left for four, then returned. I've been back a year."

"Why'd you leave?" Simone asked.

"I was invited to work for an elite top-secret agency, but it wasn't the right fit," Nina said. "Plus, I'm too much of an explosives junkie. I'm fascinated with the psychology behind why people like to blow things up."

Simone nodded. "I get that."

"When I returned here, I was tasked with helping Scotland Yard implement a new system for tracking terrorists who are explosives experts. It's been a great project, but it forced me to spend a lot of time away from my family."

Simone spotted a framed photo of three children. "Are those your kids?"

"Yes, but that's an outdated picture. My son is in college and my daughters are in high school. I'm blessed that my husband is a very hands-on dad, so they were probably better off without their helicopter mom." She smiled. "Still, I missed them."

"Were you out of the country recently?" Simone asked.

"Yes, I spent the last two months finishing up the project in

London, so I was gone more than I was home. Today is my second day back."

"I'm curious, as an ATF agent, what are your thoughts on The Bomb Maker?"

Nina leaned back. "I haven't heard that name in a few years now. Is he back?"

Unfortunately, yes.

"In doing my research on ATF, some were calling that case an epic fail," Simone said. "I'm not sure I'd label it as such. Like too many criminals, he was able to outsmart law enforcement."

"I wasn't assigned that case, but it fascinated me as well," Nina replied. "He had a tremendous knowledge of how explosives work along with being able to executive his hits at just the right time." She shut her office door. "I mentioned I worked for an elite agency. He killed several of their special forces operatives. Rumor has it that he's back." She waved a dismissive hand. "I'm not buying that, but some of the agents think he's planning something big."

"Why do they think that?"

Nina's phone rang and she glanced at the screen. "Excuse me, it's my boss." She answered. "Nina Roy." She listened, then said, "I'm wrapping up a meeting. Five minutes." Nina hung up.

"Nina, why do some of your coworkers think The Bomb Maker is back?"

"I have no idea. Might be conspiracy theorists, could be that someone working a case leaked the info. Everyone needs to feel important and significant." She shrugged. "I'm just happy that I'm back." She shifted on the chair. "I hope I've been helpful."

"Absolutely. Thank you again for your time."

"Who are you interviewing with?"

Simone paused. "His name escapes me. Might be a Joe. Could be a Keith."

"Well, if you take the position, let me know." Nina walked her to the elevator.

"Thank you again, Nina." The doors opened and Simone rode to the lobby.

She's not guilty of anything. I've hit another dead end.

Exiting the elevator, she almost crashed into Jerod De Clerq.

"Red, what a surprise," Jerod said as he moved away from foot traffic. "What are you doing here?"

"I was talking with Nina Roy," she replied.

He furrowed his brow. "I don't know her. Anyways, I was going to text you. My girlfriend, Becca, is coming into town this afternoon. I managed to get a res at Carole Jean's in Tysons tonight. Am I the luckiest guy or what? They had a cancelation and I snagged it. I want you to join us. Tell me you're free."

Simone thought about the case and her lack of progress. She couldn't afford to spend two hours meeting someone's girlfriend.

"I'm sorry—"

"Nope, wrong answer." He shot her a smile. "Have you ever been to Carole Jean's?"

"No, but I've heard—"

"It's Michelin-starred. You *have* to go. I need you to meet her... you know, for selfish reasons. If you don't like her, she's out."

Simone smiled. "No pressure there."

"It's kismet. She decided to fly down. I got a table at Carole Jean's. I bump into you. C'mon, Red."

"Fine, but—"

"Perfect," he said cutting her off. "Six-thirty." He grinned. "Don't be late."

As she drove toward the restaurant for lunch with Peter, she thought about Nina Roy. She wasn't in the country when Frederica and her team were killed, and Nina Roy didn't appear to hold a grudge against ALPHA. She was forthright with information and had no obvious tells. As far as Simone was concerned, Nina Roy was not a person of interest.

Frustration had her white-knuckling the steering wheel. She had no viable leads, not a single suspect, and a dead man who was forced to make passports for terrorists who'd been marching into the country like ants through a pinhole at the kitchen window.

Her phone rang. It was Luciano.

"Hey," she answered. "Missing me like crazy, huh?"

"You know I am," he said. "Can you talk?"

"I'm in my car," she said. "Peter invited me for lunch."

"That oughta be interesting," he replied. "Sin thinks he can put the squeeze on Chenkus's boss's boss, the exec at State. He set up a meeting today at one. Can you join us?"

It was twelve-fifty. "Not unless I cancel Peter."

"Where are you meeting him?"

"The restaurant in Hotel Dillinger."

"That's Rebel's hotel," Luciano said. "Do you think he's gonna make a move—"

She laughed. "Thank you, I needed that. No, Peter Hirzog is not going to make a move." She laughed again. "I have updates for later."

"All I heard was 'later'."

She smiled. "I gotta go, charmer. I hope you and Sin put the squeeze on that jackass."

Simone parked in the hotel lot, made her way into the luxury boutique hotel near Dupont Circle that bore Rebel's name. She loved the bohemian-styled hotel with the chill vibe. The lounge caught her eye, and she stopped to admire. Purple microfiber sofas flanked by bright orange chairs filled the room. One entire wall housed cabinets of vinyl records. She sauntered over to check out the album collections. Rebel had every kind of music imaginable.

The bartender said hello. "First time?" she asked.

"Yeah, I'm meeting someone for lunch," Simone replied.

"Bring your lunch in here. You can choose an album to play on the spinner." She nodded toward the stereo.

"Thanks," Simone said.

She entered the restaurant and found Peter waiting near the hostess stand. He offered a friendly smile, but instead of a hug, he extended his hand.

As she shook it, he said, "Thanks for meeting me."

The hostess seated them in a booth, handed them menus, and left. Simone eyed the options, selected something, then set the menu aside. *Something* needed to go her way so, with a tactic in mind, she shifted her attention to Peter.

The server approached, told them the lunch specials. After they ordered, he scooted off.

"Simone, I invited you to lunch to apologize," Peter said. "I'm very sorry I asked you to spy on Luciano. It was out of character and I've been disappointed with myself ever since."

She smiled. Not too big, but enough that his shoulders relaxed. "Peter, it's totally okay. Even you couldn't keep up a perfect track record—"

He mimed stabbing himself in the heart. "Ouch."

"You feel passionate about it and I appreciate that."

"Jerod was so angry with me. That never happens, so I knew I'd really messed up."

The server delivered their beverages and left.

After sipping her iced tea, Simone said, "Are you happy with Lucy?"

"Very," he replied.

"I've never been married, so I can't begin to know how you felt, but I am sorry about what happened with your first wife."

His rueful smile told Simone that he probably still had feelings for his ex. "I don't care about Santini, but Jerod's right. If I'd paid my first wife more attention, she might not have gone looking elsewhere."

Simone wanted to tell him that Luciano Santini was a man that most women probably wouldn't refuse... her included. But that was not the plan she'd laid out for their meeting. Instead, she leaned forward. "I completely forgive you. It's all behind us now."

This time, his smile touched his eyes. "Thank you."

"So, since we're having a heart-to-heart, I wanted to confide something to you." She cleared her throat. "You were right, I was with ALPHA."

His eyebrows jutted up. "You have the best poker face of *anyone* I have ever met."

"Thank you." She sipped her drink.

"Are you still with them?"

"No, I really did leave five years ago. I was only with ALPHA for a year." She looked around, pretending to check if anyone was eavesdropping. "I was the lead Op on The Bomb Maker case. Everyone on my team got killed. I got PTSD, left the group, and went into private industry."

She was studying his reactions, like he was under a microscope.

Empathy filled his eyes. "I'm sorry. That must've been rough for you."

"It was awful. I'm better now, so that's good."

"Do you miss the group?"

"I miss the closeness we had. It was like the team you built under your leadership."

"That's nice of you to say." After taking a swig of soda, he said, "I worked for ALPHA."

Elated that he'd shared that, she smiled. "I'm disappointed our paths didn't cross there as well. Why did you leave?"

"I was Philip Skye's first hire. Did you know he goes by Z now?"

"No," she lied, "I lost touch after I left."

"I worked there for a year. Philip hired me to manage the

newly-formed Ops team. I got along fine with Luther, but Philip and I, we didn't mix. He let me go and I returned to the Bureau. They've grown a lot since I left. You wouldn't believe it's the same organization."

"If it's still top-secret, how do you know?"

He blinked in slow motion, as if closing his eyes to shut her out. Then, he paused to drink.

He's buying time to come up with an answer.

He pinched his nostrils together, then wiped his nose. "I keep in touch with a few."

You're lying.

"Anyone I'd know?"

"I don't think so." Peter forced a laugh. "But I couldn't tell you who they are anyway."

"No, I guess not."

The server returned with their lunches, topped off their beverages, and left.

"Do you hold a grudge against Philip like you do against Luciano Santini?" Simone asked before digging into her Niçoise salad.

"I did. It worked out in the end for me, but I would have liked to make a career there. It's very cutting-edge."

He's talking about it in the present. How does he know what's going on with ALPHA?

"Like what?"

"I can't say," he replied. "In fact, we shouldn't even be talking about them now, but I appreciate that you told me the truth."

She forced a smile. "Same, Peter."

"I'm going to throw something out there," he said. "Don't dismiss it. Promise me you'll think about it."

"Sure."

"Come back to work for me."

"I'll consider it," she replied.

As they ate, she asked about his wife, Lucy, and the conversation moved on. She couldn't help wonder who, at ALPHA, would be leaking information to him... and was any of this related to The Bomb Maker? After lunch, she and Peter said goodbye in the hotel lobby. He asked her to consider his work offer, then headed toward the exit. Rather than leave, she retreated into the lounge. She wanted to jot notes from the meeting on her phone. While sitting in an oversized orange chair, she glanced into the hotel lobby, and her brain stuttered. Instead of leaving, Peter strode over to the elevator bank and waited. An elevator door opened, and he vanished inside.

He must've parked in the underground garage.

She walked over to the front desk. "Excuse me," she asked a clerk. "Is there parking underground?"

"No," the employee replied. "We have the lot next to the building, and there's street parking."

After shouldering into her jacket, she made her way through the lobby. As she approached the exit, someone entered through the revolving door. She glanced over, did a double take, then turned away.

Ohmygod.

Keeping her head down, she reversed direction, then lasered-in on her target. Jerod strode to the elevators, tapped the up button. Elevator doors opened and he vanished inside.

As the elevator ascended, Simone murmured, "What the fucking fuck."

19

ONE STEP AT A TIME

LUCIANO

After Stuart pulled up in front of the State Department, Sin handed Luciano a badge.

"Looks legit." Luciano read the name—Malvagio Peccatore—and laughed. In Italian, his name meant Wicked Sinner.

"And I work for the FBI. That's irony." Luciano glanced at Stuart's reflection in the rearview mirror. "Stuart, I'll text you on the way out."

"I'll park around the corner." His driver opened Luciano's door and both men exited the Range Rover.

They made their way through security without issue.

"How'd you do it?" Luciano asked as they walked to the elevator. "Malvagio Peccatore doesn't exist."

"Sure he does," Sin replied. "Check the system, you'll see he's there. I gave you a hella title too. It's equivalent to King of the Universe."

"I knew I liked you for a reason."

They rode the elevator to the fourth floor, entered the Bureau of Consular Affairs, stopping at reception.

"Sinclair Develin and Malvagio Peccatore for Cary Newburg," Sin said.

The woman slid her gaze from one man to the other and color flooded her cheeks. With her eyes locked on Luciano, she made a call. When finished, she said to Sin, "Mr. Newburg is in a meeting."

"It's about Guy Chenkus," Sin said.

The men stepped away from the desk, and the receptionist made another call. Seconds later, she said, "Someone will be right out."

Of course someone will be right out.

A different woman bustled over, escorted them through the department and over to a small waiting area near a corner office. "Mr. Newburg is finishing a call." She returned to her seat and popped a piece of chocolate into her mouth.

A moment later, the door opened. A pudgy man wearing a hideous light gray suit exited his office. He eyed both men. "Cary Newburg."

After he shook his hand, Luciano wanted to wipe the dampness off, but he sure as hell wasn't using his suit for that.

Mr. Newburg ushered them into his office. "What can I help you with today?"

After Luciano sat, he stuck a micro listening device to the underside of the guest chair as Mr. Newburg hollered for his assistant to come in and take notes.

"No," Luciano said, the smell of mildew turning his stomach.

Mr. Newburg glared at him. "Did you just tell me no?"

Luciano nodded, once.

"Why the hell not?"

Sin sat, crossed his legs. "Because we say so."

"Never mind," Newburg yelled out before shutting the door.

When he lowered himself into his desk chair, the furniture creaked from his weight. "Are you law enforcement?"

"I'm Sinclair Develin with Develin and Associates."

"The Fixer, right?"

An acknowledgment nod from Sin. "This is Malvagio Peccatore with the Bureau. We spoke with Guy Chenkus about his side gig here."

Newburg's elbow jerked out, like a nervous tic. "What side gig?"

"You forced him to create passports for Haqazzii terrorists on the No-Fly list." Luciano said.

"Now, wait one goddamn minute. I didn't force anyone to do anything, and I have no idea what you're talkin' about." Beads of sweat broke out on Newburg's temples.

"Who do you work for?" Luciano said. "Who's behind this?"

"Behind what? I have no idea what you're talking about."

Silence.

Mr. Newburg fidgeted in his chair, the creaking sound bouncing off the walls of his drab government office.

"I get why you're scared," Luciano said. "Chenkus is dead. Let us help you. Tell us who you work with."

"If you don't, we'll open an IG investigation," Sin said.

"I... um, er... Guy was lying," Newburg said.

"This is a serious offense that carries jail time," Luciano said. "And the Bureau will come down hard on a traitor."

Newburg feigned surprise, but his open mouth and wide eyes only made Luciano want to shove him against a wall and knock the answers out of him. This was a total shit show and a complete waste of his time, but they had to do it this way first. When this failed, they'd do it *his* way. That would get them the answers they needed.

"If you don't cooperate, not only will the Inspector General be on your ass, you might find your investment accounts have a zero balance," Sin growled.

A sound, like the air being released by a balloon seeped out of Newburg. "This is much bigger than me and the small part you *think* I played. If I were you, I would march your asses out and crawl back under the rock from where you came."

Luciano and Sin exchanged glances.

"Wrong answer," Luciano bit out.

Sin flashed a smile. "You have no idea who you're dealing with."

"Get out!" Newburg shoved out of his chair and waddled to his door. He threw it open and glared at them.

The second they exited, he slammed the door shut.

As Luciano and Sin strode down the hall, Sin said, "He should have told us."

"He is." Luciano checked his watch. "My money says he's making a call right now."

That ten-minute visit would start a chain reaction that would blow the case wide open.

Luciano handed Sin an earpiece. They slipped the tiny devices into their ears and listened.

"We got snoopers," Newburg said. "Sinclair Develin and Malvagio Peccatore dropped by to ask me about Chenkus. How the hell do I know? Look, I was freaking the hell out, so I didn't ask a lot of questions. No, he didn't leave his card. Shut the hell up for a minute. You gotta make this problem go away. Do you hear me?" Silence then, "What do you mean take a few days off? I've got a goddamn department to run." Newburg slammed the phone on his desk.

Luciano smiled. "Now, we're gonna have some fun."

Sin chuckled. "Here comes the shit storm."

After dropping Sin at his office, Luciano checked his phone. Over a dozen texts waited for his review, but he scrolled until he found the one from Simone.

Call me

He tapped her number, the phone rang.

"Mr. Santini," she answered, her whisper-soft voice making him smile.

"Ms. Redding, should I pay you a house call?"

"That depends," she murmured. "Will you be a help or a distraction?"

"That's up to you."

"Swing by." The line went dead.

Blood whooshed through his veins. He couldn't wait to see her. He lowered the privacy screen, instructed Stuart to drive to Simone's. Fifteen minutes later, Stuart pulled into her driveway.

"Would you like me to carry the clothing inside, sir?" Stuart asked.

Luciano had his assistant put together a collection of Santini Originals for her. Not wanting to overwhelm her, he said, "Only the shoes now. The rest can wait."

Luciano rang her doorbell. She opened it, and a punch of adrenaline powered through him. The effect she was having on him was addictive. He kissed her hello, letting his lips linger on hers.

"Can't stay away, can you?" Her playful smile sent another hit of energy through him.

He held out the gift bag.

She didn't take it. "You don't have to—"

"Open it," he urged.

Before she closed the door, she peered outside. "Is Stuart waiting?"

"Yes."

"Ask him to come inside," she said. "I can make us a pot of coffee."

"I was hoping I could convince you to work at my place today."

She hitched her hands on her hips. "Go ahead."

"And?"

"Convince me."

He snaked his arm around her waist, this time kissing her breathless. "Should I continue?"

She sucked down a deep breath. "I'll get my laptop."

Again, he offered her the gift bag. "You don't need to buy me gifts," she said as she took the bag.

"These are for me." He winked.

She pulled out the Christian Louboutin shoe box, opened the lid. "They're stunning."

"Feet as talented as yours deserve a pair of luxury leather platform sandals."

"These are too much."

"Too high?"

"No, too expensive."

They were a grand. That was nothing to him.

As soon as she slipped them onto her bare feet, he started to harden. Being around Simone was too damn easy. She sashayed toward the kitchen, turned slowly, and walked back, her heated gaze making his balls ache with need. When he eyed the shoes on her gorgeous feet, he bit back a groan.

"They're perfect for you." He pulled a small black jewelry box from his pants pocket, opened it, and displayed a silver toe ring.

She laughed, then kissed him. "I love it. Toe jewelry."

"I wanted to get you one with diamonds—"

"Ouch," she said. "That could have hurt."

He knelt, removed one of the sandals, and slid on the simple, gold ring. Then, he kissed her foot, appreciating her silky skin before he slid the shoe back on. When he stood, she ran her hand over his bulging crotch.

"I definitely appreciate your fetish. You're easy."

"It's you," he said. "It's all you."

"Work now, play later," she said.

"I'll hold you to it."

She smiled. "And I'll deliver."

With her computer bag in one hand and her handbag over her shoulder, she paused in front of him. "Thank you for these gifts. Gotta say, I'm not used to being spoiled like this."

"Spoiling you would be buying you a car... for fun."

"Thank God I don't need one," she murmured. "I'm having dinner with Jerod tonight. He's introducing me to his girlfriend who's in from Atlanta. Let me grab a change of clothes."

She set down her bags and trotted upstairs. It took every ounce of strength *not* to follow her. A few minutes later, she returned, pausing to kiss him.

Her presence soothed his soul and kick-started his libido. Her sweet smile should have made him happy, but the guilt and grief crept back in. Would he ever forgive himself and allow himself to feel joy? It was his job to *protect* his family, not send them to their deaths. He shook his head as he took her overnight bag from her.

Pausing, she furrowed her brows at him. "You just shook your head at me." She ran a gentle hand down his whiskered cheek. "You okay?"

"All good," he replied.

After she locked up, they made their way down the walkway, but she stopped at her SUV. "I have to drive. I'm meeting Jerod at Carole Jean's in Tysons."

"I'll take you there," he said. "Ride with me."

"Thank you." She continued on to his Range Rover.

Stuart opened the trunk.

"Hello, Stuart," Simone said.

"Ma'am."

In went her bags before they climbed into the SUV. There, she crossed her legs, eyed the shoes. "These are beautiful."

He laid a possessive hand on her shapely thigh. "They look great on you."

"I'm not dating you for your money," she murmured.

When his gaze found hers, worry filled her eyes. "I know that," he said. "You have money."

"How do you know?"

"I ran a background check—"

Her eyebrows crashed into her forehead. "On my finances?"

"You were stalking me for weeks. I had no idea who you were."

She nuzzled close, leaned up, and murmured, "And now you know my brother got all the fashion sense. You saw his condo. He has a sense of style I don't have."

"You know what looks good on you and what doesn't."

"That's kind of basic, don't you think?"

"You'd be surprised."

She smiled. He loved the way her eyes lit up, the way she held his gaze. "I'm more like my dad. He's very practical when it comes to clothing. And you're right, I have money, but I'm more of a saver than a spender. I spent more in my twenties—"

"Wait, you aren't still in your twenties?" Luciano asked. "I can't date a woman—"

She shot him a little smile. "If you know how much money I have, then you definitely know how old I am."

He kissed her hand, then set their clasped hands on his lap. "I know I like being with you." They came together in a tender kiss, her soft moan filling his ears. "I like how you respond to me, how you feel in my arms."

"I like you, Luciano Santini. You zhuzh me up like no one I've ever known."

"You make me feel hopeful," he murmured.

She shifted toward him. "I have to tell you something."

He waited.

"It's about Peter Hirzog."

He curled his lip. "Was I right about him?"

"You might be."

That got his full attention.

"I went in with a plan—"

"I would expect nothing less."

She smiled. "He invited me to lunch to apologize for the spying thing. I confided that I'd left the Bureau for ALPHA, headed up The Bomb Maker mission, and was the lone survivor."

"You put it out there."

She tucked her hair behind her ear. "I did it so he'd feel like he could trust me."

"Did it work?"

"It did. He told me he worked at ALPHA, but Z fired him. He mentioned how much the group has grown over the years, like he keeps up with it."

"The Director could have told Hirzog about ALPHA."

"I still don't think he's The Bomb Maker, but he's on my radar." After a beat, she said, "I ruled everyone else out." She updated him on ATF agent Nina Roy.

"Follow the white rabbit," he said. "That's Hirzog."

"I did see something. After lunch, I said goodbye to Peter in the hotel lobby, but he circled back and took the elevator upstairs. First, I thought he parked under the building—"

"There is no underground parking."

"I know. Turns out, he was meeting someone."

"A woman."

"No, a man."

"Who?"

"Jerod De Clerq, my friend from ATF. The one at the dinner party who told Peter to stop obsessing over you."

∼

SIMONE

"Do you think they had a meeting there?" Luciano asked.

"My gut says no," she replied. "That's a pretty upscale hotel to hold an off-site government meeting."

"You think they're lovers?"

"Why else would you meet someone in a hotel guest room in the middle of the day?"

"Would either confide in you?" he asked.

She hesitated. "Hard to say, and I'm not sure its relevant. I just found it intriguing."

Stuart pulled up to the gates of Luciano's home.

Luciano unrolled the window, rattled off a code, said hello to his guardsman, and they drove onto the property. Today, the yard was bustling with workers. Several were blowing leaves while others were manicuring the gardens. Being there felt familiar and comforting. Never did she imagine she'd ever be back. Stuart parked at the fountain.

As she and Luciano collected her bags, Stuart said, "I'll be in the gym if you need me."

They all went inside.

Stuart headed toward the lower level as Luciano escorted her down the hall and into his office. It had been redone since Colton had lived there. He'd removed the dark paneling, had the walls painted white, and hung an oversized piece of abstract art. The room felt open and airy, and filled with natural light.

Her gaze floated over the desk and executive chair with the built-ins behind them. Nearby stood a small conference table with four chairs. A large white sofa took up real estate in the center of the room, but it was the second desk near the French doors that caught her eye. That one stood completely empty, the first had a closed laptop on it.

"Take whichever desk you want," he said.

"Have you always had that second desk?"

"No, I had it moved in here for you, but if you need your own space, you can work next door."

Her heart expanded in her chest. *He did that for me.*

She pointed to a closed door nearby. "Brigit worked in there."

"That's the size of a closet, so I converted it to one of my safe rooms," he explained. "Can I get you something to drink?"

On their way toward the kitchen, he showed her the room next door. Like his office, it housed a desk, an executive chair, a wall of built-ins, and a love seat.

"If you need privacy, you can work in here," he said.

"I'm good with you," she replied.

His smile made her heart quicken.

In the quiet kitchen, he pulled a bottle of sparkling water, but she filled a glass with water from the beverage center in the refrigerator. With drinks in hand, they returned to his office. She pulled out her laptop, set it up on the desk by the patio.

"Sin and I met with Chenkus's boss, Cary Newburg," Luciano began. "We threatened him, but he wouldn't talk."

"Of course."

"I left a micro surveillance device in his office—"

She shook her head. "That's not a federal offense or anything."

"And he made a call right after we left."

"Nice," she said. "I'll check his desk phone and his cell, but he probably used a burner. It's gonna take me some time to get that info. If I'm on the phone, will it bother you?"

He placed his palms on her desk, leaned down and said, "No, Simone, it won't."

His hushed, compelling voice, paired with the fire in his gaze, made her heart flutter. "I'll let you know if you're a distraction."

With a wink, he returned to his desk. She admired his broad shoulders and nice, tight ass.

Maybe I should work next door. I'm never gonna get anything done in here.

She dragged her gaze to her computer, logged in to ALPHA, and requested Cary Newburg's phone records.

Her money was on a burner, but she had to go for the low-hanging fruit. Ten short minutes later, an employee on ALPHA's Internet team called.

"I've got Mr. Newburg's phone numbers and I'm uploading his recent calls to the portal, but I can't help you with a burner this fast. It's gonna take time for me to triangulate it in DC."

"Thanks for the heads up," Simone replied. "I appreciate the help."

Simone hung up and read the report.

Shortly after Luciano and Sin left Newburg's office, he made three calls from his desk phone to other employees at State. She added their names to her follow-up list. Next, he sent two texts from his personal phone, both to the same number. That number was assigned to a woman. After more digging, Simone discovered the woman was his longtime girlfriend, Trish Benderson. She worked at Social Security Administration.

One text said, "I'm thinking of using up some leave. Maybe head out of town. Can you join me?"

She replied with, "Talk later?"

He'd replied with a thumbs-up.

Simone continued working, her attention diverted when Chef Louis entered pushing a cart. A platter loaded with sliced apples, peeled Mandarin oranges, plump raspberries and vibrant blackberries. The second platter offered a variety of cheeses and crackers. There were two sparkling waters, a teapot and two mugs.

Cookies or chocolate would have gotten her vote.

"Hello, Chef," she said.

"Simone, how are you? If you don't like tea, I can make you a coffee, a cappuccino, espresso, whatever you'd like."

She sauntered over. "This looks great." She slipped a raspberry into her mouth.

"Are you staying for dinner?" he asked.

"No, I'm just working here this afternoon."

He acknowledged her with a nod before leaving.

She poured herself tea, added a little honey before sipping the hot beverage. With the mug in hand, she returned to her desk and paused to feast on her delicious-looking office mate. He was on a video chat, doing more listening than talking.

"What's the bottom line?" he asked. After listening, he said, "Tell them they're price gouging and shop that around."

He ended the call, answered another. "Santini."

As he listened to the caller, his gaze found hers. Even from across the room, she could feel the magnitude of his strength. It permeated everything around him, her included.

The call ended and he rose. She stayed focused on him as he stalked toward her.

The power he exuded stole her breath. Everything from his walk, to the sophisticated way he carried himself, to the intensity in his bright eyes. Even the air crackled with an invisible fire that held her complete attention.

"What's Newburg up to?" he asked.

"He might be headed out of town."

"Running from the devil, but I'll still find him." He eyed the food on the conference table.

"We need to put a tracker on his car."

A devilish smile filled his face. "I like the way you think."

Unable to stay away, she sauntered close. He picked up a blackberry, slipped it into his mouth. Her attention jumped to his perfect lips, his chiseled jaw.

"Try one." He held out a blackberry.

With a tender touch, he placed the bulbous fruit in her mouth. She bit down and a burst of tartness tickled her tongue.

He brushed his lips against hers, the jolt of energy careening through her.

His phone started ringing. One more kiss before he answered. "Santini."

"Hey, brother," said a man Simone recognized as Liv's husband, Jericho Savage. "I gotta switch up our meeting from tomorrow to tonight. You good with that?"

"I'll be there," Luciano replied, his attention still on Simone.

"Come hungry."

After he hung up, he said to Simone, "I can take you to Carole Jean's. I have a meeting in Jericho's wine cellar."

"When you're finished, join us for dessert," she said. "You can meet Jerod and his girlfriend."

"*You* are dessert."

She dropped a light kiss on his lips. "Mmm... I can't wait."

He stole one more kiss before walking over to his safe room. There, he punched in a code, stood in front of the scanner, and vanished inside. Curious, she stood in the doorway.

Instead of finding cases of bottled water and non-perishable foods, stacks of cash lined the shelves.

What the hell?

He opened a black container, pulled out a small device. When he turned, he chuffed out a laugh. "You look surprised."

"Don't you use a bank like everyone else?"

"This is boodle."

"What?"

"Counterfeit," he replied, before closing the door. "My contribution to my family's business."

He held out a tracking device. "For Newburg's vehicle."

"I should get ready," she said. "Where can I change?"

He collected her overnight bag, brought her upstairs into a guest room. As he was about to leave, she said, "Stay."

She unzipped the duffle, pulled out a folded pair of pants and noticed a tear in the seam. "I can't wear these."

"I got you." He left the bedroom.

She slipped off her new designer shoes, removed her shirt and her pants. With her essentials bag in hand, she went into the bathroom. What she really wanted to do was go for a swim —unless Luciano had removed the indoor pool in the lower level—or go for a run on a treadmill—unless Luciano had taken out the gym. But she didn't have time to fit in a workout and get to Carole Jean's by six-thirty.

After brushing her teeth, she returned to the bedroom to find Luciano hanging up a pair of black pants and two shirts in the closet.

"Those are nice."

"They're from my design center. I thought you'd look beautiful in them."

"I'll wear something tonight, but I can't accept them."

"Simone, Simone," he murmured. "The clothing is made to be worn."

He did this special... for me.

"I'm sorry. You're being generous and I'm feeling uncomfortable."

"If you feel smothered or like I'm trying to control what you wear—"

"It's not that. I'm not used to someone being so generous."

His wicked-handsome smile set his eyes alight. "It's my pleasure."

She leaned close, kissed him. "The clothing is beautiful. Thank you." One more kiss before she eyed the items on the bed. "I'm going to wear the pink shirt with the black camisole and black skirt."

After zipping into the skirt, she pulled on the camisole, shouldered into the pink shirt and zipped it halfway. "These are luxurious... and comfortable." She stared at herself in the full-length mirror. "Form fitting without being too tight."

"It's a proprietary blend of fabrics."

She could see the pride in his eyes. He'd built his empire from nothing. Of course he would want to share his success with others.

"All these gifts, and I have nothing for you."

The divot between his brows softened. "You bring me peace, you challenge me, you give me hope. Those are far greater gifts, and something I never expected."

They came together in a hug, their connection so strong, she felt like she could melt into him. They shared a passionate kiss filled with love. It was real, it was happening, and she couldn't stop it if she tried. For the first time in a long, long time, she would accept the joy.

"I've felt so guilty and sad for so long," she murmured as she stared into his eyes, "it feels foreign to feel anything else."

"I know. One step at a time."

"One step at a time, *together*," she said.

As he kissed her, his lips lifted in a smile.

She liked that... she liked that a lot.

20

EXPECT THE UNEXPECTED

SIMONE

A t six-twenty that evening, Simone and Luciano entered Carole Jean's restaurant.
"I'm meeting Jerod De Clerq," she said to the maître d'. "Six-thirty reservation."
"Yes, ma'am, I can bring you right in." The maître d' tipped his head to Luciano. "Good to see you, Mr. Santini. May I seat the lady first, then escort you to the elevator?"
"I got this," Luciano replied.
"You'll need the elevator code," the maître d' said.
"Jericho texted it to me." Luciano regarded Simone. "I'll see you shortly." He kissed one cheek, then the other before taking off toward the elevator.
"Ma'am." As the maître d' escorted Simone, she soaked up the décor. Soft-glowing chandeliers set the romantic tone. Charcoal-colored walls complemented the light black table cloths. Servers dressed in black flitted silently around the large room attending to their diners. Each table boasted a small vase

with a bouquet of freshly-cut, short-stemmed roses, a vibrant display of beauty in the popular, Michelin-starred restaurant.

Simone spotted Jerod sitting beside a brunette, their backs to her. As the maître d' pulled to a stop at their table, Jerod's gaze jumped to her. With an exuberant smile, he stood, offered her a warm hug.

After Simone sat, the maître d' handed her a menu. "We have just received our third Michelin star." He beamed. "We're celebrating with a complimentary glass of champagne. May we bring them to you?"

Yeses all around. With a slight bow, the attendant wished them, "Bon appétit," and left.

"It's good to meet you," Becca said. "Jerod said he's stoked you're friends again."

Simone smiled. "Same."

"I'm a little nervous," Becca confessed. "He said you didn't like his last girlfriend and he broke up with her."

"Jerod. Not helpful," Simone scolded.

He laughed. "I love you, Becca, and I didn't end things because Simone didn't like her."

After they looked at their menus, the friendly banter continued. Their server brought their bubbly, mentioned the specials, and took their orders. After she left, they toasted, and sipped the chilled champagne.

"I hate to talk shop, but I promise it'll only be for a few minutes," Jerod said.

"Perfect timing." Becca glanced around the room. "Be right back."

After Becca left, Jerod said, "Someone in my department has a reliable source who said Frederica's death *wasn't* from a gas leak explosion," Jerod leaned across the table toward Simone. "It was The BM."

Simone wasn't surprised word had gotten out. People talked, especially about someone who'd harmed so many. Years earlier, when The Bomb Maker decimated government buildings in four metropolitan cities, he'd claimed responsibility for his heinous crimes, then taunted law enforcement. But after her failed mission, he'd done the opposite, by going silent for years.

She shook her head. "No, Frederica left law enforcement," she lied.

"Red, it's me you're talking to," Jerod pushed back. "Look, I wanted you to know the truth, but I don't want to ruin our fun vibe."

Too late.

Her heart ached at the mention of Frederica, the festive mood squelched. But he *had* started the conversation, so she'd follow the white rabbit and see where it led.

"Did your agent verify the source?"

"I don't have details, but I did assign a team to follow up. If you have any interest in joining, I'd hire you like that." He snapped his fingers.

The server returned with their appetizers, and Simone opted to change the subject. Now wasn't the right time—or the right place—to discuss the case.

"We'll talk," she said as Becca returned to the table. "Becca, are you thinking of relocating here?"

Becca beamed at Jerod. "We've been talking about living together. I'm starting a new job and can work remotely. The company is based in Manhattan and I'd need to spend a week every quarter at their headquarters. It's a quick train ride from DC."

"Sounds perfect," Simone said. "Jerod you must be excited for Becca to move here."

He blew her a kiss. "I'd marry her tomorrow if she was ready."

"Let's live together and see how that goes," Becca said.

"How does Peter feel about you and Becca?" Simone asked.

A flash of surprise darkened Jerod's eyes. "I'm sure he'd be thrilled."

"Have you met Peter?" Simone asked Becca.

"No, I haven't," Becca replied. "Is he a friend of yours, honey?"

"Just a work friend."

Simone held his gaze.

Jerod's pink cheeks turned a deep red, the color spreading to his nose. He drained the water from the crystal glass before eying Becca.

If he was going to poke the bear, she'd poke it right back. While she might have backed down then, she was *not* backing down now.

LUCIANO

LUCIANO GLANCED from Jericho's laptop—where he'd been eyeing the faces of the men—to Sin, then Carrera before finally settling on Teddy.

"This really pisses me off," Jericho said. "How the hell are we going to stop them?"

"Their passports are legit," Teddy said.

"Their aliases are good," Carrera said. "They're getting in completely undetected. Not a single stop by Customs."

"When seven *known* terrorists enter my country pretending to be upstanding US citizens, I get angry," Jericho said.

"These men are on the No-Fly list," Sin said. "They should've been stopped."

"They're barely disguising themselves," Carrera said.

"Simone has been following up on every lead, no matter how small, but it's been frustrating as hell," Luciano said.

"She's upstairs having dinner with friends," Teddy bit out.

"She's not work—"

"Chiudi la bocca, Theodore," Luciano growled. "Non una parola in più."

"No fighting," Jericho barked. "I'm assuming that wasn't nice."

"Luciano told Teddy to shut his mouth," Carrera translated.

"Help her, Teddy," Luciano said, the bite gone from his voice. "We've got nothing solid. Find these monsters."

"Yeah, it's like chasing the wind," Teddy said. "I can't find any of them."

"They land at Dulles and they disappear," Sin added.

"We know they're working for The Bomb Maker," Luciano said, "or they've got some kind of partnership with him."

The conversation continued while Luciano's frustration grew. The men's faces plastered on the laptop were the latest in the growing number of internationally-wanted men who were entering the country without anyone giving them a second glance.

"I've asked a few trusted people about The Bomb Maker," Sin said. "No one knows much. He works alone—"

The elevator doors opened and Jericho's younger sister Georgia rolled out a food cart. Luciano closed Jericho's laptop.

One by one, Georgia set down their entrees, but her gaze kept jumping to Teddy. "Can I get anyone anything?"

Luciano regarded his brother who appeared unaware that a pretty woman was checking him out. Teddy pushed out of his chair, raked his hands through his long hair, and began pacing.

"Is he okay?" Georgia asked.

"No," Carrera replied. "He's insane."

The group laughed, but Georgia was too busy staring at Teddy to pay them any attention. She pushed the empty cart out of the way, topped off their water goblets, said goodbye to Teddy, and left.

"Teddy, she's cute, don't you think?" Luciano asked.

Teddy stopped pacing, stared at him. "Who, Georgia? Yeah, she's super-hot. I have an idea. I need photos of everyone on the No-Fly list."

Carrera got busy on his laptop. Seconds later, he said, "I sent it over."

"I'll scrub this against the men we think got in," Teddy said.

"A lot of them are stopping at Heathrow," Luciano said. "They might use the same passport or they could be swapping out their first one for a different one."

"It's a fucked-up world," Jericho said.

"And we're in the center of it," Sin added.

"After you scrub that list, send me the ones you *know* are here," Luciano said.

Teddy nodded before he dug into his steak. After chewing and swallowing, he guzzled his beer, then glanced at each of them. "Aren't you eating? I'm starving."

The men raised their wine glasses. "Let's get it done," Luciano said.

Thirty-minutes later, the meeting had ended, their meals finished. Luciano shook everyone's hand, except Teddy who pulled him in for a bro-hug.

"I love you, Lulu," Teddy said. "Sorry about earlier. I like Simone. She's cool. Foxy too."

"Teddy—"

"Relax, I'm not gonna say how I met her."

"How did you meet her?" Jericho asked.

"Lulu had his face between her legs, and I interrupted."

A chorus of laughter echoed through the wine cellar.

Luciano bit back a smile. "Teddy, why can't you be discreet?"

Teddy chuckled. "It's funny. It's not like they've never had sex before."

Georgia appeared with several desserts on a rolling cart.

"Talk to her," Luciano urged.

"I clam up around pretty women," Teddy whispered.

"You don't have to talk," Jericho said. "My sister will."

"Will what?" Georgia asked.

"Teddy wants to say hey," Luciano said, then tossed his brother a nod toward Jericho's sister.

Georgia beamed. "I've got a few minutes."

Luciano folded two hundred-dollar bills, offered them to Georgia. "I know you're the GM, but you took good care of us tonight."

Georgia accepted the money, kissed his cheek. "You're sweet. Thank you."

After taking the elevator, Luciano spoke with the maître d'. As the attendant escorted him to Simone's table, he glanced around the room until he found his target.

Simone was sitting across from a brunette and a man with military-short blond hair. As he approached the table, Simone glanced over. Their connection was unlike anything he'd ever experienced. A jolt of energy shot through him and the desire to touch her took hold. He hadn't felt such an overwhelming need to protect someone in a long time, but he felt it now.

He thanked the maître d', who'd pulled out his chair.

Simone rose, pressed her lips to his cheek and kissed him. "Perfect timing. We just ordered coffee." He kissed her other cheek before turning to face the couple.

"This is my friend, Jerod, and his girlfriend Becca," Simone said. "This is Luciano."

Jerod rose, shook Luciano's hand. "Red didn't mention anyone joining us."

"I hope I'm not interrupting," Luciano said.

"Of course not." Becca gestured to the chair. "Are you hungry?"

"I had a working dinner." Luciano seated Simone before easing down next to her.

The server hurried over. "Sir, welcome. Can I bring you a menu?" She topped off Simone's coffee.

"Espresso," Luciano said.

"Did we decide on a dessert?" the server asked the others.

"The chocolate mousse cake sounds amazing," Becca said. "Jerod, share?"

"Two forks," Jerod said to the server.

After she left, Simone said, "Becca's moving to the area from Atlanta."

As Becca chatted about her decision, Luciano glanced at Jerod. He looked vaguely familiar, but Luciano had never met him and couldn't place where he'd seen him.

When Becca finished talking, Jerod said, "How do you two know each other?"

"We met at a party," Simone said.

"You look familiar," Luciano said.

Jerod fiddled with his utensils. "I work in the federal space. You?"

"I run Santini International."

Becca grinned. "Wait, no way. I love your chianti and have a subscription to your Once-a-Month Club."

"What's that?" Jerod asked.

"I receive a surprise gift every month. One month it was a Santini Original cashmere scarf. The next, a bottle of Santini Whiskey, the next a man's sweater. You benefitted from that. I gave you the sweater for your birthday."

"Grazie," Luciano said. "That's a very popular club."

Jerod pulled out his phone. "Excuse me, I've got to make a quick call." He strode toward the front of the restaurant.

"He's always working," Becca said.

"Where does he work?" Luciano asked.

"ATF," Becca answered. "He's very dedicated to his group."

"Have you been dating long?" Simone asked.

"A year, then he moved, and it's been long distance ever

since." Becca rolled her eyes. "That put a strain on things, but I'm hoping we get back on track once I move here."

"When are you looking to do that?" Simone asked.

"Right after Thanksgiving, which is crazy." Becca pulled out her phone. "I won't know anyone here but Jerod. Can we exchange numbers?"

"Absolutely." Simone rattled off her number and Becca shot her a text.

Jerod returned. "Becca, I'm sorry, but I have a work thing. We need to leave."

"But my dessert," Becca protested.

"I asked our server to wrap it." Jerod smiled at Simone. "Thanks for joining us. I'm sorry I have to bolt. I took care of the bill, but please stay and enjoy your coffee." He extended his hand to Luciano. "I'll have to try your whiskey."

Luciano stood and shook Jerod's hand.

Simone hugged Becca. "I'm glad we met." Then, she hugged Jerod. "Thanks for inviting me."

"So, you're giving her a thumbs-up?" Jerod asked.

"Two thumbs-up," Simone replied.

The server appeared with a small bag and a demitasse for Luciano. "Thank you for dining with us."

Jerod took the bag, ushered Becca toward the door. After setting Luciano's espresso on the table, the waiter left.

"How was your dinner meeting?" Simone asked.

"Productive. Did you like Carole Jean's?"

"The food is delicious," she replied. "Jerod bolted pretty fast."

"What's his story?"

"He's with ATF. He was an agent, now he runs a department there."

Luciano sipped the strong coffee. "Do you think he's having an affair with Hirzog?"

"I asked how Peter felt about Becca."

He cocked an eyebrow. "That had to get a reaction."

"He turned super red." She sighed. "Maybe they are, but how do they go from having an affair to being involved in a terror plot?"

"I still think we need to follow the white rabbit."

"Hirzog," she murmured as the server returned.

"Can I get you anything else?"

"We're good, thanks," Luciano replied.

"I hope everything was to your satisfaction,"

"It was perfect." Simone thanked her. After she left, Simone said, "We should go."

"What's the rush?"

"I want to attach the tracker," she whispered.

He chuffed out a laugh. "You're as driven as I am."

"No, Mr. Santini, no one is *that* driven."

They exited the restaurant, and she shivered from the chill. He removed his suit jacket, placed it over her shoulders. "Do you want to wait inside while I get the car?"

"I'll stay with you." She entwined her fingers through his. "Why don't you valet park?"

"Not safe."

After tucking her into the SUV, he leaned in, and kissed her. As they stared into each other's eyes, hope started to take root. One more kiss before he closed the door, got behind the wheel.

He drove out, wrapped his hand around her thigh, and glanced over. Her gaze met his.

"Love," she murmured.

"Love," he replied.

After a beat, he asked. "Did that just happen?"

She shot him an adorable smile. "It's just a word."

"It's *the* word," he murmured. After a pause, he asked, "Should I talk shop or wait?"

She caressed his hand. "Tell me."

"Teddy's going to scrub the No-Fly list. That'll help us figure out who got in so we can stop everyone else."

"That's good," she replied. "Jerod told me Frederica's death wasn't an accident. He said that a reliable source told one of his agents it was The Bomb Maker."

"What did he think?"

"Becca returned to the table, so we stopped talking about it."

He turned into a DC neighborhood, cut the headlights, and called Teddy.

"Yo, baby," Teddy answered.

"I'm attaching the tracker to Newburg's car. Where should I park?"

"Pass his house on the right, turn left at the corner," Teddy said. "There's a house for sale on the right. It's vacant. Park there."

"How 'bout I place the tracker and you drive around the block?" Simone asked.

"I'm not leaving you," Luciano said to her.

"Hey, Simone," Teddy said.

"Hi, Teddy."

"Newburg parks in his garage," Teddy continued. "He's home. His girlfriend is there. She parked in the driveway. I'll override the garage door opener, so you can open the garage enough to get inside, then attach the tracker."

"Grazie, fratello," Luciano said before ending the call.

As instructed, he parked in front of the vacant house, handed Simone a ski mask and black gloves before pulling on his own.

"We'll jog down the middle of the street," he said. "Do you want to open the garage door or attach the tracker?"

"I'll attach the tracker," she replied. "What should I do if they come out while we're there?"

"Get out of the garage if you can and we'll hide around the side of his house."

"And if they enter the garage from the house?"

"You're screwed," he said and flashed her a smile.

She laughed.

"Get out. If you can't, hide in the garage."

With their simple plan in place, they exited the vehicle. Simone started jogging down the middle of the street and he pulled up alongside her.

This wasn't normal. It wasn't how most people began a healthy relationship, but he wouldn't change a thing.

This was *their* story, no matter how extreme.

As he approached Newburg's cozy, two-story home, he slowed. One car sat in the driveway. The front porch light was on, as were two lights on the first floor and one upstairs. He pulled the tracker, handed it to Simone. As he lifted the door, it squeaked on its hinges.

"Fuck," he murmured.

Simone knelt, then vanished inside while he held the garage door in place.

The front door opened, Newburg's voice filtered into the night. "Honey, I wish you'd stay."

"You snore and I can't sleep," said a woman. "Plus, I've gotta get up at four."

Simone hurried out. He lowered the garage door, clasped her hand, and they bolted into the shadows, but the crunch of dry leaves on the side lawn stopped them.

His heart beat slow and steady in his chest.

"Did you hear that?" asked the girlfriend.

"Hear what?" Newburg asked.

"Like an animal running through the grass or something," she said.

"Maybe you heard a deer," Newburg replied.

"Crouch," Luciano whispered.

Together, they turned toward the backyard and squatted.

If Newburg or his girlfriend approached the side of the house, they'd run. No way could Newburg catch them. As they hid in the shadows and waited, a surge of excitement powered through him.

Newbury's girlfriend started her car, turned on the headlights, and drove away. Newburg coughed, the thick phlegm catching in his throat. After he spit, he shut his front door. Luciano waited to be sure he'd gone inside.

"Let's go," she whispered.

Still holding hands, they took off toward his car, parked around the corner. Once there, they jumped into the vehicle, but neither removed their mask. He started the car and drove out in silence. On the main road, he turned on the headlights. She pulled of her mask, he pulled off his.

"That was fun," she said.

"Were you nervous?"

"Not at all," she replied.

She's the one.

In the dark car, they regarded each other. "I love you, Simone."

She smiled. "I love you too."

SIMONE

Simone was buzzing with excitement. She loved working with Luciano. His energy was contagious, his confidence radiated off him. When she'd heard the voices, her heart started galloping in her chest, but knowing Luciano was on the other side of the garage door kept her calm. Working with him was exhilarating. She hadn't felt this alive in a long, long time.

Rather than obsess over every little thing that might go

wrong with the case, she forced herself to stay on point. One small win at a time. She hoped Newburg would lead them to something relevant because she had nothing.

Absolutely nothing.

Luciano drove to Simone's, parked in the driveway, and got out. As she exited the SUV, they made their way up the walkway.

"I don't need an invitation," he said. "I'm staying."

She wrapped her arms around him and kissed him.

As she fished out her keys, Luciano said, "Simone." The sternness of his voice had her following his gaze.

A large piece of white paper had been taped to her front door. On it, the word:

BOOM!

He grasped her hand, ushered her into his vehicle. She felt numb, then angry and overcome with dread. Luciano drove around the corner and pulled over.

"What about my things?" she asked. The second those words were out there, she wanted to retract them. "Never mind."

Luciano made a call.

"How'd it go?" Teddy answered.

"No problem," Luciano replied. "You did good."

"We all set?"

"No," Luciano replied. "There's a sign on Simone's front door. Boom. The place needs to be swept. Hawk has a robot for explosives. Simone, can you wait until tomorrow—"

"Of course, but I don't want Teddy putting himself at risk."

"Thank you, Simone," Teddy said. "My brother doesn't care about me."

Luciano chuckled. The calmness in his voice, paired with his relaxed expression, settled her down. He had this magical ability to insulate her from the reality of the situation. She couldn't enter her home. Everything she owned might be lost if the house exploded—

I lost my ALPHA team. I lost Fred. I might lose my home.
Stop. Breathe.

She inhaled a slow, lung-filled breath. And another.

"Teddy, do whatever you need to do to ensure your safety," she said. "Should I be there?"

"I got this. You need to find The Bomb Maker, though I kinda think he found you first."

"Fuck," she bit out.

Teddy was right. He had found her.

"Do you have security cameras?" Luciano asked her.

"I have one out front and one out back," she replied as she clicked on the security app on her phone. "Same with my neighbors next door and across the street." She opened the app, scrolled. "I got a hit." She showed Luciano the short video.

"Someone dressed in black," Luciano said.

"Forward it to me," Teddy said.

Simone did.

"Teddy—" Luciano said. "I texted Hawk."

"I'm on it."

"Use a body cam and let us know when the robot goes in." Luciano hung up and drove away.

The Bomb Maker is taunting me.

That simple sign taped to her front door had rendered her homeless without a thing in the world but the clothing on her back—which was from Luciano—plus a few items in her essentials bag.

He clasped her hand. "I got you."

Those three words reminded her that she wasn't alone. She was leaving, but she wasn't running scared. Not this time. "I'm okay."

"Nothing is going to happen to you, Simone. *Nothing.*" The power in his voice had her kissing his cheek.

"I can stay with my brother—"

"I'm not letting you out of my sight. You'll be safe in my home."

She grew silent as she thought about everything that had happened over the past month. She went over every conversation she'd had with every single person.

"Maybe you're right," she said, as he sped toward home. "Maybe Peter Hirzog isn't the good guy I think he is."

"Why would you say that?"

"I don't know." She shrugged. "Honestly, I'm not thinking clearly."

"Let's get you home and we'll think this through... together."

In the dark car, he squeezed her hand. His power seeped into her bones and filled her with hope.

"Do you get scared?" she asked.

"No," he replied. "I've looked into the eyes of the devil himself."

She shuddered. "What did you see?"

"Hell," he replied. "I saw hell."

"How are we going to win?"

"By letting the devil think he has all the power."

"Doesn't he?"

"No," Luciano replied, a sinister smile filling his face. "I do."

Silence accompanied them the rest of the way, Simone reviewing every aspect of the case in her mind. She remembered the anonymous texts. The death threats she'd so brashly dismissed.

Once past the gates, he drove into his underground garage. Up the elevator they went and into the kitchen. There, he offered her an array of beverages. She picked his whisky. After pouring two glasses, they sat at the island. He opened his laptop. She tossed back a mouthful, then another. The subtle flavors ignited her taste buds. Warmth filled her belly.

"This is robust, yet delicate. So many tastes."

"What did you experience?"

"Chocolate, then espresso. After I swallowed, it tasted creamy and a little sweet, like honey or vanilla."

His smile soothed her. "That's exactly what you should have tasted."

She peered into his eyes for a beat. *You gotta tell him.*

"I haven't been completely up front with you."

His eyebrow arched, ever so slightly.

"I'm pretty independent and take a lot of pride in that. It was hard for me to open up to my therapist, but I didn't have a choice. I couldn't burden my family or friends with what I was going through because I couldn't talk about the mission. When I worked for Colton, my focus was on mergers, acquisitions, and helping him grow his business. As a watcher, I worked alone."

"Simone, what do you want to tell me?"

She showed him the two text messages she'd received.

> If you take that case, you're a dead woman.

> I warned you not to take the job. Now, I have to kill you. I will win. I always do. Mass destruction and chaos will be mine.

His expression didn't change, except when he stared into her eyes. To her surprise, his were filled with love. "You don't have to go through this alone."

"I shouldn't have dismissed them."

"This is The Bomb Maker."

She shuddered in a breath. "I've been in denial."

"Let's geolocate the burner phone." He guided her to his

office, logged into his computer. He was able to narrow the location to Northwest DC, but nothing closer.

Teddy called and Luciano put the call on speaker. "Go."

"Hawk is with me," Teddy said.

"Hawk, thanks for doing this," Luciano said.

"Hey, Luciano. Simone, no worries, okay?"

"Thank you," she replied.

"Hawk sent a robot around to clear the exterior," Teddy said. "We found nothing. From what we can tell—the house hasn't been breached. No entry points were disturbed."

"Good news," Simone said.

"How many spare keys are out there?" Teddy continued.

"My brother has one."

"What about a cleaning service?"

"No."

"Any hidden outside?"

"No. Just the one with Gary."

"Okay, so we're going to clear the interior," Teddy said. "Lulu, I sent you a link for live feed."

Luciano clicked on the link and Simone's house came into view.

"Since we cleared the exterior, we were able to remove the hinges, so we didn't blow your door," Teddy continued. "We checked ducts that opened to the outside, like the dryer. All clear."

"You're very thorough," Simone said.

Teddy chuffed out a laugh. "Yeah, well, we got no room for error."

She and Luciano watched as Hawk piloted a robot that walked on two legs. "Mr. Metal has cameras for eyeballs," Teddy explained. "We're showing you live feed on the front-facing camera, but there're back-facing cams too."

Hawk guided the robot into the foyer.

"I'm looking for an obvious package or stacks of dynamite," Hawk said as he piloted the robot into the living room. "But I've also gotta confirm nothing has been hidden. Again, I'm not sure how the bomber would do that since he never breached your home."

"Sounds like a power move," Luciano said.

"That's what I'm thinking," Hawk agreed.

Everyone grew silent as Hawk maneuvered the robot from room to room, opening every cupboard, every closet. As the minutes ticked by, Simone was overcome with gratitude for their commitment to her safety.

In her bedroom, Teddy asked, "Anything disturbed?"

Through the eyes of the robot, Simone viewed her bedroom. "Nothing."

"Mr. Metal has been programmed to detect subtle changes in a room," Hawk explained. "If an explosive was set to blow, the computer could sense it."

Two hours later, Hawk and Teddy finished their extensive search.

"The asshole who did this might be watching," Teddy said. "You know, getting his rocks off from all the attention. I've got two of my guys combing the neighborhood for him."

"Teddy, Hawk, thank you," she said. "Do you bill me or do I pay you now?"

"Hawk, I got you," Luciano said.

"No charge," Hawk pushed back. "You're ALPHA, so you're family."

Tears pricked Simone's eyes, but she shoved down the emotion. "Thank you so much for having my back."

"We're gonna shut things down, then I gotta tell your neighbors everything's okay," Teddy said "A bunch of 'em have been watching this shit go down."

"Did you see anything on my surveillance cams?" Simone asked.

"Just the man in black," Teddy said. "I'll let you know if that changes."

The picture went dark and Simone released a long exhale. "What a relief."

"This is good," Luciano said. "The Bomb Maker's creating chaos, something he thrives on. Think about the mass bombings on those government buildings."

"That sent the whole country into panic."

"Anytime, he gets attention for something bomb-related, he feels empowered. We need to draw him out, let him think he's winning. Then, once we know who it is, we take him out."

"Sounds simple," she said, "but we don't have anything to go on."

"We will," he said. "Everything takes longer than we'd like, but we'll get there."

Simone regarded Luciano. He was the pillar of strength. He wasn't worried, he felt no fear. He stayed in control, he stayed focused, and he got the situation addressed and resolved in a matter of hours.

She dropped a light kiss on his lips. "Thank you for treating me with respect, despite my idiotic denial. I should have told you about the threat texts. Thank you for handling this and for insisting that I stay safe. I'm so used to keeping things bottled up, handling things on my own." She kissed him again. "I'm so indebted to Z for the assignment."

His smile sent a streak of energy powering through her. "Me too, babe, but please, Simone, no more secrets. We're a team."

He logged into a tracker site and clicked over to several active trackers, marking Cary Newburg as CN. "Anytime he goes anywhere, I'll get notified."

Her gaze dropped to the list of people he was tracking, then she circled back to the one he'd labeled SR. "Am I SR?"

"Yes."

"Were you planning on removing the tracker from my vehicle?"

"I'd turned off the alerts, but based on what happened tonight, I'm reactivating it."

"And I thought the damn chip in my neck was intrusive."

"I had no idea who you were or why you were following me," he said. "I had to protect myself."

"I get it."

"You're not angry?"

"At you? Hell, no." She stood, shot him a little smile. "I'm not completely stupid."

He pushed out of his desk chair. "Time to sleep. We can get your clothes tomorrow."

"Five years ago, I moved into this mansion for protection from The Bomb Maker. And here I am, hiding behind the iron gates all over again."

"You're not hiding. You're staying alive. He found you. He knows you're hunting him. I have no idea how he knows, but he does." He ran the back of his hand over her cheek, dipped down and kissed her. "I need to know you're safe. I can't protect you unless you're with me—"

"Like twenty-four seven? That's crazy." Then, she realized what he'd been through, what he was still dealing with, and would always struggle with. "I'm sorry. I would love to stay here with you."

"We'll get whatever you need tomorrow. Maybe you'd consider some new clothes. A woman as stunning as you—"

She pulled him into her arms, kissed him. "I love you. I don't know what you're doing with someone like me."

"The same thing you're doing with someone like me—"

"You're very wealthy, extremely successful—"

"I'm surrounded by brilliant people who are very loyal. And now I can add you to my inner circle."

"You're so humble," she whispered. "I'm not wealthy. I haven't amassed the power you have."

"You're successful, you're driven, you have smarts and intelligence. You're well liked. You follow the rules a little too closely for me—" He winked— "but we can work on that."

She laughed.

"We've both experienced great loss," he continued. "We understand the fragility of life. We have family we love and friends who've become family. And I have a weakness for leggy brunettes named Simone."

She nuzzled close. "Let's go upstairs."

As they ascended the sweeping staircase, she put her arm on his back and caressed him. "You do so much for everyone. All the time. When was the last time someone did something—anything—for you?"

At the top of the stairs, he stopped. "Elsa has always been there for me. She's been my one constant."

"Tonight, let me do something for you."

He continued toward his bedroom at the end of the long hallway. She didn't move. After a few steps, he turned around, spread his arms out, and continued walking backwards. "You have ten bedrooms to choose from."

"I choose you," she said. "But I'm going to massage you."

He stopped walking. "You don't have to, caro."

"What does caro mean?"

"Dear one."

"I love that." After a second, she asked, "Wouldn't you like to be pampered?"

"Of course," he replied.

"Then, I'm going to take good, good care of my man."

21

FOLLOW THE WHITE RABBIT

LUCIANO

Luciano was concerned for Simone, but he needed to play this one chill. She was being hunted by The Bomb Maker and her denial was blinding her to the harsh reality. As long as they were together, he would keep her safe.

In his bedroom, she stripped him bare, directed him to lie face down on his king-sized bed. She removed her pants, then her shirt and camisole, leaving her in a lace bra and panties. She climbed onto his back, drizzled oil into her hands, and pressed her warm palms against his back.

Her touch was soft, but the pressure firmer than he'd expected. She ran her fingers across his shoulders, slowly.

"Wow, you're tight," she murmured.

When she switched to using her knuckles, the pressure intensified. "Breathe," she said and he inhaled through the discomfort.

One knot at a time, she worked his shoulders before pausing for more oil. Her hands felt like a gift from the gods.

Yes, he'd paid for massages, but he'd never received one as a gift.

Despite the late hour—it was almost three in the morning—he didn't object. This was her loving him, and he was grateful. As she worked out the tension in his shoulder blades, he couldn't stop his mind from racing.

How did The Bomb Maker know she was offered the case? How did he know she'd taken it? And if he had access to that, finding her home address had been easy.

"Deep breath," she murmured.

He inhaled and she dug her knuckle into an especially painful spot on his lower back.

"Are you okay?" he asked.

"Doing great," she replied. "How's the pressure?"

"Perfect, like you." He craned his neck so he could see her. Her sweet smile was the medicine his vengeful soul needed.

He laid his head on the pillow, tried to stop himself from obsessing over the case, but he couldn't.

"Guy Chenkus got the false passport info from Cary Newburg," Luciano began. "Newburg has to be getting his information from someone. Is that person working with someone in the Haqazzii terror cell or is there a go-between? How big is this network?"

She dipped down and kissed his cheek. "Turn your head the other way, so your neck doesn't get stiff."

After he did, she rubbed his traps before massaging his glutes. "That feels amazing. You've got the hands of a goddess."

"All for you," she murmured and started rubbing the back of his thigh. "You've got a great butt. Very muscular. Great legs too."

"Thank you, baby."

"I love that." He could hear the smile in her voice. "I'm your baby. My heart is happy, but the anger is consuming me."

"That's good. We're going to need it when we unleash it on the devil."

She grew silent.

"Simone?"

"Yeah."

"Do you think there's a crime ring in the government?" he asked.

She stilled for a few seconds before resuming her rubbing. "When you put it like that, yeah, it's possible."

"How far up do you think it goes?"

"Far enough so that these terrorists are sailing into the country with real passports and believable aliases."

"What's the connection between them and The Bomb Maker?" he asked.

"No shop talk. Try to relax."

Relax? I never relax.

He continued running through questions without answers, trying to follow an invisible trail that led to the guilty.

The massage continued for much longer than he'd anticipated. He figured she'd rub him for ten, maybe fifteen minutes. When she got off him and told him to roll onto his back, he glanced at the time. She'd been at it for over forty-five minutes.

She was laser-focused on whatever area she was working on. While rubbing his biceps, her eyebrows pinched together, then she'd spend a few seconds chewing on the inside of her cheek. Was she thinking about this case… a case with no viable suspects who was taunting law enforcement and hiding in plain sight?

"Talk to me about Jerod," Luciano said.

"He and I worked a few cases when I was with the Bureau and he was an agent with ATF. We got along well, became work friends. I saw him at Peter's dinner party. We had lunch at Rudy's—"

"Did you tell him anything?"

"I told him I was the agent who went after The Bomb Maker and lived." Her gaze found his. "You're not thinking—"

"Check him," he replied. "He looked familiar, but I'd never met him before tonight."

"I'll see what I can find." Simone finished by caressing his foot. "I hope you liked your little massage."

"Thank you. That was amazing." He patted the mattress next to him. "Sleep, Simone. We've got time for a nap."

"Not yet," she said. "Now, you get a happy ending."

A bolt of heat shot through him. "You're taking very good care of me."

"You're keeping me alive. I'm keeping you happy." She smiled. "Sounds perfect to me." Straddling him, she stroked his shaft with her lubricated fingers. A tender touch to jump-start his engine. Back and forth she rubbed before leaning down and, on a loan ardent moan, she took him inside her mouth.

Her warm, talented mouth.

His insides roared to life, his attention pinned on her abilities. He loved how she stroked his shaft while running her tongue over the head. Jolt after jolt of electricity thrummed through him, while her whisper-soft moans urged him onward.

Slowly, she pulled off, and with half-hooded eyes, murmured, "You taste good."

The ache in her voice turned him harder, the excitement whipped through him in a torrent of energy. Then, she was back on him, devouring him with greed while she massaged his balls and raked her lips over his cock.

Up and down, she took him into her mouth, ran her skilled tongue over him, then licked him like a popsicle. Her blowjobs turned him wild with need as he raced toward a climax.

His groans meshed with the garbled sounds coming from her as she quickened her pace. Her hand tightened around his hardness while she pumped him again and again. Then, she pressed him in until he vanished inside her mouth, but when he hit the back of her throat, the orgasm took hold.

"Fuck, Simone, I'm gonna come."

While fondling his balls, she raked her teeth over his shaft while flicking her tongue across the head, her guttural groans launching him over the edge.

On a groan, the orgasm shot out of him, glorious waves of ecstasy pounding through him. In those seconds, every broken piece of him became whole... and healed. Life was perfect and simple. There was nothing but blinding white goodness.

Until it was over, and the darkness began to seep in.

She slunk out of bed and vanished into the bathroom, returning shortly wearing nothing at all. She crawled in beside him, pulled up the linens, and snuggled close.

He pulled her onto him. Large pupils blown with lust peered into his eyes. "Thank you for taking care of me," he murmured before kissing her.

Her kiss was passionate... and loving. In their embrace, he felt the power of her love. The strength of what she could bring to his life. He was so used to taking care of everyone, allowing someone to take care of him felt foreign.

But also fantastic.

"Thank you for becoming such an important person in my life," she whispered. "Thank you for allowing me to be me. Damaged, vengeful me."

"I got you," he murmured.

They shared another kiss.

"I got you too," she replied.

~

SIMONE

AT SEVEN-THIRTY THAT MORNING, Stuart parked the Range Rover in Simone's driveway. She, Luciano, and Stuart made their way toward the front door. All three were armed. All three wore Kevlar protection.

"Here comes a neighbor," Luciano murmured.

Simone turned, painted on a friendly smile and waved. "Hello, Lorraine."

"Simone." Lorraine hurried over, still wearing her bathrobe. "What happened? Is everything okay?"

"All good," Simone said. "Someone left a note on my front door that turned out to be a hoax."

Lorraine's eyes widened. "Yikes. I'm glad you're okay."

"Did you see anyone before the team showed up in the middle of the night?" Simone asked.

"No, but I talked to the man in charge. His name is Tank—" She broke into a broad smile—"and he looked like one. Anyway, I forwarded my videos to him. I had several dings last night, but didn't pay any attention. It's usually just a deer in my yard."

"Thanks for helping," Simone said before she hurried onto the front porch where Luciano and Stuart waited.

Teddy had taken the BOOM sign to dust for prints, but Luciano doubted they'd find any. This was a simple job that would take a complete fuck-up to screw up. The Bomb Maker was not that. He was skilled, cunning, and one step ahead of them, leading them down the rabbit hole to the depths of hell.

After clearing the first floor, they went upstairs. While Stuart cleared the second floor, Simone retreated into the bathroom to change into fresh clothes. After she packed two suitcases, Luciano and Stuart carried them downstairs. As Stuart loaded the suitcases into the Range Rover, Luciano's phone pinged.

He opened the tracking app. "Newburg is on the move."

He showed Simone. "Looks like he's going to work," she said.

Into the car they went.

"Are we headed to your company?" she asked.

"We're going to Springfield."

"What's there?" she asked.

"A chemical supply company run by Igor Stachko. He supplies materials to bomb enthusiasts."

"Nice. How'd you get his name?"

"From Carlo Garibaldi."

"The head of the Garibaldi crime family?"

"We were rivals. After I left, we became close."

Simone wasn't going to ask any more questions. Sometimes less was more, especially when it came to her criminal boyfriend.

Luciano's phone rang, he answered. A work-related problem that snagged his attention allowed Simone to review the notes she'd made on her phone. Thirty-minutes later, Stuart drove into an industrial section of Springfield, pulled into a lot and parked. They made their way toward Stachko Chemical Supply Company.

As soon as Stuart opened the door, the stench of chemicals made her grimace. The pungent odor aside, she couldn't wait to see Luciano in action. How would he get Mr. Stachko to talk?

Luciano smiled at the receptionist. "I'm looking for Mr. Stachko."

"Do you have an appointment?"

"Do I need one?" Luciano replied.

The woman glanced at Simone. "Did *you* make an appointment?" Her haughty attitude caught Simone by surprise.

What a B.

"This is my boss, Joelle James," Luciano said.

The woman swallowed. "Sorry." She rose. "Let me check with Igor. What's your name?"

"Malvagio Peccatore."

She hurried off and Luciano murmured, "How am I doing, boss?"

"Smooth, charming." Simone shot him a little smile. "Perfect." Then, she turned toward him, lowered her head, and whispered, "Cameras everywhere."

"Saw them."

A small man with spindly arms and wire-framed glasses too big for his narrow face joined them. He glanced at Simone, then at Stuart, settling on Luciano. "What can I help you with?"

"I have a business proposition for you, Mr. Stachko," Luciano said.

"'Bout what?"

"I don't conduct business in a lobby," Luciano said. "Do you have five minutes?"

"Yeah, sure, c'mon back." Igor led them into his office, which had a thick layer of dirt on any surface that wasn't cluttered with papers, old paper cups, and bottles of chemicals. He sat behind his desk, gestured to the two chairs.

"Is he your bodyguard?" Igor asked of Stuart.

As Luciano sat, he said, "Yes, he's a member of my security detail."

"What can I do for you, Mr…"

"Malvagio Peccatore. I need information." The tone in Luciano's voice had changed from a charming lilt to a harsh staccato.

Stuart shut Igor's office door.

Igor narrowed his gaze at Luciano. "I sell chemical supplies. That's the business I'm in."

"You're working with The Bomb Maker," Luciano said. "Who is he?"

Igor shifted in his chair.

Stuart pulled his Glock. "Don't open that drawer," Stuart growled.

"Ah, fuck," Igor bleated. "I don't need no trouble." He shifted his attention to Luciano. "Look Mr. Pecker, he never told me his name, but I'm sure if he did, it wouldn't be real. You know what I mean?"

"When was the last time you saw him?" Luciano asked.

Igor glanced up at Stuart, his weapon still drawn. "A few weeks ago. Maybe a month. He paid in cash—"

"How much?"

"A quarter of a mil. Said he'd be back for more and I should expect the same large order."

"Does he come alone?"

"Yup."

"What does he look like?"

Igor leaned back and his chair squawked on its old hinges. "Now, Mr. Pecker, that's gonna cost you. I don't give that kinda information away for nothing. I run a business."

"I can call Carlo Garibaldi or I can call the FBI. Either way, you'll have unfriendly visitors on your doorstep in hours. One would slit your throat, the other would arrest you."

"Ah, crap," Igor mumbled.

Luciano walked around the desk, yanked Igor out of his chair, and shoved him against the back wall. "What does he look like?" he growled.

"Dark hair to about here—" Igor touched his shoulder. "Sharp dresser. Real nice clothes. He was tan, but it didn't look legit. Maybe he wore makeup 'cause his face was kinda orange."

Luciano released his hold, but he didn't step away. "Did you see his car?"

"He had a truck, you know, for supplies."

"Who loaded everything?"

"He did, but I helped him, a little."

"Any tats? Piercings?" Luciano raked his hand through his hair.

"None that I saw, but he was—wait, yeah, he had this super

flashy pinky ring. Lotsa diamonds and the band was a pink color. He kept playing with it, you know, spinning it around, and it caught my eye. How 'bout you give me your number and I'll let you know when he swings by?"

"Did he call you?"

"No, he showed up, like you." Igor tried to smile, but he looked like he'd shit his pants. "Look, Mr. Pecker, I don't want you to call anyone. I told you what I know, 'kay?

Luciano glared at Igor. "If you supply him with any more bomb-making materials, you're a dead man. Capiche?"

Visibly shaking, Igor hugged himself. "Sounds like I'm a dead man either way."

"Remember what I said." Luciano opened the door, waited for Simone to exit, then followed with Stuart close behind.

They got in the vehicle, and Stuart drove out of the lot. "That was good, boss," he said.

"I went easy on him."

"We need to get this guy off the street," Simone said. "And pull him in for questioning."

"I know who The Bomb Maker is," Luciano said, a sly smile temping his lips upward.

She stared at him for a few seconds. "From that description?"

"My cousin introduced me to someone named Dante who wanted a mil in boodle. I refused him, twice. Time to let Dante know I'm ready to do business."

"How do you know Dante is The Bomb Maker?"

"He wore a rose gold pinky ring loaded with diamonds," Luciano said, "and he fiddled with it during our meeting."

Simone nodded. "Finally, a break. *Now*, you're being helpful."

He and Stuart laughed out loud.

Stuart gained speed on the entrance ramp to the beltway.

After a moment, Simone asked, "Where'd you get the name Malvagio Peccatore?"

"From Sin." Luciano showed her his FBI badge. "It's Italian for Wicked Sinner."

She laughed. "Mygod, that's perfect."

Luciano made a call, kept it on speaker.

"Hey, Lulu," Willie Boy answered. "What's happenin', fratello?"

"I need Dante's number."

"What for?"

"I changed my mind about doing business with him. You trust him, so I trust him."

"That's great! I'll let him know."

"Text him now. I'll wait."

"He shows up when he needs somethin'."

"Willie Boy, you run a business," Luciano bit out. "Why don't you have his number?"

"He's discreet. I don't push."

"Maybe if you did, you'd be a respected boss."

"Fuck you."

"There's twenty G's in it for you," Luciano said, the bite in his voice replaced with the charm Simone had come to appreciate.

"I don't want boodle."

"Twenty *legit*, Willie Boy. But you gotta set up a meeting for tomorrow. If not, the deal's off."

"Christ, why do you have to be such a dick?"

Luciano cracked a smile. "Make it happen." He hung up, regarded Simone. "If Willie Boy doesn't come through, I'll put the heat on Newburg. Either he ordered the hit on Guy Chenkus or he knows who did. I'm out of patience."

Simone couldn't agree more.

. . .

LATER THAT AFTERNOON, while squirreled away in Luciano's office, Simone was reading through posts in a private chat group on the dark web. Luciano had accessed several groups that supported terrorism. Some were haters of democracy, others were disrupters—anarchist groups and conspiracy theorists.

As she was reading, one comment caught her eye. "Who loves creating chaos and destruction?" It was authored by Inferno531.

Several members of the group had responded, but it was Inferno531's response that prompted her to say, "Luciano, come check this out."

He stood behind her, his charisma and essence filling the small space. He wrapped his arms around her, pulled aside her hair, and kissed her ear.

"What did you find?" The irresistible timbre of his voice, paired with his warm lips pressed against her skin, sent a frisson of delight racing through her.

She swiveled toward him, placed her hands on his cheeks, and kissed him. "Hi." She kissed him again. "I found two comments by Inferno531." She read the first comment to him, "'Who loves creating chaos and destruction?' and his response, "I'm going to create terror in America that will be remembered for centuries. It's a project of epic proportion and I'm working day and night to make it happen. Get ready, 'cause here I come.'"

Simone started typing in the chat. "I want in. I want to be a part of a history where America gets crippled to its knees. No, its ass. LOL!"

"Nice," Luciano said.

"He's never responded to anyone," Simone said. "He just rants and posts threats, but I've gotta try." She hit, Post Comment. Seconds later, her post went live in the group under Luciano's group name, TheDevil.

Luciano's phone rang. He answered. "Santini."

"Don't you see it's me calling?" Teddy asked, his booming voice filling the room.

"I was talking to Simone and—"

"With gaga eyes?"

Simone laughed. "I'm not sure I'd use that to describe your brother."

"He's pussy whipped."

Luciano smiled. "There's a lady here, Theodore."

"Yeah, the one who's got you whipped."

Again, Simone laughed. "Thank you, Teddy. That was perfect."

"Rough afternoon?"

"Slow going," she replied.

"I've got good news and bad news," Teddy said. "Which first?"

"You decide," Luciano replied.

"Bad news first. I couldn't lift a print from the sign on Simone's front door. He wasn't wearing gloves, but I got nothing."

"Dammit," Luciano bit out.

"Here's the good news," Teddy continued. "I got a hit from your surveillance cam, created pics, and enlarged them. I'm sending everything your way."

They sat side-by-side at Luciano's desk. Seconds later, the encrypted emails came over. He started the video.

A man with shoulder-length, dark hair and sunglasses walked into frame. He strode to Simone's front door, pressed the piece of paper against it, hurried down the driveway, and vanished out of frame. Luciano opened the enlarged still shots.

"Check out his right pinky," Teddy said.

"Flashy pavé diamond," Simone added.

"Son of a bitch," Luciano growled. "It's Dante."

"The one who bought the supplies from Igor?" Simone asked. "And wants to do business with you?"

"That's the one," Luciano said.

"And that's why I get paid the big bucks," Teddy said.

"Nice work," Luciano said. "I met him at Willie Boy's, but Willie Boy says he doesn't have a way to contact him."

"He probably doesn't," Teddy said. "I have more business acumen in my *other* head than he does—"

Simone laughed. "Good one."

"I like you, Simone," Teddy said. "You laugh at all my jokes."

"We need to find Dante," Luciano said.

"Why don't you and Teddy put pressure on Cary Newburg?" Simone asked. "Santini style."

"She's catching on," Teddy said.

"She sure as hell is," Luciano replied.

"Watch your six, yeah?" Teddy said.

"Absolutely." Simone pushed out of her chair. "Luciano, do you still have the indoor pool and gym in the lower level?"

"Yes."

"I'm going to work out before dinner."

"Simone," Teddy said.

"Yeah."

"Lulu's gonna be your shadow."

"Thanks for the heads up. What should I do about it?"

"Nothing you can do," Teddy replied. "When my brother sets his mind on something, it's a done deal."

At the doorway, she turned back. Luciano winked. "I'll meet you in the gym."

Up the stairs she went. Earlier, Stuart had brought her luggage into her old bedroom. The décor had been updated, but not the furniture. A comforting familiarity washed over her.

She changed into her swimsuit, threw on sweats, and hurried to the lower level. After a good run on the treadmill, she did a quick circuit with a few weights, then headed to the pool. Colton had one rule. Never swim alone. So they didn't. As she contemplated whether she should venture into the water, the door opened and Luciano entered.

And all the air got sucked from her lungs.

Luciano Santini in a bathing suit was eye candy perfection. An Adonis of a man with muscles for days. She was transfixed by the way he commanded the space, how his mere presence affected her in the absolute best way. She had been struggling with the lack of progress she'd been making, but seeing him was like finding a lighthouse in the middle of a violent ocean storm.

Is he my salvation?

He was a man, a god of a man who consumed power like people consumed food. Yet, in his company, she felt like she could do anything, be anything, accomplish anything. It felt like he was sharing his power with her.

He went to her, pulled her into his arms. "Ciao, mia bella, Simone."

Their kiss was filled with love, but it was over too soon. When he broke away, there was a sadness in his expression. A melancholy that touched the deepest part of her.

She ran her fingers lightly down his shoulders. "Is your heart feeling heavy?"

He sighed. "I don't want to forget them."

She offered an encouraging smile. "You won't." She pressed her hand to his chest, over his heart. "They live here. They will always be your first loves. Maybe even your true ones. But you have room to love others. You just have to forgive yourself first."

He kissed her forehead. "Let's swim, yes?"

She didn't want to push him, didn't want to force him to speak when his heart was heavy. People process love and loss differently. She couldn't begin to understand the depth of his anguish, but she would do whatever she could to support him.

He walked to the diving board, dove in. She followed. The warm water refreshed her skin. Not too cold, not too hot. Just right. Like Luciano.

A broken, flawed, beautiful man with so much to offer.

She swam for as long as she could. Feeling more out of shape than she'd anticipated, she stopped against the wall to catch her breath. But he continued swimming. Back and forth until she joined him again.

When they finished, they swam to each other. Staying apart was impossible. The need to be close, the invisible string kept tugging her toward him. The passion in his kiss and the strength in his embrace made her feel alive... and so safe. His touch ignited her need, his kisses electrified her. When the kiss ended, she swam away. She *wanted* to get lost in him, but she *needed* to work.

It wasn't her first choice, but it was the right choice.

After a quick shower, she dressed in yoga pants and a comfortable sweater and made her way downstairs. Despite the enormity of the house, she felt like she'd come home.

Following the delicious aroma, and the sounds of voices, she found Luciano sipping a glass of chianti in the kitchen while chatting with Chef Louis and his wife, Therese.

When Louis finished cooking, he and Therese retreated downstairs.

"Do you ever eat together?" Simone asked.

"No." Luciano held up the bottle of wine.

"Just a half."

He poured her wine, topped off his own. "I keep my personal and work lives separate."

"Thank you for breaking your rule for me."

He stepped so close she could see the streaks of dark green in his eyes. "I miss you." He brushed his lips against hers.

"I miss you too." She kissed him back.

He pulled her close, the power in his embrace made her

gasp. Being in his arms was a powerful aphrodisiac and the perfect escape. He kissed the top of her forehead, broke away.

"Dinner, then we'll work, yes?" he asked.

She didn't *want* to say yes, but she needed to stay on point. "Dinner, work, then us."

The intensity of his kiss filled her with anticipation. "I can't wait for more zhuzhing," she whispered before breaking away.

Chef Louis had prepared a delicious meal. Baked chicken, wild rice, a garden salad packed with fresh vegetables. "This looks fantastic... and it's very health conscious."

"Louis is excellent."

"Do you eat alone?" she asked while they ate.

"When I'm home, yes. You?"

"Same."

"Do you want children?"

Whoa.

"Where'd that come from?" she asked.

"I never saw myself falling in love again," he said. "But I have, and these are questions I need answers to." His phone buzzed. "Newburg is on the move."

"Follow the white rabbit," she said.

"To wherever it may lead," he replied.

22

LOVE, LOVE, AND MORE LOVE

LUCIANO

Luciano was ready to move their relationship forward. He'd found a woman he could build a life with and he wanted her to know. If she didn't see a possible future together, he would work the case with her and walk away.

Sooner is always better. Later might never come.

Simone had grown silent after he'd asked her about children. Was he pushing?

Only for information.

With a soft hand on his, she said, "I do want children. What about you?"

"Depends on the day," he replied.

They watched the blip on the tracker as Newburg drove to a bar in Arlington.

"He's at Mac's on Lee Highway," she said. "That place has been around for decades. It's a landmark."

He grimaced.

"Not your jam?"

"It's a shithole."

"It's a dive bar. You know, French fries are dripping in decades-old grease. The beer on tap is probably laden with bacteria." She shot him a smile. "Not everything in life can be a Santini Original. Not *everything* can be first class."

He arched an eyebrow.

"Luciano Santini, ruler over all," she declared.

That made him smile.

∼

SIMONE

LUCIANO DROVE TO MAC'S, backed into a parking spot in a dark corner of the lot. After they fitted comms into their ears, Simone slid on a dark baseball cap. Luciano pulled on a black knit cap, showed her a photo of Newburg on the State Department website.

"I'm armed, I'm wearing body armor, and I'm ready," she said.

"You got this." he replied.

On a nod, she exited the vehicle, squared her shoulders, and headed toward the entrance. The place was busy, but not packed. There were two open seats at the bar, one open table, and two unoccupied booths. After a quick sweep of the patrons, she found Newburg sitting alone in a booth nursing a beer. She kept her head down as she passed him, slid into the back booth, and sat facing out.

Once there, she whispered, "I've got eyes on him."

"Is he alone?" Luciano asked through the comm.

"Yeah."

The server appeared. "Can I getcha something?"

"Whatever's light on tap."

The server moseyed off and she flicked her gaze to the front door. A couple entered, made their way to the bar.

"I used to come in here," she said to Luciano through the comm.

"When?"

"In my twenties with Frederica. We'd toss back a beer, talk about how much we loved being Special Agents."

The server returned, set down a napkin and the beer. "Those guys at the bar wanna know if you're with someone."

Two guys were waving her over.

"One of the dudes said the drink's on him."

"I got this," Simone said.

"Hey, it's a free beer."

"They're gonna want something for it. I'll pass."

"What's going on?" Luciano asked as one of the men from the bar walked over.

"A guy's hitting on me," Simone whispered.

"I'm coming in."

"I got this."

"You sure do," said the stranger.

Simone glared at him. "Not interested."

"You look like you could use some company," the stranger pressed.

"I wouldn't sit there if I were you," she warned.

"Why the hell not? I can sit wherever I want."

The door to Mac's flew open. Luciano's striking presence hit her like a bolt of lightning. Two seconds later, he was by her side.

"The lady said no," Luciano growled.

"Fuck off."

Luciano's nostrils flared, his eyes turned black, and his fingers curled into fists.

Oh, boy, here we go.

"Walk. Away," Luciano growled.

The front door opened, Simone glanced over and gasped. "Ohgod."

Both men turned in her direction.

"Sit," she said to Luciano. "Now."

Luciano slid into the booth.

"What the hell?" blurted the stranger.

Simone glared at him. "Get lost before some real shit goes down."

The guy raised his hands. "Yo, bitch, you don't need to get all jacked up." He spun around and walked away.

Simone flicked her gaze to Luciano and her heart beat faster for a very different reason. "I found the white rabbit," she murmured. "Hirzog's here."

Excitement danced in his eyes. "We should say hello."

Her mouth fell open. "Are you insane?"

His devilish smile sent adrenaline pounding through her. "Yes, I am."

She snuck a peek at Hirzog. "He's sitting with Newburg."

"The white rabbit." Luciano's smug expression had her shaking her head.

The server returned to take Luciano's order. "We're out." Luciano paid for Simone's beer.

"Knowing he's involved makes me sick to my stomach," she said.

"He'll lead us to the next person."

Simone's guts churned. "Unless he's the end of the road." She glanced over. "We shouldn't be seen together."

"I'll be outside." He pointed a finger at her. "Don't make me wait."

"What will you do if I'm a bad girl?"

"I'll punish you."

"All night long?" she asked.

"Until the cock crows in the morning."

"Lucky me," she murmured while her gaze drilled into his.

He drew her hand to his and kissed her palm.

"Thank you," he murmured.

"For what?"

"Helping me heal."

Her heart filled with love. "Whatever you need. I'm here for you."

"Goes both ways, baby." Luciano pushed out of the booth, but instead of walked past Hirzog and Newburg, he vanished into the busy bar area… and was gone.

I've fallen and I've fallen hard.

Minutes passed while the two men sat and talked. Her attention was diverted when Newburg shoved his large frame out of the booth and headed toward the door.

Simone whispered, "Newburg's leaving."

"What about Hirzog?" Luciano murmured through the comm.

"He just stood."

Hirzog started toward the back of the bar, glanced over, and stopped. "Red!"

"Peter, hi. What a surprise."

"Are you alone?"

"My brother Gary was supposed to meet me, but he was running late so we just rescheduled."

"I've got to use the restroom. Can you stay for a minute?"

"Do it," Luciano said into her ear.

"Of course," she replied.

"You were right," she whispered into the comm.

"I got lucky," Luciano replied.

"Damn straight. You met *me*."

"Very lucky." She could hear the smile in his voice. "Bait him to talk."

"I got this," she whispered.

Two minutes later, Peter slid into the booth across from her.

"What a fun surprise," Simone said. "Are you here by yourself?"

"I met a friend for a beer."

She pulled off her baseball cap, ran her fingers through her hair. "You're looking great. How are you? How's work?"

"Never better." He leaned forward. "Can I confide in you?"

Her pulse quickened. "I got you."

"I've been seeing someone, you know, on the side. It's been a whirlwind, crazy-ass, ride."

Jerod popped into her thoughts.

"I never pegged you for stepping out of your marriage, especially after what you said about your first wife."

Peter's shoulder's fell. "I know, I know, but I can't help myself." His face turned bright red. "It's not like anything I've ever done before."

"Shit happens."

"I'm not gay," he blurted.

"Okkkkaaaaay."

"I've been seeing Jerod. Jerod De Clerq."

"Jesus," Luciano murmured in her ear. "Fucking hypocrite."

"Are you in love?" Simone asked.

"It's lust. One-hundred percent. He has this kind of psychosexual hold over me. It's like nothing I've ever experienced. I've been going to the gym five nights a week. I'm in the best shape of my life. I can't stop thinking about him. It's hard to put into words the kind of spell he's cast on me."

Simone wasn't sure where to go with this. "Are you thinking of leaving Lucy?"

He reared back. "God, no. I love my wife, but I can't stop myself from seeing Jerod. I know I need to break it off with him."

"No fucking kidding," Luciano growled.

The situation was *not* funny, but Luciano's reactions made her want to laugh.

"How does Jerod feel?" she asked.

He stared at her for the longest time. "I don't know."

"That's a good place to start."

"Nice," Luciano whispered.

"Maybe *you* could talk to him," Peter said. "Find out how he feels."

What the hell...

She felt spidery. This was *not* something she would take on. Jerod had Becca, she was moving to the area for him. Was Jerod bisexual? Was he a closet homosexual? Was his relationship with Peter a manipulation play?

Playing dumb, she asked, "Is Jerod also having an affair?"

"He's never talked about anyone, so I assumed he's single," Peter replied.

"What a cluster fuck," Luciano whispered.

"I didn't know his sexual orientation until he came on to me." Peter leaned close again. "It was the most intense sex I'd ever had in my life. I thought I was gonna lose my mind."

She wanted to scream, "TMI! TMI!", but she just nodded. "Sounds like you should talk to him. Find out what next steps could look like for you both."

At this point, she was channeling her friend and former therapist, Liv Savage.

He heaved in a deep breath, released a long sigh. "You must think I'm a monster."

"Because you're gay?" She laughed. "My brother is gay. I adore him and his husband."

"Because I'm having an affair and I was so angry because my ex had had one."

"Karma, asshole," Luciano murmured.

Simone bit back a smile.

"Relationships are complicated," she said. "I'm the last person who should be giving advice, but I do know that talking helps. Find out where his head and his heart are. Think about your own feelings."

"I feel intense passion and the worst guilt." Peter hung his head.

She ran a comforting hand over his. "It's gonna be okay."

When he lifted his face, tears glistened in his eyes. "You've been so gracious. I'm very grateful you've come back into my life."

She pasted on a smile. "I feel the same way."

She wanted to ask him about Newburg. She wanted to ask him if he knew anything about a covert crime ring in the government. Did he know about these passports for terrorists who were entering the country?

She would *never* play her hand, but she *would* encourage him to continue confiding in her.

"I'm a phone call or text away. I'm here for you, like you were for me."

"Thank you, Red."

She shot him a smile. "Of course."

"I was such a jerk about Luciano Santini. I have no idea why, but Jerod bit my head off. You'd think he and Santini were friends."

"Are they?" Simone asked.

Peter chuckled. "They don't even know each other."

"Hirzog knows nothing," Luciano murmured. "I met Jerod at Carole Jean's."

"I'm sure if you talk to him about your relationship, you'll know how to move forward," Simone suggested.

His eyes grew large. "You mean, consider leaving Lucy?"

"If you see a future with Jerod, then, yes. Does she have any idea you've been having an affair?"

"God, I hope not."

"Let me know how your talk with Jerod goes," she said.

"Thanks for listening," he said.

She had found the white rabbit. It *was* Hirzog. Luciano and Z had been right all along. Disappointment tinged her thoughts. Peter used to be one of her heroes.

As they left the bar, the blast of chilly air felt great against her heated skin. She glanced over to where Luciano had backed into the space. Across the lot, their eyes met. In that split second, she could see a life with him. A future with children. She could see it all, maybe even have it all.

He had her heart for as long as he wanted it. But if he couldn't share a small portion of his with her, she'd have to let him go.

"Thank you, Red," Peter said. "Can I walk you to your car?"

"I was going to walk you to yours."

"I want to make sure you get to your car safely."

Simone stalled. "Hmm, where did I park?"

After Luciano slunk out and vanished into the shadows, she walked over to Luciano's Range Rover.

There, she hugged Peter. "I'm just a phone call away if you need a friend. You've got a great job you've worked hard for. Don't do something you'll regret."

He scrunched up his face. "What do you mean?"

"Sometimes affairs make people do crazy things. You've earned your position at the Bureau and you're well respected."

He nodded. "Great advice."

She got into the car, started the engine.

Once Hirzog was in his car, she whispered into the comm, "All clear."

"I'm sitting right behind you," Luciano said.

She startled, then glanced into the rearview mirror. With a smoldering gaze, Luciano winked.

"How'd you get back in?" she asked.

"Ninja."

She drove out. "He said Jerod's got a psychosexual hold on him."

"They're both lying, cheating scumbags," Luciano bit out.

"Sounds like Peter's being manipulated."

"Or he's doing the manipulating. Either way, we need some damn answers."

LUCIANO

Simone stopped at the mansion gates. Luciano gave the guard the code, the gates opened, and she drove up the driveway. Rather than park at the fountain, she continued around back to the underground garage.

As she drove in, Luciano contemplated the irony of Simone's life. Years earlier, the mansion had been her home. Was she ready to make it her home again?

I want her to live here with me.

With clasped hands, they walked to the elevator. Their breathing had fallen into sync, the pull to draw her into his arms and love her had his blood pounding through his veins. But, tonight, he wanted her to know his true feelings. The ones he'd barely admitted to himself.

In the elevator, she said, "I could use a nightcap."

The door opened, she took off toward the kitchen. Rather than sit, she pulled a glass from his cabinet. "Am I drinking alone? And don't think I won't."

He loved that, despite the intense pressure she was under, there was a playful tone in her voice.

"Brandy?" he asked.

"Perfect."

He pulled a bottle of aged brandy from his cabinet, poured two glasses. Together, they sat at the center island.

She raised her glass. "To you, for being so damn patient."

They tapped glasses, sipped the after-dinner liquor.

"How am I patient?"

"Your methods are different from mine. Mine take time. I have to gather information, build a case, find evidence. Your ways are cunning, manipulative, forceful. They get results fast."

"You have skill and finesse. You threw Hirzog a lifeline. I

would never have done that. I would have taken advantage of the situation and gone for his jugular. Forced a confession."

Her shoulders fell. "Maybe I should have—"

"No, you're handling this right. You can't force him to give you information. You *don't* play your hand, Simone. I love that about you."

Her pupils dilated, a shadow fell over her face. "*I* love how you say my name. It's the sexiest thing ever."

He shot her a smile. "No." He stroked her cheek with the back of his hand, combed his fingers through her long hair. "You, naked, beneath me is the sexiest thing ever."

A raspy growl shot out of her.

He pushed off the stool. "You. Come with me."

Up the stairs they went, the urgency to their pace turning him hard with desire. "I want you in my bedroom, in my bed."

"I want that too."

He opened his bedroom door, closed it behind her. She was in his arms, kissing him with a passion that had him moaning through their embrace. She was on fire, stroking his tongue with a wild, wild greed.

He slowed the kiss, ended it. "Naked." He stripped her bare, paused to admire her beautiful feminine form.

"You don't get to have all the fun," she rasped. With nimble fingers, she worked to undress him. Seconds later, they were pressed against each other, the heat of her skin on his turning him into a beast.

She raked her fingernails down his back, grabbed his ass and squeezed. His erection was pressed against her, his desire to mate turning him into an animal.

The intensity in her gaze had him growling her name. "Simone, I need you." He threw back the linens and they tumbled into bed.

"In me," she gasped between kisses. "I need you in me."

While fondling her breast, he covered her nipple with his

mouth and sucked. The harder he sucked, the firmer her nipple, the more ardent her moans. So much lust passed between them, he ached to bury himself inside her and surrender to the need.

"Ohgod, that feels good," she bleated. "I love that."

She moved her hand between her legs.

"My sexy, sexy Simone."

While he licked her other nipple, she caressed her clit. He stroked her drenched pussy, delicately teasing her sensitive skin. She began undulating beneath him, her growly moans sending jolt after jolt of pure lust pounding through him.

He could come from the way she moved, the erotic way she touched herself, the fucking hot sounds she made.

And then, she started bucking. He kissed her, hard. When she shoved her tongue into his mouth, she convulsed beneath him, crying out. Watching her climax, seeing the ecstasy on her face, made him happy.

In those few seconds, he knew he needed to lean into Simone. She was his second chance at having a life filled with meaning and love… and he was going to take it.

Seconds passed. Her eyes fluttered open and she peered at him with half-hooded eyes.

Never before had he felt so connected to anyone.

She stilled, breathed deep. "Mygod, you undo me."

"Zhuzhing?"

She smiled. "So much zhuzhing." Then, she nudged him off her and mounted him. After curling her long fingers around his wet shaft, she took him inside her in one glorious glide. The onslaught of pleasure sent him flying high.

"Fucking good," he rasped.

She fondled her tits, pulled on her engorged nipples, while she rode his shaft. Hit after hit of euphoria shot through him.

"Do you like the way I'm fucking you, Mr. Santini? Do you like how my pussy is devouring your huge cock?"

Her dirty talk had him grabbing her hips. "You fuck good, baby."

She stroked her chest, pinched her nipples, and started moving faster. Up and down while the rush filtered into every part of him. So much pleasure. Then, she raised her arms over her head and came down on him completely.

And she stilled. She peered at him with lusty eyes, slickened her pouty lips with her tongue.

"Sit up."

He did.

She pressed her nipple into his mouth and started moving again, her intensity turning him into a savage beast.

"Fuck me," she ground out. "And fuck me hard."

He grabbed her hips, controlled her thrusting. Back and forth faster and faster. Her moans turned desperate, her gaze never leaving his. She was his. All his. And he was hers.

The orgasm started deep inside him, building slowly.

"Come so hard in me," she rasped.

His juices shot out of him, the blinding, deafening ecstasy had him releasing a long, loud series of groans while he stared into her eyes and poured himself into her.

"I love you," he murmured, before their mouths came together in another wild kiss.

"I love you." A tear spilled down her cheek. "That terrifies me more than anything."

He wrapped his arms around her. "Why are you afraid?"

"Love makes us vulnerable. I'm like a turtle, and I like having a shell I can hide in."

"Like this house."

Still locked in an embrace, she peered into his eyes. "Yes, this house. Feeling scared won't stop me from loving you. I want this. Whatever this is, for as long as it lasts. I love loving you." Her adorable smile made him smile.

"I feel complete with you," he said, "and the closest I've felt to being whole."

"I want to help you find the person who killed your family."

He shook his head. "It's okay."

"Let me help you. Maybe, then, you can start to heal."

The truth might push her away, but he needed her to know...

"Loving me puts you at risk. Someone wanted me dead, and my family was collateral damage. That can't happen to you. I won't let it."

"Luciano, I can't stay here in your ivory tower, surrounded by a tall fence and armed guards. I have to live my life."

"I know, caro."

He said nothing more. Why ruin their perfect moment? Until he found the person who killed his family, he would always be looking over his shoulder, always be doing everything he could to keep her safe.

Even if it meant taking a bullet for her.

23

MURDER AND …

SIMONE

At nine-thirty in the morning, Simone entered the Metropolitan Police Station in DC and walked over to the check-in counter.

A woman sidled over. "Special Agent Joelle James?"

"Yes," Simone replied.

"I'm Nikki Cardoso." After they shook hands, Nikki held up a shopping bag. "Perfect timing. My weekly junk food run."

"Please tell me you share, Commander Cardoso," Simone said.

Nikki laughed. "Hell, yes. I'm stress eating, so I buy way too much."

The Homicide department was bustling with detectives and uniformed police officers. Once in her office, Nikki sat behind her desk while Simone eased onto a chair.

A man wearing a suit strolled in, a sheepish smile filling his round, clean-shaven face.

"How's it going?" He extended his hand. "Detective Blake Hull."

Simone shook it. "Special Agent Joelle James."

Nikki pulled out a candy bar and handed it to him. The detective nodded at Simone before leaving.

Nikki closed her office door, sat back down.

"Are you seeing someone?" Nikki asked.

Jus thinking about Luciano made her smile. "Yes, why?"

"The detective who just came in wanted me to ask."

"How do you know that?"

"He threw you a head toss, which is *his* male speak for 'ask if she's seeing anyone.'"

"He moves fast."

"He's definitely not a procrastinator, but he's been married four times, so he's not a horse I'd bet on."

Simone laughed.

Nikki pulled out three small bags of chips, several candy bars, then extracted a package of six glazed donuts. "I like working with the Bureau, so take your pick."

"Gotta have a donut."

"Definitely." Nikki opened the package, Simone selected a chocolate frosted and bit into it. As the delicious sugary dough titillated her taste buds, she said, "I love you, Commander Cardoso."

Nikki laughed. "Stress eating is the best, especially when you do it with someone who appreciates it."

"Nothing like being a strung-out LEO."

"So true," Nikki replied, before biting into her own glazed donut.

Simone asked, "Any progress with the Guy Chenkus case?"

Nikki got busy on her computer. "The gun casings were sent to forensics. Our witness, Sinclair Develin, saw a man in a hoodie approach the car from the east side, open fire, and bolt. One of my detectives followed up with Mr. Chenkus' family and his boss. He worked for State and his record there was clean."

Not exactly.

"I'd love to know why you're following up on this case," Nikki said. "Especially since we don't have much to go on."

If Simone told Nikki what she knew—and if Chenkus' death was related to The Bomb Maker—she'd be thrusting him into the limelight. That could result in him blowing up the government buildings faster than he'd planned, simply to outrun law enforcement.

"I will as soon as I can," Simone replied. "I'm sorry I'm not being more helpful, but I'm not at liberty to discuss. Don't hate on the messenger."

"I get it, but it would be good if we could work together."

"Until recently, I had nothing. I'm concerned if word gets out, we're just giving the unsub the attention he craves."

Nikki leaned back in the chair. "I get that." She bit into the donut.

"There's a cold case from five years ago that I'd like to review."

"Is it related to the Chenkus case?"

"No," Simone replied.

"I'm having a terrific sugar high, so lay it on me."

"The Santini murders."

Nikki hopped on her computer. "When?"

After Simone gave her the details, Nikki pulled it up and spun the monitor so they could read the file together.

In August, five years earlier, a car exploded at the Santini home, killing all three occupants. Twenty-five-year-old Linda Santini and her two children, four-year-old Marco Santini and two-year-old Caterina Santini, were killed in the explosion. Luciano Santini, the alleged head of the Santini crime family, had taken his wife's vehicle to the mechanic for repairs. He was at the repair shop at the time of the explosion. Cleared as a suspect, he was presumed by police to be the intended target. There were no persons of interest and no leads from those brought in for questioning."

"That's tragic," Nikki said. "They were all so young."

"Yeah," Simone murmured, her chest tightening.

These three were his entire world. His heart would never completely be hers. She would always share it with them, but she understood that it had to be this way.

His grief and survivor guilt must be overwhelming.

"I can forward everything to you." Nikki shifted her attention to Simone. "Are you okay?"

"Yeah, sure."

"You don't look okay. You wanna talk about it?"

"Mr. Santini is a friend of mine. He's gone legit and now runs Santini International."

"No way," Nikki said. "I love his clothes and treat myself to something nice when stress-eating isn't enough."

Simone was wearing one of the pantsuits he'd bought for her. "The clothes *are* beautiful."

"It's good you're looking into it," Nikki said. "Cold cases need fresh eyes."

"I'll see what I can dig up, and I'll keep you posted," Simone said.

"I'm happy to help out any way I can." Nikki glanced at the report. "The arson detective is still around, but the homicide detective isn't."

Nikki's desk phone rang. "Excuse me one second." She answered, "Commander Cardoso." As she listened, she jotted a few notes, asked a few questions, then hung up.

"I've gotta head out," Nikki said. "Possible suicide, but it's high profile, so I've been called to the scene."

"So much for that donut," Simone said.

"I know. Suicides are tough for me." The color drained from Nikki's face. "My dad committed suicide."

"I'm so sorry." Simone's gaze dropped to Nikki's notes, and

the name of the deceased caught her attention. "Does that say Cary Newburg?"

"Yeah, I'm surprised you can read my writing."

Her guts twisted.

Peter, are you behind this?

"We need to talk, off the record," Simone said.

"Can you ride with me?" Nikki asked.

"Absolutely."

Simone had to confide in Commander Cardoso. She needed Nikki to walk into the crime scene with eyes wide open.

En route to Newburg's, Simone said, "I think Cary Newburg's death is related to Guy Chenkus' murder."

"How?"

"Both men worked at State," Simone explained. "Newburg was having Chenkus create passports that could be passed on to the Haqazzii terror cell."

Nikki's eyebrows jutted up. "Oh. My. God."

"This is something a *very* small group of people are keeping a tight lid on."

"Got it." Nikki turned into the neighborhood, the street swarming with cop cars and an ambulance.

Nikki parked, the women got out, made their way down the street. The air was chilly, the sky blue, and the pit in Simone's stomach was the size of the donut she'd eaten. She'd left a tracker on Cary Newburg's car. If someone checked that car *carefully*, they might find it.

I need to pull it before someone else does.

They gloved up, covered their shoes, and entered the home. A beat cop asked for their IDs.

After displaying their badges, Nikki said, "I need to talk to the responding officer."

"Where's the victim?" Simone asked the officer.

"His office, down that hall." He pointed Simone in the right direction, and she took off.

Simone found Cary Newburg on the floor, a bullet wound to his right temple, a gun on the floor next to his right hand. He was dressed in cotton pajamas and a bathrobe. His face ashen, his eyes lifeless.

Her chest tightened.

Death was difficult, regardless of the situation. She walked around his office, eyed the papers on his desk. A sticky note was taped to a framed picture of he and a middle-aged woman.

Love you always, Trish

Simone made her way into the kitchen and over to Nikki who was speaking with two officers.

"Who called this in?" Nikki asked.

"Welfare check from his girlfriend. She said he was supposed to pick her up this morning, but didn't show."

"Where'd she call from?" Nikki asked.

"She said she was home. They were taking the day off from work."

"Was anything breached?" Nikki asked.

"Nothing," replied one of the officers. "Negative on B&E."

Simone walked around the kitchen, pausing to read a handwritten note. It was a list of handyman items for the house. A grocery list sat next to that one. She spotted the pen. It was to the left of the papers.

Was Newburg left handed?

"Was anything moved?" Simone called out.

Nikki and the officers regarded her. "No, ma'am," said one of the officers. "Not by us, but we've had some traffic through here."

Simone walked into the garage. She was alone, the garage door was closed. She hurried to the car and removed the tracker. As she shoved it into her handbag, the door to the garage opened and Detective Blake Hull walked in.

"Joelle James, right? We just met back at the station. What are you doing out here?"

Simone brushed past him. "Same thing you are, looking for evidence."

"Actually, I was following you," he said.

She stepped into the house, turned back. "Why?"

"I thought maybe we could have coffee, or a drink, and discuss the case."

"No, but thanks." His smile dropped as she walked back inside.

That was close.

Back in Newburg's office, she eyed the short stack of papers on his desk. There was nothing that would answer her question about whether he was left or right handed.

A piercing scream from the foyer had her hurrying out of the room. The woman from the photo—Newburg's girlfriend, Trish Henderson—was being consoled by Nikki.

"I want to see him!"

"Ms. Benderson," Nikki said, "let's sit down."

"Tell me what happened!" Trish protested. "Who killed him? Who would do this to him?" Tears streaked down her cheeks.

"Was Mr. Newburg under a lot of stress at work?" Nikki asked.

"Just the usual job stress. We were talking about taking a cruise in January." Tears spilled down her cheeks. "I can't believe he's gone."

"Do you have any reason to think he would commit suicide?" Nikki asked.

Shock filled Trish's face. "Suicide? Are you kidding me? He would never kill himself. Why would you even ask that?"

"Ms. Benderson, Joelle James, FBI. I'm very sorry for your loss. Was Mr. Newburg left or right handed?"

"Left, why?"

There it is.

"We're just being thorough in our investigation." Simone stepped away, asked Nikki if she could speak to her for a quick second.

Nikki asked one of the female officers to sit with Ms. Benderson, then followed Simone into the home office where Newburg's body had been covered with a sheet.

Simone pulled back the cloth. "Entry wound on the right side of his head, gun laying by his right hand."

Nikki's slid her gaze from Newburg to Simone. "She just told us he's left handed."

"There are two lists on his kitchen counter," Simone said. "The pen is on the left side of those lists."

They returned to the kitchen. Nikki stared down at the papers, along with the pen. "Nice work, Joelle."

"Newburg was murdered, just like Chenkus," Simone said to Nikki. "Someone has a short fuse. There's no room for mistakes, no room for pushing back. If someone steps out of line, they're dead."

She thought about the sign on her front door.

BOOM!

Despite the intensity of the case, she was not backing down. Fear would not win... not this time.

She told Nikki she had a few more questions for Ms. Benderson. Together, the women returned to the living room.

"Ms. Benderson, where do you work?" Simone asked.

"SSA," Trish replied. "Social Security Administration."

"What department?" Simone pressed.

"I don't see how that's relevant. My boyfriend was *murdered* and I'm being told it was a suicide."

"We believe you," Nikki said. "Please answer Special Agent James's question. What department do you work in at SSA?"

"I run the Office of Systems. My department manages the computers that generate and assign social security numbers."

"Are you an SES like Mr. Newburg?" Simone asked.

"I am," she replied.

"You wouldn't happen to know a good friend of mine, Peter Hirzog, Deputy Director with the Bureau," Simone asked.

Trish's ashen-white face morphed from pink to crimson, the color brightening her cheeks and her nose. "No, I don't know him."

Yes, you do.

"You sure about that? He and Mr. Newburg are friends."

"No, they're not."

"I saw them together at Mac's bar in Arlington."

"Why ask me if you already knew," Trish snipped. "Look, this is not a good day for me."

"Ms. Benderson, do you know Peter Hirzog?" Simone pressed.

"I... um... I've met him."

Still lying. She knows him.

"If it would make it easier on you, I can tell Peter about Mr. Newburg."

"I'll do it," Trish's beady eyes drilled into Simone. "You'd think it was a crime to know someone," she snapped.

"It's only a crime if you do something illegal," Nikki said. "Have you done anything illegal, Ms. Benderson?"

"Of course not," Trish quipped. "My boyfriend is dead. I don't remember who I know, who I don't know, and I don't give a damn about any of it!"

"Thank you for talking to me." Simone slid her attention from Trish to Nikki. "I'm gonna take off."

"Excuse me, Ms. Benderson," Nikki said. "I'll be right back."

At the front door, Nikki said, "Let me get an officer to drive you back to the station."

"I'm good. Thanks for letting me tag along. I'll be in touch."

"You were super helpful." Nikki opened the front door and they went outside. "Are you calling an Uber?"

"No," Simone said removing her shoe coverings. "See that black SUV parked up the street. "He's with me."

Nikki's eyebrow arched. "What do you mean?"

"He's my security detail."

"*What?*"

"Yeah, it's a long story. After we solve this case—hopefully before the end of time—we'll share a bottle of Santini Chianti and I'll fill you in."

"Oh, wow. I didn't know he made wine."

"He does it all, including ensuring my safety."

Nikki smiled. "Sounds like a good friend."

Simone's heart blossomed. "He's the best."

Nikki went back inside, Simone removed her gloves before hurrying up the street. After climbing into the SUV, she said, "Thanks for doing this."

"Whad'ya find out?" Teddy asked.

"Newburg was murdered, but it was made to look like a suicide. Sloppy job though."

"How's that?"

"Newburg was left handed, but the killer shot him in the right temple."

Teddy laughed. "What kind of an idiot does that?"

"Maybe he was impatient, but I'm thinking he assumed Newburg was right handed."

"They always fuck up. But they don't always get caught."

"I appreciate the ride today," she said. "I know your brother wants me safe, but you have more important things to do than to drive me around."

"He wanted to do it himself, but I told him no. He's going to be like this, so you better get used to it."

"Forever?"

Teddy shrugged. "I dunno. He's not okay, you know that, right?"

"I know his family will always have his heart. I think he's capable of loving me and continuing to love them."

"You're cool. I like that 'bout you."

"I'm just faking it."

He chuffed out a laugh. "Where to?"

"I could use your help with something."

"Being your driver isn't enough?"

She laughed. "You're doing *too* much, but you've got your laptop. Any chance we can hop online?"

He logged in. "Whatcha need?"

"Do you have any names of the terrorists who got into the country?"

"Got 'em all." He got busy typing. Seconds later, he spun the laptop toward her.

She eyed the list. "Pull up the two Haqazzii men."

He pulled up one. His passport said he was a British citizen, here on a teaching assignment at the University of Virginia.

"A history teacher," she grumbled. "He sailed through customs, no problem. How is that even possible?"

"No one checked."

"Right," she replied. "And why is that?"

She continued reading, then stopped at the nine-digit number. "He's got a social security number. He's not an actual US citizen, but there's his number, which makes him—"

"Totally legit," Teddy said.

"I just met the woman at SSA who runs the department that issues social security numbers."

"Nice work, Sherlock."

She chuckled. "Looks like your brilliant brother was right."

"I'm the brilliant one. The other three are dummies."

"Three? Are you including Carrera?"

"Luciano, Gabriel, Greystone—he's the black sheep—and me." He shot her a cheesy grin. "I'm the baby."

"Luciano never mentioned Greystone."

"Bad blood," Teddy replied as he pulled up the second Haqazzii terrorist.

"This one claims he's an oil company exec." Simone ground her teeth as she continued reading. "He's got a legit passport and an SSN." Heat infused her chest and she cracked the window. "We need to head over to the Hoover Building."

He threw the vehicle into gear and headed out of the neighborhood.

"Do you need me to pull up directions?" she asked.

"Nope."

"Been there before?"

"Yup."

"Why?" she asked.

"For fun," he replied with a wink.

Teddy kept his eyes on the road. She couldn't tell if he worked there, had special access to the building, or what his deal was. Her poker face was amateur compared to his.

"Do you think Peter Hirzog is involved?" she asked.

"Walk me through the deets."

"Chenkus worked for Cary Newburg at State. Chenkus was shot dead driving out of Develin & Associates. Now, Newburg's dead, gunshot wound to the head. Newburg's girlfriend—Trish Benderson—denied knowing Deputy Director Peter Hirzog with the Bureau, then changed her answer several times."

"Red faced?"

"Yeah."

"Did you say, 'liar liar pants on fire'?"

Simone smiled. "You should take your act on the road."

"Nah, I like what I do too much."

"And what, *exactly*, do you do?"

He waggled his eyebrows at her. "I do it all, baby. I do it all."
He stopped at a red light. "So Benderson knows him."

"Then, there's The Bomb Maker," she continued. "He asked Luciano for a million in counterfeit. He threatened me if I took the case, then put that note on my front door after I did."

"Working with Mr. Steel Balls was great," Teddy said. "I know you were worried about your home, but I gotta get me a robot like that. Super handy."

"Are you always this laid back?"

"Yeah, pretty much," he replied. "Why?"

"It's good."

"No point in getting worked up about any of this. You're up against a lot. Better to give yourself a break, than to beat yourself up."

"You really are the brilliant one in the group."

Teddy grinned over at her. "You've got a network of execs at different federal agencies. We go with the theory that they're helping terrorists get into the country and providing them with legit paperwork. From the ones I looked into, they haven't even changed-up their appearances. They're clearing customs, no prob. The Bomb Maker's planning something epic. Hard to pull that off alone."

"Too much pressure," she murmured.

"Can't stress about what you can't control. Your job is to chase the leads, follow the evidence. Right now, you've got dead people, a possible corrupt group in the government, a lone bomber hiding in the shadows, and an unknown number of Haqazzii terrorists in the US." Another shrug from Teddy. "Unless Hirzog or that woman with SSA are gonna talk, you got nothing."

She rubbed her forehead to help calm the bass drum pounding out a frenetic rhythm. "Luciano put a call in to Willie Boy. I need to bring Dante in for questioning."

"Willie Boy is a fucked-up mess. He has no loyalty to the

fam. Never has. He'll only give up this Dante guy if it serves him."

"Can you take me to his restaurant?"

"Lulu will." Teddy turned onto Pennsylvania Ave. "I'll talk to him while you're meeting with Hirzog."

Teddy was super chill and easy to talk to. Hard not to like him, but she was seeing his soft side. He was large, like six-three, jacked-up muscles, and long blond hair. She couldn't begin to imagine what he'd do to someone he *didn't* like.

Teddy pulled up in front of the FBI building.

"You can't park here," she said.

He flashed her a smile. "Sure, I can."

She left the warmth of his vehicle for the biting November air, hurried inside and over to security. She was there on official ALPHA business, so she pulled out her Joelle James FBI badge, held it under the scanner. The light turned green and she proceeded through employee security. Once through, she made her way toward the elevator bank.

She had questions, and she was confident Peter had answers. She *hadn't* wanted to believe Luciano was right about him... but the farther down the rabbit hole she went, the more convinced she was that Peter was somehow involved.

∼

LUCIANO

Luciano's phone rang. "Santini," he answered.

"She's talking to Hirzog," Teddy said.

"How's she doing?"

"Good, but she's feeling the pressure. She wants to talk to Willie Boy. Should I bring my brass knuckles?"

"We need answers, so bring whatever the hell you want. Swing by and pick me up."

The line went dead, and Luciano turned his attention back to work. He was on edge. He had meetings he couldn't miss and several execs flying in from Italy for a showing. While Simone had agreed to spend the day with Teddy, she wouldn't do that for the rest of her life.

What choice did he have?

She was in danger every moment she was with him. While he knew she'd be safer if he ended things with her, he couldn't.

I'm in love with her.

Linda, I will never stop loving you, but I can't spend my life alone. Please forgive me for loving again.

SIMONE

On the elevator ride upstairs to Peter Hirzog's office, Simone's phone buzzed with a text.

> You're a naughty girl, Simone Redding. You're chasing me, but you won't catch me. If I were you, I would STOP. The mighty gates of the Santini mansion won't stop me. Nothing will stop me!

Her blood turned to ice in her veins.

Refusing to let the fear creep in, she snapped a screenshot of the threat and texted it to Luciano.

The elevator doors opened on the top floor, she stepped out, and her phone rang. It was Luciano. Despite loving that he was calling, she couldn't have him worrying.

"I'm fine," she answered. "I'm about to talk to Peter."

"You're vulnerable," Luciano said. "I don't like that."

"I'm okay, and I've gotta work."

"You're wearing body armor, yes?"

"You watched me put it on." After a brief pause, she said, "Luciano, I can't let him bully me into submission. He already did that. Maybe if I hadn't gone into hiding, Frederica and her team would be alive. Maybe that son of a bitch would be long dead and a postscript in the history of American lunatics."

"I'm sorry, Simone, but—"

"No buts. I got this. I love you, and I'm hanging up now."

"I love you too," he said.

She ended the call, entered the executive division, and stopped at reception. "Simone Redding for Peter Hirzog."

"Hey," said a familiar voice. "I thought that was you." Carrera walked over. "What brings you by?"

She stepped away from the check-in desk. "I need to talk to Peter. How are you? How's Slash and Elsa?"

He smiled. "All good. We'll see you next week."

She blanked.

"Thanksgiving," Carrera said. "You're coming to dinner with Lulu."

"Right. Thanksgiving with the Santini's." She stepped close. "Peter doesn't know I'm seeing Luciano."

"He's not hearing about that from me," Carrera replied.

"Ms. Redding," called out the receptionist.

Carrera said goodbye, and Simone returned to reception.

"Mr. Hirzog isn't here," said the receptionist.

"When do you expect him back?"

"Normally, he lets me know when he's off-site, but it looks like he never came in today."

"Please let him know I stopped by."

On her way toward the elevator, Simone texted Teddy. "On my way down. Where can I find you?"

"Right where you left me," Teddy replied.

She found Teddy standing next to the SUV, talking with two people in suits. She waited in his vehicle while they finished their hushed conversation.

"Special Agent friends of yours?" she asked as he pulled into traffic.

"Maybe," he replied. "Whad'ya learn from Hirzog? Lemme guess? Deny, deny, deny."

"He wasn't there," Simone pulled out her phone. "I'm calling him." The phone rang several times before rolling to voicemail. She hung up and sent him a text.

> Are you okay? Call me

Teddy turned onto 11th street, made a right on H, a left on 10th, and a right on Palmer Alley. He drove under the building, parked in a VIP spot along the front row, and cut the engine.

"C'mon, let's go inside." He was out the door and moving toward the building entrance, so she kicked up the pace to catch up.

He opened the door for her, she stepped into the upscale building, and stopped short to take in the magnificent lobby.

SANTINI INTERNATIONAL
US Headquarters

The white neon company sign brightened the black wall behind reception. The long counter was manned by two men and three women. Dressed in their Santini duds, everyone was using bright pink earbuds. Some were talking while others typed away on their keyboards.

Polished white marble reflected the pendant lights dangling from the second story. Bursts of bright colors, from oversized abstract art, clung to the dark walls.

The expansive waiting area boasted modern white sofas with rounded edges and several stunning black chairs situated in a corner facing a round coffee table. There was a state-of-the-art coffee machine, giant-sized indoor plants staged throughout the space, and the entire company was abuzz with unbridled energy.

Simone's headache went away, the excitement running rampant through her.

"Is this the nexus of the universe?" she murmured to Teddy.

He chuffed out a laugh.

One of the receptionists ran over. She threw her arms around him, hugged him hard, then stepped away. "Hey, Tank. I haven't seen you in so long."

"What's goin' on?" he asked.

The young woman batted her lashes at him, and Simone bit back a smile. "Nothing. You?"

"Hangin'. Can you check us in?"

"Sure. How's things?"

"Busy," he replied.

She ran behind the counter. "I'm hoping we can get together soon."

"Same," he replied before ushering Simone through the door.

"She was cute," Simone murmured.

Teddy said nothing as he guided her to the elevator bank where they were whisked to the top floor. Down the hall he took her, past offices and cubicles. The incessant hum made the air sizzle. People were talking fast, they were scurrying around. Everything was urgent, needing to be handled right away. The positivity was outright contagious.

"You like it here, don'tcha?" Teddy asked.

"How can you tell?"

"You're smiling. It's crazy, huh? It's like Lulu releases his power into this space and they gobble it up. If I didn't know better, I'd say they were all on something."

Simone laughed.

Teddy ushered her into a small waiting room at the end of the hall. On the other side were two offices. One had its door closed, the other open. A pleasant-looking man emerged wearing a suit, a black shirt, and a bold orange, yellow, and red tie.

He grinned at Teddy and hurried over. "There he is. The man of the hour."

"Are you keeping the boss man in line?"

"He's doing a million things at once. I don't know how he does it. He's got another new line coming out, so it's been nonstop all morning. We've got the contingency here from Milan." He smiled at her. "I'm Dominic, Mr. Santini's assistant. Who have you modeled for?"

"This is Simone," Teddy said.

"I'm not a model," Simone replied.

Dominic's mouth dropped open. "What a complete waste of stunning beauty. Wow." He shook his head. "You would look fab—totally fab—in anything from our new line."

A door opened, Luciano stepped into the waiting area. His attention slid from Dominic to Teddy to her, and in that split-second, his expression changed. His eyes softened, the look of love impossible to miss. It was as if he was projecting his power into her. The light shining from his eyes made her want to jump into his arms, kiss him for days, and never, ever leave his side.

In that moment, she melted from the intensity of everything Luciano.

"Ms. Redding," he murmured as if no one else was in the room. With his hands bracing her shoulders, he kissed one cheek, then the other. His smile turned her inside out, but it was the fire in his eyes that scorched her soul.

"Mr. Santini." She extended her hand because she had to touch him. Had to feel his skin on hers, his fingers against hers.

He slipped his hand into hers, but he didn't shake it. He just held it. For those few glorious seconds, everything faded away. Nothing mattered, but the man in her direct line of sight. Handsome, powerful, and sizzling with unparalleled energy. Being in his presence made her believe that everything would be okay.

As she tugged her hand away, she offered a little smile.

"Okay, so I'm gonna need a cold shower," Dominic said. "Whew, there is some crazy thing happening between you two. Tell me this isn't the first time you've met."

"No," Luciano said. "Not the first time." He hadn't even acknowledged his brother, his attention still anchored on her. "Are you hungry? Can we get you a coffee?"

"I'm starving," Teddy blurted. "Not feeling a coffee, though. How 'bout one of those protein drinks you've got in the cafeteria?"

"I'm on that," Dominic said.

"Simone," Luciano said. "Are you hungry?"

The morning had been intense, but the donut was keeping her hunger pangs at bay. "I'm fine," she replied.

"We'll eat when we return." Luciano shifted his attention to Teddy. "I'll drive."

"Ohmygod, what the hell was that?" Teddy barked out. "That's how you greet me?"

"Oh, boy." Dominic smiled at Simone. "Lovely to meet you." He retreated into his office.

Luciano directed them to a different elevator near his office. His *private* elevator. On the ride down, Luciano clasped Simone's hand, gave her a tender squeeze, and let go. A bolt of electricity shot through her. He could send her to the moon with very little effort.

She was a goner. A forever goner.

They left through the parking garage in Luciano's Range Rover. Through the streets of DC he drove. His focus was on the road, his lips slashed in a thin line. After a few minutes, he broke his silence. "What did Hirzog say?"

"He wasn't there," she replied. "His assistant didn't know where he was, so I texted him."

"How was your morning?" Luciano continued.

"Cary Newburg is dead," she said.

Silence.

Deafening, wicked silence.

He glanced over. "Details."

"Murder made to look like a suicide. I was with Commander Nikki Cardoso of MPD when she got the call."

"This is fucking unreal," he bit out. "And Hirzog's MIA. He's lost it and he's on some kind of killing spree. Maybe his plan is unravelling. People want out, so he's killing them."

"I pulled the tracker from Newburg's car."

"Nice," he said.

"And I met his girlfriend, Trish Benderson. She runs the Office of Systems at Social Security. Teddy and I learned that the terrorists who are coming in don't just have legit passports and aliases, they have social security numbers."

"Figli di puttana succhiacazzi," Luciano growled.

"Translate," she said to Teddy.

"He's swearing pretty good," Teddy replied.

"Teddy, thank you for spending the day with Simone. I appreciate it."

"You got it."

Luciano made a call.

"Yes, sir," Dominic answered.

"Send a car to pick up Teddy," Luciano gave him the address to Willie Boy's restaurant in Old Town, then hung up.

"What's going on?" Teddy asked.

"After we're done beating our douche of a cousin for answers, Simone and I are going to hunt down Hirzog," Luciano said.

When his gaze found hers, she couldn't miss the anger in his eyes. Luciano was furious. She had no doubt he'd unleash some of that on his cousin... and save the rest for Hirzog.

24

... MAYHEM

LUCIANO

The only reason Luciano wasn't going to break Willie Boy's face was because Simone was there. Had she not been, this would have been the end for his cousin.

They entered the restaurant. Tara greeted them with a smile, then lit up when she saw Teddy.

"Tara, is Willie Boy here?" Luciano asked.

"Of course. He's playing pool. Let me take you back."

He hated that Simone was going to see his darker side, but his patience had run out. Even for family, he had his limits.

Tara led them through the restaurant, past the patrons who were there for a decent meal. Luciano wanted to tell them to get out, to find a better restaurant. He wanted to torch the building and bury the past. Instead, he steeled his spine and followed the hostess.

She walked into the back room, stepped aside so they could enter. His cousin was smoking a cigar and playing pool with someone while a few people watched. Luciano released a string of obscenities under his breath. He couldn't believe how damn lazy his cousin was. His hands tightened into fists he wanted to launch at Willie Boy's stupid fucking face.

"Hey, cousins," Willie Boy said. "What do I owe the honor?" The second Simone came into view, he sucked his stomach in.

Luciano swallowed down a laugh.

"Yo, I remember you, pretty lady. Simone, right? I never forget a hot chick or a super-rad name."

"That's some talent you've got," Simone bit out.

"Tara, get them drinks," Willie Boy barked.

"How 'bout some beer?" Tara asked.

They declined, and Tara left, shutting the door behind her.

"Gentlemen, I need a word with my cousin," Luciano said.

"Ah, Jesus," Willie Boy said. "I got money riding on this game, Lulu, and I'm finally winning. If you knew how much I'm in the hole—"

Luciano glared at his cousin. "*Now*."

"Yeah, yeah, okay. Don't get your panties in a fucking wad." Willie Boy shooed the men out, then sat at his usual table, like he was holding court.

"I've got a problem," Luciano said, "and family help family, right?"

"Oh, yeah, sure, of course. What's going on?" Willie Boy drained his glass of beer, then shouted for Tara.

"Dante never called me," Luciano said.

"Sit," Willie Boy said.

He sat across from Willie Boy. Simone eased down to his left, Teddy sat to his right.

"Call Dante," Luciano said.

"I told you, I don't have his number."

"Dante's a dangerous killer," Luciano said. "Did you know that?"

"I know he's done that kinda thing before." Willie Boy wiped the perspiration from his brow with his sleeve.

"Break his finger," Luciano said to Teddy.

Simone tensed. It was subtle, but even in the dimly-lit room, he could see her back stiffen.

Teddy shoved out of his chair so hard, it hit the floor behind him.

"Happy to," Teddy replied. "Whad'ya say WB? Should I start with the pinky? It's such a defenseless little finger. Or I could start with your thumb, which, technically, isn't a finger, but that would fuck up your day pretty good, huh?"

Luciano leaned back. He loved watching Teddy. Everything with Teddy was larger than life, a damn performance. He would have already broken Willie Boy's finger and would have him pinned against the wall.

But everyone did torture differently.

"Fuck, no!" Willie Boy screamed. "I don't have his number and he hasn't been by. What do you want from me?"

"The truth," Luciano said. "How do you know him?"

"I told you the truth. I hired him to do a job for me a few years ago."

"Did he do the job?"

"Kinda. He did it, but he fucked it up."

"Then, what?"

"I never heard from him until a few months ago. He came 'round like he'd never been gone. He was askin' for boodle, I introduced him to you. He stopped by a few times more, but that was it."

"If you needed him to do another job for you, how would you contact him?" Luciano asked.

Fear flashed in Willie Boy's eyes. "I wouldn't hire him again."

"Because he fucked up the job."

Willie Boy hugged himself, hiding his hands in his armpits. "Yeah, right."

"What was that job?" Luciano asked.

"What was that job?" Willie Boy parroted back. "I, um... I... I don't remember."

Luciano flicked his gaze to Teddy. "Cosa ne pensi?"

"Si ricorda del lavoro," Teddy replied.

"Tienilo fermo."

Teddy grabbed Willie Boy's wrist, slammed his palm hand-down on the table, and held it there. Luciano snapped his pinky like a twig.

"AAAAAIIIIEEEEE!!!!" Willie Boy squealed.

Simone turned away.

"Gestisci questo," Luciano said to Teddy.

"Vuoi che lo uccida?" Teddy asked.

Luciano growled at his cousin. "He's a traitor. Non mi interessa cosa gli fai."

"Lulu!" Willie Boy screamed. "I'm gonna fuckin' kill you."

Without another word, Luciano guided Simone out. They waited in the SUV until a car pulled in for Teddy.

Luciano spoke with the driver, then he drove out of the parking lot. He felt nothing. No fear, no sense of satisfaction. He did what needed to be done because his cousin was a liar. You lie to the family, you get punished. It was that simple.

After a few silent moments, she asked, "What did you and Teddy say to each other?"

He laughed. "I just broke my cousin's finger, left him in the hands of Teddy, and you want to know what we said?"

She shot him a little smile. "Yes. I'm going to have to brush up on my Italian, but in the meantime, help a girl out."

He wrapped his hand around her muscular thigh. "Not just any girl. *My* girl. My *woman*."

She leaned over, kissed his cheek.

"I asked Teddy what he thought of Willie Boy's lie. Teddy said, 'si ricorda del lavoro', which means, 'he remembers the job.'"

"What does gestisci questo mean?" she asked.

"Handle this," he replied.

"Will he kill him?"

"No, but I told Teddy I don't care what he does to him."

"You're ruthless," she murmured.

He smiled. "Sì, amore mio, lo sono. Yes, my love, I am."

Simone's phone rang. "It's Peter." She answered, put the call on speaker. "Hi, Peter."

"The office said you stopped by."

"Yeah, I did." He sounded like he'd just woken up. "Are you not feeling well?"

Peter choked back a sob. "Jerod ended things. He broke it off with me last night. I'm devastated."

She exchanged glances with Luciano. "I'm sorry."

"I'm a mess." He paused to blow his nose. "I didn't think it would affect me like this. I mean, I knew it would end. Maybe I didn't. Hell, I don't know. I called in sick today. Fortunately, Lucy is at work. I begged Jerod to come over so we could talk it out—"

"He broke up with you over the phone?"

"Yeah, it was brutal. It started with a text, then we talked." He started crying again. "I have to go."

The line went dead.

"Here's your chance," Luciano said.

"I'm going for his jugular," Simone replied.

"Now, you sound like a Santini."

She shot him a little smile. "Thank you."

After she plugged Peter's address into her GPS, Luciano took the on-ramp to the beltway and slowed. It was rush hour and traffic was crawling.

"I thought Peter was a good guy—one of the best," she said. "Now, I think he's helping terrorists get into the country. How fucked up is that? I thought *you* were a bad guy. You're one of the best men I have ever known."

"I just broke my cousin's finger."

"He deserved it."

Luciano clasped her hand in his, rested them on her lap. "You know what we should do together?"

"Go to target practice?"

He smiled. "No. Fly to my Milan headquarters, then vacation on the Italian coast."

"That sounds incredible."

"The family has a condo in the city and a home on the coast. You would love it there."

"I'm sure I would."

"First, we deal with Hirzog, we find this Dante monster, and we play in Italy for as long as we want."

"Forever sounds good," she replied.

"Forever it is."

She stared out the passenger window as they slogged through heavy traffic. After a long moment, she said, "Why would Peter risk his career to get involved in a government crime ring?" she asked. "Money, right? Certainly not power."

"Definitely money."

"If he hates his country, then bringing terrorists in would bring him great satisfaction."

"Does he?"

"I never got that impression, not when I worked for him," she said.

"What about Jerod and his pyschosexual hold?"

"Absolutely," she replied. "Money, love, manipulation. I need to check Peter's finances. Can you help me?"

"Of course."

Forty-five minutes later, Luciano drove down Peter's street as the sun dipped into the horizon.

"His wife just got home," she said.

A petite woman with shoulder-length blonde hair was opening the back hatch of her vehicle. Several bags of groceries waited in the cargo area. Luciano parked in the driveway and they got out.

"Hi, Lucy," Simone called.

"Simone, what a lovely surprise. I hope you can stay for dinner." She smiled warmly at Luciano. "Hi, I'm Lucy Hirzog."

"Luciano Santini. Let me get those for you."

Loaded down with bags, Luciano followed Lucy and Simone into the house. Beneath his jacket was his Glock. Since Lucy was there, he doubted Hirzog would ambush Simone, but he wasn't dropping his guard.

Too much crazy shit was happening for him to relax... even for a minute.

The lights in the kitchen and adjoining family room were on, but no Hirzog. He set the groceries on the center island. A laptop sat open on the counter, the screen lit up to a page that looked familiar. Luciano strolled over and a shock of adrenaline charged through him.

The browser window was open to ALPHA, the screen displaying the current mission tracker. All ALPHA missions were on stand-down due to recent attack by The Bomb Maker. He skimmed the page. A single line item turned his veins to ice.

The Bomb Maker Case: Operative Simone Redding.

Figlio di puttana.

"Thanks for helping with the groceries," Lucy said. "It looks like Peter's here, but I didn't see his car."

"I talked to him an hour ago, and he said he was here," Simone said.

"Hmm, I didn't realize he was coming home early. He's been putting in a lot of hours at the office. It'll be nice to have dinner together." She put a few things in the refrigerator. "Let me tell him you're here."

She excused herself and left the room.

Luciano snapped a picture, then snapped a second that included the interior of the home. "Check this out."

She stood beside him, stared down at the laptop.

"He shouldn't have access to this and what the hell is the laptop doing open?" Simone also snapped several pictures, then shot Luciano a smile. "This is enough to bring him in for questioning. It's incriminating as hell."

Lucy returned to the kitchen. "He's not here." She checked her phone. "Maybe he ran to the store real quick."

"Please let him know we stopped by," Simone said.

They showed themselves out.

As Luciano drove toward home, he said, "I'll check Hirzog's finances when we get home."

In the dark car, she glanced over. "What happened to Peter? He used to be this amazing lawman, a respected leader, and total team player."

"I know what happened to him," Luciano replied. "Jerod happened. We need to find this Jerod De Clerq and squeeze him for answers."

"Santini style?"

"I'll start by breaking his fucking knees. I'm done being Mr. Nice Guy. So fucking done."

Thirty-minutes later, they were sitting at their desks in his home office, their covered dinner plates waiting on the conference table.

"I requested a background check on Peter," she said. "Is there anything I can do to help you with his finances?"

Luciano had all three computer screens lit up. He was searching for Hirzog's online bank accounts. Once he found out where Peter banked, he'd access them by impersonating Peter. After he explained to Simone what he was doing, he said, "It's going to take me a couple of hours, maybe longer. If I find nothing, I'll search for offshore accounts."

She pushed out of her chair, walked across the room, her

intense gaze pinned on him. "Thank you." She dipped down, kissed him. "While I wait for Hirzog's background check, I'll read the cold-case file on your family."

He had no expectations she'd find anything. The homicide detective had come up with very little, the arson detective even less.

An hour passed, then another. Every now and then, she'd comment to herself. He loved having her in his office, appreciated how focused she was, how committed she was to finding his family's killer, despite the odds stacked against her.

"Luciano," she said breaking her silence.

"Yeah, baby."

A hint of a smile tugged on the corners of her mouth. "Did the arson detective contact you?"

"No, but the homicide detective did. Once, in the beginning and several months later. He said the bomb materials were untraceable. They were common substances like hydrogen peroxide and ammonium nitrate that couldn't be traced to a specific seller."

One nod, then she continued working. She spent the next thirty minutes typing, then reading, more typing, more reading. At one point, she pushed out of her chair, walked onto the back patio, and stood in the yard staring up at the night sky.

A few minutes later, she came inside and rubbed her arms. "It's chilly tonight." Then, she sat on the sofa. "Can you sit with me for a minute?"

He'd located Hirzog's bank, then accessed his checking and savings accounts, but had found nothing suspicious. Both were joint accounts he shared with his wife.

"One minute." He called Teddy. "How'd it go?"

"It was fun."

Luciano smiled. "Is he alive?"

"Unfortunately."

"I need your help."

"Go," Teddy said.

After he told Teddy what he'd found, he said, "I'm looking for an account Hirzog *doesn't* share with his wife. It's not at this bank. I've searched several others, but there's nothing."

"What about a credit union?" Teddy asked.

"I didn't check those."

"Lemme see what I can do."

The line went dead. Luciano joined Simone on the sofa.

The rosy color had drained from her cheeks and she was nibbling on her fingernail. "I'm going to need a bomb expert to confirm what I found in the case file." She paused. "From what I'm learning, bomb makers—especially the good ones—leave like a signature in their explosives. They use specific materials, blended in a unique way. They're masters at knowing how much to use to create the exact level of destruction they need. Like with Frederica, The Bomb Maker used just enough dynamite and other materials to blow up his house, but the explosives did no damage to any of the other houses on the street. It was the same when my team got ambushed by him." She shifted on the sofa, but she was struggling to look at him.

"Simone," he murmured. "I'm right here. Talk to me."

She fixed her gaze on him, concern radiating from her eyes. "The same materials, with the same signature components, were found at the scene with your family. I'm *not* one-hundred-percent certain, and I'm not a chemist, but the types of materials match up. Even the proportions are the same. Less for the car explosion than the houses, but it's the same."

Luciano stared at her, trying to absorb her words. Several seconds passed. "Why would The Bomb Maker come after me?"

"I don't know," she replied.

"My thing was boodle," he said. "Counterfeit money."

The fury, the pain, the grief were always there, lurking

below the surface. As he ran through the countless deals in his mind, he'd never once interacted with an explosive's expert.

His phone rang. It was Teddy. He put the call on speaker. "Tell me something good."

"Are you in front of your computer?"

He and Simone moved to his desk. He pulled a chair around for her and they sat side by side.

"Hirzog has an account at a credit union in DC," Teddy said. "He opened it several months ago. There have been ten deposits, each one for twenty-five grand. I'm sharing my screen."

Seconds later, he and Simone were staring at Hirzog's bank account.

"Jesus," Luciano bit out.

Simone's smile lit up the night. "Teddy, I love you,"

"I'm good, huh?" Teddy asked.

"The best," she replied. "This is huge. Thank you." While Luciano took a screenshot, she hurried back over to her desk, retrieved her phone, and made a call.

"Cooper, it's Red. I got a break in the case."

SIMONE

The next morning, Simone was ready to rock it. To say she was fired up was an understatement. She'd hardly slept, which worked out to her and Luciano's favor. After he'd zhuzhed her up good at four in the morning, she was still buzzing with energy.

It was eight o'clock. She was sitting at her desk in Luciano's office ready to execute her plan. All she needed was her star player.

She texted Hirzog.

> I'm worried about you. Can we talk?

> ...

> I have an all-day meeting with the Director. How's 4 today?

> I'll be there

Simone called Cooper. "I'm meeting Hirzog at the Bureau, four o'clock."

"Nice work. What do you need from me?"

"I'll let you know." Simone hung up, called Commander Nikki Cardoso. After she brought Nikki up to speed, Nikki suggested Simone meet her at the police station so they could work out the details. Though elated, Simone wasn't getting ahead of herself. This wasn't a win, but things were moving in the right direction.

She pushed out of the chair, sat across from Luciano. "How are we going to do this so I'm safe, and you can go to work and not worry?"

"Stuart and I can drop you at the police station. He'll take me to the office, then come back and drive you to your meeting with Hirzog."

"That'll work."

As planned, they drove her to the DC police station.

She and Nikki talked strategy, discussed options, reviewed Guy Chenkus's and Cary Newburg's cases. She loved bouncing ideas off Nikki, feeling confident she was making headway. If her plan worked, she'd be arresting more than one person in the next twenty-four hours.

Even more so, she felt thrilled to be back in the game. She'd missed her life and was done hiding in the wings, watching from the shadows.

By three forty-five, Nikki had secured a court order. Armed

with a pen capable of recording their conversation, Simone left the station and ducked into the Range Rover waiting at the curb.

Five-minutes later, Stuart dropped her at FBI headquarters.

As she rode the elevator, her heart pounded faster than usual. There were so many ways her conversation with Peter could go. She was hoping for his cooperation, but expected pushback. Deputy Director Hirzog would *not* come quietly.

Upstairs in the executive department, while waiting in reception, a calmness settled over her. She was there to get answers and she wasn't leaving until she had them.

At just after four, several people exited a nearby conference room, one of them Carrera.

"Good luck," Carrera murmured before heading toward his office.

Simone didn't need luck. She needed the madness stopped and the bad actors locked away. It sounded like a lot, but she just wanted to do her damn job. And do it well. She had enough to arrest Hirzog, but she wasn't sure if she had enough to get a conviction.

Peter had just broken away from the group. Their eyes met. She pasted on a cheery smile. "There he is."

"Red, good to see you." Bags hung heavy under Peter's eyes, his rueful smile telling the real story. He ushered her into his office, shut the door.

"How are you doing?" she asked.

"It's been rough." After a beat, he said, "Lucy told me *you* stopped by with Santini. What was that about?"

She was there to question him, not be questioned by him. Instead of answering, she pulled a photo from her computer bag, set it on his desk. It was the picture she'd taken of Peter's laptop, open to ALPHA's secure website. In the photo's background was his home.

"How do you have access to ALPHAnet?" she began.

He stared at the picture, furrowed his brow. "What is that?"

"Seriously? You're asking me? It's from your house. Your laptop was open and ALPHA's website had been accessed." She pulled out another photo, this one with a close-up showing the line item for her working The Bomb Maker case. "Why are you tracking this?"

He read it, then shook his head. "I have no idea what that is."

"Is that your home?"

"Yes. Why are you questioning me about this?"

"Peter, why are you tracking ALPHA?"

"I'm *not*."

"Isn't that your laptop?" she asked.

He pulled a laptop from his computer bag. "*This* is my laptop. That's an old one I let Jerod use when he'd swing by."

Anger streaked through her. "Then, why is Jerod tracking ALPHA?"

"I have no idea," he replied.

She studied his face. It didn't appear that he was lying, but her trust of him had been shattered. She slapped her Joelle James FBI badge on his desk.

"I'm working The Bomb Maker case, and you're a suspect."

His eyes bulged, his surprise uncontainable. He stared at her for so long, he looked catatonic. "I would laugh, but that's not funny. That is an egregious accusation. I take personal and professional offense with that. I'm going to ask someone to step in here."

He opened his office door and his jaw dropped when Carrera and Nikki Cardoso appeared in his doorway.

"Mr. Hirzog, I'm Commander Nikki Cardoso, Metropolitan PD."

Carrera glared at Peter. "Deputy Director Carrera Santini."

"Fuck me," Peter grumbled.

Nikki eased into the second guest chair while Carrera stood like a sentry, arms crossed. He wore no smile, he said nothing.

A peace settled into Simone's troubled soul. She felt hopeful she was on the right path to getting justice and to healing her heart.

"Peter, sit back down," Simone demanded.

Peter crumpled into his chair, his gaze jumping from Carrera to Nikki, then back to her. "Why the ambush?"

"You have a bank account with ten deposits of twenty-five thousand dollars each," Simone continued. "Where did that money come from?"

"Jerod paid me," he said.

"For what?"

"I helped him bring his family into the country." Peter pulled out his phone, showed her several pictures of people, but Jerod wasn't in any of the shots.

Simone's brain skidded to a stop. "That's what he told you?"

"Yes, he wanted to help them, especially his mother." Peter pulled up a picture of an older woman. "I put him in touch with several people who could make that happen."

"Like?" Simone asked.

"Cary Newburg at State, Trish Benderson at SSA. I created an entire network for him."

"Peter, you've created an intragovernmental crime ring to bring terrorists with the Haqazzii terror cell into the country."

Peter recoiled. "No, that's not true—"

"Is his family's name Haqazzii?"

"Jesus, no."

"Jerod manipulated you, worked you for information," Simone said. "With your help, he brought an unknown number of terrorists into the United States. Where the hell did you think all that money was coming from?"

Peter swallowed. "He told me his family had money." He glanced furtively at Carrera. "I was too caught up in the excitement of the relationship." A growl shot out of him. "That son of a bitch used me."

"Peter Hirzog, you're under arrest for treason," Simone said.

"No, wait," Peter blurted. "Let me help you. I'll do anything. Anything so that I don't get arrested for *that*. I've worked here my entire career. I don't deserve this. I'm guilty, but not of losing my allegiance to my country or its government." He paused, his eyes shifting left and right, as if searching for a way out. Then, he sat ramrod straight. "If I'm arrested, the press will find out, and Jerod will bolt. I'll help you catch him, if you don't arrest me for treason."

"Go on," Simone said.

"He's money obsessed. I'll offer him the quarter of a mil he paid me if he'll meet me one more time. Then, you can arrest him." Hirzog exhaled a squeaky breath like the air was being released from a balloon.

The two women exchanged glances.

"We'll consider that," Simone said. "Where would you meet?"

"My house," Hirzog said. "Lucy left today to visit her sister. She stocked the fridge for me, made me a casserole last night."

Simone's stomach dropped. His sweet wife doted on him, loved him, yet he was a lying cheat and corrupt government worker.

"Text him," Simone said. "Show us the text before you send it, then we'll hold onto your phone so you don't warn him."

Hirzog's eyes widened. "Warn him? Why would I do that? He's just ruined my life. I never want to see the SOB again. This is my Hail Mary."

He typed out a text, showed it to them.

"Send it," Simone said.

> Jerod, I don't want the money. You can have it if you come by tonight so we can talk. One last time

Seconds later, his phone binged.

> 8 tonight. You can transfer the money when I'm there

Peter's shoulders fell. "I can't believe he used me."

Outside, Nikki placed Hirzog into the back seat of a waiting police car. Simone and Nikki slipped into Nikki's unmarked cruiser, and the caravan took off for Hirzog's home in Chevy Chase.

"I'm not convinced Jerod will show," Simone said. "If he's funded by terrorists, he doesn't need Peter's money."

"I'm not sure I agree with that," Nikki pushed back. "If he's in it for the money, he will. I don't know a lot of people who *wouldn't*. Two hundred fifty thousand is a lot of money for a fifteen-minute meeting."

It was six-thirty when they arrived at Hirzog's. Two police officers entered, cleared the home, then waited outside. Simone was surprised that Peter heated the casserole, opened a bottle of wine. Both she and Nikki declined the alcohol, but Nikki ate some of the enchilada casserole.

"Your wife is an excellent cook," Nikki said.

"Yeah, she's a great woman," Peter said. "I really blew it with her. When she finds out, she'll leave me."

Simone had been seated at the kitchen table, studying Hirzog. She wasn't sure what to make of her former mentor. He appeared as relaxed as could be, but maybe he was good at hiding his emotions.

I wouldn't be able to eat if I was accused of helping terrorists into the country.

Peter turned on the television to watch the news broadcast.

When it ended, he turned it off. "I'm relieved I wasn't on it." He regarded Nikki. "I'd like to call my lawyer."

"After you're arrested," Nikki replied. "You don't get special treatment just because you offered me a piece of your wife's casserole. Doesn't work like that."

Hirzog went to the counter and got busy making a pot of coffee.

At seven-thirty Luciano texted her.

> How are you doing?

> Quiet here. Hirzog is acting like things are normal. Denial???

> Body armor, yes?

> Yes

> Service weapon?

> In my handbag

> Not good enough. Wear it! See you in 45. Love you, baby.

> I love you

Luciano brought her joy, plain and simple.

"This situation feels surreal," Peter said. "I should never have had an affair with Jerod."

"Why did you?" Nikki asked.

"Jerod's very handsome and he paid me a lot of attention. We worked out together, played pickleball, met for dinner."

"Yeah, so? Friends do that," Nikki replied.

"He seduced me, led me to believe what we had was real."

Hirzog brought over a tray with three coffees, a small pitcher with creamer, and a bowl of sugar. He set a mug down for Simone, one for Nikki, then joined them at the table.

Simone pushed hers away. She couldn't stomach a thing. Nikki drizzled in cream, added a little sugar. In silence, they sipped their hot drinks. When Nikki had finished hers, Hirzog held up the carafe, but she waved it away.

"Excuse me," Nikki said. "I'm going to the restroom."

Simone checked the time. Five past eight. Adrenaline powered through her. She was ready to arrest Jerod, Hirzog too. She'd followed the white rabbit and it had led her to these two men, but there were so many others she *didn't* know about.

I'll find them too.

She and Hirzog sat in silence. She had nothing left to say to him. A few minutes passed, but Nikki hadn't returned.

THUD!

"What was that?" Simone asked.

"I didn't hear anything," Hirzog replied.

She hurried to the closed bathroom door. "Nikki, you okay?"

The door opened. A glassy-eyed Nikki said, "I lost my balance."

Simone helped her back to the table. Nikki sat in the chair and slumped over. "I don't feel so good," she mumbled.

After a quick glance at Hirzog—who appeared oblivious to Nikki's situation—Simone hurried to her handbag, rifled through it, but her Glock was missing. A punch of fear pounded through her.

"I moved your gun," Peter said. "I don't want things to get violent."

A growl shot out of her. "Where's my service weapon, Peter?"

"You won't be needing that."

POP! POP! POP! POP!

Simone jerked her head toward the sound. The front door

burst open and a man strode into the kitchen, eyed the three of them, and drew his lips back into a sinister smile, like a dog baring its teeth.

Dread filled her to the depths of her soul.

His dark hair fell to his shoulders. He wore tinted eyeglasses, dressed in an expensive-looking suit, bright white shirt, and shiny, black loafers. In the low-lit kitchen, he appeared very tan, but his complexion looked more orange than sun-kissed.

She glanced at his hand. On his pinky, he wore a flashy diamond ring.

Her heart dropped.

Ohgod, It's The Bomb Maker.

Hirzog looked flat-out confused. "Who the hell are you?"

"Who am I?" barked the stranger.

Ohgod, no.

Simone staggered back.

It was Jerod De Clerq.

"It's me, honey baby, but I prefer my chosen name, Dante." Jerod removed his tinted glasses, walked over to Hirzog, and kissed him on the mouth. "Surprise, lover man!"

Adrenaline-fueled fear spread through Simone like wildfire.

Jerod is Dante... and Dante is The Bomb Maker.

LUCIANO

Luciano was seething. Traffic had come to a standstill. An accident had shut down one of two northbound lanes on Connecticut Ave in DC.

As he inched his way toward Maryland, he thought about everything that had transpired over the past few months. From

Simone spying on him to their first erotic meeting at Burke and Morticia's. How they'd fallen in love while hunting down a madman, then found themselves following a trail of corrupt government workers. Hirzog had blamed him for his ex-wife's infidelity, then he'd cheated on his current wife with Jerod.

What a snake.

He thought about Jerod's quick exit from Carole Jean's minutes after meeting him.

Why did I think I'd met him before?

There was something about Jerod that reminded him of someone, but who?

His voice.

"Jesus," he bit out as reality rained down on him.

He didn't look familiar... he *sounded* familiar.

Jerod De Clerq is Dante The Bomb Maker.

Dread crept in, but he shoved it out.

Luciano texted Simone, got no response, and called her. Her phone rang. "C'mon, answer."

She didn't.

He searched for an alternative route, but nothing would get him to Hirzog's any faster. According to the nav app, the accident was just up ahead. Once he got past that, he'd be there in fifteen minutes, tops.

Despite the situation, he would not let fear take control.

He called Teddy.

"Yo," Teddy replied. "I can't talk."

"Why the hell did you answer?" Luciano snapped.

"Whoa, whoa, you gotta take it down a few."

"Simone may be in trouble, and I'm stuck in traffic."

"Sorry, bro. I'm in Virginia Beach." Teddy hung up.

Luciano started swearing in Italian.

As he drove past the accident that had caused the major delay, cop cars, an ambulance and a fire truck blocked both southbound lanes. A tarp had been laid over one of the vehicles. His stomach dropped, his heart ached. Whoever was in that vehicle had not survived.

"Tragic," he murmured.

Once past, he picked up speed. He called Simone, again. Still, no answer. In his gut, he knew something was wrong. Something was very, very wrong.

Simone's walked into another ambush.

SIMONE

HIRZOG BEAMED. "I love the disguise and I love the name, *Dante*. Very impressive. I'm ecstatic to see you. I want us to work things out."

"Shhh, honey baby," Dante said. "We'll have lots of time for chatting once we take care of business." He glanced over at Nikki, then glared at Simone. "First, those annoying officers out front are down."

Peter stilled. "Down, as in dead?"

"Of course," Dante replied. "*Killing* is my specialty, *not* all the blowjobs I gave you. That was Dante doing whatever it took to get the job done." Dante bowed. "Mission accomplished."

Dante regarded Simone and his eyes turned black with hatred. "Red, Red, Red." He pointed his gun at her. "You just wouldn't stop coming after me, no matter how many times I warned you. Now, you're going to pay, which is a bummer, 'cause I really like you. And thank you, honey, for confiding in me. That made me so happy. I get that we're friends—well, you're friends with Jerod—but Dante is all business, so don't take this personally."

Simone's heart was pounding out of her chest, but she refused to surrender to the fear. She would fight to her death if she had to.

"You're insane," she snapped. "Fucking insane."

"I'm just leading two very different lives, but I can assure you I'm sane. Very sane and very, very evil." His satanic grin sent a shiver whipping down her spine.

"And don't get me started on Becca," Dante continued. "She can't wait to move here so you two can become buds." He made a sad face. "You don't get to be her friend because you'll be DEAD!"

Simone lunged for him, but Hirzog grabbed her. "You need to have a seat." He shoved her down on the chair.

"Actually, I need our lovely Simone to do me a favor," Dante cooed.

She wanted to spit in his face, but she needed to stay calm. Her first priority? Find her Glock or take Dante's from him.

He pulled rope from his shoulder bag, held it out to her. "Tie up my lover."

"*What?*" Hirzog bellowed. "Are you out of your mind?"

Dante pointed the gun at him, his cold eyes spewing venom. "Sit, your ass down, you old fucker."

Hirzog dropped into the kitchen chair.

"Tie him up, sweetie."

Hirzog put his hands behind the chair and Simone loosely tied them together, then she tapped his wrists hoping he would know. Though a risk, she still believed he was the lesser of two evils.

"Sit," Dante instructed her. "We have to get caught up."

Dante glanced over at Nikki still slumped on the kitchen table. "What's her story?"

"I drugged her, like you told me," Hirzog said.

Dammit. Jerod got to him.

"Is she dead?"

Simone stifled a gasp.

"No, she's passed out," Hirzog said. "What is up with you?"

"Do you know who I am?" Dante asked.

"Yes," Hirzog replied. "You're Jerod in disguise."

"*I'm Dante.* Jerod is like Clarke Kent. Jerod works for ATF, chasing bad guys. All bad guys except The Bomb Maker. Do you know why that is?"

"Because *you're* The Bomb Maker," Simone said, keeping her voice steady so he wouldn't hear her fear. "Dante is a killing machine. Dante killed Guy Chenkus. Dante killed Cary Newburg."

"Ding! Ding! Ding!" Dante beamed. "I'm that person. I create mayhem and destruction wherever I go. Years ago, I bombed all those government buildings—"

Tears spilled down Hirzog's cheeks. "Why?"

"Because it's fun! I *love* making explosives and watching people suffer. The more the merrier. I love seeing my success play out on the news, on social media. No one could catch me, but ALPHA—fucking ALPHA—was on to me. So, I killed them." He slunk over to Simone, grabbed her face in his gun-free hand, and squeezed. Hard. "This cutie pie lived, but I didn't know that. I thought *everyone* had died."

"Ohgod, this is bad," Peter bleated.

Dante kept his wild-eyed gaze on Simone.

"Imagine how surprised I was when you returned from the dead, like a Phoenix rising from the ashes. What a fab reunion! Thanks to Peter and his laptop, I had access to ALPHA. Happy day! And here you are, again. Finally, I get to finish the job I started, make a cool quarter mil then vanish into thin air, just like I did five years ago. Only this time, I'm going to make sure you, Simone Redding, are dead."

"You killed my team," Simone bit out. "You sent me into hiding, you stole my life, then you killed Frederica and her team."

"My motto is destruction and mayhem—"

"I thought you said mayhem and destruction," she hissed.

Dante smacked her cheek. "You're annoying me. I wouldn't do that if I were you."

Simone's face burned from his slap, but she stayed silent. He had the power *and* the weapon... until she took them both from him.

"Don't hit her," Hirzog growled, the tone catching her ear.

"Seriously, big guy, you're in no position to tell *me* what to do."

"You want the money," Hirzog said. "Take it and get the hell out! Crawl back under the fucking rock from where you came."

"Speaking of fucking... you, lover man, liked it rough," Dante said. "Is that what's happening now? You're putting on a tough-guy attitude with me? I wasn't interested in you then. I'm not interested in you now. You were such an easy mark. I fawned all over you. I stroked your massive ego and I stroked your dick. And you fell for me." He grinned. "I was playing a part to get you to create that incredible network of yo-yos who gave me what I needed. A government-based crime ring where I gave open access to the world's most ruthless criminals. And they're here. They're all here! Our day is coming and, when it does, we will be immortalized as the most destructive power in the universe!"

To her absolute horror, Dante did a happy dance.

Bile rose in her throat while nausea rolled through her. She wanted to throw up.

"I'm going to quote Jerod," Dante said. "Death is the ultimate loss. It messes with people in a way that nothing else does." His face split into a terrifying grin. "Don't you just love that quote? I do!"

Hirzog jumped out of the chair, the rope dangling loosely from one of his wrists. He lunged for Jerod.

BANG!

"AAAAAAIIEEEEEEEE!!!" Hirzog shrieked, falling to the kitchen floor.

"Shut up, old man. Shut the hell up! While I couldn't have done it without you, I can do without you now. Now, you're a cling-on. You're a fucking nuisance and you're expendable."

Groaning in pain, Hirzog lay bleeding from a leg wound, blood oozing onto his pants.

The front door banged open, Luciano rushed into the kitchen, his Glock drawn. Dante yanked Simone out of the chair, pulled her in front of him like a shield. One arm around her neck, the gun to her temple.

"Welcome to the party, handsome," Dante said. "I believe we've already met."

Luciano growled, his fury-filled gaze sliding from Simone to Hirzog to Nikki, still slumped at the table.

"I'll kill her," Dante said. "Because I love watching people suffer. So, Mr. Richie Rich, put the weapon on the counter and step away."

To Simone's surprise, Luciano set down his gun.

All her hope faded away.

He devours power, so why did he just give it all away?

LUCIANO

LUCIANO SMILED AT DANTE. "Do you want to die quickly or do you want to die slowly and suffer?"

"Oooooh, I love forced choices, don't you?" Dante rolled his eyes, as if contemplating his question. "I'm the one holding the gun, so I'm *not* going to die. Nope, not me. I'm going to wreak havoc here, then vanish until... drumroll please...May thirty-first. Five thirty-one."

Simone was alive. That was Luciano's primary concern.

Luciano relaxed his stance, loosened the fists he'd made. "I know who you are, Dante. You're Jerod, Inferno531, The Bomb Maker."

"Congratulations, shithead! You wouldn't sell me counterfeit money, but you did become *very* interested in me, Mr. Santini. After a little detective work of my own, I realized you were helping our lovely Red. Red, who's about to be dead. How are you, the great and mighty Santini, going to handle the death of yet another loved one? I mean, the pain must still be so raw all these years later. I've seen you at the cemetery visiting your dead family. I'm sure it's very touching, but I don't have any empathy. I'm not an empath. I'm a sociopath." He grinned. "Life's short. If you cross me, it's *really* short." He cackled, his high-pitch laugh slicing through the air. "I'm the one who killed your beautiful wife and two kiddies."

A hatred so consuming filled every cell in Luciano's body. Fury and revenge had him primed to release a maelstrom of violence, but he had a plan.

Time to put it into play.

"Dante—or should I call you Jerod?"

"I like that about you. You're very couth. I prefer Dante."

"Alright, Dante, let's talk. Man-to-man, yes?"

"Aren't we doing that now?"

"You're hiding behind a woman, so no, you're not."

Dante stared at Luciano. "You're not gonna pull any funny business, are you? You do, she gets it."

"You have my word. Just a simple conversation, then you can kill me. You can finish Hirzog off too, but please, let Simone live."

"You're a gentleman."

Dante moved Simone to a chair at the table, pointed his Glock at her. "Don't move or I shoot."

Simone glared at him.

"Okay, what do you want to talk to me about?" Dante asked as he re-aimed the gun at Luciano.

"Why the counterfeit money?" Luciano asked.

"My middle-east friends have paid me millions, but I had to fork out a huge chunk to Hirzog and his nincompoop network. If I had counterfeit to pay them with, I'd cut my expenses, amass a fortune, then vanish, leaving my army of minions to carry out my orders." A heinous smile filled his wretched face. "Ingenious, don'tcha think? The perfect crime."

Dante didn't get the boodle and he was about to die, so no, it was *not* the perfect crime. Instead of disclosing that, Luciano continued with his line of questioning. Slowly, slowly amassing the power he needed before he took this monster out.

"Why did you kill my family? We didn't know each other, we'd never done business together."

Luciano slid his gaze to Simone. She was waiting. As terrifying as this situation was, she looked as calm as he felt. Calmer, maybe. They stared into each other's eyes for a brief second and, in that fleeting moment, time stood still. He saw his future. With her, and their children. He saw a life overflowing with love and laughter. And he saw an eternity with both his families. Peace settled into his soul. He shifted his attention back to Dante.

"It was an oopsie," Dante said. "The hit was meant for you."

"Which rival family ordered it?"

"That's a yes—and a no—answer." Dante pointed his weapon at Simone, then back at Luciano. "I don't know who I'm going to kill first. Simone, what do you think? All four of you will die. You choose who goes first!"

She didn't respond.

"Simone, if you don't answer—"

"Me. Take my life, but spare Luciano."

"Why? You haven't even known him that long."

"I love him. That's what you do when you love someone. You want them to live, to thrive, to make the most out of this one life that we have."

"Very noble. I'm impressed. As Jerod, I did love being friends with you. You were always the coolest agent in the room."

"Thank you. I felt the same about you."

"Dante," Luciano said. "Who ordered the hit?"

"Are you ready for this?" He glared at Luciano. "I don't think you are, but I'm going to tell you, and then, I'm gonna kill you."

"Understood," Luciano said.

"Please, no," Simone whispered.

"I've held it in for five long years. Only one other person knows the truth." He puffed out his chest. "I'm bursting to tell you... are you sure you're ready?"

"Tell me."

"Your cousin, Willie Boy, ordered the hit. He wanted you dead, so he could run the business without you. But I killed your fam instead. My bad!"

"Slowly," Luciano said, devoid of any emotion.

"What the fuck does that mean?" Dante asked. "C'mon, I just told you that your cousin—*your own family*—ordered the hit on you. And all you can say is slowly? What does that even mean?"

"It means, you will die slowly and painfully. Very, very painfully."

"Dante, Commander Cardoso is waking up," Simone said.

Dante glanced over. Luciano whipped his second Glock from the holster hidden beneath his jacket.

BANG!

Luciano shot the gun out of Dante's hand. Simone leapt out of the chair, grabbed it, and pointed it at Dante.

BANG!

Luciano shot him in the abdomen.

"FUCK! You son of a bitch." Dante pressed his hand against his torso as blood poured from the wound.

BANG!

Simone shot him in the upper thigh. "That's for killing *my* team."

"AAAAIIIIIEEE!!!" Dante shrieked.

Then, she fired off a round into his other femoral artery.

BANG!

"That's for killing Frederica and her team."

Dante crumpled to the floor, landing on his back, blood flowing from his wounds.

Luciano knelt beside him and glared into his eyes. "I want my face to be the last you see before you spend eternity with the devil."

"This isn't over," Dante rasped out.

Simone stared down at Dante. "Any last words?"

Gasping for breath, Dante said, "May thirty-first will be memorialized forever. My name will be remembered as the king of mass destruction. I've set into motion something that not even the great Santini can stop." An evil smile contorted his face.

She held the gun steady. "This is for killing Luciano's family."

BANG!

The bullet pierced Dante's heart, his eyes went flat, and his breathing stopped.

It was over... for now.

Luciano knew the real nightmare was to come. Dante had deployed a ruthless team of terrorists throughout the country, with plans for a major attack against the US.

He rose, pulled Simone into his arms, held her tightly, and breathed. "Are you okay?" he asked.

"Yes. You?"

"You're in my arms, so it's all good."

"Thank you for the save," she murmured.

"Thank you for having my back, and for avenging my family."

She nodded.

"Partners always, yes?" he asked.

"Always," she replied.

One more hug before she checked on Nikki while Luciano called for an ambulance.

After seeing that Nikki was coming around, Simone grabbed a towel, hurried over to Hirzog, and pressed gently against his wound.

"You're going to be okay, Peter," she said. "You were very brave."

"I'm sorry," Hirzog murmured.

Luciano called Carrera, added Sin to their call. "The Bomb Maker is dead. Hirzog is wounded. Simone was a rock star. The Bomb Maker gave me the Day of Destruction."

"When?" Sin asked.

"May thirty-first."

"In six months?"

"Yes."

"We're not gonna get much sleep, are we?" Carrera asked. "Does Teddy know?"

"I'm calling him next."

"We'll talk," Sin said.

Luciano hung up, called his brother.

"Hold on," Teddy answered. After several seconds, he said, "What's the latest?"

"Willie Boy ordered the hit on me, the one that killed my family."

Teddy released a string of obscenities in Italian. "How are we handling it?"

"The Santini way. You in?"

"Don't ask stupid questions, fratello," Teddy said. "Of course I'm in."

Luciano hung up as the wail of sirens grew louder.

The next hour was mayhem, but when Cooper and Dakota

appeared on the scene, Luciano collected Simone and vanished into the night.

He tucked her into his Range Rover, got in behind the wheel. "Ready to go home?"

"So ready."

"Yours or mine?"

"As long as we're together, does it make a difference?"

He collected her hand in his, kissed her warm skin. Grateful she was alive and unharmed, he smiled. "Together."

"Absolutely."

Simone stayed quiet on the ride home. She held his hand in her lap and stared out the windshield. He pulled up to the gates of his home, the guard cleared them to enter, and he drove up the long driveway. After parking at the fountain, he cut the engine and turned to her.

"You were brave and composed under pressure," he said.

That elicited a smile. "I trusted you. I believed we'd get the job done."

"I saw our life together," he murmured. "Children too."

She leaned over, kissed him. "Do you even want to bring children into this world? There's so much evil."

He lifted her hand to his lips, dotted her skin with kisses. "And love. If you could help me feel whole again, then I think a family would only make our lives better."

"I'll have your children, Mr. Santini."

He smiled. How could he not? They'd come face-to-face with the devil and they'd cheated death. He believed their love would heal them, and they'd have a long and happy life together.

They went inside, sat on the sofa in the family room, staring at the flames dancing in the gas fireplace. She turned toward him, draped her legs over his lap, and ran delicate fingers through his hair.

"I love your touch, Simone."

A whisper-soft smile graced her beautiful face. "What are you doing about Willie Boy?"

"What would you do?"

"I'm not an assassin," she replied, directing her attention back to the roaring flames, "but it's a dead man's word against your cousin's. Without evidence, it would be hard to arrest him. Even if he was arrested, a conviction might be impossible."

"You didn't answer my question," he said.

She regarded him, the light from the fire reflected in her eyes. "I will love you no matter what you choose."

"He got what he wanted," Luciano said. "I left for Italy, he took over the family business."

"You'll know what you have to do when you see him," she said.

She's right. I'll know when I confront him with the truth.

25

WILLIE BOY

SIMONE

Simone spent the day at ALPHA HQ. She was being hailed a hero, but she didn't feel like one. She was relieved the case had been solved, but deeply troubled about Dante's Day of Destruction.

After spending the morning in a debriefing with Dakota, Providence, and Cooper, Slash whisked her into the conference room where the female Ops waited to officially welcome her to the team.

After Slash made the introductions to—Emerson, Danielle, Addison, Jacqueline, and Brit—they feasted on carry-out from a nearby restaurant. They wanted to hear every detail of the case, then they toasted her.

"We're thrilled to be back here," Slash said.

"I loved working from home," Addison said, "but I missed my ALPHA team so much."

"Especially my ALPHA girls," Brit added. "I'm all about the girl power."

An echo of agreement filled the room.

"Red, do you think you'll be assigned lead for the Day of Destruction case?" Danielle asked.

Simone shrugged. "I think fresh eyes need to run with this one, but if leadership puts a team together, I'd love in on that."

"We should suggest it," Jacqueline added.

While the team cleaned up the conference room, Slash said, "You're sharing an office with me."

Simone smiled. "I love that."

Slash slung an arm around her. "Makes me happy too."

Once there, Simone pulled out her laptop, plugged it into the large display on her desk. "It'll be great bouncing ideas off you."

"Same," Slash said. "It's gonna take me a while to get used to seeing you. It's good to have you back, Red."

"It's good to be back."

Her phone buzzed with a text from Luciano.

> How's my love's first day going?

> Great. Are you at work?

> All day. One more stop before I see my baby. Love you Simone.

> Love you Luciano

Cooper had assigned her a heavy case load, so she spent the afternoon reading through the files.

At the end of the workday, Slash said, "I'll see you for Thanksgiving *and* for Friendsgiving."

Simone peered over at her. "Friendsgiving?"

"Saturday, everyone's getting together at Jericho Road."

"Luciano hasn't invited me," Simone said.

"With everything going on, he probably just forgot," Slash said. "So, if he pops the question, what's your answer?"

Simone grinned.

"That rocks." Slash stood, slung her computer bag over her shoulder. "Let's get outta here."

"I'm gonna stay a little longer. Thanks for the warm welcome. See you tomorrow."

Slash left, and Simone turned her attention back to her computer.

An hour later, she packed up her laptop, headed out. Since she hadn't heard from Luciano, she drove to her house.

It felt fantastic to be home. She turned on lights, walked around surveying each room. While she hadn't been gone long, it felt like forever.

Entering the kitchen, she eyed the box of mini cakes Fred had brought over. So much had happened since their fun evening. Her entire life had changed in ways she could never have imagined.

Loss, pain, destruction, death... and love.

"I miss you, Frederica. My life isn't the same without you." She couldn't eat the cake, couldn't throw it away either, so she placed the box in the freezer. "I got the monster who killed you. And I fell in love. I fell in love with Luciano. Crazy huh? Who would have imagined?"

In the silence that followed, she heard her front door click shut.

"Luciano, is that you?"

No answer.

Still wearing her shoulder holster, she withdrew her Glock, flipped off the kitchen light, and stood with her back against the wall. The creaking of the wooden floor had blood whooshing through her. Was she being burglarized? Was this a targeted hit?

Someone wearing a ski mask appeared in the doorway, a large gleaming kitchen knife in their outstretched hand.

"Drop it or I'll blow your head off!" Simone shouted.

"AAAAIIIEEE!" The assailant startled, then dropped their weapon.

It's a woman.

Simone grabbed her shirt, shoved her against the wall, then yanked off her mask.

Trish Benderson, the SSA Manager and Cary Newburg's girlfriend, glared at her. "Because of you, my Cary is dead," she hissed. "You should have walked away from this. It's bigger—way bigger—than any of us. You pissed off a lot of people, you stupid, stupid woman."

Simone shoved her to the ground, pointed her Glock at her. "Don't you fucking move. If you think I'm messing around, I pumped three bullets into Jerod De Clerq."

"Who?"

"Dante. Dante is dead. And I'll fucking kill you too."

"Oh, fuck me," Trish grumbled.

With her gun pointed at Trish, Simone called 911.

The police arrived, placed Trish in the back seat of a cruiser, then returned to talk to Simone. She showed them her badge, gave her statement, and told them Benderson was part of a corrupt crime ring.

An hour later, Simone was alone again, but she was gutted, furious, and fully anticipating a cyclone of continued fallout. In truth, Jerod's death and Peter's arrest were only beginning. The Bomb Maker might be dead, but his work was just revving up. The looming date—May thirty-first—was a deadline of overwhelming magnitude.

No way was she staying there by herself. Word had gotten out that she was the agent who'd eliminated Dante. Now, there was a bounty on her head. She climbed into her SUV, glanced up at her home one more time, and drove away.

Luciano was right. She wasn't running scared. She was ensuring she stayed alive. When she arrived at Luciano's, the guard waved her in, and she parked at the fountain.

At least, here, I'm protected.

∾

LUCIANO

Luciano pulled up to Willie Boy's restaurant in Alexandria, drove around back. The hatred he'd been carrying around finally had a target. Never once did he suspect his own cousin was behind the deaths of his family.

Teddy parked beside him. In silence, the men got out. Luciano keyed their way in through the back fire door. They entered Willy Boy's private salon to find it dark. Teddy flipped on the lights. No one was there.

"He's always here," Teddy said. "Do you think someone tipped him off?"

"Who?" Luciano said. "Dante is dead. No one else knew."

They exited, walked through the restaurant. It was empty. No patrons, no waitstaff.

"What the hell is going on?" Teddy asked.

"He's on the run," Luciano said.

"Maybe someone offed him," Teddy said.

"And his entire staff?"

Just then, the front door opened and Tara the hostess entered, then startled. "Oooh, you surprised me."

"Where's Willie Boy?" Luciano asked.

"A few days ago, he told us he'd gotten a job in Las Vegas and went to live with his aunt. Anyway, he took off, leaving me in charge. I would have called you, Mr. Santini, but I didn't have your number."

"Where is everyone?" Teddy asked.

"The staff freaked out when they saw Willie Boy," Tara explained. "He'd been roughed up good. Two black eyes. His nose looked broken. He might have lost a tooth too."

"Don't forget about his arm—" Teddy blurted.

"Right," Tara replied. "His arm was broken. Oh, and his pinky. Anyway, everyone freaked and bolted. I just came in to get my things. I got a new job and wanted to clean out my locker." She handed Luciano the key. "Do you mind?"

"Go ahead," Luciano said.

Tara made her way toward the back.

"We've got ourselves a rabbit," Luciano said.

"You gonna chase him?" Teddy asked.

"Hell, no. He'll run out of money or get into trouble and come crawling back."

"Is the restaurant in your name?" Teddy asked.

"The family owns it," Luciano replied. "Do you want to run it?"

"Hell, yeah."

"You got time? You're already spread pretty thin."

"This is our family's restaurant, and it's gone to shit," Teddy said. "I would update the hell out of it. If I can't turn it around, we'll sell it."

Luciano extended his hand and Teddy shook it.

Tara returned carrying a small box. "Do you want to make sure I'm not taking anything?"

"Teddy runs the restaurant now," Luciano replied.

"I trust you," Teddy said. "You wanna work here when I reopen?"

Tara beamed. "Sure." She gave Teddy her phone number and left.

"You trust her?" Luciano asked. "You hardly know her."

"What's she gonna steal?" Teddy asked. "The place is a dump." He eyed the restaurant. "I'll see if Greystone wants to manage it."

Luciano stilled. "You can't be serious."

Teddy grinned sheepishly. "He's been in touch with me."

"What for?"

"He's our brother."

"Not *my* brother."

"Leaving town doesn't end a relationship," Teddy pushed back.

"He walked out and we never saw him again. That's not what family does. What do you know about him?"

"I know he's family."

"Willie Boy was family."

"I'm giving him the benefit of the doubt."

"Not me. Guilty until proven innocent."

"Let's get outta here." Teddy locked up and they left.

A streak of frustration had Luciano growling. Willie Boy had gotten away with killing his family, then he skipped town when it was time to man up.

Did someone tell Willie Boy I was coming for him?

Luciano drove home in a sea of frustration, but when he saw Simone's SUV parked at the fountain, the anger slipped away. He found her sitting at the kitchen table, her plate empty, her glass of iced tea half full.

She went to him, and he whisked her into his arms. "I'm sorry you're here alone."

He kissed her, relishing the way their lips came together, the way she caressed the back of his neck. When the kiss ended, he paused to appreciate the look of love streaming from her eyes.

Killing Willie Boy wouldn't have changed a thing.

Let him run. His demons will catch up to him. They always do.

"I hear we're spending Friendsgiving together," she said.

"Absolutely." He furrowed his brow. "Did I forgot to tell you?"

She nodded.

"How does Thanksgiving with the Santinis and Friendsgiving with the ALPHA family sound?"

"Perfetto," she replied before holding him close.

"Qualcuno sta imparando l'italiano. Someone is learning Italian."

She sat with him while he ate dinner and told him about her day.

His anger jumped to the forefront when he learned about Trish Benderson, but she deescalated him.

"Luciano. I'm fine."

"Baby, we should have a security detail on you—"

"Luciano, I was armed, I'm wearing my Kevlar, and I took her down."

"My kick-ass woman," he said.

"What happened with Willie Boy?"

"He left town or he could be hiding in plain sight. He abandoned the restaurant."

Her eyes grew large. "So, he's alive."

"For now."

"Are you going to chase him?"

"No. I'm going to celebrate the holidays with my love, then we're going to stop the destruction Dante set into motion."

She lifted her glass and clinked his. "Sounds like a plan."

"I would love it if you moved in here."

She smiled. "I would love that too."

"Step one," he said.

"What's step two?"

"A proposal," he replied.

"Then what?"

"A big, over-the-top wedding on the coast of Italy."

She grinned. "I like the way you think, Mr. Santini."

"I like *you*, Ms. Redding. I like *all* of you."

"We've come a long way since our sketchy beginning."

"When you were following me around with a pair of binos."

He pulled her onto his lap, kissed her. "Thank you for bringing joy into my life and peace to my heart."

She placed her hand on her chest. "How romantic."

"Always," he said and kissed her.

"Always," she replied and kissed him back.

EPILOGUE

One Month Later, Christmas Weekend

LUCIANO

While eating an early breakfast together on Christmas Eve, Luciano glanced over at Simone. "You've been quiet."

She swallowed down the oatmeal. "I'd like to do something special today."

"Wrap gifts?"

"All done," she replied before sipping her coffee. "I'd like to visit your family."

"But we're spending Christmas with them tomorrow."

"No, Luciano." She placed her warm hand on his. "Your family at the cemetery." Love poured from her eyes.

"That's very kind, Simone."

"They're important to you and I'd like to acknowledge them."

She continued to amaze him. "We can stop on the way to Carole Jean's."

Her smile brightened his day. He loved making Simone happy... he just hadn't expected this would be one of those ways. That's what made her unique. She went out of her way to include his past and he was grateful for that.

"I spoke with my realtor," she said. "We're putting my house on the market January twenty-third, so if you have *any* doubts about my moving in—"

He captured her face in his hands. "None, baby. Are you sure you want to live here? It's a big house—"

"I've always loved the mansion, plus, I definitely feel safer here... and with everything going on, it's the perfect solution."

He pushed out of his chair and kissed her. "Not gonna argue with perfect."

"Elsa told me she's thinking of visiting us," Simone said as they cleared the dishes.

Luciano started cleaning a pot.

"Domestic Luciano is super-hot." She ran her fingers down his back, stopped on his ass, and squeezed. "My sexy, sexy boyfriend." She leaned up, kissed his cheek.

"Elsa's concerned she's a burden to Carrera and Slash," he replied.

"Maybe she'd like living here part of the year with us."

"Are you sure about that?" he asked.

"Absolutely." She smacked his backside with the dishtowel. "I'm going to grab a change of clothes, then head over to my place for an hour or two. I've got a ton to do before the house goes on the market."

"I'll go with you," he said.

"Luciano—"

He pulled her close, wrapped his arms around her. "You're the one who killed Jerod De Clerq. I just shot the gun out of his hand."

She laughed. "Ohgod, what kind of sick mess am I to laugh over that?"

He kissed her. "My sick mess."

Then, his smile fell away. "Trish Benderson attacked you—"

"*Tried* to attack me," Simone pushed back, "and she failed."

"There are dozens of terrorists out there who could be plotting their revenge. I'm coming with you."

Upstairs, she pulled her body armor over her shirt while he dressed for their lunch. He pulled on a black shirt, black dress pants, and a sport coat while she tucked a Santini Original cocktail dress and stilettos into a garment bag.

After slipping into his shoe boots, he said, "How do I look, baby?"

"You, Mr. Santini, are eye candy for days." She went to him, kissed him. "You gotta wear your vest.

"Simone—"

She crossed her arms. "I'll wait."

"I'm not going to win this one, am I?"

"Nope."

Off came his sport coat, then his shirt. He pulled on his Kevlar vest, redressed, and they returned downstairs.

"Bring your laptop," she insisted. "You can work while I go through my things."

"Let me grab that." Alone in his office, he extracted the small jewelry box from his safe. After slipping it and his laptop into his computer bag, he found her in the kitchen staring out at the expansive backyard.

He stood behind her, wrapped his arms around her, and looked outside.

"I see children running around out there," she murmured.

Still standing behind her, he hugged her. "For real?" he teased. "I don't see anyone."

Laughing, she turned to face him. "In our future, but I'm getting way ahead of myself." Her smile fell away. "I used to stare out these French doors and miss ALPHA. I wondered where The Bomb Maker was hiding. I used to fantasize about finding him and avenging my team, but I was too scared to do it."

"My badass babe isn't scared anymore."

"No, I'm not."

He drove them to her house where he worked at her kitchen table while she got busy sorting through everything.

Over the next two hours, his mind kept wandering. This was a big weekend for him... the biggest in a long, long time. He was asking her to marry him. He might pop the question at their holiday lunch, or wait until that evening. Or... he could propose on Christmas Day. He would know when the time was right.

Simone came downstairs looking stunning. She'd pulled her hair into a messy updo, placed a diamond cuff on her ear. Her black cocktail dress was the perfect combination of classy and sultry. On her feet, she'd kept on her low-heeled, black leather boots, the stilettos dangling from her finger.

Taking his time, he checked her out. Twice. "You look hot, baby." He rose, went to her.

She modeled the dress for him.

"Sembri abbastanza buono da mangiare," he murmured.

"Something about eating," she replied.

"Very good. I said, 'you look good enough to eat.'"

"Mmm," she murmured. "I like that, but you gotta wait for the good stuff. Santa only comes once a year."

"Poor Santa."

She laughed.

Before leaving, she confirmed all the security cams were functioning, then she activated the alarm, and they left.

On the way to the cemetery, she clasped his hand, rested it in her lap. But she said nothing. The only sound was the eclectic mix of holiday tunes coming from one of his playlists.

He drove into the cemetery, parking near his family's gravesites.

"You sure about this, babe?" he asked.

"I am, but I think you should go first, without me. They should hear about me from you, not from me."

One quick kiss before he made his way over to their graves.

He knelt at Marco's grave, brushed away some errant leaves, and laid his hand on the stone marker. "Hello, son. It's almost Christmas. You had so much energy on Christmas eve. Mommy and I could not get you to sleep. Every two hours, you'd wake up, tell us it was time to open presents." He smiled at the memories. "I know you're in a better place, surrounded by a love that we can't understand. Doesn't take away from how much I love you and will always love you. Marco, you are my firstborn, my beloved son, and you always will be."

He ran his fingers over Marco's name, the familiar pang of loss finding its way into his heart.

After a few seconds, he moved to his daughter's gravesite. "Caterina, my angel, your days must be filled with singing and rejoicing as you praise the Lord. Your time here was too short, but I will keep you alive in my heart for the rest of my life. You were such a happy baby. Hearing you laugh brought me so much joy. Being your daddy gave my life purpose. I wanted to protect you and keep you safe."

Emotion gripped his throat, but he pushed on. "I will love you always. One day, we'll be together again. That will be a happy day filled with your laughter. Daddy loves you so much, honey." He laid his hand on the stone.

"Heavenly Father, I failed my family. I did not protect them like I vowed to you I would. Evil stepped in and stole them from me, but I know you've made them whole again, and keep them safe in your loving arms. Amen." He made the sign of the cross, kissed his fingers, and pressed his hand to each of his children's gravestones.

Then, he moved on to Linda's, and pain slashed his heart.

She had been his first and only love. And he believed that his punishment on earth would be to walk the rest of his life alone.

But he had found love again, and he dared to take that next step.

"Linda, my love, I think about you and our babies every day. You know the truth about what happened... and now I do too. I'm sorry it wasn't me who was taken, and I hope you've forgiven me for what happened. If I could do one day over, it would be that day. I would gladly give up my life for yours and the children's."

He ran his fingers over her name—Linda Anne Santini—on the black slab of granite. After several quiet seconds, he said, "I found someone to love. She's someone you'd like. She is not your replacement. You are my first and should have been my only. She is my chance to step out of the darkness and live a life filled with love. I hope you would have wanted that for me. She wants to speak to you, maybe to Marco and Caterina too. I will always love you, my sweet, sweet Linda."

With a heavy heart, he rose and returned to the SUV.

"Can I bring you over?" he asked.

Simone exited the vehicle, buttoned her cashmere coat. "I was thinking I'd go over alone, if you're okay with that."

He kissed her cheek, then the other, and he let her go.

SIMONE

SIMONE STOOD BACK several feet and eyed the three gravestones. Her heart broke as she read their names and each of the engravings.

She walked over to Luciano's wife's grave and knelt down. "Hello, Mrs. Santini. I'm Simone. I wanted to pay my respects to you and tell you that I've fallen in love with Luciano. I'm not going to take your place. No one could ever do that. I promise that I will help keep the memory of you and your children alive in Luciano's heart for as long as we're together."

She paused.

"I love him and want to help him have a happy life."

A gust of wind blew past her, swirling the leaves away from the graves.

Simone moved her hair away from her face before moving to the children's graves. She bowed her head and stayed silent for a long moment.

"I'm so sorry," she whispered.

She rose and walked back to the car. As she got closer, he emerged. She went to him and he pulled her into his arms.

"Thank you," he murmured. "That meant a lot to me."

"I'm sorry for your loss. I want us to find our own happiness while still remembering and honoring our pasts."

He opened her door for her, waited while she slipped inside. Then, he leaned in and kissed her softly, before shutting her door and getting behind the wheel.

They pulled into Carole Jean's at one o'clock. Jericho and Liv had suggested they all spend the holiday celebrating before spending it with their families.

Inside the restaurant, they were escorted to the Copper room, the private dining room in the back. An oversized gas fireplace threw dancing shadow-flames on the shiny black hearth while copper-tiled walls reflected the warm, amber glow. Soft lighting, multiple tea candles, and bouquets of short-stemmed roses added charm to the Michelin-starred eatery. The tables had been arranged in a large square so everyone felt like they were seated together.

Simone's heart overflowed with love as her gaze fell over her coworkers and friends. Carrera and Slash were talking with Cooper and Danielle. Nearby Sin, Dakota, and Jericho were speaking in hushed tones while their wives—Evangeline, Providence, and Liv—chatted nearby.

Prescott and Jaqueline, Hawk and Addison, and Rebel and Brit were toasting their champagne flutes, their joyous laughter making her smile.

"There they are!" Carrera broke away to greet them.

After saying hi to him, Simone walked over to speak with Evangeline, Providence, and Liv.

"Congratulations," Evangeline said. "Providence was just telling us how you jumped back in full throttle."

Simone smiled. "Red's back, baby."

"We told the guys we wouldn't talk shop—" Providence murmured.

"I know my husband," Liv said, "and he's over there talking strategy."

"Same," Simone said. "Luciano's obsessed with the Day of Destruction. He's been totally focused on chatter on the dark web. And he's been talking with someone at The Agency."

"I think Sin has been on some of those calls," Evangeline added.

Slash and Danielle joined them.

"What are we talking about?" Slash asked.

"What we're all talking about," Simone replied.

"The Day of Destruction," Danielle said.

"May thirty-first doesn't leave us much time," Providence said.

Emerson and Stryker walked into the private dining room and joined the group.

Jericho whistled. "Hey, fam, everyone's here. Time to get our Christmas Eve luncheon started. First, welcome to Carole Jean's, my *three*-Michelin-starred restaurant."

The group applauded.

"The chef has prepared a five-course meal," Jericho

boomed. "You better be hungry." He gestured to the tables. "Please."

Simone made her way back to Luciano. After kissing her cheek, he seated her, then sat beside her.

Luciano raised his champagne flute. "Per chiudere gli amici che sono famiglia."

"To close friends who are family," Carrera translated.

They clinked glasses, sipped the champagne.

"Red, are you joining Luciano on any of his jobs?" Sin asked.

As Simone regarded her man, she smiled. "Depends on who he's going after."

"I'm sure Simone can be persuaded to join me," Luciano said.

"I'm in if it's the terrorists," Simone said.

"I think we're all-in on that one," Jericho replied.

"Hell, yeah," Slash added.

Luciano's phone buzzed. After reading the text, a growl shot out of him, and he showed Simone his phone. It was a text from Willie Boy.

> I lived in your shadow my hole life. No more, cousin. I will have my revenge. Everyone thinks I'm too stupid to do anything right. I'll prove you all wrong!

"Are you worried?" Simone asked.

"Worried? No, but I am concerned he can't spell the word whole."

She chuckled. "I'm being serious."

"You know I don't get scared," he replied.

"Everything okay?" Carrera asked.

Luciano nodded. "All good."

But Luciano's jawline was ticking and he re-read the text before setting his phone down. Though he shot her a loving smile, his eyes had gone flat. Thanks to Willie Boy, Luciano had one more thing to deal with.

For today, she was stepping away from the grind, from the pressure, and from the intensity of their lives to enjoy their friends for a few hours.

"What's the latest on Hirzog," Sin asked her.

"He's out of the hospital and awaiting trial in jail," Simone replied.

"Did you visit him?" Evangeline asked.

"I went to see him in the hospital," she said. "Luciano didn't want me to, but I needed closure."

"How'd that go?" Slash asked.

"He's a mess," she replied. "He's devastated over having been manipulated. He's being charged with multiple counts that might put him in prison for life. It's hard to believe he's the same man who mentored my career."

"He brought it on himself," Carrera said.

"I know I'm in the minority," Addison said, "but I feel sorry for him. He got scammed real good."

"He did," Simone added.

"Still, he shouldn't have cheated," Sin said. "If Hirzog had said no, he wouldn't have given De Clerq all the power."

"Red, what happened with Hirzog's wife?" Addison asked.

"I talked to her a few days ago. She filed for divorce and is putting their home on the market."

"Okay, guys," Liv said. "No more shop talk. I think we should plan a big, crazy vacation together."

As the waitstaff delivered their first course, the conversation shifted to how much fun it would be if all twenty of them—and their children—took an exotic two-week trip.

The group began tossing out travel ideas. Everything from renting a castle in Europe to staying in a mansion in Italy to vacationing in The Maldives or in South Florida.

Though the tone of the conversation had shifted, the divot

between Luciano's brow had not gone away. She typed out a text to him, then sent it.

> I can't wait to massage your cock with my feet until you come all over my toes

His phone buzzed, he read the text, and slid his gaze to her. She was waiting with a sly smile and an arched eyebrow. Within seconds, the spark in his eyes returned.

"You're a million miles away," she murmured.

"Not anymore, baby. I'm all yours."

Despite his latest obsession with the Day of Destruction and, now, his cousin's threat, she would help him find balance between work and play. She would support him through it all and she would love him fiercely.

For the rest of her days.

LUCIANO

LUCIANO WAS ANGRY. Stupid fucking Willie Boy was trying to exert his power from the shadows. He wasn't scared of Willie Boy, but he was concerned for his family. Rather than wait for Willie Boy to strike, he would put out feelers and track the son of a bitch down. Shouldn't be hard. If he did bolt to Vegas, he'd be acting like he was a Santini somebody.

He's a nobody who's accomplished nothing. He shames the Santini name.

As the conversations continued, Luciano shifted his attention to Simone. She was talking with Evangeline, but she glanced over. They shared a smile before she returned her attention to her friend.

She was his second chance at having a full and meaningful

life, and he wasn't going to let a scumbag like Willie Boy ruin another moment of their evening.

After the servers cleared away the first course, Liv asked everyone what they were grateful for. "I know it's not Thanksgiving, but we can show gratitude on any day."

"I love that, babe," Jericho said. "Why don't you start?"

"I was thinking we should offer up something different than what we usually say—"

"So, not me?" Jericho teased, and the group laughed.

"I'm so grateful for my husband, but this year, I'm grateful for my children. Liam accepted our foster children, Owen and Layla, with such grace. He shared his toys, he was so friendly and excited when they came to our home." Liv smiled. "He was so loving toward them, I couldn't believe it."

Jericho swiped the tear from his eye. "I'm grateful for you, Liv. You handle our children with so much love and you take every chance to show them how to treat others with kindness. I'm out there taking out the monsters and you remind me that there are amazing, good people in the world."

She put her hand on her heart.

One by one, the conversations of gratitude continued.

"I'm grateful that Evangeline and I run our home for runaway children *together*," Sin said. "To do it right, we have to put in a lot of time. We don't have children of our own, but Evan works hard at Develin, then puts in time at The Center. She believes that all these kids—no matter what life has thrown at them—can be productive adults. I love you, Evan."

"I'm grateful for my girlfriends—" Evangeline said.

"What about me?" Sin asked, and the group laughed.

She grinned at him. "I adore you Sinclair Develin. You know that. Every single one of you has got my back and I've got yours. I've called Providence at three in the morning and she's been there for me. I've reached out to Liv countless times and she's been my rock."

Evangeline smiled at Simone. "Your turn, Red."

Simone glanced around at everyone. "I'm grateful to Z. He sent me on a mission that led me back here, to all of you. I wasn't sure returning to an organization I love was possible, but here I am. I'm also grateful to Providence and Cooper for giving me a second chance. And I'm grateful for the friendship I had with Frederica. I miss her, but I feel her with me, especially when I think I can't do something. I hear her cheering me on."

She rested her hand on Luciano's thigh. "You're up, baby."

This is my opportunity.

"I'm grateful to Z as well," Luciano began. "He put Simone in my path, and we took it from there."

"Brit and I had no idea our dad played a part in your lives," Addison said.

"Z is always there behind the scenes, like the puppet master," Sin said, and the group laughed.

"I thought *you* were the puppet master," Dakota said to his twin.

"Turns out, the real puppet master is Luciano," Sin said.

More laughter erupted.

"Simone, the night we met is unforgettable," Luciano continued. "Being with you is the best part of my day. Falling in love with you has been intense and beautiful. I know we've been working nonstop, but I wouldn't change anything, except for the death of your friend, and all the Operatives."

She acknowledged him with a nod.

He knelt beside her.

Gasps filled the room, then silence.

"Simone, you are my entire world. You give me hope, make me feel excited about living again. I want to build a life with you, my beautiful, brilliant, badass babe." He pulled the ring box from his sport coat pocket, opened the box, and said, "Marry me, Simone."

Her gaze never left his as a breathtaking smile erupted on

her face. She pressed her hands to his face, kissed him. "Yes, absolutely."

They came together in tender kiss while everyone started applauding and hooting.

"That's what we're talking about," Carrera said.

Luciano slid the ring onto her finger, but she still hadn't broken her gaze. "I will love you forever," she whispered.

"I'm yours." He kissed her. "And you're mine."

She grinned. "I love that."

He smiled out at the group. "She said yes!"

Everyone came over to congratulate them, but Simone stayed glued to his side. To his surprise, she still hadn't looked at the ring, something he hadn't expected. After the commotion died down, and everyone sat back down, Carrera stood with his champagne flute.

"Congratulations to my cousin and to Red. They're a great match."

"It's perfect," Slash added.

"I'm going with what my wife said," Carrera said. "She's *always* right."

The group cracked up.

"You figured out the secret to a good marriage," Stryker said. "My wife is always right too."

"Same," the men echoed around the room.

While everyone toasted with their bubbly, the servers returned with the entrées.

Simone leaned over, kissed Luciano's cheek. "Thank you for turning Christmas Eve into something we celebrate every year. I did not expect that."

"I love surprising you," he replied.

"Oh, the ring!" Simone eyed the six-carat emerald-cut diamond, flanked by a halo of smaller diamonds, with baguettes running down the sides of the band. "This is stunning. And too much."

He laughed. "I wanted to go bigger, but I knew you'd object."

"It's beautiful. Seriously. Gorgeous." She kissed him.

He leaned over, whispered, "I bought you a second ring, in case—"

She laughed. "You did not."

He nodded. "But if you like this one."

"It's perfect. I love it, and I can't wait to show you my gratitude when we get home."

"A Christmas Eve celebration," he said.

"Of the best kind," she replied. "Love, love, and more love."

"I couldn't agree more," he replied.

March, the following year

LUCIANO

STUART PARKED in front of the brand new, two-story building. As Luciano exited the Rolls Royce, he glanced up at the restaurant sign.

Santini

Unlike Willie Boy's shithole, he was proud to be associated with this new, upscale eatery. Luciano walked inside, removed his shades. The place looked fantastic. Teddy had gutted the building and created a first-class restaurant that served Italian cuisine. A mix of classic dishes and modern creations. Teddy had thrown himself into this project, and Luciano was damn proud of what his baby brother had accomplished.

Teddy bounded over with the biggest grin on his face. "Whad'ya think?"

"You did good," Luciano replied.

Teddy puffed out his chest. "I got it done!" Then, he chuffed out a laugh. "I'm in serious sleep deficit, but otherwise, all good."

Luciano chuckled. "Who says the words 'sleep deficit'?"

"Me. I do," Teddy said. "The grand reopening is in two weeks. Are you coming?"

"Of course."

Movement had Luciano glancing over Teddy's shoulder, then he did a double take. "No fucking way."

A tall, muscular man in a paint-smeared tank and tattered jeans sauntered into view. His long hair had been pulled into a ponytail, but most had fallen out. A shock of wild hair framed his familiar face.

His brother, Greystone Santini, was back.

"Yo, Lulu." Greystone pulled to a stop.

"The renegade returns," Luciano bit out.

Greystone didn't extend his hand, didn't try to hug him either. He just slipped his hand into his jeans pocket and shot him a cool stare.

"I told you I was hiring Grey to run the restaurant," Teddy said.

"Cool joint, don'tcha think?" Greystone shoved his hair out of his eyes.

"This *joint* cost me several million to renovate," Luciano said.

"Yeah, whatever." Greystone slid his relaxed gaze from him to Teddy. "It's got the vibe goin' on, huh, Teddy?"

Teddy just stood there grinning. "Gotta say, Grey really came through for me. He helped with the build-out, kept the contractors on time, and made sure we stayed on budget. With everything I got going on, he saved my ass."

"Sounds too good to be true," Luciano said. "Are you gonna show me around?"

"I've got a meeting," Teddy said before taking off toward the front door, leaving Luciano alone with a brother he hadn't seen in over a decade.

"I got you, Lulu," Greystone said. "It's your basic food stop for people with dinero to burn." Grey gestured to the plush leather booths lining the walls and the tables throughout the main dining room. Luciano spotted a skull and crossbones tat on his brother's shoulder and a sword running the length of his forearm.

As kids, he and Grey had been the closest. Not anymore. Luciano was staring at a stranger.

Greystone moseyed toward the back, turned, and continued walking backwards. "You comin'?"

Luciano wanted to tell his brother to get lost, to go back to wherever the hell he'd come from, but he said nothing as he made his way toward the kitchen.

Grey pointed out all the upgrades. "Your money, so there you go. Teddy did a good job."

"Where've you been Grey?" Luciano asked.

"Around. You?"

"For fuck's sake," Luciano bit out. "You take off without a goodbye. We thought you went missing."

Greystone shrugged. "I did. Now, I'm found."

"Why are you back?" Luciano asked.

"Why the hell not. I was passin' through, thought I'd stop for a few. Teddy offered me a job, so I stayed. Ain't no thing."

Of all his brothers, he and Grey had fought the most, but they had been the closest. Neither liked the other telling him what to do. They were always trying to out-boss each other. But, at the end of the day, they were brothers, and they had each other's backs.

"Where are you staying?" Luciano asked.

Greystone opened the professional-grade refrigerator. Luciano was nonplussed. Next, his brother showed him the pristine cabinets and high-end meat locker. The place was brand new. He expected it to be first class.

"Been stayin' at diffrent places," Greystone replied. "Crashed at Teddy's for a while."

Back in the main room, Luciano said, "Were you planning on contacting me?"

"Look, I get it. You're pissed. I couldn't take it no more. That life wasn't for me, so I bolted."

"Dad's dead," Luciano said.

"Yup."

"Mom moved to Las Vegas."

"Gotcha."

"Have you seen her?"

"Nope. You?"

"I call her, send her money," Luciano said.

"She's probably pissin' it away at the tables."

"Not my problem," Luciano replied.

"Teddy said you got outta the family biz." Greyson's phone buzzed. He lifted it from his back pocket, read the text, and chuckled. "You cuttin' the ribbon for the big reopening?"

"Teddy can do that." Luciano slid on his sunglasses. "It's good to have you home, Grey."

"Yup."

As Luciano pushed out the front door of the restaurant that bore their name, he glanced over his shoulder. Grey was sauntering toward the kitchen, head down on his phone.

Frustration slithered down his spine. Luciano hoped that whatever skeletons his brother was carrying around didn't follow him back here.

"You probably should have stayed gone, brother," Luciano said before he slid into the waiting Rolls Royce.

Back home, Luciano went on an Internet search of his brother, but Greystone Santini didn't exist. It's not like he hadn't looked for him before. There'd been plenty of times that he'd tried to find him to make sure he was okay. But Greystone Santini had dropped off the planet.

Simone breezed into his office.

"And now he's back." Luciano said.

"Who's back?" she asked.

Simone was wearing workout sweats, her hair clipped on top of her head.

Her beautiful smile melted his frustration away.

"Hey, baby." He rolled the desk chair back, patted his leg. She eased onto his lap, draped her arm around his shoulder, and kissed him. "Hello, handsome. How was the restaurant?"

"Looks great. How was work?"

"Busy, busy. I've got my first actual mission next week."

"Local or out of town?"

"DC, so local."

"Arrest or elimination," she replied.

"Arrest."

"When should I start worrying?"

She laughed. "This home is a no-worry zone, so never. I've got this and I'm part of a great team."

He kissed her. "Are you working out?"

"Yeah, can I tear you away to join me?"

"I'll change and meet you downstairs."

She waggled her eyebrows. "I'll help you."

He smiled. She knew *exactly* what to say to redirect his frustration.

She pressed her lips to the small space between his eyebrows, then ran her finger over the spot. "What's got you?"

"My brother, Greystone, is back."

"Teddy mentioned a black sheep—"

"That's the one."

"Where's he been?"

"Didn't say."

"Why is he back?"

"Wouldn't tell me."

"What's he doing?"

"Working for Teddy."

"At the new restaurant?"

"Looks like Teddy made Greystone the GM."

"Nice." She kissed him. "What's the problem?"

"I don't trust him."

Simone smiled. "Baby, you don't trust anyone at first. Maybe, if you get to know him again, he'll actually answer your questions."

"Maybe you're right. You'll meet him at the grand reopening."

"Fine, whatever. We've got so much going on with trying to track down the Haqazzii terrorists, with our work, with planning our wedding, your brother should be the last person you spend any time thinking about."

He put his arms around her, kissed her, letting his lips linger on his. "What would I do without my Simone?"

"Be a lot more angry," she replied. "I've got a fun evening planned for us. It starts with a workout and ends with one too." She winked.

"Does it involve your talented toes?"

She stood, offered her hand. He placed his hand in hers and rose. "It involves all of me, Mr. Santini. Body, mind, and soul."

"Forever," he murmured before pulling her into his arms.

"Forever," she replied with a beautiful, loving smile.

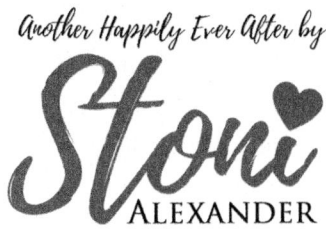

Another Happily Ever After by **Stoni Alexander**

A Note from Stoni

Storytelling is my passion, so I'm always very appreciative and humbled when someone takes that journey with me into my twisted, wild, and borderline-obsessive imagination.

Oftentimes, my characters wake me in the middle of the night because my muse is in a completely different time zone. I've learned—the hard way—that I have to get those words down... and fast. Then, when I put my story out there, it's akin to putting my beloved kindergartener on the school bus and watching him carried away... along with my heart.

Writing Luciano and Simone's story filled me with great joy. I had more than usual going on in my life, so stepping into their world kept me grounded and gave my imagination the freedom to play. Building the fictitious family of ALPHA Operatives and my cadre of powerful, wealthy alpha men has been my sanctuary. That world has also brought happiness to my loyal readers. If you're among them, thank you so much for loving my stories.

I especially love bringing back characters from other stories and giving them their happily ever after! Finding Simone was fun. Early on, in the plotting process, I'd chosen the name Simone and had been working on her character arc.

One night, Johnny said, "You already have a Simone. She was Colton's business manager in MITUS." I remembered her as Red because that's who she was to me... *and* I was extremely impressed with my husband's memory!

I revisited Red's storyline in THE MITUS TOUCH and everything fell into place. In POWER, when Simone returned to Mitus mansion and felt like she'd come home, so did I.

Now, it's time to turn my attention to my next adventure... and I've got many yummy options. There's bigger-than-life and shy-around-women Teddy Santini, our lady-eater Gabriel Santini, and our resident bad boy Greystone Santini. So much fabulous testosterone to choose from!

I love hearing from readers. If you'd like to say hello, you can send me an email at Contact@StoniAlexander.com. And if you want to receive my occasional newsletter, sign up at Stoni-Alexander.com. You'll receive my free and very steamy short story, MetroMan.

Thanks for traveling with me on my writer's journey. It's a pleasure having you with me!

Stoni Alexander

ACKNOWLEDGMENTS

Always first, my beloved **Johnny**, I owe you a debt of gratitude for everything you do to get my stories out into the world. Our own love story will forever be my favorite, and I love reliving it over and over in the characters I write.

Whenever you called Luciano, Lucy-anno, I laughed. Then, you started calling him Lulu… which I loved. Thank you for being my hero *and* for being the plucky comic relief. We laugh a lot together and I love that about us. Going through this crazy life together is the best. It just is. ∞

Son, thank you for having my back, for being a genius at so many things, and for continuing to recognize that "My mom is always right."

Michele Woodward, I have known you for decades and admired you throughout them all. Even when we were sorority sisters, you had your act together. And you still do. It's a joy to call you my friend all these years later!
    Words matter. They change us, mold us, help us grow, or they suffocate us. Your words to me— back when I was miserable in my day job—stayed with me. They affected me in the best way, weaving their magic into my soul as I started plugging away on my craft. You inspire so many with your coaching and with your smarts. Your smile has forever been something that

makes my day and, as I sit here writing this, I think of you doing just that... and I smile right back. In the bonds, always.

To the many new **friends** I've made while crafting this love story. While I'm perfectly happy living in my imagination, stepping out is equally important, so thank you for ensuring I have balance in my life.

Thank you to **Stoni's Fabulous ARC Team** for helping me get the word out!

To my wonderful **readers and fans,** thank you so much! I am so appreciative that you choose to read my stories. Knowing they bring you joy makes me happy. Bless you all.

Muse, we did good... in spite of life's insanity while writing the first draft. Time to take a breather, then we'll figure out who takes the lead on the next story. I'm very excited to delve into bad boy Greystone... but Teddy already has my heart. Which direction will you lead me? I can't wait to find out!

NOVELS BY STONI ALEXANDER

THE TOUCH SERIES

The Mitus Touch

The Wilde Touch

The Loving Touch

The Hott Touch

In Walked Sin

Dakota Luck

THE VIGILANTES SERIES

Damaged

Vengeance

Savage

Wrecked

Broken

Rebel

Fury

THE SANTINI ASSASSINS

Power

BEAUTIFUL MEN COLLECTION

Beautiful Stepbrother

Beautiful Disaster

Available on Amazon or Read FREE with Kindle Unlimited

ABOUT THE AUTHOR

Stoni Alexander writes sexy romantic suspense and contemporary romance about tortured alpha males and independent, strong-willed females. Her passion is creating love stories where the hero and heroine help each other through a crisis so that, in the end, they're equal partners in more ways than love alone. The heat level is high, the romance is forever, and the suspense keeps readers guessing until the very end.

Visit Stoni's website:
StoniAlexander.com

Sign up for Stoni's newsletter on her website and she'll gift you a free steamy short story, only available to her Inner Circle.

Here's where you can follow Stoni online. She looks forward to connecting with you!

- amazon.com/author/stonialexander
- bookbub.com/authors/stoni-alexander
- facebook.com/StoniBooks
- goodreads.com/stonialexander
- instagram.com/stonialexander

Printed in Great Britain
by Amazon